# A CAPTIVE FREEDOM

# A Captive Freedom

## Emma Drummond

St. Martin's Press
New York

Library of Congress Cataloging-in-Publication Data

Drummond, Emma, 1931-
    A captive freedom.

    I. Title.
PR6054.R785C3  1987        823'.914        87-1650
ISBN 0-312-00575-X

First published in Great Britain by Victor Gollancz Ltd.

First U.S. Edition

10 9 8 7 6 5 4 3 2 1

*FOR MY MOTHER, WITH LOVE*

*Part One*

# CHAPTER ONE

London theatre audiences had never seen anything like it before. The initial performance had been greeted with a breathless hush followed by a standing ovation. Now, the people went wild every evening, but no matter how long they applauded and called for an encore, one was never forthcoming. If they wanted a repeat performance they had to come again; and come again they did.

It had become the latest rage, and those who had not seen it laboured under a social handicap. It had changed public attitudes, launched fashions, and broken hearts. It delighted both sexes—albeit for different reasons—and charmed those of all classes. The wealthy attempted to emulate it; the poor saw it as the embodiment of a dream. Other theatre managers sought to copy it, but it was to Lindley's that the crowds flocked night after night. They wanted the original.

As so often happened in theatrical history, one trivial item in a production full of colour, musical delight, and talent, had somehow become the highlight that would never be forgotten long after the show and its stars had faded into obscurity. That it had happened purely by chance also followed theatrical history. However, to the great theatre-going public in that year of 1896 who crowded the gallery in their best stepping-out clothes, or graced the stalls and boxes with silks, furs and jewels, the whys and wherefores did not matter. They flocked to Lindley's to see it again and again.

The group of young men in a box that evening were waiting impatiently for that special moment to come, and for just one of them it would be a new experience. The deeply tanned complexion, contrasting so strikingly with the extreme fairness of his hair, betrayed the fact that he had recently returned from a trip abroad. Many eyes had been drawn to that box because all six were in merry mood as they noisily roistered the evening away with little consideration for others, but even they fell silent when the soft throbbing lilt of music purporting to have originated from the peasants of South America began to fill the auditorium, and brought about the usual hush. The fair-haired man leant forward eagerly in response to nudges from his companions. Dark memories of his past two years in one of the most savage areas of the world were being forced from his mind by the determined pursuit of wine, women and gaiety, making him ripe for total enchantment that evening.

The lights had dimmed. The music was strange and compulsive, with a slow insistent beat that matched the one in his temples during those few moments of anticipation. Then, all around him, came the sound of a concerted sigh as first one, then another, and another, and another stepped from the wings—in all, thirty girls of identical stature, each with the darkest shade of brunette hair swept up into an intricacy of curls that added a further six inches to her height. They resembled a veritable troupe of Amazons as they weaved in kaleidoscopic patterns about a stage decorated starkly with black velvet backcloth and wings.

All they did was walk, but it was the way they moved and how they were dressed that caught the imagination and held in thrall those who were watching. It was not so much a walk as a sway: a sinuous movement from shoulders and hips that was full of sedate grace, yet acutely sexual. It gave the girls an air of subdued sensuality that was tantalisingly belied by the haughty angle of their heads and almost total lack of expression on their faces, which were strikingly beautiful. That alone was enough to excite the young man in the box, without the additional allure of costumes composed entirely of white ostrich feathers, which cleverly contrived to suggest that the slender female bodies were naked beneath. Here and there, a bare shoulder, a shapely calf, a slender forearm was momentarily revealed as the light-as-air feathers floated and quivered in a stage zephyr caused by the moving patterns. Those glimpses were so tantalisingly brief, they had the young man on the edge of his chair wondering if he had imagined them. The slow beat of the music became almost hypnotic as he watched spellbound, wanting the moment to go on and on.

The whole sequence had been brilliantly conceived, and was magnetic in its simplicity. More subtly sexual than the tights and low-cut costumes of the burlesque queens, it was also more alluring than the usual chorus of girls in elaborate befrilled, beribboned dresses, with enormous confections of hats, who sang or danced their way through catchy numbers beloved by whistling errand-boys. The burlesque and musical-comedy girls had won the hearts of their audiences through the warmth and liveliness of their personalities, but the Lindley Girls, as they had come to be known, did not reach out across the footlights. Instead, they challenged. They seemed to say: We are here, and we know you are out there, but if you wish to know us better *you* must make all the approaches.

The popular girls like Ellaline Terris, Marie Tempest, Ada Reeve, and the lead of this show at Lindley's, Adeline Tait, were successful because they managed to give the impression that they were performing for every single person in the auditorium, from duchess to shop-girl. But this parade of tall aloof girls, with enormous waving plumes fastened into their hair with jewelled combs, managed to suggest that there was just one beau somewhere out there in the darkness who *might* win one of them, if he dared to try.

Each man watching told himself he would be the one, if it were not for his wife or girlfriend beside him, his lack of wealth, his lack of height, his lack of youth. Each woman was telling herself she could be like the Lindley Girls, with the ability to hold all men at arms' length, if it were not for her husband or boyfriend beside her, her strict father, her blonde or auburn hair, her lack of ostrich feathers . . . her lack of will power!

The number was coming to an end; the girls were swaying off through the wings as the music rose to a voluptuous rhythmic climax, until there was only one girl left. She hesitated momentarily, stared haughtily into the auditorium, then lifted her head in an imperious gesture before stepping from sight behind the draped black velvet.

Those occupying the stalls were already on their feet clamouring for more; the balcony was exploding into cheers. The bewitched young man in the box knew there would be no encore no matter how loudly he called, because he had been forewarned by his friends. But he knew the excitement was not yet over for him. He had already chosen his girl. They might all be tall, slender and brunette, but one had caught his eye the moment she had walked on. The seventh, according to his programme, was called Leila Duncan. There had been something about her face that had defied her deliberate aloofness of expression; something about the defiant tilt of her head that suggested she was telling life, not merely the audience, that to know her better it must make all the moves. Cool, lethargically swaying, haughty she might have appeared, but a close study of her through his opera-glasses had shown that her eyes, a startling deep blue amid so many pairs of brown ones, had been filled with the intoxication of the moment. Beneath the sublime pose she adopted that girl had a fiery temperament, he told himself. He would enjoy encountering it.

The remainder of the show seemed to fall flat, despite the lavish costumes and the gaiety of the music. Even the final spirited number by Adeline Tait, dressed as a South American princess, failed to lift the sense of anticlimax. The "strolling" number had been moved further and further into the running of the show by Lester Gilbert, the impressario, but the runaway success of what had been intended as no more than a time-filler showpiece now demanded that it become the finale or be scrapped altogether. Audiences would not countenance the cutting of their favourite scene, yet Adeline Tait, a *petite* girl with tremendous verve and personality, could not possibly appear in the midst of floating ostrich feathers and *sing* to that seductive music as the curtain fell. Miss Tait was decidedly not happy, and neither was Lester Gilbert. But all the time the show ran to packed houses he had to let the dilemma remain.

There was a scramble at curtain time, but the six young men in the box were busily scribbling notes to attach to the flowers they had brought with them. Each had selected a different girl, after a short spell of bickering, and intended making up a party at Romano's to celebrate the coincidental birthdays of two of their number. Notes written, they vacated the red plushness of the box, collected cloaks and hats, then strolled round to the stage-door to slip Monkton, the door-keeper, a sovereign each to deliver their floral tributes to the chosen girls. With such generous palm-greasing Monkton expressed his willingness to oblige the gentlemen, and they dashed out to secure hansoms in readiness for the jaunt to the famous café for supper.

Only five couples went there, after all. Leila Duncan returned the posy of flowers, still with the flattering note attached. The call-boy who brought them back smiled cheekily and said, "Sorry, guv'nor, Miss Duncan 'as another hengagement . . . and says to tell you it will be the same hevery other night."

He took the flowers automatically. It was unknown for a girl ever to refuse an invitation from him, and the set-back was all the more severe in the face of his five companions' success. But their cheery advice to pick another girl fell on deaf ears. He was damned if he would go through the remaining twenty-four girls, offering the same spray of cream and apricot hothouse roses until one of them deigned to accept. It would make him a laughing-stock in front of Leila Duncan. Telling his friends to go on, he added that he would look up a girl he used to know before going overseas and join them later.

He set off in the hansom he had called, giving the driver the address of a milliner who had once been his mistress. Then he sat back to discover that he was ridiculously angry. The Duncan girl knew nothing about him; had never set eyes on him before. Who did she think she was to fling his flowers back in his face so ungraciously? He stared from the cab window, trying to forget that tantalising swaying body, and the blue eyes that had appeared to be looking right at him as he stared through the opera-glasses.

Outside, the November fog began to swirl up from the surface of the Thames to make its way through lamplit streets leading to the West

End. As it spread, the face of London changed. Hansoms that had been rattling freely through the streets now slowed, and the clamour of ringing hooves grew muffled. Vehicles appeared without warning from the grey obscurity, making the horses toss their heads uneasily and rear with nervous excitement at the sight of another emerging from the opposite direction. What had been a normal late evening scene now took on a mysterious, even sinister, aspect. The horse-drawn travellers of a while ago, who had been no more than politicians returning home after a late sitting at the House, dinner guests departing from their hosts, theatre-goers heading for supper-rooms, now seemed more like hidden Machiavellian passengers on errands of grim fantasy.

At street corners, hot-chestnut sellers cried their wares through throats made hoarse by the fog, and people gathered round them to glean warmth from their braziers as much as from the palm-scorching chestnuts. Ladies of the night glided from doorways to accost passers-by, frightening the virtuous and offending the holy before coming across a potential client more by luck than by their usual infallible judgement, now confused by the damp greyness of the night.

By the time the hansom drew up at the address he had given, the fog had grown so thick it was impossible even to see if a light was burning in the upper windows.

"'Ere it is, sir. Fourteen Lissing Lane," called the driver with a voice like gravel.

The fair-haired passenger stayed where he was, slumped in the corner, staring at the dismal unwelcoming night outside. Then he shivered and turned up the collar of his cloak.

"I've changed my mind. Drive on to Mayfair!"

"Mayfair, guv'nor? That'll take a long time in weather like this."

"Take as long as you damned well like. I'm in no particular hurry," came the sharp rejoinder. "There'll be a handsome tip if you get me there in one piece . . . and you can take these home for your wife." He held up the expensive spray of roses toward the face that peered down at him through the flap in the roof.

"Well now, sir, I'll do me best, thanking you werry much on be'arf of me missus."

But giving away the flowers did not drive the thought of Leila Duncan from his mind, and she continued to spoil his evening long after he had drowned his sorrows in the empty house and gone to bed.

Leila poured Nellie a cup of tea and made her sit down to drink it. The poor girl looked exhausted, and raw with the cold in a coat that was only fit to wear in the summer. Strong dislike of her former employers, for whom Nellie still worked, made Leila's voice sharp as she asked if the Clivedons were giving the girl extra tasks now their grandchild had been born.

Nellie's pinched face took on an expression of doubt as she looked back at Leila, her reddened hands seeking warmth around the cup. Blind loyalty made her fear speaking her mind.

"Well, little Miss Emma do need a lot of attention, and there's that much extra washin', you wouldn't believe. Miss Benedict, wot took your place, don't seem to do nothin' but change the baby's clo's ev'ry five minutes, and ring for 'ot water all day long."

Leila sipped her tea angrily. As scullery-maid Nellie was given all the fetching and carrying to do, regardless of her lack of robustness. Girls like her were easily come by, and just as easily thrown onto the streets if they did not have the stamina or temperament to survive their lot.

"*Miss Benedict!*" she exclaimed in derision. "First names were always good enough for the rest of us. What has she to be so high and mighty about?"

Nellie looked almost scared, even though Leila was uttering such sacrilege in her cosy basement rooms at least ten miles from Clivedon Place.

"Mrs 'ildreth calls 'er Miss Benedict, so does Lady Clivedon. I s'pose even Sir Frederick does. Cook says it's because she's been trained as a proper nurse, and come to us from the Medlars who took 'er to Switzerland when they went four years ago." Nellie's pale eyes were full of awe. "She speaks fluent French, Cook says."

"Ha!" exclaimed Leila scornfully. "I'd like to hear how she'd get on with some of the gentlemen who come to the theatre. They change from one language to another without a moment's thought."

"Oooh!" marvelled Nellie. "'Owever d'you manage when you're talkin' to them, then?"

"I don't," came her firm answer. "I keep myself to myself, and my mouth shut. I don't want anything to do with their sort."

"Oh, I nearly forgot. There's another letter come." Nellie began fumbling in her handbag that had been rescued from the rag-and-bone cart last year, and dragged out a crumpled envelope to lay on the chenille table-cloth. "It's from a place wiv ever such a funny name." She grew dreamy. "Fancy your Frank seein' somewhere abroad, and 'im only ordinary like us. Don't you wish you could 'ave gone wiv 'im?"

Leila got up and went to the hob. The old iron kettle was sizzling with steam that lifted the lid to rattle against the rim, and she took up the pad to wrap around the handle as she poured more water into the brown earthenware pot. Nellie had disconcerted her. A year ago she might have answered "yes" to that question. Now she avoided making one.

"What does Dastardly Desmond call Miss Benedict?" she asked, returning to the table. "I bet he doesn't dare to pinch her bottom like he used to mine. Sometimes I was black and blue from his wicked fingers."

Nellie looked around nervously, as if there might be hidden spies waiting to report back to her employers. "You shouldn't call Mr 'ildreth that," she whispered.

Leila smiled as she sat down. "I can call him anything I like now, and it's nothing to what others call him, I can tell you. He's well-known as a bounder and a libertine."

"What's that?"

"A libertine? Someone who does all the things a real gentleman shouldn't do, and far too often." She put her hand on Nellie's work-worn one as it lay on the table. "When is Jim going to marry you and get you out of that place?"

The pale face with its permanently red nose looked woeful. "Never —not on them wages. Mr Marks keeps sayin' 'e'll push Jim up to checker, which would bring in anuvver ninepence, but there's always an excuse when Jim asks about it. It's 'eavy work liftin' them barrels all day, and Jim's none too strong since 'e 'ad the pewmonia last winter. A shillin' goes to 'is ma's rent." She looked at Leila appealingly. "'E can't do nothin' else wiv 'er a widder. Now 'e's got the doctor's bills to pay after one of them barrels fell on 'is foot and crushed 'is toes. Can't barely walk on it now."

Leila sighed. "Mr Marks should pay the doctor if the accident happened on his premises."

Nellie's head wagged gloomily. "'E says Jim was careless and stacked the barrels wrong."

"Yes, I expect he did," replied Leila tartly, used to the ways of employers. "But your Jim should stand up for himself more. People like Mr Marks will always have the last word if we let them." Seeing Nellie looking longingly at the plate of biscuits she pushed them toward her. "Go on, have some more."

"You live ever so grand now," the girl commented, helping herself to another gingersnap. "Biscuits on a *plate*, like Lady C and Mrs 'ildreth. When they 'ad the last word wiv you, it did you a bit of good, reely, didn't it? I mean, you bein' a Lindley Girl and 'avin' this place all to yourself. It's better'n bein' Mrs 'ildreth's maid, I bet."

Leila resisted the biscuits. She had to keep her shape. "Yes. But they weren't to know I'd get work at Lindley's when they gave me my notice, Nellie; and for six months I lived in a bare freezing attic with only tea and buns to keep me going, don't forget. This basement is the first warm home I've had since they put me out on the street." Her voice grew more vigorous. "I'm going to have it just the way I've always wanted it before long, Nellie, my girl."

The little scullery-maid munched another biscuit, asking through the crumbs in her mouth, "Does that mean you've got a . . . *a gentleman friend,* then?"

"No, I haven't," replied Leila sharply. "You should know better than to ask that." She got to her feet again restlessly and walked around the tiny apartment, made darker on that November afternoon by the wall that rose to street level only three feet from her sole window. "This place had a few bits of furniture in it when I came, but I have bought the other things myself." As she walked her fingers trailed lightly across the japanned tray, the brass clock, the tallboy with its blond lace doily edged with glass beads, the patchwork cushions, the tasselled lamp-shades, and the china epergne filled with wax fruit. "I'm going to transform this place into a real home. I'm going to be warm on cold days, I'm going to eat from plates that aren't chipped and have beautiful patterns on them, and I'm going to have lamps lit during the daytime when it's a dark dreary day outside."

She swung round on the other girl, carried away by her own dreams. "As a Lindley Girl I earn more than I did as a lady's maid, but I have to spend more on clothes and cabs. Mr Gilbert won't have us arriving at the theatre by tram, and we always have to dress smartly in case we're recognised. But I'm moving up the line and, when I get to the front and lead them all in, my wages will go up." She walked back to the table and leant on it the better to impress Nellie with her next statement. "I'm going to buy a carpet then—a red Turkey carpet that will cover the whole room."

"You're *never!*" gasped Nellie. "What'll Frank think about it when 'e comes 'ome?"

In an instant, the vision of a luxury room shattered; reality came crashing through the frail fabric of her dreams. She sank back on her chair, filled with apprehension as dark as the autumn gloom seeping into her basement. The room suddenly seemed cold and dingy.

"The show will probably come off before I ever get to the front of the line," she said with heavy pessimism. "Miss Tait is playing merry hell with Mr Gilbert over her final number, and the novelty of our sequence will fade before long, I shouldn't wonder."

Nellie took another biscuit automatically and bit into it with gusto. "Cook says the papers claim you're all as naked as you was born under them feathers. Is that right?"

"Of course not, you silly. We'd have the censor after us if we were. Mr Gilbert had to show them the costumes before we could appear on stage in them."

"I wish I was as beautiful as wot you are," sighed the scrawny girl.

"Don't," advised Leila with a shake of her head. "Beauty can lead a girl into all sorts of things too quickly. Men are only out for what they can get. All of them—including your Jim. So watch it, young Nellie, and don't let him take you into any dark corners tonight."

The warning brought a blush to the young girl's cheeks as she stood up to go, full of thanks for the tea and biscuits. Leila began walking to the door with her.

"You know I'm always pleased to see you on your afternoon off—or any other time, of course."

The little servant-girl looked almost embarrassed as she confessed, "When you become a Lindley Girl, I didn't fink you'd want to be bovvered wiv me no more. You talks all la-di-dah now and wears frocks almost as good as wot the Clivedons wear, so it's 'ard to remember we once used to giggle togevver in that attic room."

"But I'm the same person underneath," Leila assured her, knowing it was a lie even as she said it. "Thanks for bringing me the letter . . . and for keeping the secret all this time."

Nellie turned impulsively in the doorway. "'E's goin' to come 'ome sometime and find 'e's bin writin' to the wrong place. Why don't you tell 'im the trufe, Lily? Deceivin' your 'usband is more sinful than goin' into dark corners wiv my Jim . . . and not 'arf as much fun!"

After Nellie had gone Leila did not open the letter immediately. It lay on the table, reminding her of something that now seemed unreal. All the time it remained unread Frank was a myth. The minute she slit the envelope and read, "Dear Lil . . ." the unalterable fact would be there confronting her. Drawing up the rocking-chair she had bought at the pawnbrokers, she sat enjoying the warmth from the range as she rocked back and forth, deep in thought. After this lapse in time she wondered yet again how it could have all happened.

Lily Lowe had been employed by Sir Frederick Clivedon as a member of his household staff. Because she had an attractive appearance, enough height to make her graceful in the long black or grey silk uniform of a lady's-maid, and some education, she had very quickly been promoted to the position of personal maid to Sir Frederick's only daughter after the young débutante's marriage to the handsome race-going philanderer, Desmond Hildreth. Doted on by her parents, Penelope Clivedon had only been allowed the husband of her choice because she had created a distressing scene when refused. But Sir

Frederick had insisted on the newly-weds living beneath his own roof, so that he could ensure that his beloved daughter had those things to which she was accustomed, and so that he could keep an eye on his unwelcome son-in-law. Desmond Hildreth had taken this penance with bad grace. He had wanted a town house, a seat on the board of Sir Frederick's mining company, and the continued freedom of a born philanderer. Denied these, the marriage was rocky from the start.

Despite that, a child was conceived almost immediately. It was wise strategy on Desmond's part because it would give him more freedom and his wife a "pet" to console her during his absences. But, as the pregnancy had advanced, it had brought extravagant coddling and anxiety from the grandparents-to-be. Because Lily Lowe had had no training as a children's nanny, they decided one had to be found, and only the best would do. The best cost correspondingly more than a lady's-maid and that, together with the expense of their parasitic son-in-law, forced them to cut their expenditure in other ways. Lily was dismissed after six years loyal service, but the Clivedons had been unaware that their maid had married two months earlier.

Frank Duncan had crossed Lily's path on one of her free afternoons. He had immediately swept her off her feet with his impressive build, his riot of black curly hair, and his wicked brown eyes. A trooper in a cavalry regiment, he had been full of swagger and tales of daring. Young, lonely and impressionable, Lily had thought him the most exciting person she had ever met. Realising this, Frank had pursued her with ardent and flattering determination until, on a summer afternoon four months later, he had taken her to the country for a picnic. She had been lethargic with sunshine and sandwiches; he had looked irresistibly virile with his open tunic revealing the muscles in his throat and a hint of dark hair on his chest. Later, she had realised that it must have been his intention to seduce her that day, but her own unbidden flare of passion had been responsible for her surrender. With fragrant hay all around her, and larks arising with songs of aching sweetness, sexual temptation had been so strong, so tremendous, Lily had lost her head. Only when passion had been spent had her sense of shame outweighed the alien pleasure to set her weeping.

During the following weeks, she had alternated between inbred fear and the furtive pleasure of what she was doing, powerless to refuse Frank's demands lest he turn to another girl instead. Then, on a rainy afternoon in a park, he had told her that his regiment was ordered to India for a spell of four years. The shattering announcement had coincided with Lily's dismayed discovery that she could be in the same condition as her mistress. Distraught, she had confessed this to him, and vowed that she would kill herself if her fears were confirmed. To her astonishment and relief, Frank had offered to marry her on her next free afternoon.

It had not been as simple as she had thought. After the civil ceremony, Frank had told his new bride that she could not go to India with the regiment, because he had not obtained permission to marry from his commanding officer. There had not been time, he had declared. With his persuasive charm, he had convinced her that she would be better off remaining with the Clivedons until he returned. There, she would have a roof over her head, decent food, and a little money of her own. It would mean that he would not be obliged to make her an allowance from his pay. He would save as much as he could during his four-year absence, because they would need funds to set up in style as a married couple when he sailed home, he had pointed out firmly. To this end, she must also keep her marriage a secret. The upper classes tended only to employ widows, or wives of men also in their households.

Bearing in mind her fears, he had given her the address of his mother in Scotland, and thirty shillings, which were his savings. If she was pregnant, he had told her, she could go to his mother for a home and help with the baby. Dazed, Lily had taken the money and the scrap of paper, promising that she would remain in her present employment until her condition became obvious. Then she would take the train to Scotland.

Frank had departed, having first made her swear to be true to him whilst he was away, leaving her, frightened and confused, to wait hand and foot on a young woman of wealth who was being pampered by an entire household. The feared pregnancy had been a false alarm, probably caused by Lily's first sexual activity, and she had breathed a sigh of relief. But what she and her roguish husband had not allowed for was the possibility of her being dismissed from the Clivedon household. It had seemed the most unlikely thing in the world.

With sexual temptation removed from her life by the departure of Frank, Lily had recovered her pride and self-possession. They had made her determined not to throw herself on the mercy of some strange woman in Scotland who did not even know of her existence, nor put her reliance on her husband on the other side of the world fighting savage tribesmen. She had been forced to set about finding other employment but, with no training in anything other than domestic work, it had not been easy. The Clivedons' reference had thoughtlessly stated that she had been dismissed because she was unequal to the post, failing to mention that the post in question was that of registered children's nurse, not a lady's-maid.

Desperate when Frank's money had finally been spent, she had joined the queue outside Lindley's Theatre where auditions were being held for chorus-girls. She had no experience in acting or dancing, but she could sing—and sing quite well. Yet she had put paid to her chances of letting them hear her voice, due to her training as a lady's-maid. Watching from the wings during a rehearsal of a scene from the new show, she had been reprimanded by an angry red-faced man for talking non-stop and too loudly to a girl called Rose standing next to her in the queue. Resentment at his tone had increased when he told her that she was distracting Miss Tait in the middle of a difficult scene. She had hotly replied that she could hardly put the girl *off* when she did not even know how to walk *on*.

"She's supposed to be a princess, isn't she?" she had challenged. "Well, real ladies don't walk with quick jerky steps like she is— prancing about like a pearly queen."

"So how *do* they walk, Miss Clever?" the man had retorted.

"Slow . . . and sort of wiggly. They hold their skirts like this with one hand when they turn around."

Her demonstration had been made with such exaggerated verve it had taken her out onto the stage itself, where the impressario Lester Gilbert had been watching the rehearsal. He had immediately demanded an explanation, which had sown the seed of an idea there and then in his mind. The result was the "Lindley Stroll".

Lily, who had given her name as "Leila" Duncan, had been engaged on the spot. But, although she had been the inspiration for the scene that now took London by storm, it had taken her nine months and a concentrated course of elocution, dancing, and acting lessons to earn even seventh place in that line of thirty girls. Lester Gilbert did not believe in overnight success for anyone but himself.

Leila Duncan was now poised, elegant, well-spoken and immensely independent. She was not in the least like Lily Lowe to whom Frank addressed the letters that Nellie brought round from Clivedon Place. That Leila had told him nothing of her present life was not due to a wish to spare him worry or concern whilst he was away fighting. It was because he was part of a past that had ended when she had entered the stage-door of Lindley's. Time had dulled the fire of sexual attraction, and also her memory. She could hardly now picture his face, recall the sound of his voice. Least of all could she remember what had made her feel the way she had about him; what could possibly have made her surrender so easily each time he had asked.

In truth, it was as if Frank Duncan had never existed, and it was only when his infrequent letters arrived that she remembered him at all. Then, as at the present moment, she felt guilty, ashamed, and a fraud. Most of all, she felt trapped and very afraid. Would she open the letter to find he was coming back earlier than she had thought?

Knowing she had to face the contents sooner or later, she took up the crumpled envelope Nellie had brought. It had been posted in a place called Peshawar. The letter, on a page torn from a book, began, "Dear Lil . . ." But her glance flew over the words looking for what she dreaded. Then she let out a sigh of relief. Leila Duncan had been given another reprieve.

She sank back in the chair, shutting her eyes against the gathering darkness. One day he would come back . . . unless a spear or a bullet . . . Oh no, *no!* Turning her head on the patchwork cushion she tried to banish such wicked thoughts from her mind.

Monty Monkton greeted Leila from his box just inside the stage-door that evening.

She smiled back at him. "The fog's just as thick as it was last night, Monty. Hope it doesn't keep people away."

"Nah!" he countered energetically. "It'd take an earthquake to keep them away from Lindley's right now. The gents *insist* on coming, and the ladies won't let them come alone." He gave a broad wink. "They know that if they do, they won't leave alone."

She walked on through the buff-painted corridor leading to the dressing-room, where the familiar warmth and combined smells of fustiness, grease paint, and perspiration greeted her. It was impossible not to be caught up in the excitement that backstage atmosphere invoked in her these days. Those, like Leila, who appeared in the concerted numbers of the first half were already there. They liked to be made-up and in costume before those who only appeared in the Lindley Stroll arrived, needing space. Leila went to her usual corner, further excited by the rows of bright lights shimmering the mirrors, and enhancing the vivid faces reflected in them.

"Hallo, girls," she warbled gaily. "Stand up all those who forgot to clap once and spit three times before entering tonight."

"Spit once and clap three times," corrected a full-bosomed girl in a pink corset.

"Ah, no wonder Jack Spratt gave me a strange look," she joked.

Jack Spratt was the stage-manager, who had reprimanded Leila at her audition. Although a hard taskmaster, he could spot true talent a mile away. Last month, he had told Leila that she would be leading in that line of girls before the run ended, and after that she would be walking on alone. He had meant solo parts, of course, but Leila just concentrated on the prospect of getting to the head of the line first. The solo parts she would tackle afterward.

Rose Heywood, Leila's friend, looked up at her as she took off her hat and coat. "Wotcher, ducky."

"Rose, Rose, where was your mind during the elocution lessons?" she scolded in mock severity.

"You know only too bloody well."

A bright voice from the other side of the dressing-room piped up, "Don't let Mr Gilbert hear you swear, Rose, or you'll be out on your ear . . . and I'll move up one place in the line."

"Wouldn't you just *love* that, dearie," came Rose's sour comment.

Leila put down her bag and looked closely at Rose. There was a tug at the corners of her mouth that was not disguised by the gaiety of her make-up.

"As bad as that, is it?" she asked her friend gently.

Rose flung down her hare's-foot and said in an explosive undertone, "I don't know what he really wants, Lei. I just don't know. One minute he tells me not to change in any way because it's the *real* me he fell in love with. Then he turns quiet and speaks as if his lips are glued together when we meet friends of his who look at me as though I came from Old Nog's dust-cart. Yesterday was the last straw. One of his Foreign Office pals asked me if I was one of the Dorsetshire Heywoods, and I'm just about to open my mouth when Miles says, all prissy like, 'Eoh yes, of *course*, old bean.' I was so angry I upped and said it was the bastard branch of the family I came from. They all laughed, except Miles. We had the most awful row." She slumped forward on her bent arms. "I sent all his presents back today, and told him never to visit me again. Now I'm so afraid he won't."

Leila looked helplessly at her bent head. "I'm so sorry, but nothing at all might be better than going up and down like a seesaw over him. There are plenty more fish in the sea."

"Wait until some man really takes your fancy, and try telling yourself that," came the muffled reply.

Leila left well alone and began preparing for the first number. Beauty was a curse. It led a girl into more problems than she should have to encounter. As she stroked rouge onto her cheeks and worked it in smoothly, she reflected that if Lily Lowe had been plain she would never have attracted the attention of Frank Duncan as he had passed by.

"Leila, you're wanted," called a voice. "Interview with Mr Gilbert right away."

She looked sideways to the end of the room, make-up stick poised. "Are you sure?"

"Message from Jack Spratt. Must be right."

Her heart jumped. Surely it could not be every chorus-girl's dream —the offer of a duet, or even a solo? Understudy to Adeline Tait? No, that was too ridiculous even for a dream. But why else would he send for her just before the show started, unless he had picked her out for something special? She flung on a kimono and made her way through the criss-cross of girls just as more arrived to change.

"What have you done, naughty girl?" one called after her.

"Put in a good word for me," called another.

"I hear dear Adeline has just walked out because of the 'Stroll' and someone has to go on for her tonight," joked another.

"If you go on in her costumes, Mrs Grundy will be after you," warned a girl as tall and statuesque as Leila. "They'll only cover half of you, ducky . . . but the Mashers will love it!"

She hurried across the backstage area, dodging stage-hands who were erecting flats, and telling her heart to be still. The others might chaff her, but Lester Gilbert did not send for members of his cast on trivial matters. He left those to his stage-manager. This *must* be something important.

The impressario's office could have been a room taken from a house and dropped into the theatre. Carpeted, wallpapered, and hung with expensive lighting, it was furnished with tasselled velvet chairs representing affluence and good taste. It was intended to impress visitors and satisfy the owner's vanity. It put the fear of God into mere chorus-girls.

He greeted her effusively, calling her Miss Duncan and inviting her to sit down. Lester Gilbert was a large man who could have made the perfect Falstaff if he had been able to act. But, like many professional people, he was brilliant at showing others how best to do something he could not do himself. Bushy greying eyebrows rose up and down comically as he complimented her on her beauty and graceful movements on stage.

"I never make a mistake, Miss Duncan," he told her proudly. "I knew you had that special quality the moment you stepped so ill-manneredly onto my stage and interrupted the rehearsal." He smiled revealing several gold teeth. "All my girls are beautiful, but you have a light from within, my dear."

Leila well knew his penchant for waxing poetic, and schooled her expression to attentive gravity.

"Small wonder my patrons have also noticed that special quality." He sat to the accompaniment of grunts, then leant back to ease the strain on his stomach. "A theatre, my dear, is a place where magic is created. It turns the tawdry into the exquisite, the beautiful into the tragic, age into youth. We who work in the theatre have a duty to perform, not only within its plush sanctity, but outside in the harsh reality of life."

She wondered what was coming, but dared not interrupt him in full flow. He placed the tips of his fingers together and assumed a frown as he studied her beneath the bushy brows.

"It was made known to me last night that you were ungracious enough to decline a gentleman's invitation to supper by returning his flowers with the invitation still attached, and further relaying to him the advice that you would treat any other such invitations the same way. I can hardly believe it of you, but my Mercury is extremely trustworthy. Do you care to give an explanation of this extraordinary business?"

Leila was so full of disappointment, so let down after her high expectations, she could not speak for a moment. He read her silence as guilt and continued.

"I understand the gentleman in question was a stranger to you, so you cannot have been offended by his behaviour in the past. I also understand that he went about the affair in the most courteous manner, and intended that you should join a party with five of your friends. There was certainly no hint of anything to which I could take the slightest exception."

Leila now found her voice, and it was sharpened by her disappointment. "But *I* took exception to it. He had paid for his ticket and seen the show. He then thought he could buy his entertainment for the rest of the night, with a bunch of flowers and some meat with vegetables."

"*A bunch of flowers, and meat with vegetables!*" echoed the aesthete, his sensibilities immeasurably bruised by such a description of hothouse roses and a supper at Romano's.

Undeterred, she went on. "Mr Gilbert, I perform on stage as well, and probably better, than most of the others. That is what you pay me for. Nothing else."

He shook his head sadly. "You are wrong. Dear me, how wrong you are." A flourish of his hand indicated her from top to toe. "I have created *this* Leila Duncan from a pert, rather brash lady's-maid. You have no right to destroy her when the curtain falls. You must maintain the magic at all times, or the house will soon be empty, I assure you. This is the third time I have been told of your refusal to extend the pleasure of your admirers' evenings with a little wine and supper." At the sight of her caustic expression, he smiled faintly. "Miss Duncan, these gentlemen are not to be compared with ruffians from the gallery.

24

They are generous, cultured, and intelligent. They know better than to misplace their affections where *my* girls are concerned."

She stood up, not caring whether he wanted to end the interview or not. "This isn't a job, Mr Gilbert, but an entire life. You ask a lot for your two pounds a week."

He rose lengthily. "Not ask, but *give*, my dear young lady. You are doing well here. I might find a duet—even a solo—for you one day. A public reputation for ungraciousness would defeat all that. You obviously have ambition, so use your admirers to that end. Popularity can vie with talent, you know. There is nothing wrong with aloofness —I expect it of Lindley Girls—but, tempered with charm, it becomes a most irresistible combination." He came across and patted her arm. "Now run along and get into your costume. A beautiful girl is born to be admired, and there is a full house out there, despite the fog. They have not braved the elements in order to be rebuffed with ill manners. Bear that in mind and remember my words this evening. After a little reflection, I am sure you will see the wisdom in them."

Leila walked slowly to the dressing-room, despite the sounds of the overture out front. She had little choice but to do as he asked. He was a gentle-mannered man, but he had not climbed to where he was through sentimentality. She still thought he asked an unreasonable return for his wages, but he had made it clear that she must be prepared to conduct flirtations or leave.

Climbing frantically into her costume as the other girls all filed out for the opening number, she muttered darkly to herself, "All right, Mr Gushing Gilbert, you hold all the aces . . . but woe betide the first generous, cultured, intelligent 'gentleman' who tries to get more for his hothouse roses than a supper companion!"

# CHAPTER TWO

Having made the break from her wealthy lover, Rose Heywood set about showing him and the rest of the world that she did not care. On Sunday morning, she persuaded Leila to accompany her to Brighton, where Miss Agatha Heywood, the aunt who had mothered Rose, ran a boarding-house for theatrical people.

After the foggy days of the previous week, November sprung a surprise, producing a golden-russet day overhung with arctic-blue skies. Autumn sunshine brought a vivid sparkling clarity of form and colour to everything. The air was still and chill, blushing the cheeks of children and the noses of the elderly, as the population of Brighton came from their houses to stroll along the promenade.

Leila and Rose wore coats with fur trimming at their throats and wrists, and hats of soft matching fur, tilted provocatively over one eye and held in place with long pearl-topped hatpins.

"We might be glad of these," Rose had commented, re-pinning her hat prior to arrival at the station. "If we should happen to be pestered by one of those creatures who call themselves 'gentlemen', a good poke with one of these should do the trick."

Leila had giggled. "What I'd give to have a go with mine on Dastardly Desmond Hildreth. Remembering all those pinches he gave me in the past, I'd know exactly where to poke it."

Rose's lovely face had assumed an expression of shock. "Really, Miss Duncan, Lindley Girls should not only *never* speak of such things, they should not even know of the existence of the best place to poke it."

They had collapsed into laughter, which had set their mood for the day. A warming breakfast of bacon and pan potatoes with Aunt Agatha, was the prelude to their spell in the Court playground of yesteryear. They next strolled around the Royal Pavilion, where trees in the surrounding gardens were in their last glory of reds, golds, and browns against the clear sky, and their kid boots crunched the crisp leaves that had already fallen along the paths.

It was not long before they heard the sound of a distant band, and realised that everyone was walking in the direction of it. Rose turned to Leila, her face aglow with the freshness of the day.

"It must be the regiments returning from church parade! The bands give a concert afterwards. Come on, let's go with all these others."

They followed the crowd and soon the walls of the barracks came in sight. There was something about the swelling sound as the band drew nearer that aroused excitement in those awaiting the marching column. In the two chorus-girls it awoke an answering call of showmanship. Then the front ranks turned the corner of the long street. Brass instruments flashed in the sunshine; scarlet and blue uniforms were a blaze of colour against grey buildings, the gold epaulettes on the jackets glinting impressively. Shining black boots thumped on the road, bugles rang with strident calls, tubas oompah-pah'd richly, and the regimental drummers twirled their sticks with great panache between each rataplan.

Rose nudged Leila. "Beats anything Lester Gilbert ever thought up."

But Leila was far away. The uniforms, the military music, the sound of marching feet reminded her that she had a husband in India, who imagined that she was still a lady's-maid at Clivedon Place. The chill of the day was suddenly in her heart, the beauty of the autumn went unseen by her now. The wedding-ring she had worn on a thread around her neck, at the start, had lain in the bottom of her trinket box for over a year. With young Nellie the only person in England who knew her secret, it was all too easy to pretend that it did not exist.

"What's up? You look as though you've seen a ghost," said Rose beside her. "Cast your eyes over there and see which one you fancy. I always think the cavalry are more exciting than the infantry. Trouble is," she added incorrigibly, "they can get away faster."

Leila tried to recapture her earlier feeling of carefree enthusiasm, and gave a smile. "I thought you had a hatpin to keep the creatures at bay."

Rose pulled a face. "A girl can change her mind, can't she? *They* are forever doing it."

Leila knew that her friend was eaten up with misery over Miles Lampton, and told herself she must emulate Rose's attempt to drive away low spirits with gaiety. So she watched the cavalry clop past, the riders' faces aloof and impersonal beneath helmets that looked, to her, like coal-scuttles turned upside-down, with a stiff peak added. She admired the glossy animals they rode, while she tried hard not to think of Frank Duncan.

The column turned in through the barrack gates and marched in to form up on the square in immaculate and colourful ranks whilst the ceremony of dismissal took place. The crowd followed them in and, when the parade was allowed to fall out on the imperious commands of

27

the officers, the band played on while soldiers met up with their best girls, or their proud parents, or their wives pushing perambulators.

The square then became a kaleidoscope of colour as people strolled about in the sunshine, enjoying melodies by Signor Tosti, marches by Herr Strauss, and ballads by Mr German. Birds sang in the unexpected warmth. The mellow notes of brass instruments were given added roundness by the still, brisk temperatures, and the soft shuffle of feet as the promenaders circled again and again gave the whole scene an air of peaceful contentment.

Leila was charmed, despite her sobering thoughts of a moment before, as she and Rose strolled in Lindley style past young girls dressed in their smartest coats and hats, past trim wives pushing babies soothed by the music and the rocking of their perambulators, past elderly couples in their Sunday best, who were defying the autumn of their lives on a day that defied the autumn of the year. Youth and excitement stirred within her again to the sound of the music. She had become one of the famous Lindley Girls; she had been told she had talent. If accepting invitations from "toffs" meant Lester Gilbert would promote her, then she would do it. Frank would not be home for a couple of years yet, and anything could happen by then.

Only vaguely aware that one of the soldiers was riding past very close to them, she and Rose were brought to a sudden terrified halt when the horse pranced sideways out of control, and reared up with a loud whinney right in front of them. A huge beast, it looked truly fearsome when rampant no more than a few feet away. Leila shrieked as she saw the polished hooves waving above her head; so did Rose. The animal's front legs crashed down just short of them, and the rider used voice and hands to bring the mettlesome stallion under control. Still it danced and sidled for a few moments, eyes rolling, blowing breath from its nostrils in frightening snorts. The incident had scattered people, leaving the two girls clutching each other, too scared to move. All eyes were now on them, and some nearby soldiers left their companions to make their way over to the shaken pair.

"Are you all right, miss?"

"Come away, ladies, he's still a bit restive."

They were coaxed from the vicinity of the high-spirited beast toward a semi-circle of spectators, all of whom looked shocked or impressed, according to their sex. The troops exchanged significant looks.

"He'll break his neck one of these days."

"It's the horse they'll have to shoot, not him."

"Rot, he's the best rider in the regiment," said a third man to the other two.

28

Rose looked at them, saying in her inimitable way, "If that's true, then God help the rest of you."

The soldiers were affronted at such words, in such a tone, from such an elegant female—one who ought to be suffering palpitations of fright, and displaying gratitude to her gallant rescuers. Their affront lasted no more than a moment, for they suddenly stiffened to attention, their faces adopting blank expressions as they stared at something behind the girls.

Leila swung round in alarm, convinced that the uncontrollable horse was now galloping full-pelt at them, but it was being led away and it was the rider who was striding in their direction. Leila and Rose were tall girls, but this man looked a true giant in headgear which added another foot to his height. What could be seen of his face between the gold-encrusted peak and the wide ornate chinstrap, was dark-complexioned and strong. Admitting that his build was impressive, and his approach was most determined, Leila still could not understand why the men at her side should seem more afraid of him than of his horse.

He arrived before them, giving the soldiers a sharp nod. "I'll deal with this. You may go."

"Yessir!" they snapped out in unison, and turned about in smart military style to march back to their companions.

So the "best rider in the regiment" was an officer! Leila studied him with interest as he saluted with great panache.

"Ladies, my deepest apologies for submitting you to such an ordeal," he said. "I trust you are both unharmed. Oscar is a well-trained thoroughbred, but . . ." he gave a wide persuasive smile, "he is plainly no proof against beauty. The sight of you both walking past shattered his composure as badly as it did mine."

That smile, together with a low, slightly husky voice, set Leila's spine tingling with a strange excitement. His impact left her lost for words.

Rose responded unhesitatingly, however. "Are you also a well-trained thoroughbred, sir?"

Leila's colour rose at her friend's impudence, but the man chuckled, and bowed as he introduced himself.

"Vivian Veasey-Hunter, at your service, ma'am."

A sixth sense told Leila that it would be wise to put an end to the encounter as soon as possible, so she said in her most refined accent, "There was no harm done, I assure you. Come along, Rose, we shall be late for our appointment."

Her friend had no intention of being dragged from someone whom she plainly found fascinating. Looking up at the brown face partially hidden by the curious head-dress, she said, "Vivienne is a girl's name. Was your mother hoping for a daughter instead?"

He chuckled again. "I have never thought to ask her, but I should imagine her hopes were soon frustrated when I arrived, shouldn't you?"

Rose looked him over from the spurs on his polished black boots to the plume on his flat-topped helmet, saying with undisguised admiration, "Oh, very definitely."

Leila was growing annoyed with her. This man was an officer and an obvious gentleman. The longer they stood there talking to him, the more their dignity suffered. Rose was making the situation worse by encouraging him. When Lily Lowe had met a trooper in the street and walked off with him, it had been the acceptable way for those in the lower classes to get to know each other. This was vastly different and, guessing the thoughts that must be in this man's mind, Leila was determined to put an end to them as soon as possible.

"Rose, we really should be on our way," she urged.

The military man turned his full attention onto her, saying with outrageously assumed gravity, "Dear me, *you* are still angry with me, Miss . . . ?"

She was not to be drawn, however. "Not at all. Your apology was more than adequate."

"Then you must have been more shaken by the incident than your friend," he persisted. "You have not yet recovered the delightful smile I saw you wearing just before Oscar disgraced himself."

"Small wonder that you lost control of your horse, Mr Veasey-Hunter," she told him tartly. "Your attention was plainly wandering."

His mouth twitched, but he responded with continuing gravity. "There, I knew you had not forgiven me."

Feeling her colour rise at his insufferable baiting, she looked away to where the band was still playing. "You are making far too much of what was really a most trivial affair."

"No, Leila, we might have been trampled to death by Oscar," put in Rose mischievously. "There'd have been nothing trivial about two of the Lindley Girls being killed by a runaway horse."

"Dear me," he responded, taking up his opportunity with smooth expertise, "your words make me realise the full extent of the danger to which I exposed you both, Miss Lindley."

Rose laughed gaily. "Wherever have you been for the past year, Mr Veasey-Hunter?"

"Fighting the Ashantis on the Gold Coast. Why?"

"That explains why you haven't heard of the Lindley Girls. We have become the rage of London, you know."

30

His tone was even more huskily attractive as he said, "Then I have now sunk even lower in your estimation than before. A shocking horseman, and an ignoramus, to boot. A further apology will really not suffice, I see that. Yet I wonder if I have the temerity to offer more, being unaware of the extent of the honour you would be affording me by accepting."

Leila was furious. He was laughing at them, surely Rose could see that. No matter where he had been fighting for the past year, he could hardly have avoided hearing of the Lindley Stroll. Columns in newspapers were full of it and it was the talk of the West End. She decided to end the meeting immediately.

"We are actresses, Mr Veasey-Hunter—chorus-girls at Lindley's Theatre. The only honour that we can afford you is to agree with your description of yourself and bid you good-day."

"*Leila!*" exclaimed Rose, as she turned away.

Their companion was plainly equal to anything, for he said swiftly to Rose, "Now that I realise how very deeply I have offended your friend, there is really only one way in which I can make amends. I am due to meet my brother for luncheon at Gallini's. Allow me to redeem myself by showing you how well-behaved and civilised I can be. I beg you to give us the pleasure of your company."

Gallini's was exclusive, highly expensive, and very, very respectable. An invitation to join him for a meal there could in no way be translated as an insult. In fact, it was more than complimentary that he considered them fit to accompany him to such a place. Leila was momentarily disarmed, and Rose had accepted before she could say a word. Next minute, Leila found herself linking her gloved hand through his left arm, while Rose did the same with his right, to stroll the short distance to the renowned restaurant. It was only when he smiled down at her and said in a tone that she read very well, "You will find my respectable brother very much more to your taste," that she realised how completely she had been routed.

They drew many glances as they entered the street leading to their rendezvous, and he was visibly delighted by the attention caused by their progress. Rose looked stunning in a coat of amber-coloured wool trimmed with musquash, and Leila felt at her best in grey velvet, frogged with black braid and softened at throat and wrist by the blue fox fur of which her saucy hat was also made. She let Rose do all the talking as they strolled through the clear, sparkling noonday air. Her own thoughts refused to be disciplined, for it seemed that she was under the influence of a personality more determined than her own.

31

Gallini's had maintained the Regency atmosphere with striped brocaded wall-hangings, gilt spindle-legged furniture, and huge candelabra. Gallini, himself, was Italian to the core, however, and greeted their escort with Gallic deference tinged with a trace of hauteur. The hauteur vanished when he was told that his patron was the brother of Mr Veasey-Hunter, who had reserved a table, and he then led the way through a salon decorated in green and gold. Little more than half the other man's height, the Italian still managed to look impressive as he advanced through the assembling diners, an apology here, a "*scusi*" there, until he brought them up to a man dressed in fawn and brown checked trousers and a buff cutaway coat, sitting in a chair by the window.

"Your guests have arrived, sir," said Gallini bowing away gracefully, his hand circling in an expressive European gesture.

The man looked up and his expression of welcome changed to one of bewilderment as he caught sight of Leila and Rose. Immediately, the feeling that this was a grave mistake flooded through Leila once more, but their tall escort was seizing his brother by the hand and clapping him on the shoulder with the other one.

"Charles, how good to see you again! You look splendid, as usual. My dear fellow, allow me to present you to Miss Heywood and her friend Miss Duncan, who have graciously consented to lunch with us." He turned to Rose and smiled. "My younger brother Charles. Would you agree that a son must definitely have been hoped for this time?"

Leila's doubts grew as Charles Veasey-Hunter bowed over their hands, reciting all the correct things with a grave formality at odds with his youth. She felt he knew all too well that they had no place in such exclusive premises, and could probably guess the circumstances under which they had been invited. However, pride rose to her rescue, when the military man excused himself on the grounds that he had come straight from a parade and should tidy himself, then left his brother to deal with a situation he seemed unable to assimilate.

Their coats were taken and they were invited to sit before the fire, but Charles Veasey-Hunter remained standing, watching the door through which his cavalier brother had vanished. Around six feet tall he was still shorter than the other by several inches, and seemed of vastly more sober character. Smooth brown hair, a brown moustache, and sad brown eyes gave him the melancholy, trustworthy air of a faithful dog. There was nothing in the least hostile in his attitude, but he was very plainly ill at ease in their company. Leila felt that he had been shabbily treated, and decided to make everything clear to him from the start.

"Mr Veasey-Hunter, I am afraid we are intruding on a private meal between yourself and your brother. The truth of the matter is that we were watching the parade this morning, when Oscar succumbed to a bout of temperament which gave us both a bad fright. We were quite unharmed, but your brother seemed to feel it necessary to make amends in rather extravagant fashion. Mr Veasey-Hunter is a difficult man to refuse," she concluded, by way of explanation.

"He is a *captain*, you know . . . er, in the 49th Lancers. Prince Harry's Own," came the serious statement.

"We are chorus-girls," she told him firmly, "in *The Maid of Montezuma.*"

"Lester Gilbert's Own," smiled Rose teasingly, enjoying herself immensely.

He seemed even more ill at ease, but managed forced enthusiasm. "Oh, that's splendid! I'm afraid I rarely go to the theatre. Never seem to have the time when I am in Town. I don't know how Vivian manages to get around as he does. Hardly ever in barracks, I hear. Only consolation is he is hardly ever off a horse, which is essential for a cavalryman."

"The best rider in the regiment," volunteered Rose.

"Oh, indeed," agreed their host, apparently delighted that his brother's reputation should be known even to chorus-girls in a show of which he had, unbelievably, never heard. "Ah, here he is now," he added, in undisguised relief.

Leila turned, and received a shock. Without the elaborate helmet, he was still around six feet four inches tall, and she was curiously shaken by the striking combination of hair that was creamy-fair and bleached by the same sun that had darkened his skin to golden-brown, a broad intelligent face marked by pale laughter-lines, and eyes that were grey-green and full of amusement. Less handsome than his brother, Vivian Veasey-Hunter was nevertheless wickedly attractive in the tight-fitting uniform which emphasized his muscular grace. As he drew nearer, Leila could see that he was well aware of the impact he was making on her. Too late, she tried to hide it by turning to study the view from the window.

"Haven't you offered the ladies a glass of refreshment, Charles? How remiss of you," he scolded, raising a brown hand nonchalantly.

Instantly, a waiter was there to do his bidding, and that set the pattern of the occasion. Vivian was an accomplished host, his brother appearing only too happy to relinquish control of a situation that he had not expected and was hardly enjoying. Throughout the pre-luncheon period, and the meal itself, Leila was left to entertain the diffident Charles. Rose appeared to captivate Vivian, to the extent that Leila began to resent the evidence that he had only engineered the foursome so that he could pair her with his dull brother, and leave himself free to flirt with her friend.

The unique delight of eating in Gallini's luxurious chandeliered rooms soon palled, as she plodded through heavy conversation centred on Cornwall, where the Veasey-Hunter family had lived for the past two hundred years. She agreed that it was tragic about the closure of the tin mines, whilst privately being surprised at the discovery that tin was dug from the ground. Following that subject, they went on to discuss the development of the gold mines in South Africa, and the power of Cecil Rhodes. At least, Charles Veasey-Hunter discussed it. Leila had no idea who Cecil Rhodes was, or what he did. Neither was she much interested in finding out, when Rose and the lively Vivian were having so much fun beside them.

Time passed, and Leila was beginning to grow extremely resentful of the situation when Charles, having apparently said all he wished about the man called Rhodes, asked her if she lived in Brighton.

"No," she told him. "We are on a short visit to Miss Heywood's aunt, who has a large house overlooking the promenade."

A thought then appeared to strike him, and he leant forward to ask hopefully, "You are not one of the Berkshire Duncans, I suppose?"

The memory of something Rose had said during the week, prompted her to say, before she knew, "Oh, yes . . . the bastard line of the family."

Her companion flushed a surprising dull red, and studied his napkin in obvious deep embarrassment. Growing aware of silence at the table, Leila turned to find Rose staring in amazement. However, it was Vivian who took her attention. All trace of amusement had gone from his expression. His eyes now held a curious intentness as he gazed at her with an air of faint shock. Instinct told her that she had gained his interest with a vengeance, now. She took advantage of the fact immediately.

"Is something wrong, Captain Veasey-Hunter?" she asked crisply. "Oscar's tantrum this morning might have affected you more than you knew." She turned to Charles. "What is your opinion, sir? You should know your brother's constitution well enough to make a judgement."

Still visibly embarrassed, he stammered a confession that they had not met for two years, due to Vivian's service overseas which could have wreaked changes in him.

Leila immediately relented. "Oh dear, do you mean to say that this luncheon was intended as a reunion? It is really too bad of your brother not to have told us. We would never have dreamed of intruding, under such circumstances." She rose, obliging the men to do so. "It has been a

34

most enjoyable meal, but we shall now leave you to enjoy each other's company. After so long apart, there must be much you wish to speak of . . . about the mines, and Mr Rhodes," she could not help adding, despite her regret that Vivian should think so little of his brother that he had burdened him with the necessity of entertaining a pair of actresses who had taken his fancy on the way to the meeting.

"No, no really," protested the confused Charles. "I trust I did not give the impression . . . I mean, it has been truly delightful, I assure you."

Leila smiled at him warmly. "You have been more than charming, Mr Veasey-Hunter. As for your brother, I trust he rewards Oscar with more kindness over the incident than he has you, sir." A brief glance at the expression on that suntanned face, still revealing his acute awareness of her, brought a feeling of satisfaction as she said, "Come along, Rose."

Before her friend could protest, she walked from the room with no suggestion of the famous lethargic Lindley Stroll, the skirt of her strawberry-pink dress dragging the thick blue carpet of Gallini's.

They were assisted into their coats and escorted to the carriage Vivian had told the door-man to summon. The goodbyes were brief. Leila knew Rose was annoyed because she had ended the meeting so abruptly, but it was nothing to the anger she felt toward her friend over the whole incident. The carriage pulled away, heading toward Aunt Agatha's boarding-house, and Rose leant back against the squabs to fix her with a wide-eyed stare.

"Well, well, what was all that about? I've never seen you in a right royal miff before. Carry on like that and you'll soon rival Adeline Tait."

Leila was still fuming. "Rose, don't you ever force me into a situation like that again. You don't know how close I came to using the hatpin—on *you*!"

Rose made a face. "Sometimes I think you're destined to be an old maid, Leila Duncan. You're all tight mouthed and disapproving."

"And *you* are supposed to be heartbroken over Miles Lampton," she snapped back, touched on the raw by the reminder that the one thing she could never be was an old maid.

They went some distance in silence, Leila finding that she was trembling from an emotion she could not identify. Then Rose said, in comic mimicry, "He's a *captain*, you know. In the faldalal lancers."

Leila could never resist her friend's perky personality for long, and a slow smile broke on her face. "Rose dear, you must let me tell you all about Cyril Rhodes one day."

"Who the dickens is Cyril Rhodes?"

"Someone who is apparently more famous than the Lindley Girls, because Canine Charles had heard of him."

Rose exploded into giggles. "*Canine Charles*. Oh, Lei, what a laugh!"

Leila also began to giggle. "He did look rather like a sad dog, didn't he?"

"With a pedigree, of course."

"Otherwise Gushing Gallini would never have admitted him," agreed Leila, spluttering into her handkerchief as reaction to the meeting increased her laughter.

They laughed all the way to Miss Heywood's boarding-house, but neither girl mentioned *Vivian* Veasey-Hunter that day, or in the days that immediately followed.

The brothers turned from the departing carriage, and made their way to the Gentlemen's Lounge. They ordered Cognac, and Charles apologised to Vivian the moment that the waiter departed.

"If I had had the slightest notion that she would make such a confession, I swear I would never have . . ."

Vivian cut him short in irritation. "For God's sake, Charles, when will you cease wearing a hair-shirt? I came to terms years ago with my illegitimacy. Why can't you?" Lighting a cigar during his brother's resultant silence, he went on, in quieter tones, "She achieved her purpose, which was to shock us into paying her the attention she felt was due to her. I'll wager she is not a bastard. A girl of her kind would never admit the fact in public, if it were true."

Charles sat in one of the camel-hide chairs, and gave him a reproachful look. "It was really too bad of you to oblige me to entertain her, so that you could spend an hour or so with a coquette whose looks had caught your roving eye. Dash it, Viv, you know I'm no ladies' man. I hadn't the first notion of what to say to Miss Duncan."

The waiter brought their drinks, and Vivian sat in the companion chair beside his brother, stretching out his legs to the fire as he swirled the Cognac in the bulbous glass.

"Did you know that those two are actresses?" Charles asked then.

"Certainly I knew," he murmured. "You've mistaken the case, however. It is Miss Duncan who caught my roving eye."

"Miss Duncan! Then why on earth . . . ?"

Vivian smiled faintly at his brother's confusion. "I had been back in England for only two days when Biffy Hayes-Mortimer dragged me to Lindley's Theatre, where those two, along with twenty-eight other beauties, perform in a show which has taken the West End by storm. Take it from me, what they do on that stage is enough to make a man's temperature rise to fever point," he added, remembering the sight from his box four evenings before. "As I had just returned from an area aptly named 'White Man's Grave', mine shot up alarmingly. The cause of my dangerous medical condition was Leila Duncan who, when dressed in little more than white ostrich feathers, tests a man's senses severely."

Charles shook his head resignedly. "When are you going to sober up, Viv?"

He savoured the Cognac before replying. "Never, if it means finding no pleasure in the sight of girls clad in tantalising costumes. However, this particular bird of paradise revealed that she had a sharp beak. My invitation to supper was turned down, with the advice that the bastion was unassailable. She even sent back my flowers, which made me look a fool in front of a mere call-boy, to say nothing of Hayes-Mortimer and his friends. I was piqued, but decided to retire in good order. Then, as I rode past the barracks this morning, I saw that same beautiful haughty face in the crowd. It seemed too much of a coincidence, until I saw them both strolling in that same provocative style. I couldn't resist the challenge."

He sipped reflectively, enjoying the recollection of the two girls clutching each other and squealing in fright, whilst he put his stallion through his histrionic paces.

"Oscar has never forgotten a trick I taught him on manoeuvres. He performed beautifully, and those two were gratifyingly terrified. Dressed in fur, Miss Leila Duncan still affected my temperature, so I played the repentant officer and gentleman. Her response should have cooled my blood, not heated it. Luckily, her saucy friend was very receptive to my charm, and I would have lost my advantage if I hadn't brought them here. I apologise for forcing them on you, but the opportunity to oblige the frosty Miss Duncan to eat a meal in my company, after all, was too fortuitous to ignore."

Charles sighed. "If it is Miss Duncan who has taken your fancy, why did you concentrate solely on her volatile friend?"

Shifting his legs to a more comfortable position, Vivian enlightened his brother. "Cavalry tactics can be used to great effect against any adversary—even the soft, cuddlesome variety. A full-blooded charge at Miss Duncan would have been repelled, once more, but a feint had her completely disarmed. That little beauty went off with her feathers badly ruffled, which was exactly what I wanted. Perhaps she'll think twice before throwing a man's flowers back at him, even though she had no idea that they were mine that she rejected last week."

Tossing back the remainder of the Cognac, he put the subject from his mind and concentrated fully on his brother, whom he had not seen for two years. "I appreciate your coming to Brighton, Charles. I've been tied up trying to settle my affairs and find suitable lodgings. You know how it is when one returns from a spell abroad, and November is the worst month in which to encounter the change from equatorial heat. That damned fever, which almost put an end to me, did allow me the chance of recuperation in the more temperate climate of Rhodesia before returning here. I visited Mama there, of course."

"She was in good health, I trust."

"Oh, yes, and looking more lovely than I remembered. She seems so fragile compared with many women. However could she have produced men of our size?"

"We have grown, Viv," his brother pointed out.

Vivian studied Charles, who had never enjoyed a close relationship with their mother, as he had. Perhaps his brother had deliberately avoided it, for the sake of peace.

"Mama was but seventeen when she first married Father. He treated her with the most callous inconsideration, in my opinion. His reputation as a libertine was no secret, even during his lifetime."

"These things are often exaggerated," reasoned Charles, with some awkwardness.

"Exaggerated? I don't think you have ever been aware of how she suffered because of his succession of *affaires*, which he hardly conducted with discretion. After turning her first-born into a bastard, he forced her to accept the fact that he had sired others during their marriage," Vivian said with great heat. "No doubt, he treated them with the same contempt he reserved for me."

Charles regarded him for several seconds with frank speculation. "You have *not* come to terms with your damned illegitimacy, as you repeatedly claim. I think you never will, Viv."

Signalling for more Cognac, Vivian said with a bite in his voice, "I suggest that we drop the subject. It always makes us both edgy and solves nothing." Tossing his cigar butt into the fire, he went on, "I have a long letter for you, which Mama charged me to deliver. I believe it contains her hope that you will visit her before long."

To his surprise, his brother's colour rose slightly. "It is more than likely that she will come to England, at the end of next year."

Intrigued, Vivian asked, "For what reason?"

"Nothing is yet to be announced," Charles said in diffident tones, "but *The Times* will receive notification on my twenty-eighth birthday of my forthcoming marriage."

"You sly dog!" he cried, astonished to find that his introvert brother had wooed and won a suitable bride during his own two-year absence.

"Who is to be the future Lady Brancliffe? Is she a sweet country innocent, straight from the schoolroom, or a dashing society beauty, who has had every bachelor on his toes?"

Shaking his head in obvious irritation, Charles said, "This is to be a marriage, not the kind of loose liaison that you conduct with such relish. Brancliffe and Sir Kinsley think it an ideal match, and I am exceedingly happy with the situation."

Surprise was too faint a word to describe Vivian's reaction to this news. His brother, who was heir to all that should have been his but for a cruel twist of fate, was apparently set to marry the daughter of their Cornish neighbour. Julia Marchbanks was the fifth child after four sons. There would be no marriage dowry for her, so that could not have influenced such a disastrous decision.

He leant forward urgently. "For God's sake, don't allow yourself to be pushed into such a union. You say nothing has yet been announced, so all is not lost."

Charles stiffened, his colour rising again. "You could not have heard my words just now. I am exceedingly happy with the situation."

Still unable to take in the truth, Vivian sank back against the chair to study Charles thoughtfully. Unworldly, malleable, his brother had worn the yoke of his strange inheritance uneasily. Vivian had never been sure whether his advice and help with the family estate had been sought because Charles was genuinely lacking in authority, or because ingrained guilt led him to attempt reparation for something neither brother could put right. Perhaps Julia was a good choice of partner for the shy, future Lord Brancliffe, if he truly was happy with the match. As the only female in a family of men, Julia had developed sporting tastes that were known throughout the West Country. Tall and buxom, she would be hardy enough for life at Shenstone, and her forthright personality might compensate for his brother's nature, which sought peace, at any price. It was some years since Vivian had seen the girl, but he remembered her as a country dowdy, unremarkable in looks apart from very large eyes, which could do a lot for her if she ever learned to use them to advantage.

As the waiter placed fresh glasses on the table, Vivian gave a rueful smile. "My felicitations, Charles. You have more sense than I. Julia will not only make you an excellent wife, she will uphold her social position very capably. I drink to your future."

Charles looked back at him with the familiar faint guilt. "What of your future? You have passed thirty and, from all I hear even down at Shenstone, have led a rackety existence. Marriage would steady you no end."

Vivian protested heartily. "Our father's rackety existence led to you being the heir, not I. Yours is the obligation to marry, Charles. I am blessedly free of it, and have no desire to embark on anything that would steady me. I damn well enjoy being *un*steady and intend to remain that way."

"With a succession of fast females, and chorus-girls who are ill-mannered enough to return your flowers?"

"Ah, the Duncan wench is the only one who has done that," he corrected. "I'll take care that she never does so again. All the same, I'll wager she'd be eating out of my hand very soon if I chose to pursue the affair."

Rueful humour crept into his brother's eyes. "You're still a rakish devil despite the ravages of equatorial jungle."

"So I should hope," he returned, as lightly as he could.

They drank in silence for a moment, then Charles asked, "What was it really like out there?"

Keeping his gaze on the fire, Vivian felt the warmth and civilised pleasure of the day fade as he forced himself to speak of something that would live in his mind for a long time, even though he drove it from conscious thought with indulgence in every kind of pleasure.

"What was it like? About as close to hell as a man can get, possibly. There are four natural killers—heat, thirst, disease, and wild animals. All four can drive a man mad before death releases him. Then there are the natives. Every soldier vowed to keep his last bullet for himself, but some were captured before they could fire it. When we overran one village we saw what happened to hapless prisoners." The visual memory of that hideous scene disturbed him so much, he emptied his glass in one long fiery draught. "It was inconceivable that human creatures could inflict such atrocities on their fellow men," he told Charles in hollow tones. "The effect on morale was disastrous. Officers and men alike became so burdened by terrible fear of such savage adversaries, it meant all orders for small scouting parties were met with a reluctance that almost amounted to insubordination."

Frowning, he hastily explained that the troopers had not turned cowardly. "They are splendid men, all of them, and as brave as any. It was simply that the sight of those remains of former comrades had shaken them into realising that their enemies were governed by pagan beliefs and rituals far outside the rules of conventional warfare. Put my men against any number of standard foes and not one would waver, but hidden savages in a jungle festering with venomous plants and creatures filled them with an unspeakable dread of being taken alive."

"You, also, Viv?"

40

"Of course," he said swiftly, giving his brother a straight look. "That dread shadowed every minute of my life after coming upon that appalling sight. My ears rang with the imagined sound of my own screams; my heart frantically pumped the blood they would drink in triumph while I agonised. Charles, when I tell you that I believe no man could put into words what we saw that day, you will understand that even the greatest hero would have quailed at the prospect." He added urgently, at the sight of the other's expression, "You have no notion, and I pray you never will."

Looking uncomfortable again, Charles asked, "Why speak of it if it revives such feelings?"

"So that you will understand something that I feel obliged to tell you," he said tensely. "The facts are simple enough, but I have discovered, to my cost, that they are open to conflicting interpretations. My fellow officers are divided on the subject, although they have an obligation to accept the decision of the official court of inquiry, and keep to themselves their views on my honour and integrity."

Visibly dismayed, Charles shifted in his chair. "There can be only one view on that subject," he declared. "Your peccadilloes might be deplored, in certain quarters, but I know of no one who doubts that you are a true gentleman."

"Save our grandfather." It slipped out with the bitterness that had not lessened over the years.

"Viv!" remonstrated Charles feebly.

He gave a twisted smile. "A bastard cannot possibly be a gentleman, no matter on which side of the blanket he may have been born. Brancliffe has upheld that belief for thirty years. If the details of this affair were ever to reach his ears, he would claim justification for that belief. Those in my regiment who share it already have."

It was Charles who now signalled for more Cognac. Then he turned back to Vivian. "You have surely overdramatised the situation. Tell me this story of yours, and I'll make you see your error."

Suddenly, Vivian wished he had never embarked on the subject. Telling Charles would serve no really useful purpose. His fraternal support would not ease his own conscience. In that comfortable lounge, surrounded by the trappings of gracious living, the whole affair seemed more like the imaginings of a madman: a demented nightmare. Yet he had deliberately raised the subject, and must conclude it to his brother's satisfaction.

"To be brief," he began, "an Engineer officer named Brassard, accompanied by his sergeant, was detailed to make a survey ahead of our main force. I commanded a small detachment acting as their escort.

41

On the third day, we encountered native warriors in numbers too great to confront. Brassard and his man were taken captive before they could make any kind of move, but I ordered my troopers to retreat immediately. They all escaped safely." Gripping his glass tightly as he visualised that scene once more, he added, "I stayed long enough to kill the doomed pair, shooting them through the head, before leaving the clearing myself.

"Good God," breathed his brother, who knew nothing of soldiering, or its demands.

Lost in time, Vivian could again hear those shots ringing out, could see his colleagues fall from sight in the midst of shiny black bodies decorated with paint and feathers. He again felt that tingling sensation of waiting for a spear in his back as he raced away after betraying his own presence with those shots.

"The official Court of Inquiry ruled that my action had been taken in the sincere and humane belief that I was sparing the captured men hours, even days, of indescribable agony before dying."

"So you were cleared!" exclaimed Charles, making no attempt to hide his relief. "I told you you had the situation too black."

"The unofficial court of inquiry amongst my fellow officers returned a mixed verdict," Vivian informed him harshly. "Unfortunately, there had been some rivalry between Brassard and myself during the voyage to Africa, over the favours of a female passenger. Those few of my regiment who have always felt that I have no place amongst gentlemen have chosen to attach a different motive to my deliberate murder of two Englishmen."

Charles registered shock at the use of the word murder in connection with his older brother, but Vivian had to unburden himself completely now.

"One of the first things that I did on arrival in England was to visit the families of both Brassard and his sergeant, who have been told that their sons were killed in action. I explained that I was the last man to see them alive, and reassured them that they were brave in battle, dying painlessly." He drained his glass swiftly, feeling the need of warming liquor. Then he sighed. "Their touching gratitude for my visit somehow then turned me into the murderer I have been dubbed. The faces of those two mothers haunt me, Charles. I am no longer sure of my own motives for what I did."Leaning back in his chair, he said quietly, "The only way to put the affair behind me is to fill my hours with all the things that gratify a man's body and deaden his mind. That's what the Leila Duncans of the world are for. Perhaps you now understand my behaviour this morning."

42

When the brothers left Gallini's, they strolled through paling sunshine to the lodgings Vivian had recently occupied. He found the chill excessive now that the afternoon was so advanced, although he appreciated the civilised graciousness of the popular resort after the barbarity of the Gold Coast. A slight wound, together with a prolonged bout of tropical fever, had put him on the sick list. He had used his leave to cross Africa to the new state of Rhodesia, where his mother had visited cousins, then decided to make her permanent home near them.

Vivian supported her decision, which she had explained to her younger son in the letter he had brought for Charles. Settling before the fire lit by Vivian's batman, they discussed the subject as soon as his brother had read the thick wad of pages in the letter.

"I suppose I half expected a decision of this nature," he confessed, still managing to look upset. "Mama was never happy at Shenstone."

"Were any of us happy?" Vivian asked bluntly. "Brancliffe had not the slightest understanding of females like Mama, who are gentle, artistic, and immensely compassionate. He always regarded her musical talent as namby-pamby, her slender build as a sign of physical weakness, and her deep maternal love for us as a lamentable lack of discipline."

"Well, yes, I suppose the old man never ceased comparing her with Father's first wife, who apparently had possessed all the right qualities for life in the country."

"Like Julia?"

"I . . . yes, like Julia," he hesitantly agreed.

Thinking of the hardy sporting girl he had known for many years, Vivian realised that Julia Marchbanks would thrive in a home he personally regarded as oppressive and full of desperately unhappy memories.

"Mama will almost certainly come to your wedding, but don't expect her to stay in Cornwall, Charles. The change in her is incredible. I always considered her a handsome woman, but there is a glow, a latent beauty now emerging that is quite striking. Even so, I believe Brancliffe could banish it in an instant with one of his cruel jibes. I have no hopes that age is mellowing him."

"It is making him eccentric—*very* eccentric, in fact."

Vivian frowned. "Do you mean that he is halfway to Bedlam?"

"Good God, no." Such bluntness was unacceptable to his placid brother. "His years are beginning to tell, that is all. He has grown very tight-fisted."

"He always was."

"Only over your impossible extravagances."

43

"They hardly affected him," Vivian pointed out dryly.

"This is something different altogether," said Charles, choosing not to pursue that thorny subject. "He refuses to have fires lit until evening, and then only in the main rooms. I don't think his constitution will stand the rigours of winter without adequate heating."

Vivian shrugged. "Then all your problems will be solved."

"*Viv!*"

"Oh, don't look so damned affronted. The old fellow is eighty-nine and has ruled quite long enough to make everyone's life a misery. How you have tolerated his selfishness and plain cruelty all these years I don't know . . . although he likes you, so you've escaped the worst aspects of his harsh personality."

Deciding to ignore that, his brother continued. "The latest plan for economy is to sell off half the horses. He maintains that they are unnecessary for the size of our household."

"Of course they are, but how does he expect visitors to get around the estate? He *is* getting eccentric."

"He does have a point, in fact. We rarely have visitors."

"I'm not surprised, if there are no fires," said Vivian emphatically. "My dear fellow, life must be deucedly dull for you down there. For God's sake, marry Julia soon. She'll give you some light relief from all this thrift and pessimism."

"You won't treat this so lightly, I'll wager," Charles went on sharply. "He's all set to accept Sir Kinsley's offer to buy Maxted's farm and the land west of it as far as the old mill. You know he's been after it for years."

Vivian sobered instantly. "He can't sell part of the estate against your wishes."

"Yes, he can. All the time he holds the title, he owns the entire estate."

"But, dammit, that land allows access to Shenstone from the west. If Sir Kinsley adds it to his, we shall end up having to ask permission to cross the Marchbanks' estate on the only road leading to ours."

"I'm sure Sir Kinsley wouldn't make an issue of it," came the uneasy response.

"Maybe not, but Randolph will when he takes over. He's that kind of man." Getting to his feet Vivian looked at his brother in exasperation. "Level-headed tact and diplomacy might have served you well in your past dealings with our irascible grandparent, but it will no longer work with a man whose mind is failing. I suggest that you have him certified and take over before it's too late."

44

Charles stood up, also. "I'll pretend you didn't say that."

"Why? In your shoes, it's precisely what he would do."

The look on his brother's face told Vivian he had gone too far, yet he could hardly believe Charles had forgotten those terrible childhood years and did not still bear the scars, as he did.

"Persuade him to come up to town and live in his club, along with all the other old buffers," he suggested in a milder tone. "He'd be with others as eccentric as himself there."

"He would never leave Shenstone."

"He'll damn well have to before long—to take his place in the Brancliffe tomb. It'll all be yours then, unless you allow him to rob you of it, acre by acre. Eccentric be damned! He's playing one of his cat-and-mouse games with you, Charles. It's his greatest pleasure in life to see us all squirm."

Charles stared hard at him. "You've grown frighteningly bitter."

"I always have been bitter," he retorted with some heat. "However, the important thing is to stop him from letting the place run down, and prevent him from cutting that land from the estate, even if it means employing an agent to purchase it on your behalf."

"Unfortunately, I can't do that. Fact is, I'm a little short of funds. The time to buy into gold is now, so I've recently tied up all my available capital, leaving myself with just enough to run the town house and cover personal expenses."

Vivian sighed. "Well, something will have to be done. As it happens, I could help with some cash, for once. A man can't go through much of a fortune in the midst of equatorial jungle, and my banker has never smiled so favourably on me as he does at present."

Apparently regretting the slight crossing of swords, his brother smiled faintly. "Wonders will never cease! I wouldn't expect you to provide financial help, Viv. Shenstone is my responsibility. I hoped that you might come down soon and help me to persuade Brancliffe to hold on to that land, that's all."

"My dear fellow, one word from me would induce him to sell it immediately."

"Then come down and talk him *into* selling. If you are so certain he revels in crossing you, that surely is the answer."

A reluctant smile broke across Vivian's face. "When a man like you resorts to guile, I know the situation is quite out of hand."

"Will you come?"

"A freezing room, and no horse to ride? No thank you."

"He hasn't sold the horses yet."

"I should hope not. Some of them are mine."

"Julia has expressed an interest in one or two of yours, for her own use."

"They're too mettlesome for her," he said instantly.

Charles gave him a curious look. "No, they're not. While you have been away she has turned into a most accomplished rider, who will have even you impressed. You'll see when you come to Shenstone."

Vivian shook his head. "I should need more inducement than the sight of your beloved in the saddle to persuade me to visit Cornwall. Can you offer me one of the Lindley girls to soften up the rigours of the old house during winter? I thought not." Growing serious again, he said, "I do feel you've been a little unwise to put all your capital into gold. The Boers have had one shot at making us look foolish, and succeeded. I don't think they have given up their attempt to assert their rights in southern Africa, and people I spoke to in Rhodesia feel that the war sixteen years ago settled nothing. It left a lot of bitterness, and the ill-timed Jameson Raid last year has made things worse. If anything blew up there suddenly the prices of shares would plummet, despite all the assurances by his friends that Rhodes has everything under control." Charles appeared to have gone into a trance, and Vivian teased, "Are my words so profound that they have reduced you to a stupor?"

A smile curved the gentle mouth beneath the moustache, and a twinkle lit his brother's dark eyes. "Sorry, Viv, didn't mean to appear rude, but that girl you fancy—Miss Duncan, wasn't it?—had no idea who Cecil Rhodes was. She tried her best to look intelligent when I spoke to her, but it was plain that she was all at sea. Can you imagine it? One of the greatest men of our time, and she knew nothing about him. Dash it all, he even has a country named after him."

Vivian leant forward to touch his brother's arm. "You, my dear Charles, had never heard of one of the greatest *titillations* of our time. The Lindley Girls have a walk named after them. Imagine that, if you can."

"A walk! You can hardly compare that . . ."

"How do you know that you can hardly compare it? I tell you, it is more exciting than anything Cecil Rhodes could ever do. You should go to see *The Maid of Montezuma*, and witness it for yourself."

There was a vigorous negative from the other man. "You'll never get me inside a variety theatre. The opera I can just about stomach, but a *walk . . . in ostrich feathers?* Oh no, Viv, very definitely not!"

# CHAPTER THREE

Rumours began flying around Lindley's Theatre during the following two weeks. In the dressing-room the girls talked and speculated constantly. Someone had heard that the Lindley Stroll was to be replaced by a concerted number featuring Adeline Tait, due to her threat to walk out. Others had heard that *The Maid of Montezuma* was being taken off after Christmas.

"That's nonsense," declared Leila, as they were all struggling to dress for their first appearance as peasants in a crowd scene. "No man in his right mind would end the run of a show that is playing to packed houses."

"Lester Gilbert would," mumbled her neighbour, who was applying lip-colour. She turned to Leila, the red wax in her hand. "Jack Spratt told me only today that our revered boss believes in the philosophy of leaving an audience wanting more. They'll flock to fill the house for the next show, then."

"That's what you think," said a cynic, pushing past them to reach her colourful costume on a hook above their heads. "All these rumours are eyewash to satisfy dear Adeline. Even she knows that the show would collapse if the Stroll was taken out."

"Why doesn't Adeline Tait collapse?" muttered a brunette busily buckling her shoes. "That would solve the problem."

"Why, ducky!" exclaimed her companion in tones of mock refined horror, "Do not tell me you cannot perceive the angelic and virtuous nature of our wonderful leading lady."

"Angelic!" cried a red-head in disgust.

"Virtuous?" scowled a half-dressed peasant. "Her language last night when the cut-out of Popocatepetl wobbled would have made a bargee blush."

"I'm not surprised that it wobbled," commented Leila's neighbour, now smoothing her hare's-foot carefully over her cheek-bones. "What a daft name to give to a mountain. Whoever thought it up?"

"It's a real mountain. Jack Spratt said he'd actually seen pictures of it," the red-head told her.

"Well, *I* have never heard it mentioned before."

The conversation put a memory in Leila's mind, and she looked up. "By the way, has any one of you heard of a man called Cyril Rhodes?"

A peasant behind her finished tying her headscarf. "Isn't he playing the lead at Daly's?"

A knock on the door broke up the subject, and the call-boy handed in another bouquet of flowers—the third that evening, so far. Leila was surprised to find that they were for her. She was reading the attached note when Rose slipped in, unusually late, and began stripping off her warm woollen dress and side-buttoned boots. The flowers were a tasteful posy of white gardenias and fern, which she thought was typical of the sender. A warm feeling spread through her as she remembered his shy, courteous manner. Fancy summoning sufficient courage to make this gesture!

She turned to Rose, holding out the flowers. "Aren't they lovely? You'll never guess who they're from. Canine Charles."

Rose looked astonished. "Well, who's a dark horse, then? Watch out, my girl. Those kind can easily ruin a good girl."

Momentary clouds passed over Leila's pleasure, but she tried to ignore them as she handed over the note, so that her friend could read the characteristic words.

Dear Miss Duncan,

In order to repair my abysmal ignorance of cultural affairs, I have secured a box for Thursday night. May I hope that you will give me the great honour and pleasure of your company at supper, after the performance?

With the greatest respect,
Veasey-Hunter

Rose looked at her. "I don't like it, at all. A man like him is likely to go doolally over his first bag of wild oats, and you might find him too much to handle. He's the sort who'd put a pistol to his brain if you scorned him."

Leila laughed. "You've seen too many melodramas, Rose. He's just a rather dear old dog, with too much conscience. He's probably been worrying in case he offended me by not knowing about the Lindley Girls, and this is his way of making up for it. I'm sure he'll hate the show."

"Are you going to accept?" asked Rose, dropping her petticoat and reaching for the peasant blouse.

"Yes, why not? I've been instructed to be pleasant to gentleman patrons, and I know that I'll be perfectly safe with this one. We shall

48

probably spend the whole evening talking about the Faldalal Lancers and that man Cyril Rhodes, who has something to do with gold or diamond mines."

Rose emerged from the voluminous costume, and began tying laces with quick fingers. "Canine Charles probably owns one—of *each!*"

Leila shook her head. "Not him. There'd be so many well-to-do ladies after him, you wouldn't see him for scheming mamas." She started to tie the kerchief over the elaborate *coiffure* needed later for the strolling number, taking great care not to disturb it any more than necessary. "But it's sure to be a nice supper . . . and he's really quite a sweet old thing."

"Please Lord, save all innocent maidens from the clutches of 'sweet old things'," chanted Rose, then drew in her breath sharply as she doubled forward.

Leila turned from the mirror. "What's up? Here, are you all right?" She took her friend's shoulders in concern. Rose's lovely features were drawn, and Leila could now see that she was paler than usual. "Are you all right?" she repeated gently.

Rose nodded. "It's this damned indigestion. It gives me gyp, lately." She sank onto the bench running along in front of the mirrored tables, gripping her stomach. "It's bloody hot in here, which doesn't help."

The perspiration stood on Rose's smooth brow, and Leila dabbed at it with a cloth. "Can't do much about the heat," she said, "but is there anything I can get for you? I'll send Jimmy out to the chemist along the road for a powder, if you like."

"No, it'll go off in a minute. It always does. But it's as bad as Carrie's Curse while it lasts."

Leila sat beside her, worried. "How long have you been having this?"

The hazel eyes gave her a frank look. "It isn't that, Lei. In a way, I wish it was. I might get him back."

"You wouldn't," Leila told her swiftly, remembering her own fears well over a year before. "Not a toff, you wouldn't. He'd just offer you a handful of money, and the address of a quiet little place he knew, where you could go for several months until it was over." She got to her feet. "I'll tell Jack Spratt you can't go on tonight."

"Don't bother. I'll be all right by curtain time." Rose sighed heavily. "It's my own fault. I don't eat, then feel a bit dicky just before I come here and gobble anything I can find, just to keep me going."

Leila sat again, taking Rose's hands. "Men are brutes. We'd all be far better off without them. Merry Miles is sure to be consoling himself elsewhere. Don't let him bring you down, Rose. You're too special for that."

49

"Don't go on, love, you'll have me in tears," her friend said roughly. "Oh gawd, there's overture and beginners!" She got swiftly to her feet, snatching her headscarf from the hook above them. "Do you think anyone'll notice if I don't have a South American complexion tonight?"

"Jack Spratt will," said Leila immediately. "So will Mr Gilbert, if he happens to be watching the opening tonight. Even so, I reckon both would sooner have a sickly-looking peasant than no peasant at all." Picking up their props, she started for the door. "Do you want the basket of fruit, or the fish?"

Rose shuddered. "The fruit, I suppose. If all the rumours about the show closing are true, a Lindley Girl who throws up into a basket of cardboard fish will be the first one out on her ear, with no hope of re-engagement."

A round of excited applause greeted the raising of the curtain. Lights blazed into Leila's eyes, and the dark red of the velvet drapes was replaced by a blackness that concealed rows and rows of eager faces. The audience was invisible, yet she could sense them, hear them, smell them, even. Coughs, murmurs, shuffling feet; the aroma of tobacco, perfume, and the chill of night that still clung to overcoats and wraps. The knowledge of their concealed presence filled her with the usual excitement, as she moved around the stage to the familiar music. How she longed to lead in that line of thirty girls; longed to be the first to step onto the empty stage when the throbbing music began. She wanted the thrill of hearing that sighing gasp that always ran through the crowded hidden tiers, as the first statuesque brunette in a breathtaking feather costume appeared, to signal the start of something for which they had all been waiting. As she wandered around in the background of that opening scene, Leila prayed that Lester Gilbert would not close the show before she had had time to move up six places in the line.

On that Thursday evening, she managed the first step to her goal. The girl who was second was given a few days off in order to settle her brothers and sisters with relatives, due to the death of their mother. Everyone moved up one place, and a trainee was placed at the end. To Leila, it seemed an auspicious start to her date with Charles Veasey-Hunter, and she was pleased that the temporary promotion should have occurred when he was in the audience. During the performance she had taken surreptitious peeps at the boxes, but as so many of their occupants were moustached and dressed in evening attire it was impossible to pick out any one person in the dimness.

Her own wardrobe was bare of dresses suitable for such an occasion, so Rose had lent her one, of primrose satin with a *décolletage* of daring proportions, tiny puffs of sleeves, a bodice embroidered with silver beading, and a long sweeping skirt.

'Miles bought it for me, of course,'' she told Leila breezily, as they returned to the dressing-room after the final curtain. "When I sent back his presents, I decided to hang on to the clothes. His next girlfriend is welcome to a diamond bracelet, ivory hair-ornaments, a musical box, several half-empty bottles of French perfume, and a hand-painted fan. But I vowed she wouldn't walk around looking like me . . . or wearing my silk drawers.'' She kissed Leila's cheek impulsively. ''Oh, Lei, what fools we are where men are concerned. Go and enjoy your supper with Canine Charles, but don't get fond of him. *Please* . . . for my sake.''

Leila laughed self-consciously. ''Don't worry. I can't see the dear old dog buying silk drawers for a girl, no matter how fond of him she grew.''

''You look better in this dress than ever I did,'' Rose told her generously, as she fastened the hooks at the back. ''Blue is more my colour.''

Leila felt too nervous to answer. She had sent a brief note of acceptance to the London address at the top of the invitation, but now she wished she had not. Performing was tiring. She longed to return to the basement apartment, make herself a cup of cocoa, then go to bed. Talking to this man was going to be a strain—he was so well-informed —and she was now more than a little apprehensive about the end of the evening. The fact that Miles Lampton had gone the whole way with Rose had been the girl's decision. Most of the mashers knew that an invitation to supper was limited to no more than that. But what if Rose were right, and this shy bachelor let things go to his head? What if he were not a bachelor?

''Stop shaking,'' grumbled Rose. ''How can I pin these flowers in your hair if you tremble like a jelly?''

Leila turned beseechingly, causing Rose to drop the spray of silk carnations. ''It was a great mistake. I never should have said I'd go.''

''And have Lester Gilbert after your blood again?'' Rose retrieved the flowers from the floor. ''I think you look better without these, anyway.'' She tossed them amidst the pots of cream and blocks of eyelash-darkener. ''Get out there, girl, before his courage fails and he drives off alone. *'She looks captivating'* as they say of Miss Adeline Tait. Go on, you ninny, and have a good time with your doggy friend,'' laughed Rose, giving her a push.

Leila picked up the heavy Indian silk wrap, also borrowed, and swiftly thanked her friend before walking out, leaving Rose to take off her make-up and change for home. As she walked through the wings, silent now the stage-hands had stacked the flats and cloths in place and

51

left, she called a goodnight to Jack Spratt, who never left the theatre until everyone else had departed.

Another voice answered, however. "Do you have an appointment, Miss Duncan?" It was Lester Gilbert standing in the doorway of his office, an interested spectator. He gave his gold-toothed smile. "How very charming you look, my dear. I see you noted my advice on maintaining the magic at all times."

She smiled as sweetly as she could, then went on her way, feeling like a lamb to the slaughter as she ducked ropes and stepped over spars to reach the corridor leading to the stage-door. Monty Monkton was chatting to a very tall man in evening clothes, who leaned negligently against the wall. He straightened up, and removed the silk hat as she stepped down the three stone steps to walk toward them; but her feet slowed and her heart jumped as she saw the pale shining hair, the unusually brown face, the grey-green eyes that took in her appearance from head to toe. He looked every bit as striking as before, in the beautifully-cut suit and scarlet-lined swinging cloak . . . and still he knew it!

"*You!*" she exclaimed, completely nonplussed and shaking with increased nervousness. "What are you doing here?"

He smiled, and she remembered the attraction of his husky voice when he said, "I'm waiting to take a young lady to supper."

She thought of returning to the dressing-room, but she could hardly do that with Lester Gilbert standing in his doorway. So she faced Vivian Veasey-Hunter, feeling the way she had when he had so expertly swept her and Rose off to lunch against her wishes.

"This is not in the least amusing," she accused him in cold tones. "You must have known that the note would be taken as one from your brother."

He stepped closer still, and his smile seemed even more devastating as he said, "From my *brother?* But surely he told you that he never visited the theatre, Miss Heywood."

Gazing up at him in bewilderment, she began, "I'm not Miss Heywood, I'm . . ." She got no further as the dreadful truth became apparent. He had mixed up their names, and it was Rose he was expecting to take to supper. Embarrassment flooded through her. Of course it was Rose. Had he not spent the whole of that meal at Gallini's fascinated by her? She wished the floor would open and swallow her. Standing there in Rose's gown and wrap, it must be obvious to him that she was dressed for a social engagement, yet there was no other escort waiting at the stage-door. It was a terrible situation—one she did not know how to escape with any shred of pride left. Rose was still in her petticoat and make-up. Even if she made an excuse to this man, and rushed back to the dressing-room, her friend could hardly then emerge in the same yellow dress and silk wrap to greet him. Her colour began to rise under his interested gaze, and it was clear that there was no easy way out.

"I'm afraid there has been a dreadful mix-up," she began in an undertone, hoping neither Jack Spratt nor Lester Gilbert would hear her obvious embarrassment. "*I* am Miss Duncan . . . the one to whom you sent your flowers the other night. *Rose* is Miss Heywood." He said nothing, just studied her with increasing interest. She swallowed. "I . . . well, I assumed that your brother . . . it was silly of me, I suppose, because he certainly did say that he never went to the theatre. But the note implied . . . I mean, it was written in a way . . ."

A movement behind them heralded Monty from the street. "Your cab is ready and waiting, Captain Veasey-Hunter."

"Ah, excellent." He put a hand beneath her elbow and began propelling her through the door, murmuring, "There seems no alternative left to us, but to console each other as best we can."

In a state of even deeper confusion, she was assisted into the hansom by a man who appeared to have complete control of the awkward situation. He climbed in beside her, tucked a rug over her knees, then settled back as he instructed the driver to head for the Savoy. Then he turned to smile at her in the dimness.

"Your error of judgement concerning my brother's character is perfectly understandable, on such short acquaintance. My deplorable memory for names has put you in a most uncomfortable predicament, however, so the least I can do to make amends is to act as substitute for Charles, and offer you supper as my apology."

Feeling that she had been routed in much the same way as on that day in Brighton, Leila managed to say, with less tartness than she would have liked. "You seem to be forever apologising, Captain Veasey-Hunter."

"I know," he agreed with a faint sigh. "You really would have had a far better evening with my brother, Miss Heywood."

"My name is *Duncan*," she reminded him sharply.

"Of course. I do beg your pardon. You see what a hopeless case I am?"

If it had not seemed ridiculous, Leila could have believed that there was a wobble of laughter in his voice. Her thoughts and emotions were in such a muddled state, however, she was uncertain of any aspect of his behaviour. The short drive allowed her no time to collect herself, and she was still bemused when he helped her to alight, and led her into the foyer of the Savoy, where the *maître d'hôtel* greeted her companion by name.

"Captain Veasey-Hunter, it is a great pleasure to see you again after such a long absence. I hope that we may look forward to the resumption of your frequent patronage now that your regiment has returned to England." He bowed to Leila. "Good evening, Miss Duncan, it is an honour to welcome you."

He clicked his fingers in the direction of a waiting bellboy, who then came forward carrying a waterfall bouquet of creamy camellias and yellow rosebuds, which he presented to her with showy ceremony. She took them with a growing sense of delighted unreality, then walked beside her tall escort as they were ushered to what was, apparently, his usual table in the supper-rooms. The splendour of those renowned rooms, the dazzle of diamonds adorning women in couturier dresses, and the succession of surprises which were overtaking her that evening, increased that feeling of unreality. Yet she was not so lost in it that she was unaware of the attention caused by their entry, or of the murmured comments of which she appeared to be the subject. Only then did she realise that she had unconsciously adopted the Lindley Stroll before this unexpected audience, and the effect had not been lost on them. As her wrap was taken, and she was assisted into the chair at the secluded table, her sweeping glance encountered a sea of smiling faces, and courteous half-bows from nearby gentlemen diners.

"Some of your admirers, who are doubtless wishing that they were in my place tonight," said a low voice beside her, and she turned to encounter grey-green eyes full of merriment.

"But . . . oh, that's absurd," she protested, embarrassment returning. "I'm not Adeline Tait."

"You are the more beautiful."

Giving him a frank look as he settled on the other side of their table, she said, "Shouldn't you be paying that compliment to Rose Heywood?"

"Should I?" he asked innocently.

Trying again, she indicated the bouquet on the table beside her evening bag. "These flowers were chosen by you for her, surely."

He smiled disarmingly. "They should have been chosen by my brother, for you."

He was far too clever for her, and it seemed easier to put aside the muddled aspect of the evening and allow herself to enjoy the gaiety, colour and exhilaration of being in such a place with an escort who managed to heighten each of those qualities. It also seemed easier to put aside the irritating aspects of his personality, and allow him to take

54

complete command of the evening, as he appeared determined to do.

Vivian chose from the menu for her, and Leila was glad to let him do so. Pâté de fois gras, roast chicken with asparagus and green peas, and a delicious soufflé of lemons and cream. The vast array of cutlery on the table did not alarm her, because the Clivedons had always eaten in style. Knowing when and how to use each item, she also knew that it was correct to sip the champagne that he ordered, not guzzle it like lemonade.

The diners all appeared to know one another. Leila was introduced to a relay of strangers with various impressive titles. She handled it all with confidence, having been well-drilled in the correct way to address distinguished visitors to Clivedon House. Even when Vivian presented her to a couple who had once visited the house in which she had worked as a servant, they spoke for some minutes about the delightful spectacle and music of *The Maid of Montezuma*, before they passed on without recognising Lily Lowe. Why should they? The girl in an elegant dress which revealed smooth milky shoulders, sitting with an upperclass escort who bought her champagne and expensive flowers, was nothing like the maid in a long gown of sombre taffeta, starched apron, and frilly cap atop a severe dark chignon.

The demands of the evening turned it into a testing performance for Leila, and she gave of her best. But she was not so intent on it that she did not notice Vivian Veasey-Hunter watching her speculatively, all through the evening. Neither did she fail to notice his immense attraction. He was amusing, attentive, lazily assured, and apparently undaunted by rank or titles. The waiters were deferent; those to whom he introduced her treated him with casual equality.

She began to wonder about him. The Savoy Grill was one of the most flamboyant places to which a couple could go. The evening would set him back a pretty penny: he and his brother had met at Gallini's in Brighton. Who were the Veasey-Hunters? They did not move in the same circle as the Clivedons, she knew. Did that mean that they were higher or lower in the social scale? Could they have any connection with that man Cyril Rhodes and his gold mines? Perhaps Rose was right, and she was spending the evening with a millionaire.

The thought of Rose dampened the effervescent delight of the last half-hour of that evening, and she was quiet on the way back to her basement. Now that he knew of the error over their names, it would be Rose who enjoyed his company in future. With a strange pang, she knew it was a fact that she did not want to face.

They reached her home, and she was suddenly ashamed of it. A yellow satin dress and carefully pronounced words in the Savoy Grill did not make her into a lady. Yet he handed her down from the cab, and escorted her down the stone steps to the basement yard as if she were, and the dingy surroundings somehow took on a moonlit enchantment she had never before noticed.

"Thank you for a truly delightful evening," he murmured, charming her champagne senses further by taking her gloved hand in his and kissing it.

Strange, yearning excitement filled her at the sensation of the warmth from his mouth touching her skin. Forcing herself to draw her hand away, she said, "You have been very kind, Captain Veasey-Hunter. I am only sorry that you did not have the partner that you really wanted."

"Oh, but I did," came his voice from the shadowed moonlight. "I knew very well to whom I sent the gardenias earlier this week. I further confess that I fully intended you to be misled by the note attached to them."

She was lost for words, her brain trying to wrestle with the complications of a remarkable evening.

"I sensed that, whereas my brother had appeared honourable enough in your eyes to accept an invitation from him, one from me would be flatly refused. I offer yet another apology for not being the partner that *you* really wanted tonight. Goodnight, Miss Leila Duncan."

Leila invented details of an evening with Charles Veasey-Hunter, to satisfy Rose's eager curiosity, because she did not want to talk about something she still did not understand herself. When a pearl necklet was delivered to her basement several days later, by a uniformed lackey, she made him take it back, with a note stating that she did not accept presents from gentlemen. On the following day, a small boy delivered a bunch of ragged chrysanthemums, saying that a toff had given him sixpence to bring them. The attached note was typical of the sender.

> This cannot possibly be classed as a gift, because I picked them from my brother's garden with my own hands. I have risked his wrath in order to persuade you to have supper with me on Saturday. If this urchin does not return with my humble tribute, I shall know that you consent.
>
> V.V.H.

Leila pawned the epergne of which she was so proud, in order to buy a suitable dress. It was out of the question to continue to borrow clothes from Rose.

Vivian went down to Cornwall at the start of December. The visit was in response to repeated requests from Charles, to attempt to stop their grandfather from selling land which they both considered vital to the estate. Once again, Vivian was uncertain of his brother's motives for the request. Was it prompted by that constant guilty obsession to give him rights that could never be legally his, or was Charles still unable to stand up to an old man who had ruled Shenstone for far too long? In truth, Vivian was unsure of his own motives. His protection of a younger brother during their boyhood had been instinctive, and natural enough in the circumstances. Was it a continuation of that rôle, or a deep-seated desire for the inheritance he was denied, that made him accept the responsibilities that Charles so often persuaded him to shoulder?

When Charles informed him that he would have to remain in London on pressing business, Vivian almost cancelled his plans. Shenstone would be even more unwelcome without his brother for company. However, he had arranged leave and refused pre-Christmas invitations, so he decided to get the business over and done with.

The train journey was tedious, and the carriage ride from the station was made in mist and soft rain. Since it was no more than a duty visit, small irritations and dismal weather served to make the whole thing even more irksome, and when Dobbins, the coachman, told him in a wheezy voice that Sir Kinsley and Miss Marchbanks were spending a few days at the Hall, Vivian very nearly turned back there and then. But Dobbins' further information that the visit was for the purpose of selecting horses from the stables persuaded him to continue to his family home. It seemed that his brother had been right, and Lord Brancliffe meant to sell some of the finest hunters in the county, without any thought for his heir.

Shenstone Hall was reached by way of narrow uphill tracks which in winter were extremely difficult to negotiate. Dobbins had brought along two stable lads to help push when the wheels stuck in the mud. Successive applications of stones had alleviated the problem for short periods, but the red earth soon sucked them under and the mud was back this year. After an hour of bumping and grinding, and long periods of standing still while horses and stable lads strained to clear the carriage of the mire, level ground at the top of the moor was reached. There, the old house came into view through the mist that hung low over the heights.

Vivian felt anything but pleasure at the sight. His childhood in the house had been repressive and unhappy. The Honourable James Veasey-Hunter had been absent for most of the time, campaigning in Parliament and in the four-poster beds of his many mistresses, leaving

57

his two young sons and gentle wife in the charge of his strict, uncompromising elderly father, who had never forgiven or tried to understand the unfortunate events that had robbed Vivian of the right to inherit.

Lord Brancliffe's only son and heir, the Honourable James Veasey-Hunter, had contracted an early marriage to the daughter of an American diplomat but, within a year, the young bride had been amongst those lost at sea during a cyclone whilst crossing the Atlantic. Scarcely heartbroken, but very heavily in debt, the widower had soon married a seventeen-year-old heiress, whose father was determined should have a title to go with her fortune. Vivian had been born within nine months and, his duty in providing an heir done, James had pursued his rakish life with total disregard for either his wife or his son.

Fate had a blow in store, however. Friends of his first wife, travelling the east coast of America, had come upon a young woman in a Quaker settlement. She had no identity and few wits, but was undoubtedly the Honourable Charlotte Veasey-Hunter. Lord Brancliffe's heir had been charged with bigamy; his son proclaimed illegitimate. During the subsequent trial, the hapless Charlotte, uprooted from her Quaker friends, had jumped to her death from a window in New York.

Society had found the affair marvellously diverting. All attention had been focused on Margaret and her small son when James was acquitted of the charge of wilful bigamy. What would happen next? they all asked. The Brancliffe heir had soon shown them. Badly in need of the fortune snatched from him by the dissolution of his second marriage, he had gone through another ceremony with the youthful shattered Margaret. She had then become his legal wife, but her son was doomed to remain illegitimate. James had been forced to do his duty a second time. Installing his wife and her two sons at his bleak country mansion, he had then more or less washed his hands of them all.

Lord Brancliffe had always run his house and estate with an iron hand. Contemptuous of the girl who had been through so much anxiety and humiliation recently, he was cruelly overbearing in his dominance of her two small sons, vowing that they would not inherit what he saw as her weakness of personality. He had proceeded to put them through years of harsh discipline designed to mould them to his satisfaction. From a ridiculously early age, they had been instructed in horsemanship, swordplay and shooting. The Veasey-Hunter stables had provided some of the most spirited beasts a rider could mount, the armoury had lent itself to fencing lessons, and the vast estate had provided game for marksmanship.

Other standards of behaviour had been drummed into them whilst standing to attention before him. Fidgeting had been punished with cruel raps on their knuckles, inattention had earned a caning on the buttocks, and any sign of slovenly stance had resulted in a board being strapped to the offender's back to improve it. A toss from a horse had been attributed to lax handling, the rider being ordered to remount immediately. Bad marksmanship had led to hours of compulsory practice with clay pigeons. The loser of a fencing match had been forced to stand and analyse the reasons for his defeat, admit his shortcomings, then embark on a fresh contest which he had dared not lose.

Such demands for excellence could have imbued the brothers with a competitiveness bordering on emnity. Instead, it had drawn them close in united fear of the tyrant.

Vivian had soon noticed that his grandfather not only enjoyed making him suffer, he made a point of inflicting the pain and humiliation in the presence of the timorous Charles, and their gentle mother. Only when he had innocently asked her the meaning of the word bastard, had the cause for the special persecution been revealed. Too complex for a boy of eight to fully understand, Vivian nevertheless remembered that his rebellion had been born on that day. If he was different from other children, he had decided, then he would ensure that the difference was obvious.

From then on he had defied his grandfather whenever possible, despite the punishment he received for it. New excessive harshness had brought protests from Margaret, but her attempted intervention had only increased Vivian's trials as his grandfather declared him "a misbegotten whelp who hides in his mother's skirts". Even so, as Vivian had grown to adolescence, he had maintained that refusal to break to the other man's will. When James's death on the hunting-field had temporarily stunned the ageing man, Vivian had seized his opportunity to escape to university.

Oxford had been the gateway to life itself for an athletic, unsophisticated young man. His excellence at all sporting pursuits had made him instantly popular with his fellows. His looks and physique were enough to make him highly attractive to the fair sex, without the added fascination of his strange illegitimacy. Sticklers for pedigree snubbed him but, in general, "The Gentleman Bastard" as he often dubbed himself, had aroused the greatest interest in them all. A complete novice to sexual experience, Vivian had raced through the series of lessons to take his degree in seduction with flying colours. He had taken to the delights of alcohol just as eagerly, the only thing marring his thrilling new existence being the fact that his mother and brother were still enduring the miseries of Shenstone.

On leaving university, Vivian had embarked upon a career which offered him not only a perfect outlet for the skills at which he excelled, but social standing and freedom from reminders of all he could not have. The Brancliffe title might never be his, but he would gain a military rank to add distinction to his name. The demands of a regiment would give him a legitimate reason for turning his back on the inheritance he could never claim. The heat of battle would allow him the opportunity to release the pent-up longing to avenge a boy who had been punished for the sins of his father.

He had encountered his first real evidence of social rejection in applying to the élite cavalry regiments. It had not been made obvious, of course, but the paper-thin reasons for the failure of his applications were polite reminders that, however unfortunate the circumstances, his illegitimacy was unacceptable to those who valued pedigree above all else. There were several men in the 49th Lancers who still resented his presence in their ranks, but most of the officers accepted him as the son of two high-born parents, and left it at that. The affair in Ashanti had fanned the embers of resentment into hostility; aloofness had deepened into complete ostracism from his enemies. While he did not much care about the attitude of men he had never liked, their condemnation served to increase his own doubts over the instinctive action he had taken.

As the carriage passed beneath the arched entrance of the Cornish mansion, Vivian's heart sank. He could almost feel that thin cane cutting through the tweed of his knickerbockers to raise weals on his buttocks; almost ached from the remembered weight of a board strapped to his back to make him stand straight. It seemed so short a time ago that he had suffered from this vindictiveness, directed against a child regarded as a slur on family pride. Lord Brancliffe would always hold that view.

The great grey stone house with turrets at each corner filled him with deep depression. Shrouded in mist Shenstone looked formidable. Yet it could also look magnificent on days when clear skies brought sunshine to sparkle the mullioned windows, and emphasise the grandeur of the building and surrounding moorland that gave a view for many miles around, of springy green turf, great craggy tors, and fast-flowing ice-blue streams. Filey was there at the door to greet him; so was the housekeeper, Mrs Hale. They both made a great fuss of him, while his bag was carried in and taken upstairs by a lad Vivian did not know. The two old servants had always had a particular affection for the elder son of the house, whom they viewed as the victim of cruel circumstances, and their delight in seeing him after so long was very genuine.

It was freezing in the great hall, and the mist appeared to have crept in even before the massive oak door had opened at the sound of the arriving carriage.

"It's hellish cold in here, Filey," he exclaimed, loath to relinquish his overcoat. "Have a fire lit right away."

The old retainer's face grew even longer as he stared at the huge empty stone fireplace. "It takes a great many logs to fill it, sir, and His Lordship would never agree. There's been no fire there for the past half-year."

Vivian gripped the old man's shoulder encouragingly. "Just light it, Filey, there's a good fellow. I'll deal with my grandfather. After two years on the equator, I find this cold weather much too severe."

Mrs Hale turned on Filey. "Captain Vivian'll catch his death of cold. Light the fire, as he says."

Reaching his bedroom, he discovered a roaring fire in the hearth. It could not have been alight long, for the damp chilliness seemed to have invaded even the furniture in that room that had witnessed his boyhood struggles against tears. He thought longingly of his cosy quarters in Brighton, or even the family house in London, which Charles kept warm and very comfortable.

He supposed that Sir Kinsley and Julia were hardened enough to life on the moors not to mind draughts and stone floors, but he still felt that his grandfather should have made some concessions to their presence as guests in his house. It looked very much as if he would be left to see to their comfort himself. The Marchbanks family lived no more than twenty miles from Shenstone, but the roads were difficult in December, making an overnight stay advisable.

He went downstairs half an hour before dinner, hoping to find his grandfather alone. It was a vain hope. A veritable reception committee awaited him in the dark-panelled anteroom that boasted no comfort, although he was relieved to find a good fire crackling in the hearth. Lord Brancliffe was in a carved teak chair that sported no cushion; Sir Kinsley sat opposite him. Julia had found a modicum of comfort in an old Cornish hooded chair lined with velvet squabs, the crimson of which contrasted well with the blue of her dress, which was all Vivian could see of her.

He went directly across to greet his grandfather, who rose with characteristic determination as he approached. Age had bowed him slightly, but he still stood a proud six feet tall as he stared in contempt. Topping the old man by several inches now, Vivian found the figure less imposing than he recalled. The face carved in austere lines remained as cold as ever.

"How are you, sir?" he began.

61

"You must be able to see that for yourself, unless there is something wrong with your sight," came the sharp retort. "What have you come for? You go off for years, then turn up with a complexion like that of a native of Africa. I suppose it is too much to hope that you distinguished yourself in Ashanti."

That challenging comment in the presence of the Marchbanks hit his most vulnerable spot. He had certainly distinguished himself—by killing two English captives before taking flight from their enemy. These people, who had never witnessed the sight of atrocities in a clearing that had put fear into even the most stalwart of men, would condemn him instantly. All the old sensations began to return, as the hooded eyes appeared to see right through to his uneasy conscience, and expose his guilt.

Fighting for composure, he returned lightly, "I hadn't much time for deeds of valour. I was too busy warding off venomous snakes, and native chieftains offering to sell me a wife."

"Pah! Nothing but a mounted popinjay. I always said so."

Vivian turned to greet their neighbour with a firm handshake. "Hallo, sir. Are you still having trouble with your sheep?"

"Hallo, Vivian, it's nice to see you back at Shenstone. I shall always have trouble with my sheep until Charles builds his walls higher. I estimate that half my flock is presently on your land."

Vivian grinned. "Free grazing! I always said your sheep had springs on their heels. How else would they get over our walls?"

"Perhaps curiosity spurs them on," said a low voice behind him, and he turned toward the hooded chair where a decided shock awaited him.

Julia Marchbanks had certainly changed in his absence, and not merely as an equestrienne, as Charles had indicated. Always having been statuesque rather than dainty, she now had a voluptuous figure created by the fashionable corset that made female waists tantilisingly small, and the area above and below irresistibly rounded. In a dress of sapphire-blue velvet that revealed the generous curves of her bosom, she appeared remarkably self-assured as she greeted him with a smile and a widening of the eyes.

"Hallo, Vivian," she said with lingering warmth. "Did you buy any?"

"Sheep?" he queried, temporarily confused by a welter of thoughts concerning this girl.

She laughed softly. "Native wives."

"I hadn't a big enough supply of glass beads," he murmured, interest in her deepening by the minute. "How are you, Julia?"

Her smile remained. "If you can't see for yourself, Lord Brancliffe

62

must be right about your powers of observation. To what must we attribute the honour of a visit from you after all this time? Could it be that Charles has told you we are interested in your horses?"

He wished she had not brought up the subject yet, but he had to continue now that it had been raised. "Yes, he did mention it."

Sir Kinsley pursed his lips. "Come to select the best for your own stables, have you?" He glanced at his daughter. "I told you we should have come over before this."

Vivian turned to him. "Several are already mine. I may take some of the others, if I consider them suited to my purposes."

Julia rose and came to stand beside him. "Have you enough glass beads for that?"

"Just about."

"What do you want with the horses?" demanded Lord Brancliffe in cracked tones. "All you do is prance about dressed in pretty clothes more suited to European ball-rooms."

"I'll probably leave a few here for the use of my brother's guests," he put in pointedly.

"No, you won't! I have to employ a dozen men and boys to exercise the confounded beasts. Peasants astride thoroughbreds! I won't have it, d'ye hear?" Sinking back into his chair, the old man glared at Vivian. "What have you to say about lighting a fire in the hall? Come on, explain yourself! Do you propose to drink your port there . . . or take your *bed*? Infernal impudence! Heedless extravagance is something I will not tolerate. If you weren't wheedling the servants for something, it was your soft-hearted mother. My memory is still very sharp, boy. White hair, a white face . . . and white blood!"

After all the years of freedom, Vivian was instantly back to those days of standing erect whilst being lashed by that tongue. The fair colouring he had inherited from his mother had always been seen by the old man as a sign of weakness, whereas Charles was a true dark-haired Veasey-Hunter. The child Vivian had quaked in his shoes; the youth had learned to counter fear with defiance. Nevertheless, the man felt a hint of the old humiliation at such words in front of Sir Kinsley and Julia.

"In the old days we always had a fire in the hall," he said firmly, "and you have guests, sir."

"Ha!" cried his grandfather. "They come from hardy stock, with constitutions that are apparently stronger than yours—even the girl."

Julia slipped her hand through Vivian's arm at that point, and smiled at her host. "I think some allowance must be made, sir. He has been for two years in an equatorial climate, and I understand from Charles that he is hardly on his feet again after a severe bout of fever."

63

"Weak," spat the old tyrant. "Always said he was. Like his namby-pamby mother. She couldn't even take a horse across Redstones Gap."

Vivian rose to that immediately. "There is many a horsewoman who could not perform a scale on the pianoforte, much less charm a roomful of people with an entire sonata," he said tightly. "I think you should not speak ill of my mother, who has surely suffered more than enough at the hands of this family. It is not only the height of discourtesy to condemn her in her absence, it is also an insult to me, when I have come down here at the worst time of year to see you, sir."

"You came to get your hands on my horses," came the cold contradiction, "in addition to forcing me to suffer your ill-bred manners in addressing me thus. You won't have anything from my stables, I tell you. You'd ride the heart out of them with your ramshackle neck-or-nothing cavalry methods. Seat like a peasant—always said you had."

That was so totally unjust, Vivian's anger would no longer be controlled. "My prowess in the saddle has won the regiment many a trophy, besides earning me the greatest respect from the foremost equestrian authorities in England. I think you are not qualified to judge, when all you have for comparison are county gentlemen who thunder over the moor in all weather, on brutes remarkable only for their stamina. In any case, the matter of your stables is surely a private affair that should not be discussed before guests."

"Why not?" The hawk nose lifted arrogantly. "They are *my* stables, as you have just admitted in the only significant remark you have yet made, and these people are here to negotiate the purchase of some of the brutes to which you referred."

"You should not sell them against my brother's wishes," he protested strongly. "He is your heir."

"If he objects, why don't he speak for himself?"

"He does, sir. You apparently won't listen to him."

"Then he does not express himself well enough. Splendid boy. Good strong body. Rides hard to hounds . . . and there is no doubt of the colour of *his* blood. Somewhat inarticulate, however. Always was." The lined handsome face turned toward the fire. "You are just the reverse. Insolent . . . and a wastrel."

Dinner was announced very opportunely, but Vivian sensed that he was not the only one feeling the strain of the evening as they worked their way through the courses. Conversation tended to be forced, restricted to general subjects by Julia, who displayed considerable skill in easing a difficult situation. Vivian was grateful to her, whilst cursing his brother for persuading him to make the trip. He still had to broach the subject of the land Sir Kinsley was after, and he now wondered if the

64

Marchbanks had come to Shenstone for discussions on that, as well as the sale of the horses. In his present spiteful mood, his grandfather was liable to sell his acres there and then, if Vivian tried to intervene on his brother's behalf. As Charles had hinted, success might be more certain if Vivian *urged* the sale. The old man would probably hold on to the land, just to spite him.

As Julia was the only lady present, Vivian gladly volunteered to forego his port in order to accompany her to the withdrawing-room at the end of a meal that had, at least, gone some way toward making him feel warmer. Lord Brancliffe enjoyed good food and wine, and Vivian had thankfully noted that economy was not being practised in that direction.

Julia was brought a small tray of tea, and Vivian asked her permission to enjoy a brandy.

She looked up at him, smiling. "You have no need of my permission. I am not a delicate creature shocked by the behaviour of gentlemen, you must know. Having been my father's companion since my mother died, and used to my brothers' inconsideration for females in a household where I am outnumbered five to one, I am much more at home in male company than with a gaggle of affected women who frown at cigar ash and mud-splashed breeches. Drink as much brandy as you wish, Vivian, and if your speech grows slurred and interspersed with oaths I shall not succumb to the vapours. I shall merely retire when I feel my ears can stand no more."

He frowned slightly as he studied her striking curves, and the face that was only made arresting by extraordinarily large eyes which she had learned to use most effectively since their last, brief meeting. She had been nineteen at that time, built like a country girl and somewhat overwhelmed by the recent death of her mother, which had left her the only female in a household of four brothers and a father, all vigorous men who had dominated the county scene for years. At twenty-three or four she had matured into a woman who apparently ran her household efficiently, and knew how to hold her own in a masculine world. He was deeply intrigued, and now responded as he always did to the fair sex.

"Do I detect a vixen in sheep's clothing, by any chance?"

She glanced up from pouring her tea. "If I am, it is unlikely that I will admit as much to you. You must find out for yourself."

"I shall be here too short a time for that," he replied, telling himself his brother must be totally bewitched. This creature now offering the most blatant sexual challenge he had received in a long time would be no partner for Charles. She would dominate him completely.

Taking a sip from her cup, Julia asked, "Why have you really

65

subjected yourself to insult by coming here? Would it be an attempt to prevent my father acquiring the land he has been after for years?"

"My answer to that is the same as yours to mine. You must find out for yourself."

"*Touché*," she acknowledged, with a strange excitement lighting her eyes. "Are you as skilful with the foils as your reputation claims, I wonder? We must have a contest before you leave."

"I leave that pleasure to Charles," he put in pointedly.

"Our skills have already been matched."

"So I heard. Now I am here, I confess to being somewhat confused about the outcome."

Deftly avoiding that, she launched a new attack. "Is it really your intention to buy horses for professional use, as Brancliffe graphically described before dinner?"

Tensing he replied, "Until I see what Charles presently has in the stables, I cannot judge whether or not they would be suitable."

She leant back gracefully in her chair. "They are not suitable, I assure you. What's more, I don't believe, for one moment, that you came to Shenstone merely to buy horses."

"Oh, really?" he commented lightly, trying to get back into his stride with the help of a second brandy. "Have you divined my secret plans?"

A faint smile played around her mouth. "There is nothing secret about them surely. Isn't it an attempt to frustrate a childhood enemy in the only way open to you?"

"It is an attempt to help Charles retain what must be legally his before very long."

Her deepening smile betrayed her disbelief. "After all these years, you are still vulnerable!"

"What does that mean?" he asked stiffly.

"Envy smothered by fraternal staunchness, on any matter concerning Shenstone." Her gaze was every bit as testing as Lord Brancliffe's as she continued. "In these stables there are excellent animals being ruined for want of good handling. As a skilled rider, you should put that consideration before any other. Charles can replenish *when* he acquires the title and estate. Father will pay a fair price for the animals. There are four geldings and a mare, which he is anxious to buy. I'll have Mountfoot St George for my own use."

"That stallion is mine," he told her crisply, "and he is not for sale. In any case, he's far too mettlesome. A female could never hold him."

Her steady gaze was full of confidence. "I took him across to Trebarn Tor this morning, before the mist closed in."

66

"The devil you did!" he exclaimed in annoyance. "You should have asked my permission."

"You were not here," she reminded him softly.

"Trebarn Tor stands in country that is dangerous at this time of the year," he said accusingly.

"I know. That's why I went."

With annoyance turning into a strange kind of anger, he tossed back the rest of the brandy and said, "You were lucky to get back in clear weather. You do know what might have happened if the mist had arrived earlier?"

"I know the moor," came her calm maddening reply.

"You don't know Mountfoot St George. One uneventful hack over rough country doesn't establish a lasting trust between horse and rider. He's strong-willed and temperamental."

"Like his owner?" She shook her head, the auburn swathes gleaming in the light of low lamps. "I've brought him under control during the course of the summer. You have been away for some years, Vivian. A lot of things have changed since you were last at Shenstone."

"So I deem," he said strongly, finding his gaze fastening on the sapphire necklace that flashed against her superb breast. "But basic facts have not. A woman's hands are not as strong as a man's. I question your claim to have brought a stallion like him under control."

He was pouring another brandy when her voice, teasingly soft, asked. "Do you dare to challenge it?"

Curiously disturbed by the change in a girl he had never viewed in a sexual light before, he found himself rising to the bait. "A race to Binford Cross?"

Her eyebrows rose. "Against a rider like you? That's a challenge indeed."

Glass in hand he stretched himself out in a chair before the fire and looked at her through narrowed eyes. "It will take a rider like me to bring Mountfoot St George back after you have been tossed."

The large luminous eyes studied him slowly from head to foot in a manner bordering on that used by men when appreciating obvious female charms. Then she smiled. "What if I should win?"

The brandy and warmth, combined with the mood of defiant challenge brought on by confronting his old tormentor, aroused a dangerous response to this exciting stranger in a girl he had thought he knew.

"My dear Julia, if you should win, I would *give* you the stallion."

She stiffened, her smile fading. "Your self-assurance is almost insulting."

"Yours is extraordinarily fascinating," he murmured, enjoying the verbal duel. "Mountfoot St George is a horse, not a susceptible male, I remind you."

"Both need to be schooled."

"From what I remember of you, you lack experience with the prime of either species."

"Advice from an expert?"

"In my professional capacity, I drill my men and control my horses with a trained hand. Both have to be totally obedient in battle. Yes, I count myself an expert on such things," he agreed looking across sleepily at the striking picture she made in the mellow fireglow, thinking how interesting it would be to bring *her* to heel. Poor Charles would be the one to obey, he thought regretfully.

"In our stables we have a stallion that is uncontrollable—even by an expert."

"Nonsense," he declared, feasting his gaze on the creamy rise of her breasts above the severe neckline of her gown.

"My brothers have all tried without success."

"Then they have gone the wrong way about it. I know them. They are used to rough-handling great brutes across this area of wild country. Some animals need gentling, the soft approach, words of love whispered into their ears. Like some women," he finished with soft innuendo.

"From all I have heard, you claim to be expert in that direction, also. The saying goes: Like father, like son. In this instance, *any* kind of son."

Through the relaxed sexually-shaded mood came a shaft of wariness as he realised she had slipped a thrust in under his guard. However, their intimacy was suddenly broken by the arrival of the two older men. Vivian rose to his feet, realising how unconventional the tête-à-tête had been. Lord Brancliffe's first words to Julia dismayed and disturbed him.

"Well, my dear, the affair is satisfactorily settled. Your father has agreed to my terms for the transfer of the land."

"Sir, you can't," Vivian cried. "That land is part of the estate, and you have an heir."

Hard eyes raked him with contempt. "The estate is mine to do with as I will. I'll have no popinjay who rides decorated horses telling me what to do. The estate is none of your concern, and never will be, I'll remind you."

Vivian rounded on Sir Kinsley. "Sir, to go behind my brother's back like this is unforgivable. Allow me time to speak on his behalf with my grandfather. It is the main reason for my visit. I sincerely beg you to hold off from the transaction until I have had the opportunity to put my case."

Sir Kinsley gave a smug smile. "It is of little use to beg *me*, Vivian. It is Lord Brancliffe's land, and he has accepted my offer. We have shaken hands on it."

Vivian swung round to the old man once more. "You have cut off access to Shenstone from the west! It's madness."

"Silence!" croaked the voice used to obedience.

"I will not be silent," he declared furiously. "You have always considered yourself invincible, but even the poorest general would never cut off the only passage to his stronghold from the rear. You have made a great mistake—and you have made it when my brother is not here to prevent you."

"Your brother, as you have always cared to call him, is well aware of my reasons for what you have the effrontery to term as madness. Sir Kinsley buys this land on condition that, if his daughter should marry anyone other than my heir, it is to be given to her husband as her dowry." A cunning smile crossed the hawklike face. "It will ensure Charles a wife who is a strong, hardy woman of Cornwall; a female who can ride as well as a man, and shoot as straight as anyone. I want no more weak, feeble creatures always with faces in a handkerchief and wasting time with *music*!" he finished with a snort of derision. "Well, what have you to say to that? Where is your apology, hey? Who gave you leave to interfere in affairs that are no concern of yours?"

As he stood facing the fact that Julia Marchbanks was being "bought" for Charles, and his brother had known the fact all along, Vivian realised nothing had changed over the years. He was still standing there with a board strapped to his back, his shortcomings being recited for all to hear. Before he could speak, however, Julia's voice broke into the tingling silence.

"Father, Vivian has offered to school that wild stallion of which we have all despaired. Are we not fortunate that he is on hand just as we thought of selling the horse?"

Vivian swung round to face her, a hot denial on his lips. Then he saw in her expression an echo of what he had always seen on the face of his grandfather. There was an additional lascivious pleasure evident as she added softly, for him alone, "If I have to prove my claim to you, my dear Vivian, why shouldn't you prove yours?" Slowly removing the sapphire earrings she wore, she smiled triumphantly as she held them out in the palm of her hand. "I will *give* you these, if you break him before he breaks you."

# CHAPTER FOUR

The moor had produced one of its sinister, desolate moods that day. Sleet, interspersed with snow flurries, covered the barren distances to drive animals into the lee of tors and rocky ridges, their thick, harsh coats insufficient to withstand the penetrating wind and plunging temperature. Tracks crossing the vast moorland were obliterated, so that even those Cornishmen who knew the terrain well only ventured out from vital necessity. To yeomen, the reason for Vivian's journey that day would be considered lunatic. To men of consequence— particularly military officers—his ride to Sir Kinsley Marchbanks' estate *would* be regarded as a vital necessity. A gentleman's ability as a horseman had been questioned, he had been challenged to prove his boast, a wager had been laid on the outcome. His honour must therefore be defended, at all costs, especially before a lady.

The lady in question was determined on her pound of flesh. Julia glowed with a curious elation centred on Vivian rather than her triumphant acquisition of his stallion, Mountfoot St George. The race to Binford Cross had been marginally won by the girl who claimed mastery over the huge grey. During the subsequent luncheon, Vivian had been forced to admit that Julia was an outstanding equestrienne, with apparent control of the temperamental animal she had ridden with skill and intelligence. He had remained silent on a possible reason for his own poor performance, as suspicion hardened into certainty during the light meal prior to the contest for the second wager. Excessive exhaustion after no more than a rigorous ride, a tendency to sweat on a day of bitter temperatures, and a light-headed sensation that hampered concentration told him the swamp fever that doctors had warned him would recur had taken a grip on him again.

It had been out of the question to use the fact to cry off the afternoon's ordeal. Personal pride, aside from every code of conduct ruling such affairs, demanded that he should hide the increasing symptoms as he prepared to uphold his claim that he could school an animal dubbed untameable by the entire Marchbanks family. Consequently, he was now standing in the home paddock, buffeted by a still-rising wind

70

which threw sleet into his face like ice-needles and sent waves of alternate heat and chill through his body.

The rogue stallion looked unimpressive by equine standards, with little evidence of the thoroughbred strain from which he was descended. Short, with a coat of nondescript shade, and with a distinct lack of nobility in his blunt head, Crispin only betrayed his intractability by the wickedness of his eyes. To disturb and test such a beast on a vicious December day was an act of human folly. Removed from a warm stall to face icy conditions in a field lined with the blaspheming two-legged creatures against whom he waged perpetual war, Crispin instantly rebelled and charged in every direction, head down and furious.

Vivian watched with a mixture of admiration and growing respect, somehow identifying with this descendant from a noble line who did not conform to expectations. Unfortunately, the stallion was unaware of any rapport, and the danger ahead was soon apparent as Vivian sized up the animal's mood and muscular strength during its furious racing.

· "My dear Vivian," came a teasing voice from beside him, "I ache for the sight of you whispering words of love into his ears." Julia's eyes shone with excitement as he turned to her. "You claimed that was all that was needed, did you not? The technique which never fails with your women!"

Goaded, he murmured, "It's not my practice to embark on seduction in the midst of a snow-swept moor."

She smiled. "A faint-hearted attitude, surely? Think how success under such conditions would enhance your reputation as a true Veasey-Hunter."

Turning away abruptly, Vivian saw that the horse was now being cautiously saddled by the head groom. Crispin stood seemingly docile, his breath clouding in the icy air as it was blown from his nostrils, and he marked Vivian's firm approach with no more than nervous flicks of his ears. Quiet, confident words, a caressing hand over his neck, were tolerated by the stallion despite the wildness of his eyes as Vivian took the leading-rein from the groom, who then hastily retreated to the safety of the paddock fence. Crispin opened the attack by sidling with such force and suddenness, Vivian lost his footing and fell, losing his hold on the leading-rein as the animal charged at the man now swinging his leg over the wooden barricade. Aware that he had made a crass error right at the start, Vivian scrambled to his feet fighting waves of dizziness that told him he must keep the battle short or fever would be the victor.

Cheated of the chance to punish the groom, Crispin stood quietly

71

again, allowing Vivian to take up the long trailing leather. It was then the stallion's turn to be taken unawares. Abandoning his normal training practice, Vivian instead mounted in a swift movement and waited for the inevitable violent reaction.

What followed was a kaleidoscope of impressions which seemed to continue endlessly. Physical punishment brought pain in curiously abstract waves, his confused brain registering it some seconds after his body suffered it. Reasoned thought was supplanted by instinct; his strength grew spasmodic as the fever tightened its grip. Dizziness produced images that swirled around him, so that he was further confused by glimpses of the white sky beneath his feet, and snow-covered ground above. The blunt nose of the stallion seemed to come at him from every direction; the grooms hung over a fence that raced round and around like a carousel. Throughout it all, he was aware of Julia in a dark cloak with a fur-lined hood, watching every moment of that clash of wills. Her face was alive with an expression akin to ecstasy, which suggested that she and the horse were testing him in exactly the same manner. Anger strengthened his determination to flout them both.

With feet grown leaden and arms so tired he was alarmed at his own weakness, he stumbled time and again through driving sleet to mount a creature his numbed senses rejected, whilst inner conviction of eventual success drove him on. Then, as usual in such cases, it was over very suddenly. Snorting, but docile, Crispin responded to hands, spurs and voice, accepting the unwelcome weight on his back. Perhaps the animal had acknowledged exceptional skill; perhaps he had sensed an anger greater than his own. Perhaps he merely wished to return to the warm stall as soon as possible. Whatever the reason, he walked quietly around the paddock half a dozen times listening to a voice which, although it had grown husky from the chill, spoke a language he now recognised. Vivian hardly knew what he was saying. Indeed, he hardly knew how he remained upright in the saddle when the surrounding moorland was undulating and spinning.

Men came alongside him; hands assisted him to the frozen ground. Voices expressed admiration, even awe. His progress toward the girl in the cloak was stumbling and erratic. Exhausted, by now quite ill, he stood before her shaking with ague. Her eyes, dilated with elation, raked him from head to foot with a glance of assessement similar to that given by a sadistic old man to a small boy stammering an account of his own physical performance. There was no sense of elation within Vivian, just a longing to escape.

Julia's bold features appeared to swim in a sea of thickening snow as she said, in a tone which reflected the triumph he could not feel, "That was *magnificent!* These are too small a reward for such a display."

He stared down at the winking stones in her outstretched palm, and recognised his humiliation as complete. Pushing past her, he entered a house containing curious nightmares—nightmares concerning black tribal warriors, hideous piles of human limbs, and white men in uniform accusing him, beating his body black and blue, tying him to a devil horse that raced headlong through white clouds containing both ice and fire.

The nightmares ended when he opened his eyes to see an unfamiliar room filled with antique furniture, and a girl, in a dark-green gown, whose auburn hair glowed like the vivid embers in the fireplace near his bed. Although reading a book, Julia was instantly aware that he was awake, and sat gazing at him with an air of great satisfaction.

"The fever broke last night. You've been sleeping peacefully for almost twelve hours," she told him, rising to pull the bell-cord by the wall. "Now you must eat."

"How long have I been here?" he asked limply.

"Four days. You'll be here at least another four," she said with relish. "It has been snowing steadily and we are completely cut off." Her smile as she arrived at the bedside was all-encompassing. "How fortunate that I am well experienced at nursing my brothers. I remained with you night and day while the fever raged, and I shall continue to do so until you regain your strength."

As he lay a helpless captive to circumstance, she sat on the side of the bed and began to wipe his brow with a cool perfumed cloth. "You were ill when you arrived here, Vivian, and said nothing of the fact. That makes your performance doubly magnificent." Her voice almost purred with suppressed excitement. "Any woman would consider the experience well worth the sacrifice of two sapphires."

Vivian returned a week prior to Christmas to find London in a festive mood. He was not. When he arrived at the family house he was tired, deeply depressed, and hungry after the long train journey from Cornwall.

"Yours is the straightest face I've seen in days, Viv," greeted his brother. "I'm sorry you were obliged to act without my support down there. I didn't plan it, but the snow that kept you there also prevented my joining you at the conclusion of my business."

Vivian surrendered his coat to the footman, saying with force, "Don't ever ask me to go there again, because nothing on earth would persuade me to do so." He headed for the study, where a substantial fire heated the room. Bending to warm his hands, he threw Charles a savage look. "When I'm sent on a military mission, I expect to be given all available details on what I may expect to encounter. I am finding it extremely hard to forgive you for allowing me to return to a place that holds unhappy memories, ignorant of the fact that Julia Marchbanks has become a devious, highly sensual woman who clearly does not share your enthusiasm for the match her father and Brancliffe want. A parcel of land has just changed hands in order to secure it."

Turning his back to the flames, he continued harshly. "Knowing that Julia's marriage to any man but you would create the impossible situation of a complete stranger controlling access to both estates, you all believe you have given the girl no option. You fool, Charles! I know women; you don't. Julia will never allow herself to be *bought* as a bride for you. Unless you are a veritable Hercules, with overtones of Casanova, you won't get her any other way, either."

Standing in the centre of the book-lined room, Charles seemed initially stunned. Then he flushed darkly. "I'll have your apology for that."

"No you won't," he snapped. "You sent me there on a fool's errand. I'll have *your* apology."

His brother began to bluster. "It was merely one of Brancliffe's more eccentric ideas. Opposing them makes him impossibly stubborn, so I usually jolly him along until he's seized by a fresh enthusiasm. I certainly never agreed to his going ahead with such a scheme."

"But you didn't refuse—which amounts to the same thing, where our grandfather is concerned. Well, Maxted's Farm and the area up to the old mill are now part of the Marchbanks estate. Shenstone is approachable from the west only with Sir Kinsley's permission. He is plainly prepared to do anything in his power to make Julia go to the altar with you, but that girl has changed drastically in recent years. Like Brancliffe, she has developed a personality that will not brook being thwarted. Once a woman recognises her own powers of attraction, she is reluctant to relinquish the freedom to use them. Julia is no biddable future bride, believe me."

Charles came right up to him, as pale as he had been flushed before. "What is that supposed to mean—in plain language, if you please."

"Very well," Vivian agreed, his anger growing less at the sight of his brother's expression. "Julia made it very plain that she was as pleasantly intrigued with the changes five years had wrought in me, as I was with those wrought in her."

Charles's lip curled. "So you're no longer content with ill-mannered chorus-girls!"

74

"Oh, for God's sake, I didn't seduce the girl you are set on marrying. My sexual adventures will always be confined to those who give their somewhat tarnished charms in return for my presents. However, my gaze strays to forbidden fruit if it is tempting enough, and remains for a while if encouraged. Julia is not the girl for you, Charles."

"I believe I am well able to judge that for myself," came the stiff response.

"You are labouring under a delusion, in that case," he put in, more impatient than angry. "You might well have lost your head over that girl, but hers is still very firmly on her shoulders. If the marriage should go ahead, she will take the title and all that goes with it, but you'll have no doting wife. Day by day, you'll be stripped of your pride and authority until you are no more than a puppet. I do know females better than you do, Charles, and I strongly advise you to pull out before any official announcement is made. You sent me down there to save your land. I failed. But I can save you from the loss of your inheritance to a woman who would take up the reins relinquished by Brancliffe."

Charles nodded in grim satisfaction. "I thought as much. It's that damned law which robbed you of Shenstone and the title. You have now found an additional reason for resentment: my relationship with Julia Marchbanks."

"Now look here," grated Vivian, anger surging once more. "I went down there against my will, because you begged me to try to help. I'm still attempting to do so, so don't insult me by throwing my status in my face. I might be a bastard Veasey-Hunter, but my blood is every bit as blue as yours. I happen to be proud of my lineage. Go ahead and give away the land you are fortunate enough to inherit; marry a girl who will rob you of everything including your manhood! But I'll thank you not to treat me to that damned priggish attitude when I give you the truth. I thought you more of a man than that."

For some moments they stood confronting each other, then Charles sighed heavily. "I'm sorry, Viv. It came as a shock. I never guessed he'd carry out something I had treated as a joke—one in rather poor taste. I swear I have never given him reason to think I would . . ." he broke off in embarrassment. "Do you think Julia is under the impression that I would resort to such tricks to force her into marriage?"

"Find out for yourself," Vivian advised him wearily, heading for the nearby decanter. "Apart from making arrangements to transport the few horses I managed to save on your behalf, I now wash my hands of your affairs. Don't ask me to go to Shenstone again, Charles. It holds too many memories I'd rather forget."

He drank the warming liquor swiftly, determined to dull his mind to thoughts of something he could not relate to his brother. There was no way he could put into words how he had felt standing bruised, bloody and ill before a girl who was displaying frenzied delight in his condition. As the ladies of Rome had thrilled to the feats of gladiators in the arena, Julia had gloried in the beating he had taken as a result of her challenge. It still gave him a strange sense of shock to acknowledge that she had enjoyed watching him battle with an animal who was dangerous; had been excited by the physical punishment he had suffered. Unlike his grandfather, Julia was less interested in success than in the struggle to achieve it. She loved power; her own and that of the men she wished to control. That knowledge had given birth to the humiliation completed when she had held out the sapphires, as a reward for pain.

At that point in his thoughts Vivian became aware of his brother once more, staring at him in obvious unhappiness with a frown on his good-looking face. The visit to the scene of his childhood had revived recollections of it, so he filled a second glass to hold out persuasively to Charles.

"Come on, join me in a toast to continuing brotherhood," he invited in quiet tones. "When we were boys the old man did everything in his power to set us against each other in physical competition, hoping that it would lead to personal enmity. We always resisted it. Let's continue that way. To quarrel now would give him the greatest pleasure of his remaining years."

They drank in silence, then Charles thought to thank him for rescuing some of the horses. "I am very grateful, Viv, and I'll refund the purchase price when my gold dividends are paid shortly. When the old man finally departs this world, I'll have them back in Shenstone's stables."

"I don't believe he will ever depart the world," Vivian murmured, well into his second drink. "Brancliffe has never obliged anyone in his life."

They went in to dinner at that point. With unspoken agreement they dropped the subject of the land that had changed hands in an attempt to secure the desired bride for the next Lord Brancliffe. Instead, they spoke of finance and investments. Charles urged his brother to put money into South African gold, or diamonds, as their mother had done. As a subject, it was only a little less controversial than any they had touched upon that evening.

Because James Veasey-Hunter had died before succeeding to the title, the income from the estate that had been apportioned to him as the heir had naturally passed to *his* heir—namely, his younger son Charles. The rest of his fast-dwindling funds had been willed to his widow. With

76

Lord Brancliffe steadfastly refusing to make any provision for the grandson he saw as an unfortunate blot on the family tree, Vivian would have been left with only his army pay if it were not for his mother and her family. A very generous bequest from a great-aunt had financed his university years and set him up as a cavalry officer. His mother diverted the annual income she received from Shenstone estate to her first-born, in an attempt to compensate him for the cruelty of the Veasey-Hunter family.

In consequence, Vivian was not as wealthy as his brother, but was well able to hold his own in the circle into which he had been born. His mode of living was such that his banker, who would have remained silent if his client had been the legitimate heir to Shenstone, often sent him courteous but cautionary notes on the state of his account. That Vivian was presently able to buy horses on Charles's behalf was due to his sojourn in Ashanti, where even the greatest spendthrift would find it difficult to part with money. The subject was an additional cause of subconscious guilt for Charles, and he was consequently always trying to persuade his bother to invest and increase his capital. Vivian recognised his motives and always countered them light-heartedly. It was the only way to treat sensitive matters.

Now, he merely frowned at Charles across the table, and shook his head. "I spent a hellish two years in Ashanti fighting a war that had as its basic motivation the gold of the region. What I witnessed there, what was done to men in the name of national greed, has forced me to regard the acquisition of riches from a wider point of view. I told you not so many weeks ago that I foresee more trouble in South Africa over the gold there—and the diamonds, of course. The war against the Boers sixteen years ago only settled matters temporarily, leaving us worsted and the Dutch settlers still dissatisfied. It will flare up again, take my word for it. Anyone who has studied Cecil Rhodes' grand plan for Africa must conclude that the Boers are a great stumbling-block which must be removed if it is to succeed." He dabbed his mouth with his napkin. "If I find myself one day fighting them, the conflict will be civilised. No atrocities and pagan rituals."

Memories, as black as any man could have, absorbed him as they left the dining-table and moved back to the study. It was there that Charles broke into the dark reflections, as he lit himself a cigar.

"Talk of Cecil Rhodes reminds me of something, Viv. I think you stand in danger of losing the lady of the ostrich feathers."

"Oh?" said Vivian, surprised that Charles had even remembered that much about the girl. "You do mean Leila Duncan, don't you?"

"That's right." He got the cigar going to his satisfaction, then leant back in his chair. "I had lunch with Beefy Baxter at Richmond last Sunday, and she was there with Fairfield's youngest son. Isn't he in the 49th with you?"

"No, the 17th. Are you certain it was Leila?"

"I suppose I couldn't say that I was *certain*, just strongly inclined to trust my recollection of her. She was wearing the same hat, but a different gown. Can't remember the colour, but it was very fetching."

Vivian felt piqued. He had introduced Leila to young Fairfield. "The devil! How dare he steal a march on me like that?"

Charles wagged his head. "He's not the only one. As I was walking through St James's Park one afternoon in the week, I saw her in a passing carriage with that banker fellow Wells. Deep in conversation, they were, and he was making no secret of his delight in her company."

Vivian's pique grew. John Wells had also been presented by him, on that first evening at the Savoy Grill. His pleasure in parading an obscure chorus-girl through the elegant premises of London's leading restaurants was rebounding on him. In his present mood, it was particularly irritating. She was plainly gathering a covey of admirers through his entertaining evenings with her. His intention had merely been to amuse himself at the expense of her lack of sophistication, and possibly to make her care a little for him before leaving her snubbed, as he had been by her initial return of his flowers that had made him a butt for his friends' laughter. What the girl did after he had tired of her did not matter, but he had not foreseen the possibility of her taking on a following of which he merely formed one. He was damned if he would be the instrument of her vast popularity. If she was learning too fast, it was time she discovered the rules of the game, as he played it. Wells, Fairfield . . . and who else? Did she return *their* presents? he wondered.

"I have spoken twice to you, Viv" said a voice, bringing him from his thoughts, "but you appear to be elsewhere."

"No, just finding the warmth of the fire and the effects of a good wine at dinner telling me how tired I am."

"That girl doesn't mean anything to you, does she?" came the probing question.

"Leila Duncan? Good lord, no," he laughed as he bent to the fire to light a spill for his own cigar. "It was an exercise in tactics, I told you that."

Two nights before Christmas Vivian booked a seat in the stalls for *The Maid of Montezuma* and, after watching the strolling number with great pleasure, sent his flowers to number four in the line asking her to join him for supper after the show. Feeling it was time to take the affair a step further, he waited at the stage-door with pleasurable anticipation.

Almost the last to come from the dressing-room, there was a faint blush on her cheeks and undeniable gladness in those dark-blue eyes as she smiled a greeting.

"The flowers are lovely, and I was pleased to find that you hadn't been in Cornwall so long you had muddled up our names again."

Well satisfied with her response, he took her elbow. "If you would give me permission to call you Leila, there'd be no problem. I'm frightfully good at first names."

He had a hansom waiting and gave the name of an out-of-the-way restaurant where they were unlikely to bump into people he knew. She looked even more beautiful than he remembered in a dress of pale lavender silk, long matching gloves, and a wrap of silvery-white brocaded satin. Her dark hair was still in the elaborate style worn by the girls in the Lindley Stroll, and her skin looked flawless in the seductive dimness of the cab. His gaze lingered on the cleft between two ivory-smooth curves revealed by the *décolletage*, then travelled on to the seed-pearl and amethyst bracelet clasped around her gloved wrist.

"I hear you have become the rage since I left for Cornwall," he commented lazily.

"The rage?" she repeated rather breathlessly. "Oh, hardly."

"But you have been gracing Romano's and Oddenino's with a selection of escorts." That was a guess, because Charles rarely entered such society playgrounds.

"Yes, I suppose . . . well, I have been out to supper a few times recently. But they were all people you have introduced," she added defensively.

"Foolish of me," he murmured, deciding the time was ripe to advance the relationship a great deal further. He had no intention of vying with half a dozen of his acquaintances, and she had better realise that.

"How did you know all this if you've been away in Cornwall?" she asked suspiciously.

"My brother has seen you everywhere he has been. You are known to him and, if I remember rightly, you prefer his company to mine."

She looked away out of the cab window where the lights of the West End glittered with pre-Christmas enticement. "I never once said that. As a matter of fact, I found him too clever for me. He spoke most of the time about Cyril Rhodes."

"Who?" he asked, with amusement.

She turned back to face him. "Cyril Rhodes. I think he has something to do with gold mines. Haven't you heard of him either? I'm so glad."

Fighting his laughter with difficulty, he tried hard to control his voice as he said, "I might have heard mention of the man somewhere. Is that the only conversation my brother had?"

"Oh no. He told me about tin mines, as well."

"How deucedly dull! Poor Charles is not at his best in female company. Yet you were hoping to spend another evening with him when you accepted my first invitation," he pointed out.

She looked down at her lap. "He's very nice, really."

"Yes, he's very nice indeed," he agreed with sincerity. "Much nicer than I am."

Drawing her wrap around her she settled back in her corner before saying with a smile, "If I didn't know you already have too much self-confidence, I'd think you were asking for a compliment, Captain Veasey-Hunter."

She was learning fast, he noted with irritation. Coquettes bored him these days. "Asking in vain, it appears."

"Not really. I am very glad you're back from Cornwall."

Reaching for her hand he took it to his lips. "So am I." Pretending to notice the bracelet for the first time, he fingered it assessingly. The amethysts were of inferior quality. "I see you are now accepting presents from gentlemen."

She tried to draw her hand away, but he would not let it go. It plainly embarrassed her to have him study another man's gift when she had sent his own back.

"Mr Gilbert regards the admiration of gentlemen as part of the performance. He insists that we accept invitations," she began awkwardly. "I seem to be getting more and more, and they all send me something the following day. I can't very well return them all, can I?"

"Only mine," he said deliberately.

"But theirs are different."

"In what way?"

Casting around for words to explain something she had not the sophistication to handle, she gave him exactly the information he wanted. "Their presents are somehow just part of the show. I'm a make-believe girl they see on the stage and admire. They don't want to know the real Leila Duncan at all. Having supper with them is simply prolonging the theatrical performance, and they're all so well-off a bracelet or brooch is no more than an ordinary boy giving his girl a yard of hair-ribbon or the tram fare home. It doesn't mean a thing."

So she did not regard his invitations as no more than part of her performance, and his pearl necklace she had returned *had* meant something to her. Gratified with the way the evening was going, he embarked on the next stage.

"Am I to be allowed the privilege of knowing the real Leila Duncan?"

Even in the dimness of the cab he could see her colour had deepened, and her eyes glowed by the light of the lamps outside. "I can't think why you should want to."

He leant toward her. "Even if I now confess that I deliberately forced Oscar to throw a temperamental fit that morning in Brighton, so that I had an excuse to speak to you?"

As he had judged, she was completely thrown by his words. So, while she sat gazing at him in emotional turmoil, he took from his pocket a velvet box containing Julia Marchbanks' sapphire earrings. They were symbolic of something best banished by bestowing them on a mere chorus-girl, who would have no idea of their true value. He watched with satisfied amusement as she opened the box. That bracelet on her wrist looked no more than a gewgaw now.

"They're . . . oh, they're absolutely beautiful," she gasped.

"There is a generally accepted manner in which to thank a gentleman for a gift," he prompted softly. "Doesn't Mr Gilbert encourage that, also?"

She looked up quickly, and he bent his head with perfect timing to kiss her lingeringly on the mouth with increasing pressure until she was trembling in his arms. Then he drew away, murmuring, "You can't possibly return them now."

She seemed completely overwhelmed as she gazed up at him with more than he had even hoped for written on her face. "I . . . I don't know what to say. I've never been given anything as beautiful as this, or as valuable." Her gaze returned to the earrings flashing blue fire as the intermittent light invaded the moving cab. It was as if she were mesmerised by the beauty of the jewels. "I couldn't possibly wear them, you know."

With a sigh of satisfaction at the success of his tactics, he leant back in his corner. "Don't worry, my dear, you'll have all the right things to go with them. I'll take you to a discreet modiste I know, who will provide a selection of ensembles guaranteed to set them off beautifully."

There was a moment's complete silence, then it was as if the cab were filled with irate hens sending feathers flying in every direction.

*"Oh no you bally well won't!"* she blazed as she gathered the wrap up so that it covered her to her chin. "Their presents might seem small next to yours, but none of your friends ever insulted me by offering to buy me clothes. I always knew what you were after, but you've picked the wrong girl this time. I'm an actress not a slut. Find one of them to dress

in your *ensembles*. She'll be more than willing to do what you want, and she'll cost you a lot less than these gaudy earrings."

The velvet box was flung in his lap and, before he could say or do a thing, she had seized his silver-topped cane and thumped on the roof with it until the cabbie opened the flap to peer down at them.

"This so-called gent is getting out," she announced in less than refined accents, "and before he goes he can pay my fare to Mirtle Street."

With that she flung open the door beside her and sat back staring straight ahead, waiting for him to leave. Not to do so would be even more undignified he decided. She was no lady, so her further actions were unpredictable. Longing to put her across his knee, he had no alternative but to bend double to climb down past her. No sooner had he reached the pavement than his bouquet of winter roses and stephanotis was flung after him before the door slammed shut.

"That'll be four-and-six, guv'nor," called the cabbie from his box.

Vivian held up the fare, and received a broad wink from the man.

"She'll come round in the morning, never fear. They always do."

"Hold your tongue," snapped Vivian and walked off leaving the bouquet where it had fallen.

Mulishly refusing to hail another cab he walked back to the house, where he planned to spend Christmas. Dismissing the butler he settled in a wing chair before the fire, trying to drive the December chill from his bones. For a long time he gazed into the golden heart of the flames, while the decanter emptied and all kinds of thoughts ran through his mind. He had believed he knew all there was to know about women, but he had recently encountered two who had proved him wrong.

It had been arranged for Leila and Rose to spend Christmas with Miss Agatha Heywood in Brighton, but when Leila made her way to the apartment Miles Lampton had provided for Rose and for which he had paid advance rent, she found her friend still in her woollen dressing-gown and doubled up with pain. It was clear she had been crying, so Leila immediately took command in a no-nonsense manner by insisting that there was no question of going to Brighton. They would have their own Christmas celebration there, she declared.

With all her domestic training to help her she soon had Rose comfortable on a couch with a rug over her, and a hot drink in her hand to wash down one of the powders a chemist had given her for her indigestion. Then Leila returned to her own basement—very drab and spartan after her friend's pretty apartment—to fetch a piece of brisket, some pickles, three apples and half a cherry cake she had in her pantry.

Together with the contents of her friend's larder she was able to make a thick vegetable soup, and bubble-and-squeak to go with the cold brisket. This was rounded off with apples, dates, and walnuts.

They sat by the fire in close companionship throughout a day of early fog followed by sleety rain, and drank each other's health with a couple of bottles of stout Rose had in her cupboard. She looked brighter and greatly cheered by Leila's company; but the pain in her stomach was severe enough to keep the lines of strain on her beautiful face, which added to the personal unhappiness Leila tried to keep hidden.

"I shouldn't really drink this," joked Rose holding up the glass of stout. "It's not exactly Lindley Girl style, is it? I got a taste for it when I worked behind the bar at the Lamb and Fleece, and still enjoy a glass. Miles used to think it a huge joke when no one else was around, but went wild if I mentioned it in company." Her face, gilded and highlighted by the fire Leila had maintained, looked suddenly desolate. "He was an awful snob, Lei, and I knew as soon as I moved in here that it would end this way. Yet I couldn't help myself. I don't seem to have any pride. I'm not ashamed of being his mistress and, if he walked in here now, I'd go straight back to how it was."

"Not with me here, you wouldn't," said Leila with forced gaiety. "Now, if you've finished knocking back the stout, we'll have a game."

So they played a board-game and giggled over each other's misfortunes. At the end of that, Rose seemed slightly better and offered to provide some music on the piano Miles had installed for her. Leila wandered across to lean on the polished instrument, running her hands over the beautiful wood as her friend went through all the popular songs of the day. Would Vivian Veasey-Hunter have hired a place like this for her? A large airy apartment filled with velvet-covered furniture on graceful legs, windows giving a view of trees and a park, long amber curtains with tasselled ropes to pull when wanting to open or close them, knick-knacks in delicate porcelain, lamps with beaded shades, rich carpets in thick pile, a piano with elegant stool, and a canary in a cage. The dining-room was filled with great pieces of dark furniture that impressed on entry, and the table bore an elaborate centre-piece of ebony elephants. Miles Lampton had been many times to Africa.

The kitchen was a pure delight after her own basement range, but meant to be operated by the servant Miles had engaged. The girl had left soon after the liaison had ended, but Rose had been told she could remain until Easter, when the hire ended. Leila had not been into the bedroom and had no desire to see it. However, it was certain to be as luxurious as the rest. It would be sheer joy to live in a place like this, she reflected . . . but only if she could afford to pay the rent herself.

"Penny for them," Rose said suddenly, and Leila became aware that her friend had stopped playing.

She shook her head. "They weren't worth that much. Where did you learn to play the piano, Rose?"

"In the Lamb and Fleece. They used to have turns there every night, until the law clamped down and stopped it. I can't play from music, of course."

"It's good, though. Go on, you must know some more."

"You sure?"

"As it's Christmas, I'll sing along."

Rose was only halfway through the second chorus of one song before she stopped and stared at Leila.

"What's up?" she asked quickly. "Have you got that pain again?"

"You never told me you could sing like that. Does Mr Gilbert know?"

Leila shook her head. "If you remember, we were told off for talking too much at our audition, and I got so angry I pranced onto the stage to 'stroll' for Jack Spratt. After that, you and I were told to come back in half an hour to practise walking. I never got as far as singing anything for them."

Rose leant across the keyboard, her face very serious. "You're good, Lei. You should be singing, not strolling."

She shrugged. "Chorus-girls don't find fame overnight. What I want most of all, just at the moment, is to lead in the line."

"Pah! Anyone can do that! You should be singing—not the songs we've got in *The Maid*. You've got a different kind of voice. It's almost opera. I went to one with Miles once. The hero and heroine looked like the Strong Man and the Fat Lady from a fair-ground but, funny thing was, it didn't matter once they started to sing. I've never heard sounds like that come from a person's mouth before. I didn't understand it, of course, because it was all in foreign, but the sound of their voices was so marvellous I could have sat there twice as long to listen. I went all over goose-pimples with excitement. Have you ever been to the opera?"

"No, silly. You have to be 'taken' to opera, like you were." She moved across to put more coal on the fire. "But I'm sure I don't sound like they did."

Rose agreed. "They've had years of training to produce that kind of voice. But you've got the same *sound* in yours. Our dear Adeline squeaks and warbles her way through songs that have to be sung that way. You need grander kind of music. More like this. Come on, there aren't any words, but you can la-la-la to it."

She began to play a lovely rolling tune that was very popular with the

84

players of street corner barrel-organs, and Leila did as she was told, finding herself carried away by the new experience of singing to someone else instead of to herself as she went around the house.

"What's that called?" she asked, enchanted at the end of it.

"It's foreign. Miles used to say it beautifully," came the somewhat wistful reply. "*Leeberstrowm* or something like that, he used to call it. Isn't it lovely? Come on, Lei, sing some more."

The afternoon passed, and darkness fell as they lost themselves in music, growing more and more excited. Then they drew the curtains and sat by the firelight, holding bread to the flames on long brass toasting-forks, as they spun cobweb dreams of fame and success.

Rose looked down at Leila who sat on the floor, knees bent up as she leant against another chair, watching the bread turn golden-brown.

"When we get our names up in lights, dearie, we shall be able to hire apartments and install *men* in them for as long as they hold our interest. I wonder how they would take to that idea?" When Leila did not answer, she went on, "D'you think that time will ever come?"

"No, Rose, their feelings don't go as deep as ours. One girl's as good as another for their purposes. They don't ever seem to really *care* the way we do."

There was a silence, and Leila glanced up to find Rose's eyes glistening with unshed tears. She was immediately full of concern. Dropping the toasting-fork, she knelt up and took her friend's hands.

"I'm sorry. I didn't mean to be nasty. But, look at you! You're the most beautiful girl in the line-up, and I've never known anyone more loyal, more generous, or more full of fun. What he's done to you is wicked. Here you are on Christmas Day, tied up in knots with indigestion caused by fretting over him, and you bet he's having a marvellous time at some la-di-dah house-party with Lady Alicia, or the Honourable Miss Goldmine. They think *we* are just . . . just . . ."

"Whores?" suggested Rose harshly, then looked hard at Leila. "That speech came right from the heart, gal. Who's upset *you*? Canine Charles?"

It all had to come out then. Sinking back on her heels she told Rose that it had been Vivian who had been taking her out, ending by relating the episode of the earrings. She twirled the toasting-fork around in her hand, the half-browned piece of bread cold by now.

"I knew, that day in Brighton, what kind of man he was. Only he had a way with him that made the most ordinary things seem exciting, because he never did what I expected him to do. I vowed I wouldn't accept his next invitation, but I always found myself going with him."

"Mmm," mused Rose from her greater experience. "Used to getting his own way, that much was obvious from the start. Look how his poor brother accepted having us two forced on him for lunch without putting up any resistance."

"That's exactly it, Rose. He could smile and persuade anyone to do anything he asked. You couldn't really call him bossy, but when he said what he wanted in that confident husky sort of voice, people just did it."

Rose tapped Leila's knee with her toasting-fork in warning. "I remember that voice. It's the kind that can get a girl into a bedroom quicker than anything."

"It never got *me* there," she responded fiercely. "Now he knows!"

There was a moment of quietness before Rose said, "You've grown fond of him, haven't you?"

"No," she said, far too quickly to fool her friend, or herself. Holding the slice of bread to the flames she found there were unshed tears in her own eyes now. "Although I knew all along what a man like him would want from a chorus-girl, I never realised how . . . how *cheap* I would feel when he actually put it into words. I put on a brave show, but inside I was curling up with shame."

The fire crackled in the silence that followed, and the piece of bread on her toasting-fork blackened and began to smoke as the tears overspilled onto her cheeks.

"I never did curl up with shame," put in Rose, at last. "You are worth two of me, Lei."

"Oh, no," cried Leila, with an even deeper sense of shame. "You don't know. You just don't know what you're saying."

Longing to confess her married state and how it had come about, Leila knew she must remain silent. But her overwrought feelings since the quarrel with Vivian could no longer be contained, and both girls clasped each other while they indulged in a good cry that made them feel infinitely better. They then spent the rest of the evening playing cards, eating the chocolates Rose had bought for her aunt in Brighton, and speculating on their future by trying, somewhat hilariously, to read tea-leaves.

The laughter and abundance of food took its toll on Rose. She was violently sick and shaken with stomach pains so severe she had to take to her bed. Leila decided to stay there for the night, and spent much of it warming cloths by the fire to lay on Rose's stomach to ease the pain, and wiping the frothy vomit from her mouth each time she was sick. When morning came, Leila knew there was something more serious than indigestion afflicting the girl, and told her she must see a doctor.

"Are you quite sure it isn't the obvious?" she asked Rose again.

"Quite sure," came the weary answer. "I expect it was the stout. Miles always said I'd end up as fat as Mrs Maggs."

The doctor asked Rose the same question, and doubted her assurance while he went on to diagnose inflammation of the pancreas. Rose was given a bottle of green mixture and told not to eat late at night. Leila left her at the surgery door and returned to her basement, telling her friend she would explain the situation to Jack Spratt.

But Rose was there when Leila arrived at the theatre that evening, apparently much improved by several doses of the green medicine, and as much agog with the news as everyone else.

*The Maid of Montezuma* was to close at the end of February. Leila's heart sank. She would never make it to the head of the line before then. It seemed an unkind trick of fate, but it was a clever trick of Lester Gilbert. The predicament he had been facing had reached a point where action was called for. The Lindley Stroll had undoubtedly become the highlight of the show, and brought packed houses, but it had reached its zenith of excitement, and the impressario knew it could only be maintained for a short period. Meanwhile, the last ten minutes of the show were fast going downhill. What had begun as a gradual sense of anticlimax, had now turned into near boredom. The dénouement of the slight plot, plus Adeline Tait's grand finale, was being treated with impatience by the audiences. They wanted a reprise of the strolling girls—which they never got—and sat through the last section innattentive and audibly discussing the famous scene they had so enjoyed.

The decision by the show's owner–manager to end the run had been made when he had spotted several people leaving the theatre after they had seen what they had really come for. With visions of his temperamental lead singing her final rip-roaring number to empty seats, he took a few liberties with the script, removed the strolling number from its present place in the running order, and put it as a strange kind of apotheosis, with Adeline Tait appearing wreathed in clouds at the top of the cut-out of Mount Popocatepetl, gazing down at the beautiful seductive women of her kingdom. It was audacious, irrelevant to the plot, and a sly way of building up further enthusiasm for the famous ostrich-feather number, but he knew the Lindley patrons would let him get away with it, at least until he had the new show ready.

There was a notice in the dressing-room asking the cast to be at the theatre at nine a.m. that Sunday in order to run through the new finale, and also to audition for *Felicity May*, the new musical comedy to follow the present production.

Leila was nervous that Sunday, along with most of the other girls. It had been rumoured that the new show called for a large chorus of men, because the story concerned a colonel's daughter called Felicity May, who was known to the men of the regiment as Felicity May or Maynot. There would be a lot of colourful uniforms and rousing numbers sung by the "regiment", every member of which was naturally in love with the leading lady. It sounded vastly different from *The Maid of Montezuma*, although not one person was in doubt that Adeline Tait would be Felicity May. The question on everyone's lips was: What will happen to the famous Lindley Girls? Somehow they doubted whether a dozen or so toy soldiers in unrealistic uniforms would have the same impact as thirty tall brunettes in white ostrich feathers.

Lester Gilbert appeared to have no such worries as he thanked everyone for coming, and swept on in his usual dramatic manner to say that *The Maid of Montezuma* had shown the theatre-going public just what heights could be achieved, and *Felicity May* would now go on to achieve them. Leila listened dumbfounded as he practically dismissed *The Maid* as no more than a useful experiment in audience reaction before they went on to offer a worthwhile show.

Sitting around on props or the floor of the stage, the cast was told the story of the new musical show, mostly by Jack Spratt with interpolations by Lester Gilbert to emphasise a point he felt his stage-manager had missed. Then the pianist played some of the songs, which seemed as catchy as the ones they had been performing for the past eight months and, when Adeline Tait skipped onto the stage to sing one of them that began: "Who was kissed by who, la-la, and caused a terrible brouhaha?", it was generally accepted that no one would be asked to audition the title-rôle. Adeline already knew it by heart. Most of them were generous enough to admit that, in Regency-style dresses and bonnets, her *petite* build and high-pitched voice would suit the part of a flirtatious girl who ruled the regiment more than her father did.

The male lead, that of a handsome and heroic lieutenant, was apparently to be taken by a newcomer from Vienna, whom Lester Gilbert had engaged whilst over there some time before. The comedy and second leads were to be filled by the same men and women who played the rôles in the present show. It was then that Leila realised the whole business of "auditions" was a charade—at least, as far as leading parts were concerned. The stage was soon left holding only the "strolling" girls, several female dancers, and a large number of men who had come in response to a notice outside the theatre, before any attempt was made to compare the talents of different performers. Even then, it was purely for the strong chorus of soldiers.

As they tried desperately to pick up the tune and put their all into the singing of it, Leila turned to Rose, who was beside her in the wings.

"Poor things, they look scared to death."

Rose's finely-drawn features, sharpened even more by her spell of illness, were full of sympathy. "It's the most frightening thing on earth to have to stand there and prove you're better than the person beside you in three minutes flat. It's even worse when you know you're trying to prevent another man from saving his wife and children from the workhouse."

Leila sighed. "Mr Gilbert doesn't seem all that interested in us. I don't know what I shall do if he says we won't be wanted after February. What'll you do, Rose?"

The other girl smiled. "Worry about it in February. There are other theatres and other shows. Or I could always go back to the Lamb and Fleece."

"A Lindley Girl pulling a pint?"

The smile widened. "Might bring in custom—especially if I wore ostrich feathers."

Leila was not so easily able to smile. She still remembered the desperate days after being dismissed from Clivedon Place. What would she do if she was out of work again by March? She knew in her heart she could never go back to being a servant, and she also knew the theatre was now in her blood.

The male chorus had been selected and, such was the show's demands, every applicant had been taken on. Leila watched their happy expressions as they left, and remembered her own gladness over a year ago when she knew she had a job again. But the moment of truth had come for the girls.

Lester Gilbert, appearing as fresh and energetic as when the proceedings had begun four hours earlier, gave his gold-toothed smile and announced that he had a surprise for just one of them. In *Felicity May*, he revealed, there was a very important scene where Corporal Standabout—the comedy lead—brought a gypsy fortune-teller to the camp somewhere in Belgium so that they could all find out who the colonel's daughter really loved. Her cards reveal that the man is a Frenchman —one of the enemy—and the entire regiment is shocked at the disclosure. But, unknown to his colleagues, the dashing hero is undertaking a dangerous mission disguised as a French officer.

"As you can see, ladies, there is drama in the scene, a sense of betrayal by the soldiers, a surge of enmity toward their darling Felicity May, whom they think is consorting with the enemy. The gypsy has to have fire, acting ability beyond the call of normal musical comedy, and a singing voice that will chill the audience into believing she is really seeing the truth."

He walked the width of the stage and back, immaculate in his black coat and striped trousers, swinging his silver-knobbed cane as he worked up a sense of anticipation in each one of the girls. "I know exactly what I want, ladies, and I warn you that I shall, very regrettably, of course, look outside my own theatre if I cannot get the precise response to my requirements." He stopped dead on centre-stage and leant on his stick as he swept the row of faces with his keen glance. "Now, which of you thinks she has the ability to take upon her shoulders the success or failure of the entire show?"

"None of us, if he puts it that way," murmured Rose. "Anything that goes wrong is going to be blamed on the gypsy. I can see that a mile off."

The pianist began to play the song that formed the main part of the scene in question, which called for a solo by the gypsy before the chorus was taken up by the soldiers. It was an attractive and stirring piece of music. Before it was over four girls had scrambled to their feet, anxious to try. Leila felt a dig in the ribs from Rose.

"Go on, Lei, it's your kind of music," she urged. "Remember *Leeberstrowm*."

She felt a leap of excitement, but was still nervous. "I don't know this one, and I can't read music. I'd just make a fool of myself."

"So will the others. They can't read music either."

Still Leila hesitated, half afraid she might try and fail, then be excluded from the chorus altogether. "You said the gypsy would be blamed for everything," she reminded her friend.

Rose pushed her up to her knees. "Old Gilbert said the *success* or failure—and he's putting on the show, not me. I talk too much sometimes." She gave Leila a straight look. "Wouldn't you like the chance to show Villainous Vivian you don't need his bloody *ensembles*?"

She was on her feet and walking toward the other four at the piano, conscious of Lester Gilbert's scrutiny. Well, she was now accepting presents and invitations, as he had suggested, and been insulted because of it. Here was his chance to give her the solo he had hinted would be hers, if she did as he asked.

As the last one to go up, she was the last one to be called, which meant the tune was well into her head by the time she was handed the piece of paper containing the words and told to take centre stage. With all the lights on, the auditorium looked a daunting sight. It was enormous. Her nervousness increased as she imagined rows and rows of faces out there in the tiered red-plush crescents and the gold-decorated boxes so close to the stage one could almost reach out and touch them. Those faces would all be looking at her as she carried the success of the show on her shoulders.

Lester Gilbert's voice reached her across the stage. "The pianist has played the introduction twice, Miss Duncan. Are we to have the pleasure of hearing you sing, or not? Lola is a fiery gypsy singing about the treachery of personal emotions, not a timid postulant about to enter a convent."

It was not meant to be unkind, but inspirational, she knew, and suddenly she remembered that scene in a hansom when a sleepy arrogant voice had reduced Leila Duncan to Lily Lowe again. The deep sense of shame, the unbelievable disappointment that he had spoken those words to her, the anger that had turned her instantly back into the girl he had known all along she really was, put feelings and nuances into her voice as she sang of emotional betrayal. She appealed to all those empty seats to sympathise, not condemn; to have compassion, not contempt for those who believed too easily in the professed affection of another.

By the time the song was over she was shaken by emotion, over-whelmed by the realisation that it was possible to convey feelings, joys and agonies by letting sounds pour from the heart as well as the throat. Trembling, she turned to find the others on stage applauding, and wearing on their faces the expressions she had visualised on the invisible audience out front. Rose's natural beauty was heightened by a glow of excitement as she got to her feet, clapping energetically. Then Lester Gilbert was walking toward her, hands outstretched to take hers, a broad smile on his face.

"Miss Duncan. *Miss Duncan*," he boomed in his expansive manner. "Why have you never told me that you have such a splendid voice? I think it is some years since I have had the manifest pleasure of being the first to hear such undiluted talent. It is always a levelling and, dare I say it, *religious* experience. That the Almighty should bless any one of us with the ability to produce such sounds is surely evidence of His existence."

Leila was too choked with disbelief and the lingering emotion of singing from the heart to be able to speak, as he led her toward the others. Yet, in her imagination, she was already in gypsy costume and surrounded by a rousing chorus of soldiers.

"But, my dear," he went on, "if people want to hear opera they go to Covent Garden, not Lindley's." Smiling down at her, he patted her hands before letting them go. "My patrons are here to be entertained, not made to feel uncomfortable. I could not possibly allow you to instil feelings of guilt in every merry gentleman's breast, and the sadness of despair in the heart of every neglected wife sitting out there. The gypsy has to arouse anger or pity for the characters on the stage, not reduce the audience to an awareness of their own shortcomings. They would stay away, I assure you. You have a lovely voice, Miss Duncan, but it is completely out of place here. People want to go home warbling the songs they have heard from their long-standing favourites. They would not take to you, I fear."

They had reached the others in the wings now, and he left her with a kindly promise that there would be a place in the chorus of *Felicity May* for her. It took a moment or two for her to absorb the fact that she had been rejected, and a blonde girl with a rasping voice was being told she would be ideal for the rôle of Lola, if she wore a dark wig and had some coaching.

When the truth sank in Leila felt like bursting into tears. She had exposed her inner sense of weakness and susceptibility; she had put into that song the confession of feelings she had not dared to own even to herself. To that auditorium filled with phantom people, and to all those around her on the stage, she had laid open wounds that would not heal. Then she had been told it was *out of place . . . not wanted*. It would drive people away; it would make them feel uncomfortable. They did not want to hear the truth, just escape into a make-believe world that always had a happy ending.

She stood in the wings, deaf to Rose's protests, trying to emerge from the deeply affecting result of her performance. Then she told herself to face facts. She was no more than a lady's maid turned chorus-girl, who would never amount to anything other than an object for men's titillation. She could stroll seductively dressed in ostrich feathers, she could accompany them to supper to please their vanity. But she must not attempt to reach their souls and make them *care*.

# CHAPTER FIVE

Afternoon rehearsals for *Felicity May* began on New Year's Day. Leila was consequently fully occupied, which kept her from brooding over her disappointment and general unhappiness. Rose's health still worried her. Although her friend declared that she hardly ever suffered pain and felt much more lively, the girl's stomach remained swollen, and her face and arms were growing thin. It increased Leila's anger against Miles Lampton, and all those like him. She still had a covey of admirers who took her to supper, or driving in the park on Sundays. None of these escorts suggested buying her clothes, and it was as well for them that they did not.

Two weeks after Christmas, a letter from Vivian had coincided with the arrival of Nellie bearing another letter from Frank. Leila had returned the envelope to the Veasey-Hunter address unopened, suddenly aware of danger. Whatever she might one day feel for any man, she must never lose sight of the fact that she was married. Frank's letter could have come from a stranger. Leila knew none of the places he mentioned, none of his friends, and nothing of military routine. The girl to whom he wrote could also have been a stranger. She was someone called Lil, who worked in a house Leila Duncan had not seen for over a year. Reading the scrawled words she resented the proprietary tone he used, and burned with shame and affront at passages of coarse intimacy such as a common soldier sent to his wife. He complained that she had not written, and ended with the hope that her employers were not making her work too hard, nor that some man was taking liberties with her whilst he was away.

As usual after one of his letters, she suffered a period of depression, wondering how she could ever have given herself so easily to a person whose face she could not even remember, or how she could have been so frightened and foolish as to rush into a marriage that had given her neither security nor financial aid, yet which tied her for life. Depression was followed by fear. How could she possibly live with him as his wife when he returned? If he wished, he could put an end to her career in the theatre. In her most frightened moments, she even reversed that dread and imagined him forcing her to become the mistress of a succession of men like Vivian Veasey-Hunter, and living off the proceeds. Then she would tell herself that she was being impossibly melodramatic. She could surely never have been remotely fond of that kind of person, could she? Unfortunately, she had little recollection of the kind of person Frank Duncan really was.

During those days following Christmas, she was more deeply occupied with another problem. On the day of the so-called auditions, when she had sung the gypsy's song about love and betrayal, she had been waylaid by Jack Spratt as she had passed. He had told her very sincerely that she should go to a teacher to have her voice trained, even if it meant allowing one of her admirers to pay for the lessons. Those three minutes while she had held centre-stage still lived in her mind and heart. It had been the most exciting experience of her life, and it had created within her the desire to sing like that again, this time to tiered rows that were full of rapt faces.

She knew singing lessons would be expensive, but she also knew there would be no gentleman admirer paying for them. For the time being she had no time, no idea how to set about it, and no notion how she would get the money. She was prepared to sell some of the things she had bought to make her basement more comfortable. She could also give up buying clothes, and economise on fuel. Would that be enough?

The problem nagged at her for several weeks, until she decided to be bold. Lindley's now had two temperamental performers: Adeline Tait, and the Austrian engaged to take the male lead. Franz Mittelheiter was dark, immensely good-looking, and so splendid in the elaborate uniforms designed for the show, Leila felt no member of the audience would ever believe Felicity May could fall for any other member of the regiment, which would strain the credibility of the plot. Even so, the Austrian was very unhappy, and had crossed swords with Lester Gilbert immediately.

The impressario had told his new member of cast he was to be billed as Frank Mitten, because no one in England would be able to pronounce his name. That had caused row number one. Then, the Austrian had been sent along to an elocution coach, because Lester Gilbert believed his Germanic accent was too strong for English ears. Row number two erupted. But the biggest bone of contention between them was Franz Mittelheiter's voice. It was incredible, enthralling, and altogether too good for the rest of the cast. A pure tenor, it drowned Adeline Tait's reedy warble in the duets, and turned his melodic solos into arias of such fire and passion they showed up the insincerity of the dialogue. A request to sing more softly, and put a little jollity into the rendition, was the last straw to a man used to Viennese operetta.

It was after yet another difficult sesson that Leila saw her opportunity. The Austrian, distressed and feeling very much a stranger in the cast, had remained on stage when the rehearsal ceased, consoling himself by playing the piano with almost as much skill as he sang, and losing himself in music. Leila stood in the wings listening. She was overwhelmed with admiration for him, and felt a strange sympathy for this man who had also been told he was virtually too good. When he began to sing, softly at first, then swelling into the full glory of tenor notes, she found herself growing cold with enotion. "All over goosepimples" had been Rose's description of how she had felt at such sounds, but Leila knew exactly what she meant. Oh, to sing in duet with a voice like that!

The song was not one from *Felicity May*, nor any show like it. It was hauntingly beautiful, catching at the emotions and sweeping the listener over cadences as beguiling as a lover's words. At the end of it, she was driven forward, her footsteps ringing hollowly in the empty theatre. She felt suddenly humbled standing beside him on that enormous stage already filled with the first set of *The Maid of Montezuma*, and her voice echoed around the red-plush tiers as her feelings burst from her.

"Mr Mittelheiter, I want to apologise for some of the things that have been said to you. They are unforgiveable."

Startled, at first, by her sudden appearance from the wings, he then listened courteously as she went on to say that she felt the cast should instead struggle to reach a standard high enough to complement his talent.

He had risen as she entered, and gave a slight bow. "You are most kind, Miss . . . ?"

"Duncan. It's not kindness, but envy. You put us all to shame, that's the truth of the matter."

He shook his head sadly. "I have not know this *Felicity May* before I sign the agreement. She is wrong for me; I am wrong for her. But it is very gracious that you come to say this to me. I much appreciate."

He was about to walk off when she plucked up the courage to detain him. "Mr Mittelheiter, how long does it take to learn to sing? To sing as you do, I mean."

He turned back, a smile crossing his handsome face. "A very long while . . . and for you, I think it is impossible to sing as I do, eh?"

It was too important to her to bring a laugh. "How much would it cost, and how would I find a teacher?"

95

He frowned at her momentarily, probably trying to decide whether or not she was serious. Finally, he moved to the keyboard again, saying, "A good teacher is much money, and it is no use to have a bad one. It is a waste. But I will soon tell you if a good teacher is waste, also. Sing please!"

Unprepared for anything as daunting as that, he had played several bars without a single sound coming from her throat as she just looked at him helplessly.

"So, you are playing the silly with me," he exclaimed angrily. "I do not want you. Go away!"

She seized his arm as he made to rise. "No, please, I'm very serious, truly I am. You are the only person who can advise me. I don't read music, but I can sing the gypsy's song for you, if you like."

Even more nervous than before, the first notes came out wobbly and shortened by breathlessness, but she finished with more confidence. It vanished when she saw the look on his face, and realised what audacity it had been to approach him.

"This one I sing just now, you know it?" he asked abruptly.

"No, I'm afraid not . . . but it's beautiful."

"You soon learn. I sing; you come la-la when you can."

He broke into the haunting song once again, only softly with infinite tenderness, and she found herself able to join in tentatively, thrilled and filled with the heights of fervour at such an experience. In duet with Franz Mittelheiter!

"*Noch einer* . . . once more!" he commanded brusquely as the last notes faded.

Confidence came to the fore to make all the difference, this time, and she was beginning to know the tune well.

"And again!"

That third time she turned to face the auditorium and increased the volume of her own voice as his swelled. At the end, she was in tears, unable to turn and face him. All that had been in her life, so far, was unimportant compared with the yearning to be out there giving expression to emotions so great she could hardly bear them.

A hand fell on her shoulder. "So, you must go to an address I give you, and you must learn how to use that voice."

She turned then to look at him. There was no smile of congratulation, no surprise at her tears. He looked almost grave.

"There is no half," he told her. "It must be all. You must eat well—that is important of the utmost—and all else must be sacrifice to the voice, do you understand? If you cannot do this it is useless to start. Go now, and think of this."

On that next day, Leila was alone in the basement. The morning rehearsal had been for principals alone, so she had used the welcome break to go to the address given her by Franz Mittelheiter, only to be disappointed. Professor Halstein was out, but his housekeeper had made an appointment for her to see him on the following Thursday, and told her the approximate cost of lessons. It had been a dreadful shock to Leila, but that afternoon she hurriedly cleared away the remains of her lunch and sat down to work out ways and means of paying for something she wanted very badly.

By getting rid of all her non-essential pieces of furniture, walking to and from the theatre, and wearing her coat indoors to save lighting a fire, she reckoned she could pay for the first few lessons. Summer was coming, which meant less fuel and lighting would be needed, and if she packed her winter clothes carefully in mothballs they could come out again next year. At that thought, she added the cost of mothballs to her total expenses. It still left her with the truth that she could then only just afford the first few months' tuition. What would she do after that?

Niggling at the back of her mind was Jack Spratt's advice to get a gentleman admirer to pay for the lessons, but that would be as bad as having her clothes provided by a wealthy ne'er-do-well, surely. An inner voice asked her how much she wanted to learn to sing, and she answered aloud, thinking of Vivian Veasey-Hunter, "Not that much, thank you."

She was still totting up pounds, shillings and pence, biting the end of her pencil as she tried to reach a more encouraging total, when there was a knock on the door. Irritated at being disturbed in the midst of her calculations, she went to answer it feeling full of frustration at her lack of money. Pulling angrily on the latch she swung the door open.

Her heart lurched with momentary fear, then raced painfully as she gazed in disbelief. He was in the full dress-uniform of the 49th Lancers: polished top-boots, dark-blue breeches, grey tunic fronted with scarlet and smothered in gold braid, elaborate sword-belt, and ornate flat-topped gold helmet with curling scarlet and white plumes. Behind him in her tiny yard was his huge charger, Oscar.

Clear greenish eyes gazed at her from beneath the gold-encrusted peak of the helmet as he gave a lazy salute.

"Good afternoon, Miss Duncan."

He looked even more of a giant in that plumed head-dress, and his presence, along with a very large horse, in her yard was so overwhelming she could not begin to collect her thoughts.

"*What are you doing here?*" she breathed.

"Visiting you."

"With . . . with a *horse*?"

"I had to bring him. I would have looked ridiculous walking in this outfit." His beguiling voice was working its usual magic on her. "May I come in?"

"No."

"I'll leave Oscar out here, I swear."

"*No!*" she repeated, fighting the reaction of seeing him so unexpectedly.

He sighed with resignation. "I have a lot to say to you, and Oscar is liable to make an awful mess in your yard if he's down here for long."

Still in a flat spin, she demanded once more, "What are you doing here?"

"My company was chosen as escort to the Shah of Persia when he visited the Prince of Wales this morning. I was on my way home when I realised I was passing your door."

She was weakening more and more by the minute. "This is nowhere near your house . . . or where the Prince of Wales lives."

He adopted an expression of outrageous innocence. "I have to go wherever Oscar takes me, and his sense of direction is deplorable."

Uncertain what to do, and fearing that he would not go away even if she shut the door in his face, she hedged. "You have wasted your time. You said all there was to say in your letter."

"How do you know? You refused to read it."

It was an impossible deadlock. People passing in the street above were gaping down in astonishment, and small urchins were dancing about shrieking the news that "there's a messenger come from the Queen wiv 'is bloody great 'orse, to see a girl in Mirtle Street". Small wonder a crowd was fast gathering to witness the entertaining sight of a giant horse and a giant military man smothered in gold braid filling the area of a dingy basement apartment in a dingy street.

"Oh really, this is ridiculous," she protested breathlessly. "People are staring."

"I know," he agreed sadly. "If I came in, they'd go away. Or, at least, you wouldn't see them if they didn't."

Surrender was inescapable, he knew that. "You can't leave Oscar there," she said faintly.

"I'll give some ragamuffin half a crown to hold him for me. Have you any apples?"

"Yes," she said, feeling part of a fantasy dream. "But half a crown is more than enough for any boy."

He smiled, his teeth extremely white against the darkness of his complexion. "The apples are for Oscar. He'd sell his soul for one. For two, he might even allow some strange urchin to hold him."

In a daze she fetched several apples from a bowl and gave them to him. All those crowding the railings at street level were then treated to the delightful sight of a tall resplendent Lancer officer coaxing a thoroughbred up a flight of stone steps with a handful of red apples. Halfway through the exercise Leila realised that Vivian was about to enter her home, and dived indoors to tidy away paper and pencil, dirty dishes, and some items of underwear drying before the fire. That done, she was at the mirror tucking in a few stray ends of hair, wishing that she could have been more prepared. But who could possibly be prepared when dealing with this man?

The doorway darkened, and she turned to see him stepping inside, bending his head beneath the lintel, the plumed helmet now under his arm. She was suddenly strikingly conscious of how shabby the room was, and wished she had an apartment like Rose's in which to entertain him.

"I was just about to light the lamps," she lied quickly. "It's such a dull afternoon."

The matches were taken from her hand after she had spilled several on the floor. "Let me do it for you."

"Will you have a cup of tea?" She hurried to remove the plate and put the kettle on the open flames. The room seemed far too small with him in it, and she felt very nervous in his company in her own environment. It had been easier in his.

With both lamps lit the room seemed less stark, but he looked unbearably attractive with the soft light now sheening his hair and the gold lacing on his tunic. Wishing she had never allowed him to come in, she busied herself with making the tea, wondering why he did not start on what he had come to say. Setting the best two cups she owned on a tray with the other things, she carried it across to where he stood beside the table watching her. Only after she sat down did he do so, stretching out his long legs in the spurred boots.

She poured his tea and pushed it across the chenille cloth to him, along with the sugar bowl. "I have some seedy cake. Would you like a slice?"

"No, thank you." He took sugar and stirred his tea slowly. "What are you going to do when the show closes?"

It took her by surprise. She had been expecting further overtures, an explanation . . . an apology, even. "The show? Oh, I've got a part in the next one."

"Splendid! That means I can continue to see you, if only from the stalls. Are there ostrich feathers in this one?"

She shook her head, which felt remarkably swimmy. "Nothing like that. We are all village girls, or camp-followers. It's set just before Waterloo—that was a famous battle, you know."

"So I understand," he murmured.

Realising that it was a silly remark to make to a soldier, she said quickly, "The real sensation in this show is the male chorus, all done up in very fancy uniforms like the one you're wearing. They're all in love with Felicity May, the colonel's flirtatious daughter."

He was still regarding her in a way that made her even more nervous. "Very foolish fellows they must all be."

She laughed self-consciously. "It's a rather silly story, really. The best thing about the show is Franz Mittelheiter. His singing is so wonderful, the rest doesn't matter."

"Oh? Tell me about him."

So she explained the whole situation regarding the leadingman and his feud with Lester Gilbert, which appeared to be worsening as time went by. Vivian listened so attentively, she did not realise how she had run on until an angry gesture with her hand to emphasise the stupidity of insisting on calling the Austrian "Frank Mitten" almost had the milk jug over.

Flushing hotly, she said, "I didn't mean to bore you with all that. You didn't come here for . . ."

"You feel very strongly about it?" he asked quietly.

Fiddling with the tea-cosy, she admitted that she did. Then, with something approaching defiance, she added, "I come from a long line of nobodys, Captain Veasey-Hunter, and I had little education. That doesn't mean I want to be treated as ignorant for the rest of my life. Mr Gilbert believes in giving his audiences only what they can easily understand, time and time again. Franz Mittelheiter is splendid and exciting. Instead of trying to make him ordinary enough to fit in with the others, he should be urging the rest of us to improve our own standards. *Felicity May* is just the same as *The Maid*, with the same kind of songs, and the same comedians doing the same funny things. Yet it could be really wonderful. The people out front wouldn't think they were all 'foolish fellows', as you said, but truly desperate for love of the same girl. It's only unbelievable because they make it so." She shrugged. "Calling poor Mr Mittelheiter 'Frank Mitten' is the last straw. Of course people won't know how to say it if they're never asked to . . . and Mittelheiter is no more difficult to pronounce than presbyterian, is it?"

His eyes danced with laughter as he solemnly agreed, then added, "Have you explained your philosophy to Lester Gilbert?"

She shook her head, then reluctantly smiled at such an idea. "You don't know Mr Gilbert."

"I don't think I know you, either. I'd very much like to," he said in husky persuasive tones.

Realising how easily she had been charmed into forgetting what he was really like, she bristled. "I thought all that had been settled."

"*That* was," he agreed. "But are your high standards so rigid they allow no one to make even one mistake?"

"It was I who made the mistake," she told him hastily, hoping to end the matter. "I should never have gone out with you, in the first place."

He absorbed that for a moment or two. "Didn't you enjoy my company at all?"

Unable to stay there with him only a few feet away across the table, she jumped up and walked to stand by the spluttering kettle on the range. It obliged him to get up and, of course, he walked across to her and was nearer than before. How could she tell a man there was not one thing about him she liked, when he was standing right beside her in her own home, and when it was not true?

She tilted her head to look up at him. "I wasn't born yesterday, you know. There's only one thing men like you want from girls like me, and I shouldn't have let it get as far as it did."

"No, you shouldn't have," he agreed warmly. "Everything would have been all right if you had been yourself right from the start. Putting on that Lindley Girl pose was most unfair to me."

Utterly incredulous that he was suggesting she had been the one at fault, she choked, "Unfair to *you*?"

"*Very* unfair," he affirmed with astonishing gravity. "I went to a great deal of trouble and risked personal danger when I forced Oscar to plunge and rear on the barrack square in order to get to know you. I also damaged my reputation as a horseman in front of half the regiment, I hasten to remind you." He edged nearer, intent on impressing on her the seriousness of his words. "What did I get for my pains? A young woman who has just admitted that she should never have gone out with me in the first place, and who then set out to ruin my chances of ever asking her out again."

Completely nonplussed, she backed away from him a step or two. "I never admitted that!"

"There was nothing about my company that you enjoyed."

"I . . . I didn't say that, either!"

Putting out his hands, he took hold of her shoulders. "My dear, if you back any nearer that stove, you'll burn yourself."

She found herself being moved to the old rocker near by and seated in it with gentle but implacable pressure. It was too late to realise how smoothly he had routed her, because he was now squatting on his haunches before her, effectively trapping her.

"Leila," he began gently, "I do *not* come from a long line of nobodys, as I expect you have guessed, and I have had a great deal of education. Now, if I try very hard to forget that you are a very beautiful young woman, and you try very hard to forget that there is only one thing men like me want from girls like you, don't you think we could have a mutually interesting friendship?"

Unable to control the wild beating of her heart, she nevertheless asked suspiciously, "What would you get from it?"

"All the inside secrets of Lindley's. What goes on behind the scenes in a theatre has always fascinated me to the point of desperation."

She looked at his wickedly innocent expression and the laughter lurking in his eyes, and sighed. "You're an awful liar, Vivian Veasey-Hunter."

He smiled devastatingly. "I know that . . . but what do you say?"

What could she say?

The first-nighters were there in their silk hats and tails, their furs and satins, their medals and diamonds. They had bottles of bubbly in the boxes, caskets of the finest chocolates in the stalls. They rolled up in their broughams and landaus. They came in hired hansoms and crested carriages. There was an air of unbridled gaiety that made the auditorium restless and noisy as curtain time approached.

Yet it was not all sables and sapphires. In the pit and balcony sat those who had waited long hours at the box-office, and spent their meagre savings on the evening of a lifetime. The men were in suits shiny with wear, or their best attire kept for weddings and funerals. The girls wore their Sunday-best dresses, to which they had attached a fancy fichu or an ecru collar, and hats they had trimmed themselves. All they had on their laps was a quarter of marzipan tea-cakes, or a bag of slab toffee broken into mouth-sized pieces by the confectioner's hammer. All the same, their sense of excitement and anticipation equalled that of the wealthier patrons.

Vivian had booked the box nearest to the left-hand side of the stage, because Leila had told him that she spent most of the performance there, and his sense of anticipation was less for the show than for their tête-à-tête afterward. Knowing her had become an unexpectedly rewarding experience. As a Lindley Girl she had satisfied his sexual ego and sense of amusement. As Leila Duncan she satisfied nothing, because each meeting left him anxious for the next. The demands of their separate careers frustrated his desire to spend more time with her, and he knew every mile of the rail journey between Brighton and London, because he spent his off-duty time travelling in one direction or the other on it.

They no longer frequented the smarter places. He resented being interrupted by his numerous acquaintances, and was growing increasingly jealous of those who took her out when he was on duty. In view of their supposed friendly relationship, he could not forbid her to accept other invitations, neither dared he let her see he was upset by them. Although she appeared to have done as he suggested and forgotten what men like him wanted from girls like her, he still wanted it. It was impossible to uphold his side of the bargain and forget that she was a beautiful young woman. Her delightfully unsophisticated personality, bubbling humour, and trusting frankness had him increasingly restless, and put considerable pressure on his enforced good behaviour. As a result, he was growing short-tempered with his fellow-officers, and anyone else who crossed him at the wrong moment.

Charles had written a long missive concerning their grandfather's increasing miserliness and the fact that he had dismissed two kitchen-maids, then the cook who had complained that she could not manage without them. Vivian had dashed off a brief recommendation that his brother learn to stand up to a man shortly to be a nonagenarian, and start running the estate in an intelligent fashion.

Deeper thought on relationships, these days, had shown Vivian that his brother had probably deserved the treatment he received and, unless he began to assert himself soon, would merely transfer slavery to an old man to that of a young woman—Julia. What Vivian had always imagined to be his younger brother's guilty attempts to share his inheritance with a man who had been unfairly cheated of it, now became clear as the attempt of a weak person to share responsibility. All in all, when he was with his family Vivian was burdened by his past; when he was with his regiment he was burdened by the affair in Ashanti. When he was with Leila he forgot both.

The rising of the curtain dispelled his introspection, and he sat forward in quick anticipation. Enthusiastic applause greeted the lavish opening set of a Belgian village square full of colourful peasants and pedlars, into which marched the heroic regiment extolling the beauty and wit of their colonel's darling daughter. Vivian could not immediately see Leila, and grew anxious until he spotted her on the other side of the stage, almost masked from his view by two hefty men with a dancing bear. The bear, to everyone's delight and no one's surprise, turned out to be the comic Corporal Standabout in a skin. Vivian immediately saw Leila's point about the sameness. In *The Maid of Montezuma*, that comedian had done the same trick with a mummy-case.

Adeline Tait entered as Felicity May to rapturous applause and sang her usual kind of saucy lilting song in a high childlike voice. Vivian sat back disappointed. With Leila hardly recognisible as a peasant girl there was little to interest him. There was a shock in store, however, for him and for everyone else in that theatre, including Lester Gilbert.

One third of the way through Act One, the hero entered—billed as Franz Mittel, after a reluctant compromise—and a new Lindley precedent was born. Strolling girls in ostrich feathers were forgotten as the tenor, dressed in a gilt-glittery white and scarlet tight-fitting uniform burst into his first song. His voice rang around the red-plush tiers to bring utter silence, and all who watched his vigorous physique, his dark flashing eyes, his dazzling smile, realised that there had never been a leading man like this one.

They did not want to let him go, demanding loudly for an encore. Lester Gilbert's rule never to give one was upheld, but the Austrian recognised what was happening that evening and responded with a performance of such fire and brilliance, the audience waited breathlessly for his every entrance. Adeline Tait did her normal best to match up, but it was abundantly clear that even her most devoted followers were growing unsympathetic toward the coquettish Felicity May for giving the dashing, adorable hero such a hard time of it, particularly when it was revealed that he was undertaking a dangerous mission in order to save the regiment from defeat. Leila had been right. Franz Mittelheiter had made pretence too believable.

The new idol was brought forward time and again at the end of the show. Loud applause and roars of approval were confirmation of what had been apparent from the start, and only a curtain that remained very firmly down finally emptied the auditorium.

At the stage-door, Vivian waited impatiently, taking out his pocket watch several times, then snapping it shut when he saw that only a few minutes had passed. Because this was a first-night, he had felt obliged to reserve a table at Romano's, knowing that their supper would be interrupted by a stream of people who wished to meet Leila. More than anything, he would have preferred to reserve a room somewhere more private, or even take her back to the Veasey-Hunter house for a quiet meal. He knew, however, that he would reject either alternative. The restrictions on their relationship irked him more and more. Knowing that the only time they would have together that evening would be in the privacy of the cab, he had primed the driver to go three times around the park before heading for Romano's.

She came out glowing with excitement, looking fresh and infinitely desirable in a dress of deep rose-pink. Slipping her hand through his arm, she looked up with a luminous expression in her deep blue eyes.

"Wasn't he marvellous? Don't you agree with me that he is superb? Wasn't I right about his voice? Mr Gilbert will have to believe hundreds of people, even if he would never have listened to me."

They entered the waiting cab, and still she ran on about how thrilled she was that Franz Mittelheiter had received the adulation that he deserved, and how she hoped Mr Gilbert would urge the cast to be worthy of their new leading man.

"I should think he has no alternative, wouldn't you?" she asked, finally, pausing for breath.

"Certainly," Vivian agreed, realising that it was the first time he had spoken since they met. "I booked the box on the left, as you said. What went wrong?"

She laughed merrily, her perfume wafting to him as she shifted in her seat. "Silly! Don't you know that stage directions are always from the actor's side of the footlights? I *was* on the left."

"I don't know anything about your profession apart from what you have told me," he protested, feeling jealous of Franz Mittelheiter who could make her so alive. "I preferred you in ostrich feathers."

"Phoo," she declared. "Anyone can stroll about in feathers. Real talent lies in what Mr Mittelheiter does. I want to sing like that."

He smiled. "I think you'd find that damn near impossible."

She smiled back, leaning against the squabs in complete relaxation. "That's what he told me, too. I'm sorry, Vivian, when I get excited I say things without thinking."

He took one of her gloved hands. "Does that mean you might say something nice to me like 'I thought about you all through the performance' or 'Couldn't we go somewhere more intimate than Romano's?'?"

Her smile widened. "You don't need flattery. You have more than enough self-confidence to carry you through anything."

Lifting the hand to his mouth, he kissed it. "I was thinking of *you* all through the performance, and *I* wish we could go somewhere more intimate than Romano's."

"But it's a first-night. Everyone will be at Romano's."

"I know," he said gloomily. "A first-night is something very special, isn't it?"

"Of course . . . and this one especially. Because of Franz's success."

Ignoring the man she could not seem to forget that evening, he asked, "As it's such a special evening, will you allow me to give you a present?"

"No, Vivian."

Knowing there must be no suggestion of return favours from her —his pearls had been returned and Julia Marchbanks' earrings flung back in his lap—he realised that he would have to mention the wretched man, after all.

"Not even to celebrate the success of all your hopes for Franz Mittelheiter?"

She shook her head emphatically. "I'm not accepting presents from *anyone* any more."

"You never have accepted mine," he pointed out dryly.

The jibe went over her head. She seemed very absorbed by her thoughts as the cab made its way through the bustle of late-evening traffic, adding the clatter of hooves and the rumble of wheels to the general commotion of a metropolis growing more and more congested with vehicles. Every day there were accidents—runaway horses, entangled coach-wheels, careless handling of traces, pedestrians stepping from a pavement in front of a cab or horse-drawn tram. Something would have to be done, but the invention of the motor-vehicle did not seem to be the answer.

As they jerked and swayed through the noisy night, Vivian watched the growing frown on Leila's forehead, the troubled farawayness of her expression, the gentle biting of her lip as she appeared to be thrashing out some problem that temporarily excluded him. The curve of her jawline tempted him to trace it with his finger, the cloud of dark tendrils at the nape of her neck teased him with the desire to blow them softly before brushing her skin with his lips, the swathe of deep-pink silk across her full breasts urged him to lower it so that the full delight of curving softness would lie beneath his palm. He had never resisted such overwhelming impulses before, and was wondering what there was about this girl that made him do so now, when she turned a very serious face toward him.

"Vivian, I have been wanting to ask you this for some weeks," she began, "but I was afraid your opinion of me might suffer."

"I hardly think that's likely," he said, thrusting away the thought of her breast beneath his hand.

"You haven't heard what I'm going to say yet," she warned him. "I haven't anyone else to advise me, and you really are the obvious one to give an honest opinion on this particular matter."

"What about Rose Heywood?" he suggested. The rôle of trusty

reliable adviser was not one that suited him where women were concerned, and he had no desire to play it.

"I already know what Rose would say, but she is biased. Besides, she has enough problems of her own at the moment. You are the only other person I can trust."

"You *trust* me? Thank God my friends aren't here to witness my complete downfall."

"Please be serious," she begged. "This has been worrying me for a long time."

He saw a romantic evening falling around his ears as she embarked on a tale concerning her great desire to have her voice trained, and how Franz Mittelheiter had given her an address of an eminent teacher willing to give her lessons. The remaining problem was the cost of such lessons, and the only way of meeting it, as far as she could see, was by pawning the presents her admirers had given her.

"That's why I've decided not to accept any more," she told him frankly. "I'd take them knowing that I was going to sell them, and that would be wrong. But those I accepted before this arose are mine to do as I like with, aren't they?"

"Of course."

It did not completely satisfy her. "But they were given to me because the donors wanted me to wear pretty things. What would I say if they asked why I never wore their gifts now?" She put her hand on his arm in appeal. "That's why you are the very best person to ask. You must have given expensive presents to any number of girls. How would you feel if you discovered they had been pawned a few days later?"

The situation was worsening. She was now discussing his numerous sexual intrigues like a trusted friend, when he desperately wanted her to be his next.

"This is a ridiculous conversation," he ruled. "In fact, it is verging on the improper."

"How would you feel?" she persisted.

"I refuse to be cross-questioned on a subject you should have more sensitivity than to raise at a time like this," he said irritably. "And I wish to make it clear to you that I am *not* a person you can trust. If you could read my preent thoughts you'd know that all too well."

He had her full attention now, and she looked at him with such heightened awareness he was not sure how much longer he could trust himself.

'Oh, Vivian, we made a bargain," she breathed.

"I can't keep it. You're asking too much."

"It was your idea, not mine."

"Then I was a fool. The day I said it, I knew that I could never forget how beautiful you are. The situation has grown worse. You must surely be aware of that."

If she was not, he made very sure she would be in the future, and her response suggested that she had stopped thinking of him as a trusty friend. She had apparently also stopped worrying about what men like him wanted from girls like her, because he was getting it without any trouble right at that moment. Then he sensed that the cab had slowed, and a voice from above announced that Romano's had been reached.

Vivian raised his head. "Drive around the park, man."

"I've already done that about three times, guv'nor."

"Go round again!"

But Leila struggled free, and announced in an unsteady voice that it was growing late and she thought they should go in. He had to accept her decision, but told himself there was always the drive home afterward.

Romano himself bowed them in, greeting them in his effusive manner and deplorable English. As Vivian had feared, the famed restaurant was seething with well-known personalities, as well as many of the cast of *Felicity May*. As they were shown to their table, voices hailed them from all directions. Vivian returned most of the greetings in cordial but fleeting manner, noting Leila's flushed cheeks and almost trance-like state as she allowed the waiter to settle her in her chair.

He smiled across the table, deepening her flush, as he said softly, "I warned you I couldn't be trusted."

Waving away the menu, he ordered for them both some asparagus with brown bread-and-butter, roast chicken with garnish, some cheese for himself, and strawberries for Leila, all with champagne, of course. The din of conversation, knives and forks on china, and the boisterous laughter of those around them made a continuation of their earlier intimacy impossible. He decided to say something he would not risk in a hansom, where he could easily be ejected and forced to walk home alone.

"Are you serious about taking singing lessons, Leila?"

"Of course," she replied, visibly relieved at his line of conversation. "I always knew I had quite a good voice. Professor Halstein, the teacher Franz Mittelheitèr recommended, said I have a soprano voice hidden somewhere beneath the tones of a fishwife." She smiled. "I think he meant it to be a compliment."

"He's a bona fide teacher?"

"A what?"

He leant forward, loving the confusion on her face. "Is he qualified to teach?"

"Yes, oh yes. He used to train singers at La Scala, Milan. That's an opera-house in Italy," she explained helpfully.

He tried to look impressed, as if he had never heard of such a place before, much less attended performances there. Covering her hand with his own as it lay on the table, he said, "The most sensible thing to do would be to let me pay for the lessons."

As he had half feared, colour flamed in her cheeks at his words. Before she could say anything, he forestalled her. "Don't fly at me like a yardful of hens, my dear. I'm not suggesting anything in the least like you imagine."

The subject went no further, because a voice addressed him in vigorous tones. "Vivian! Thought I might find you here tonight. One of your favourite playgrounds, isn't it? Sorry I missed you when you were at Shenstone just before Christmas."

Vivian was intensely annoyed. Rupert Marchbanks one of Sir Kinsley's strapping, hearty sons was there, smiling broadly and showing every sign of wanting a long talk. He would have to get rid of him somehow, he decided as he got to his feet and shook the man's hand.

"Hallo, Rupert. How is the sawbones business?"

"Moderate, you know. People still keep coming into the world as fast as others leave it, despite all our efforts to kill off the human race." He cast an interested glance at Leila. "Am I interrupting something?"

"Yes," said Vivian bluntly. "We must have a chat some other time, old chap."

Julia's brother came from a long line of determined people, however, and had the bit between his teeth. "Can't be done, I'm afraid. I'm very tied up at the medical convention until Sunday. Er . . . won't you present me to your charming companion?"

Vivian was just as determined. "Sorry, but we are in the middle of an important discussion. I'm afraid you'll have to excuse us."

The lean face registered curiosity. "Important discussion? Pity. I should like to have heard about Ashanti. Young Philip is set on a military career despite opposition from Father and the rest of us, and your gallant appearance at Christmas fired him with such renewed enthusiasm nothing will now stop him from joining the colours. To that end, I've been chatting with some fellows from your regiment who came to the convention to talk about the ills that bedevilled them in Africa. They said the 49th came upon some damned tricky situations."

"Yes," said Vivian, trying to gauge whether or not there was a barb in the remark. Which men from his regiment had Rupert met? It only needed a loose tongue in one of his opposers, and the story would be out.

Rupert put a friendly hand on his shoulder. "I hear Julia did a splendid job in nursing you back to health when you collapsed whilst snowed in at our place. Tropical fever in December! Sounds ridiculous, doesn't it? Apparently you took a great deal of controlling when delirious, so she had no doubts that it was the real thing." He grinned. "Good thing my sister is used to hearing curses and oaths. She said you let fly some rich language."

"Quite probably," he murmured, reminders of that time in Cornwall making him all the more determined to send Rupert packing before he said anything more on the subject. "Well, if there's nothing that can't wait until another time . . ." he prompted pointedly.

Fixing Leila with another interested gaze, Rupert extemporised. "No, just wanted a general chat. Don't see you all that often. When are you coming down to Shenstone again?"

"I have no idea. Never, if I have my way."

The other man laughed knowingly. "Having too good a time up here, I can see that. By the by, that was a staggering feat you performed in December. That stallion was damn near untouchable. I took it for a killer; you get one now and again. Julia said it was touch and go with you until you had the brute under control. Gave me a most graphic account of the affair, blow by blow, ending with you almost out for the count, badly cut and bitten. Funny girl, Julia! Most females would have fainted away with fright, but she seemed almost to have enjoyed it." He laughed again. "More than you did, I dare say. It was an incredible piece of pluck on your part. All the same, I wish she hadn't wagered those valuable sapphire earrings on the outcome. They are part of a set which belonged to our grandmama."

Conscious of Leila growing stiff beside him, and knowing that the evening and probably their entire relationship was now ruined, Vivian began to turn away from Rupert.

"You must excuse me. I really can't ignore my guest any longer, and our behaviour has been ill-mannered enough as it is."

It did the trick, but far too late. With a slightly sardonic bow toward Leila, Rupert said farewell and departed. The immediate arrival of the waiter prevented any interchange of words for a few minutes, creating a tense atmosphere between them. Leila was staring at the far end of the room, her features set and expressionless, and Vivian had to wait until the man departed before attempting to bridge the chasm that had opened so unexpectedly and disastrously at his feet.

"I'm sorry about that," he began, wishing the other revellers were not making it impossible to speak quietly. "Rupert is the son of Sir Kinsley Marchbanks, our Cornish neighbour. He is inclined to outstay his welcome, and I thought he'd be with us all evening if he found out who you were. Do you forgive me for not presenting him?"

She turned to face him, but the stony expression was still there in her eyes. "Did his sister really nurse you while you were on that visit to Cornwall?"

"Yes. I had a recurrence of a tropical fever I suffered in Ashanti. The doctors warned me that it could return without warning, and I was trapped in the Marchbanks' home by heavy snowfall."

"Why did you try to buy me with her earrings?"

It was said quietly enough, but proved a sharply painful barb. He frowned. "Put like that, it sounds terrible."

"That was what you were trying to do, though, wasn't it?"

His ready tongue failed him, for once, and he could do no more than look with sadness at the hurt and accusation in her eyes.

"I'd like to go home," she said, picking up her beaded-net bag from the table.

He caught at the bag swiftly. "Leila, please! Let me try to explain. Hear me out, then I'll take you home if you still wish to go."

It said much for the way their relationship had progressed that she put the bag down, even if she continued to regard him with an expression that was not in the least promising. Faced with the need to exonerate something that was basically true, Vivian cast around in his mind for the right approach—one a girl of her simplicity would understand. He began tentatively.

"My father was something of a man-about-town. In consequence, he left his youthful wife and two sons in Cornwall with his father, who had very stern ideas on the rearing of children. My brother and I were made very unhappy by his almost spiteful determination to mould us to his pattern and break any sign of independence in us. Instead of setting us against each other, his scheming drew us closer together. He also failed in another direction. As I grew older, I began to defy him."

Keeping silent about the reason for his defiance, he went on in the same quiet tones. "My grandfather will not submit to being thwarted so, from then on, he has done everything in his power to frustrate or humiliate me. He did so again in December, in the presence of Julia Marchbanks and her father. Under the guise of what I foolishly took as sympathy, she then lured me into accepting a challenge by making it publicly and leaving me no alternative. I spent an entire afternoon in driving snow schooling a temperamental stallion she had claimed was impossible to control. The exercise was a physically punishing one, and I went down that night with fever that raged for almost a week. Those earrings were Julia's wager. When I had recovered sufficiently to think straight, it occurred to me that Julia had somehow emulated my grandfather with her calculated challenge. I suppose I felt those sapphires symbolised defeat rather than victory." He broke off, unwilling to put into words a suspicion so subtle he hardly understood it himself. Leila's expression was still uncompromising, so he added, "I'm not trying to excuse my behaviour that night, just explain what prompted it."

She looked back at him steadily for some moments, then asked, "If you hadn't won the earrings wouldn't you still have tried it on with some other jewellery?"

He sighed. "I thought we had passed that stage some weeks ago."

There was another long pause while she apparently tried to sort out her thoughts, and he hoped the danger had passed. That danger had, but a new brand arrived with her next words.

"A small boy being made to obey his grandfather I can understand, but not why you were prepared to half kill yourself with a wild horse just because this Julia dared you to . . . and if you felt that way about the earrings, why did you take them from her?"

This plain evidence of their differing attitudes and standards of life led him to explain quietly, "They were the stakes in a wager that I won. I had to take them."

Absorbing that, her brow creased in thought. "Well, the whole thing sounds very silly to me. Why would any girl decide to give away her valuable jewels just to make a man do something dangerous? It sounds almost cruel . . . just like your grandfather, as you said. Your father is quite as bad for letting them behave that way to his sons."

"My father is dead, Leila."

"Oh, I didn't realise. What about your mother?"

"Once Charles was a man, she went to live in Rhodesia. She's very happy now, I'm glad to say." Letting the subject rest for a moment or two, he realised that she was making no move to go. "May I signal the waiter to serve our chicken?"

Giving a slow nod she confessed, "I am rather hungry, you know. I was so excited before the show, I couldn't eat a thing."

The restraint remained between them, however, and she looked up from her plate of chicken to ask, "Are you going to marry this Julia?"

"Good God, no!" he returned swiftly, wondering what had prompted that notion.

"It sounds to me as though she hopes you are."

"You're wrong," he declared, just a little too heartily. "She is practically engaged to someone else."

"Only *practically*? I wonder why."

"It is to be a marriage of convenience. Passion doesn't enter into it, so far as I know."

"Then it won't suit *her*. She sounds like a very passionate person to me."

"Can we drop the subject of Julia Marchbanks?" he asked, in mild irritation.

Casting him a thoughtful glance Leila nodded, and devoted her attention to her meal. However, although they discussed the opening night of *Felicity May* and Franz Mittelheiter's captivation of his audience, she caught him on the wrong foot when she suddenly asked, "Have you still got those hateful earrings?"

"Yes," he replied, still wondering what was coming. "I can't throw the things away . . . and I can't send them back to her, either."

"Are they valuable?"

"Reasonably so."

"Then sell them to pay for my singing lessons."

Taken by complete surprise, he asked, "You've changed your mind about my paying for them?"

"But you wouldn't be paying for them. *She* would. This Julia, who made you do something you didn't want to do and half kill yourself. Selling them would rid you of something that bothers you, for some reason. And I wouldn't have to pawn my presents—something that bothers me. It's the perfect solution, isn't it?"

Bemused by her irrational reasoning, he murmured, "Of course."

Although paying for her singing lessons would create a stronger bond between them, he knew those earrings had brought about a set-back in their relationship that evening. She was quiet on the drive home to her basement, and she said goodnight swiftly before he could start an embrace, then ran quickly down the steps and indoors.

He continued to the Veasey-Hunter house, lost in thought. Getting to know Leila had taught him many things that had never even crossed his mind before; shown him a different set of values. She could not understand why he had had to accept Julia's challenge that day, yet she had her own brand of pride that resisted all his attempts to put a seal of ownership on her. Would she have understood any better if he had admitted that he came back to her time after time because she also challenged him; that his pride had not allowed him to be so easily dismissed by a girl of her class?

But, even as those thoughts formed in his mind, he knew the affair had changed in a subtle kind of way with which he had not yet come to terms. What had started out as "an exercise in tactics", as he had described it to his brother, had grown far more complex than he had imagined. Those earrings had added further complexity. He could not possibly sell them, of course, now that he knew they were Marchbanks heirlooms. Julia had been clever—more so than he had initially seen. The earrings put a strange kind of seal of ownership on *him*. He would have to find some way of making her take the damned things back as soon as possible.

# CHAPTER SIX

Rose Heywood took her own life three days before Good Friday. Her doctor had told her she had cancer of the stomach from which she would never recover and, as she was obliged to move from Miles Lampton's apartment after Easter, she had wanted to die surrounded by beautiful things that symbolised the happiest times of her life. The alternative had been unfaceable.

Lindley's Theatre was fully featured in the publicity that followed the suicide of one of the Lindley Girls, and details of Rose's life were spread across the pages of the daily papers. Those publications with a public conscience roundly denounced Miles Lampton, who had just become engaged to a South African millionairess. The columns called Miles, and all those like him, heartless playboys who took the weak and underprivileged for their sinful pleasures, then cast them aside for a marriage of rank that earned them undeserved respect from society. How many others like Rose Heywood died unmarked and unmourned when a high-born seducer abandoned them to their terrible fate, they asked? This courageous girl had sacrificed her hope of Christian eternity in order to draw attention to what was still a large-scale practice, even in the present age of social enlightenment.

The story touched a good many righteous hearts, and Miles Lampton was pelted with rotten eggs when he left the Foreign Office the next day. He retired to the country until the squall blew itself out.

The shock of Rose's death was more than Leila could take. Her friend had left a letter for her, in which she explained the reasons for what she had done. She ended by thanking Leila for her caring friend-ship, begged her to use the wonderful gift of her voice to the full, and wrote, defiant to the end, that she regretted nothing she had done.

The letter tore Leila apart with a grief she had never before experi-enced. Police questioning over the note, which they confiscated as evidence of suicide, exhausted and upset her so much she collapsed on stage the following night, unable to ward off the reaction of severe shock any longer. The dressing-room, the empty stool next to hers, the pots of grease, the props in the corner of the room, the costume hanging on a hook above her head, the gap in the ranks during the show, all spoke so strongly of her friend's absence it was impossible to go on.

Lester Gilbert took her home in his own carriage, and sent one of his maids to stay at the basement all night. A doctor sent by the impressario advised complete rest for a week or more, with plenty of sleep. But Leila lay wide-eyed all through the hours of darkness, when remorse and recrimination ran riot. She could see Rose's face, hear her saucy voice in mimicry, remember her sharp wit. Grief would not allow Leila to believe that the lovely young girl no longer existed; that Rose had vanished in an instant, never to be seen or heard again.

There was so much that she should have said to her friend. Why had she treated their relationship with such an air of "tomorrow will do"? Why had she never put into words the value of knowing that Rose was always there when needed; never shown the girl that she loved her as the sister she had never had; the family she had never known? Why had she left it all too late?

Moving her head from side to side on the pillow all night, Leila tortured herself with the charge that she should have known there was something significant about those terrible stomach pains; should have been there during Rose's last despairing hours. The thought of that lively young creature lying alone in the pretty apartment where they had spent Christmas together, while the poison spread slowly through her body, was one Leila could not drive from her mind. Her sense of loss was overwhelming. It seemed that, with Rose gone, she was all alone.

Next morning, she found her mistake. Lester Gilbert's maid answered a knock on the door, and Vivian walked in wearing a tweed suit and soft brown hat. He looked so large, so strong and dependable, the tears that had stayed away all night flooded her eyes. In her nightgown, she ran to him and collapsed, sobbing, into his arms. He held her tightly, stroking her hair which hung long and resting his cheek against the top of her head, as she abandoned herself to grief and remorse. Her hands gripped him in a desperate attempt to seek escape from the terrible truth, and she pressed her body against his for maximum comfort from the solid strength he represented. Making no attempt to stop her tears, he kept his close enfolding embrace around her until she was completely spent. Only then did he relax his hold and smooth back the wet strands from her eyes.

"I read in my newspaper that you had been taken ill on stage," he said in rough tones. "I came here from the station. The regiment only returned from manoeuvres in the early hours."

"You know about Rose?" she asked thickly.

He nodded, taking a handkerchief from his pocket to wipe her cheeks. "How could I not? It has caused quite a scandal."

"Oh, Vivian, it would break her heart," she cried in fresh distress. "She never stopped loving him, right to the end, and she would never have guessed it would do this to him. It wasn't out of revenge, as everyone is suggesting. Rose wasn't like that. If she knew they were throwing things at him, she'd . . ."

The tragedy of it all overcame her again as she pressed against him but, while he held her close, he was speaking over her head to the maid Leila had forgotten.

"Go into the bedroom and pack all Miss Duncan will need for a short visit to the country. I'm taking her to my home in Cornwall."

"But, sir, I don't work here."

"You're a lady's-maid, aren't you? Then you should know what to put in a suitcase for a four-day visit. Good God woman, do I have to do it myself?"

Leila struggled free. "Don't speak to her like that. She has been up all night."

"So have I," he returned firmly, looking across at the maid to nod her into action. "Be as quick as you can. We have a train to catch."

Leila was wiping her eyes with the back of her hand, since he still had the handkerchief, and asked on a shuddering breath, "What are you talking about, Vivian?"

He turned his attention back to her. "I'm taking you to Cornwall for Easter . . . and before you fly at me, I'll tell you that the presence of my brother, the housekeeper, and a bevy of minor staff will provide adequate chaperonage. You need a rest, and Shenstone is far away from any of this."

"I . . . I can't go off to Cornwall. There's the show."

"I saw Lester Gilbert on my way here. He is in full agreement with my proposal."

"You . . . saw . . . Lester Gilbert? And he is in full agreement with your proposal?" she echoed in a daze of disbelief.

"Did you think he would not be? He's a reasonable man who quickly saw the sense in it." A glance at his pocket watch brought a frown. "Get dressed as quickly as you can. I have a carriage waiting to take us to the station."

She stayed where she was, unable to take it all in. "I can't go off with you, at a moment's notice, like this."

He turned her around and pushed her toward the bedroom. "Unless you get some clothes on, that's just how you will go with me. I'd be very happy about it, but the other passengers might stare."

It was late in the afternoon when they entered the carriage Dobbins had brought to meet their train. Leila was still in a daze of unreality, and could hardly believe the truth of where she was. They had travelled in a first-class compartment all the way, and she had discovered that this man undertook a journey in much the same way he did anything else, with efficiency, self-confidence, and maximum luxury.

Unfortunately, she had missed most of the scenery on the way down, because she had fallen asleep almost immediately, lulled by the rocking of the train. On awakening, she had found herself stretched out on one seat while Vivian sat reading a newspaper on the other. He had waved aside her apology, and urged her to eat some of the dainty sandwiches and drink a little of the wine he had summoned a steward to bring. It had surprised her that she was able to do so, and she had no sooner returned from the toilet compartment, where she tidied herself as much as the movement of the train would allow, than they had arrived at their destination.

Stepping from the train she was greeted by country peace and the beautiful sun-soaked perfume of wallflowers that splashed the white of the station fence with red, yellow, and flame. The air smelt so pure; the gentle breeze was sweet with the waft of rich meadows, baking bread, and clean cows. There was a farm beside the tiny station, and cattle were mooing their desire to be milked as they filed into the barn with lumbering gait.

She hardly noticed the coachman's respectful greeting, so charmed was she by her first sight of this part of England. Everywhere she looked there was beauty. Bright luscious meadows, fields of infant crops, picturesque farms with thatch and tiny windows and, away in the distance, rising heights of paler green. As they clattered through the cobbled streets of a tiny market-town, Vivian asked if she was comfortable and offered a rug for her knees. His solicitousness passed practically unheeded, so taken was she with lanes edged by banks covered in huge clumps of pale primroses, fragrant enough in that late afternoon to fill her nostrils with further bewitching scent.

"How perfectly lovely!" she exclaimed. "Look, they're everywhere."

Yet her attention was almost immediately taken by an even more appealing sight, when the carriage began climbing from the valley and the plaintive cry of lambs was all around her. The slopes were home for hundreds of sheep, so it was inevitable that, in those last days of March, there should be long-tailed lambs galore, skipping and frisking in the warmth, full of the joys of being alive. The high frightened calls of those who had temporarily lost their mothers mingled with the deeper baas of those they sought. The rejoicing lambs rushed across and immediately nuzzled the teats of their parents for the comfort of milk. To Leila, born and bred in London, it was all utterly entrancing.

"They're absolutely beautiful," she breathed. "I'd give anything to hold one."

"Your wish shall be granted, my dear," said a teasing voice beside her. "We have plenty of sheep at Shenstone."

She turned to him eagerly. "Do you live on a farm?"

"There are several farms on the estate." He pointed ahead. "We climb to the top of that rise, then cross the moor for around half an hour. Most of that land is part of Shenstone, including the village of the same name." He smiled. "The weather seems set fair. We'll ride over there tomorrow, if you'd care to."

His words brought a lightning reversal of mood; a cold shower in the midst of glorious summer. Delight and enchantment abruptly vanished, and she turned away to look out over the side of the carriage. They had topped the rise now, and the view in every direction was wild, rugged, and extremely desolate. The sun was beginning to sink. Civilisation appeared to have been left behind. A chill wind now reached them on that exposed ridge, and the track they were following along the heights seemed to disappear into nowhere. The cry of the sheep up there sounded mournful as they clustered in the lee of rocky outcrops, and shaggy short-legged horses cropped the grass in resigned isolation. Overhead, hawk-like birds sailed or hovered, their beady eyes searching for carrion.

Leila gazed blindly as the carriage progressed through the bleak countryside. Whatever was she doing here? How could she have let herself be brought on a journey of this length, to a place in the middle of a wilderness? Vivian had just spoken of an "estate" containing several farms and a whole village. He had mentioned riding there tomorrow. Suddenly, everything seemed menacing, where it had earlier charmed. All at once, she felt full of fears, a stranger in a wide barren wilderness. A great longing for her basement, for things familiar, for the warm smell of the theatre swept over her. Then, a great longing for Rose, who always put things into perspective . . . but Rose would never be there again. She was lying cold and white on a slab somewhere.

A voice spoke; the carriage stopped. "Leila, what is wrong?" came the gentle question.

"I'd . . . I'd like to go back," she managed through the clutch of grief at her throat.

Next minute, she was being encouraged down onto the track. Then, with a rug held around her shoulders by a strong arm, she was led across the springy turf to where a cluster of rocks caught the dying rays of the sun. Once there, Vivian turned her to face him, full of concern.

"What has happened to change your mood so drastically?"

Looking up at him she cried, "I don't belong here. I should never have come, but you gave me no choice. You always sweep people along with no thought for them or their feelings. It might be a good way of getting what you want, but don't you ever think of how it might affect your victim?"

"*Victim?*" A frown furrowed his brow, and the setting sun turned his hair a dull red shade that made him seem even more a stranger.

Her urge to return to things familiar grew. "How do I know where you're taking me? This is miles from anywhere, and it's going to get dark soon."

His frown deepened. "I thought you trusted me."

"Each time I do, something happens," she said wildly. "Look at those earrings."

His arms dropped away from her slowly. "Haven't I redeemed myself over that affair yet?"

The sun began to disappear over the rim of the grassland to leave a peculiar glow across the entire landscape. Leila clutched the rug closer around her shoulders, as instinctive protection against the overwhelming loneliness of that moment.

"I don't really know anything about you, do I?" she told him in a low voice. "I have seen you parading about in an impressive uniform; I've seen you in evening-dress as a man-about-town. You spend money like the Prince of Wales, and seem to know everyone of importance. For me, you are still just someone who takes me to supper. A masher and a chorus-girl, that's what we are." When he appeared to wince at that, she went on, "We agreed that was all it would be, didn't we? Friends who have supper together, or go for a drive in the park."

"Yes . . . I suppose we did," he conceded.

"Then what am I doing here?" She was questioning herself as much as him, as she realised that it was her own fault she knew so little about him. Subconscious avoidance of her own past life had led her to avoid discussions on his. Their times together had been used by her to release all her enthusiasm for her day-to-day life at Lindley's, and discuss her hopes for eventual success as a result of her singing lessons. Only now did it occur to her that, apart from that first-night supper at Romano's when he had been forced to explain how he had won Julia Marchbanks' earrings, she had never shown much interest in him other than as a companion and adviser.

The truth then hit her with devastating force. She had been acting a part, as she did each evening on the stage. There was no real Leila Duncan for Vivian to get to know, because such a person did not exist. Lily Lowe, former lady's-maid who had given herself to someone she could not now remember and had had to marry out of temporary desperation, *dared* not show deep interest in a man who was a danger to her. Yet it was already too late, she realised. When he had walked into her basement that morning, she had run unhesitatingly to a man whom she had loved. It was that love which was now making her so afraid, not the isolation of the moors.

When he tried to take her hands, she pulled them away swiftly, as if denying what she had just acknowledged to be disastrously true. In the face of her apparent rejection, he sighed.

"I had no idea that I was trampling on your feelings, or that I was forcing you into a situation which would make you afraid of me like this. I believed we now had greater understanding between us," he said sadly. "I appear to have misread you once more."

Looking away across the desolate landscape she made no answer. She had misread herself, that was painfully clear.

"Leila, when I returned from manoeuvres I found a telegram awaiting me from my brother, which necessitated my coming to Cornwall. Sitting on the train to London I read all the details of your friend's death and your collapse on stage last night. Even a friend who merely takes you to supper wishes to be of help in such a situation," he told her urgently. "Since it was out of the question for me to take up temporary residence in your basement, it seemed to be the ideal solution to bring you here with me. At Shenstone you can rest and recover from your shock, with our housekeeper to fuss over you, and I can be with you in perfectly acceptable circumstances. I knew you had met Charles and liked him; I thought you had grown to like me. However, if you really want to go back, I will take you. There might not be a train tonight, but I can hire a carriage."

She had no idea what to do, no experience of such a situation to guide her. Clutching the rug tightly around her shivering body, she asked wildly, "An 'estate' you said. What does that mean?"

"Shenstone Hall stands in eight thousand acres, most of which is moorland. My ancestors made a fortune from tin mining. My grandfather has it now invested in South Africa."

"Ancestors?" she echoed, growing more afraid of the truth by the minute. "Just who is your grandfather?"

"Lord Brancliffe. My brother Charles is heir to the title."

Stunned by the revelation, by all that was happening that day, she demanded hotly, "Who are you, then? Who are you really?"

"Vivian Veasey-Hunter, captain of the 49th Lancers." His attempt to take her hands was more successful, this time. "Leila, have I ever pretended to be anyone else?"

She gazed back helplessly. "I suppose not."

Vivian said no more, did not attempt to solve her dilemma, which was made worse by the physical contact of their hands. Every feminine instinct urged her to seek the comfort he was offering, yet all he had just told her heightened the feeling that it would be courting disaster to do so. As he waited, his face was grave, the laughter missing from eyes that usually danced with it. If she knew it, surely his superior learning told him that it was hardly fitting for her to stay in his home, where his grandfather was a lord.

"Lord Brancliffe—is he the grandfather who hates you?"

"What has that to do with your trust in me?"

"What will *he* have to say about me?"

"He has suffered a heart attack. That is why I had to come . . . and why I had no alternative but to bring you with me. My dear girl, as you can see, Shenstone is extremely isolated. With Brancliffe very seriously ill, and only my brother present, you can follow doctor's orders and rest in complete peace and privacy in the guest wing of the house. If you prefer to remain in your rooms the whole time, you may. On the other hand, I shall be glad if you seek my company occasionally."

Casting around for some kind of guidance, she suddenly thought of what Rose would say to all this. *Canine Charles heir to a title. Oh Lei, what a laugh! I suppose he'll have the family crest on his collar when he goes for walks.*

"Rose would go with you like a shot," she told him, shivering badly in the enveloping rug by now.

He smiled faintly. "Yes, she would. If she hadn't been that kind of girl, my trick with Oscar would have been a terrible waste of effort that day in Brighton."

Gripping his hands tightly, she confessed, "I was very annoyed with her for how she behaved that day . . . but you couldn't be annoyed with her for long, you know. It's the same with you."

He let that last remark stand for a moment or two, then took her by the elbow. "Shall we carry on to Shenstone now?"

As she dressed after breakfast in a grey plaid woollen skirt, a white cambric blouse with a black floppy bow at the high neck, and a warm jacket in plum-coloured velour, Leila thought back over the previous evening. Mrs Hale, the housekeeper, had treated her like an invalid, and a girl from the village had waited on her hand and foot. Charles

Veasey-Hunter had been visibly taken aback at her arrival with his brother, but Vivian had quickly explained the situation, leaving him no chance to do more than offer politely rigid condolences on the loss of her friend. Mrs Hale had swiftly whisked her off to a set of rooms, where fires had been quickly lit on Vivian's orders. A bed had been made up by the girl, whilst Leila had drunk tea brought to her on a silver tray. Ewers of hot water had been carried in for a bath, then Leila had rested on a four-poster bed until dinner had been served to her in the sitting-room of her suite. Vivian had sat with her drinking sherry while she ate, and she had been glad of his company.

Leila had already been told by Mrs Hale that Lord Brancliffe had rallied against all medical predictions. At eighty-nine no one had expected him to live through the attack, much less show signs of recovery, as he was doing. It had been Mrs Hale's mumbled comment about adding insult to injury, by summoning Captain Vivian to the supposed death-bed, which had driven away all sorrowful thoughts of Rose as Leila lay in the bed enjoying the unusual pleasure of having firelight dancing on the walls. In this house, a small boy had been left by an uncaring father to be cruelly treated by his grandfather, until he grew old enough to escape. The mother appeared to have done little to save her son from torment. Leila did not think much of any of them. The father had died; the mother had gone off to some foreign place. This grandfather—lord or not—did not deserve to recover, in her opinion. Maybe it had been the atmosphere in this great mansion, or the discovery of a love that had taken her unawares, that had made her suddenly see something with great clarity. Too many people had hurt Vivian in the past. She must take care not to do so in the future.

It was with this thought uppermost that she greeted him that bright morning. Having confessed to him the night before that she could not ride a horse, he had promised to drive her out in a dogcart to see the lambs. He arrived to collect her at the agreed time, and immediately asked how she was feeling.

She in turn enquired after his grandfather, who was still making progress, it appeared.

Giving his irresistible smile, Vivian then said, "Now the medical bulletins have been exchanged, shall we set out?"

It was useless to deny her delight in walking beside him through a building that seemed more like a palace than a home to her. Yet Vivian trod the long corridors and numerous rooms with casual acceptance of the gigantic paintings, the hundreds of beautiful ornaments, the vast carpets in rich hues, the furniture which looked far too elegant to use. He descended the graceful curving staircases with a familiarity that denied any sense of wonder at the marble steps, intricate wrought-iron bannisters, the delicate murals. Once outside, he crunched the gravel paths beneath his boots, intent on reaching the stables where the horses stood watching the morning's activity through half-open doors. He appeared to see nothing of the splendour of sweeping lawns, ornate terraces, the enormous glasshouse containing plants and exotic trees, or the banks of shrubs bearing great blossoms of pink and red such as Leila had only before seen in London's parks.

Now she was here, it was easy to understand why Vivian should have such self-assurance and that air of command that automatically expected obedience. He looked every inch the son of such a place in fawn breeches, brown tweed jacket, and silk scarf knotted at the throat. Yet this same man had encouraged a horse to perform a dangerous trick in order to meet her, and had come to her basement with an olive branch after she had ordered him from a cab, and thrown his flowers and those fatal earrings out after him. Why? With his dashing looks and manners, he could surely win any girl worthy of all this. Why bother with a Lindley Girl?

Vivian drove the little cart out through the gates to the rear of the stables at a spanking pace. Leila loved the sensation of bowling along a narrow track winding across high-level moorland, which gave an incredible view for miles around. She had never before known such *space*. However, it made their intimacy more apparent, and therefore more dangerous, so she tried to banish her wayward thoughts by asking a succession of questions about the area they were covering.

Finally, Vivian looked at her quizzically. "My dear girl, I think it might be better to wait until we return to the Hall, when I'll give you a book to read on the subject in which you appear to have suddenly acquired an avid interest."

Flushing slightly, she tackled a fresh one. "*Felicity May* has changed since you last saw it, Vivian. Mr Gilbert has bowed to the truth that the show is not worthy of Franz Mittelheiter."

"Good God, that fellow plagues me even down here," was his comment, to accompany a warm look that deepened her flush with its implications. "May I hope the paragon with flashing eyes has been replaced by someone with a few human failings?"

Ignoring that, she went on, "Six of the original Lindley Girls have been selected for several new numbers written by the composer for women with strong voices. I am one of the six."

"You're pleased about that?"

"Of course. Oh Vivian, you must know that I am."

"Then I shall book a seat in the centre stalls as soon as I get back, taking no note of your advice on which side of the stage you appear most."

She laughed softly. "We six are supposed to be members of the regiment, and wear tight-fitting uniforms. One of the numbers might become as popular as the famous Stroll, except that a band of ladies bent on making theatres places of less wickedness have already condemned the costumes as indecent. They parade outside Lindley's with banners."

"Undoubtedly these ladies are all plain and matronly."

"They're not, as it happens, but as it is my big opportunity to sing, I don't care what costume I wear."

"I do," came the teasing response. "I see uniforms every day of the week. My vote goes to ostrich feathers. You look divine in them."

She angled her face away, knowing he could see her much more clearly than she could see him in the bright sunlight. "I enjoy my singing lessons so much, thanks to Julia's earrings. I think you said she is your neighbour here."

"Yes. The Marchbanks' property is over there to the west. You can't see the house from this point."

"Is it a big place, too?"

"Reasonably."

If he resented Franz Mittelheiter, so did she resent Julia Marchbanks —a girl who gave away heirloom earrings as a reward for physical punishment. The person who could force Vivian to do something he did not want to do, and a woman at that, must have a personality to be reckoned with.

Bringing the cart to a halt, Vivian climbed out and walked around to where she sat. "It might be better not to speak of Julia, and certainly not the earrings, in the presence of my brother. He is the probable partner in the marriage of convenience I mentioned to you."

It surprised her. Charles Veasey-Hunter was so very sober and diffident. If Julia could challenge a man like Vivian and win, she would surely *devour* his staid younger brother. At that thought something occurred to her that she had missed in her mental confusion the day before.

"You said yesterday that Mr Veasey-Hunter was your younger brother. How is it he is heir to the title instead of you?"

He made a vague gesture with his hand. "These matters are always extremely complex. Because my father died before *his* father, and therefore did not inherit, the situation was complicated further. A minor legal point makes Charles next in line."

Watching the square face she had come to know so well, her

newly-acknowledged love for him deepened her perception which told her he was not being completely honest, for some reason. Unlike his quicksilver charm that allowed him to lie so outrageously when he chose, she sensed that this particular evasion of the truth had deeper roots.

"Is it something your grandfather has done?" she asked.

He shook his head. "A legal quirk that cannot be changed."

"Don't you mind about it?"

"I was told years ago, when I hardly understood the implications, so I have grown up in acceptance of it. Poor Charles suffers from it most," he continued in a light tone. "He has to remain here a victim of the old man's eccentricities, while I am free to do as I please without bowing to obligations."

Even more convinced now that he was concocting answers he imagined she would believe, she said with deliberation, "That means you don't have to marry Julia, either."

His eyes lit with awareness as he replied slowly, "No, I don't have to marry Julia, do I?"

Next minute he had lifted her to the ground and, sandwiched between him and the dainty carriage, she found his mouth hard on hers before she was prepared for it.

"Reward for an astute girl," he murmured, lifting his head.

Trying to recover, she asked accusingly, "Are you sure it wasn't a reward for yourself?"

He smiled engagingly. "Don't you consider that I deserve one for bringing you here to see the lambs, as I promised?"

Taking her hand, he began to lead her toward a low stone wall just off the track they had travelled. There, he lifted her over into an area where sheep abounded further down the sloping meadow, and began to run toward them, pulling her with him until she was laughing and out of breath. Time passed in sheer delight as she wandered amongst the ewes with lambs galore, chuckling at the antics of the newly-born as they bounded into the air in the exhilaration of leaving the cramped womb and finding a warm grassy paradise. Leila exclaimed in enchantment over tiny fleecy twins, as she strolled hand in hand with Vivian in the spring sunshine. Then, over in the corner of the meadow, she spotted a black lamb.

"Oh Vivian, *look*. That's the one I'd cuddle, if it were possible."

No sooner had she spoken than he went toward it, arms outstretched, ready to grant her wish. Immediately, the little creature baaed loudly and scampered away, whilst Vivian was still several feet from it.

"You'll never catch it," she laughed.

"Oh, won't I?" he replied with determination, peeling off his jacket to hand to her.

There followed a scene she would never forget, as Vivian raced all over the sloping grassy area, dodging sheep and their white lambs as he pursued the nimble black bundle hither and thither, before finally seizing it as it tried to dash between his legs. Leila had flung her jacket down in the lee of a wall, and sat on it rocking with laughter, while he slipped and slid on that hillside—a giant of a man pursuing a miniature creature.

Finally, he came up to her, flushed and dishevelled, but grinning triumphantly. Then he handed the captive to her, looking deep into her eyes as he murmured, "One black sheep giving you another."

She cuddled the animal to her while her heart thumped in sudden painful awareness, and she spoke her love-words against its fleece because she could not say them to the man who now sat down beside her. Within seconds, the lamb had fallen asleep in her arms, putting an alien longing in her breast as she cradled it and rubbed her cheek on the dark wool. She did not want that moment to end . . . *ever!*

Then she became conscious of those grey-green eyes watching her intently, all the humour now gone from them. "You asked me yesterday who I really was. Now it's my turn to ask who you really are, Leila."

She concentrated on the lamb in her arms. "You know who I am—a chorus-girl who lives in a basement. I haven't a lordly grandfather to hide away."

"I didn't hide him away." When she said no more, he prompted, "Tell me about your family."

"I haven't any."

He frowned. "No parents living? No aunts or uncles who are responsible for you?"

"No."

"Brothers or sisters?"

She shook her head.

"Is that all you're prepared to tell me?"

"Why should you be interested?"

"Don't be coy, Leila. I think you know all too well why I should be interested."

She had to meet his gaze then. Leaning on one shoulder against the wall he looked very youthful, and more serious than she had ever seen him. At that moment, she desperately wanted to be someone other than Lily Lowe for him, but he demanded honesty from her now.

"My father worked as an apprentice to a hatter," she began, relating the story that had been told to her. "He no sooner completed his apprenticeship than he married a music teacher, who was a great deal older than himself. My mother died giving birth to me, and Father gave up half his wages so that his employer's housekeeper would rear me on the premises. When I was three, my father was killed in an accident. Fortunately for me, Mr Bunting, the hatter, had grown fond of me, so I stayed where I was until he died four years later. His housekeeper went back to her sister in the country, and I went to the house of an elderly neighbour, who had once been a governess. She educated me and, in return, I kept house for her."

"At the age of *seven!*" he exclaimed.

"A child can clean and wash clothes quite easily at that age. She did the cooking, of course, and fed me well. It was there that I first began to enjoy singing. Miss Gates played the piano, and I used to warble." She gave him a faint smile. "They were mostly ballads and hymns. Very different from *Felicity May* and *The Maid of Montezuma*."

"Where is she now?"

"I don't know. When I was twelve she moved away quite suddenly, and without apparent reason. At least, I was never told why she went. I then went to the Rectory helping with the eight children." She shrugged her shoulders. "The rest you know," she said, ignoring the six years of her life in domestic service with the Clivedons. "I became an actress."

He seemed unconcerned about how or when that had happened. "Do you keep in touch with the Rector and his family?"

"No."

"Were they unkind to you?"

She thought that over. "They had no interest in me. That's not unkindness. I didn't have to go through misery just to let an old man get his own way over me, like you did."

He was plainly unhappy over something he had told her under pressure. She guessed he deeply regretted that meeting with Rupert Marchbanks, in her presence.

"So you have no guardian, no one at all who might be concerned with your future welfare?"

"Rose would have been," she said quietly. "Our friendship was only a recent one, but we packed such a lot into eighteen months. She is the first person I've loved." Quick tears blurred her eyes. "If you hadn't brought me here yesterday, I don't know . . ."

The lamb stirred, realised where it was, and struggled free. She felt ridiculously bereft, and her tears increased to hang on her lashes.

Vivian's palm curved round her cheek, turning her to look at him. "Leila, do I have to tell you why I brought you here?"

Knowing she had to prevent him from telling her, she said, "You're very kind, and I'm grateful."

"Kind be damned," he swore, reaching for her.

His earlier kisses had been nothing like this. His hands were warm through the thin cambric of her blouse, and he held her so close it was almost like being a part of him. Soon, she was trembling with a desire she had felt once before, on a long-ago summer's day. But, although her body remembered it, her mind did not, as it acknowledged the power of deep love for a man for the first time in her life. Her hands moved in his blond hair, and her lips moved against his temple with the same fervour as his kisses on her throat.

Then, she was tilting backward as he gradually lowered her to the jacket spread on the ground. Bending over her he said huskily, "You've driven me hard, and this is the result. I've never had to wait this long for any woman."

He pinned her to the ground, her hands on each side of her head, while he demonstrated in breathtaking fashion the penalty for keeping him waiting. Leila wondered wildly how she could ever have done so; how she could in the future.

His face was vivid with desire when he lifted his head to gaze down at her. "Do you still think it was kindness that prompted my actions, or do I have to show you even more forcibly what my real reasons were?"

As his hold tightened again, she realised where they were heading, and struggled frantically to get up. "No, Vivian!"

He overpowered and stilled her struggles. "Don't fight me, Leila. You knew as well as I did that it was only a matter of time, and I've waited too long already."

Her resistance melted away; soon she was past caring where his demands might lead. His hands began to move over her body possessively, and she moaned her pleasure as she lay beneath him. Gradually, he unfastened the buttons of the high neck of her blouse, until his mouth was exploring the softness at the base of her throat, while her own hands gripped convulsively at his shoulders through the silk shirt. But her heart thudded in sudden fright as, over his right shoulder, she caught sight of the figure of a mounted rider watching them. From Leila's position flat on her back, the horse seemed to tower over them. The woman rider was like a statuette, so still was she. Leila guessed that she had been a spectator to their love-making for some while.

"No, Vivian," she said urgently.

"*Yes*, Vivian," he insisted, too far on the road to heed anything but his own desires.

"We're not alone," she managed to say, as his mouth chased hers. "There's someone behind you."

It took him a moment to accept that she was serious. Then he slowly pushed himself up on his hands, to glance over his shoulder. He seemed to gaze at the woman for a long time. Her return look was one that Leila could not interpret. Without a word, Vivian got to his feet and helped her up to stand beside him, her hands swiftly buttoning her blouse to the neck.

The horse the woman rode was every bit as tall and strong as the one Vivian had ridden, and a magnificent grey. She was dressed very severely in a masculine-style dark-blue habit, with a tiny black bowler-hat kept on with veiling that covered the whole of her face. Behind that veiling Leila could see very large eyes dominating a face of breeding rather than beauty. Their calculating glance raked Vivian from head to foot, missing nothing of his tumbled hair, loosened shirt, and breeches smeared with grass stains from chasing the lamb.

"Breaking in another wild creature, Vivian?"

Her voice was assured and beautifully modulated. Leila knew, without being told, that the girl was Julia Marchbanks.

# CHAPTER SEVEN

Vivian was dressing for dinner when his brother walked in, already neat and handsome in tails. His expression was grim.

"This is going to be a damned impossible evening," he declared angrily.

Vivian looked across at him in the midst of tying his bow tie. "You precipitated it by inviting Julia to stay overnight."

"I . . . my God, that's cool! Julia is to be mistress of Shenstone, and I have every right to invite her to join us. You, on the other hand, have brought one of your women here and conducted your *amours* on the open moor, with scant regard for whoever might witness your . . . your *pleasures*," he finished cuttingly. "I believe I suggested that Miss Duncan should dine in her room tonight, as she did yesterday."

Straightening up slowly, Vivian confronted Charles across his dressing-room. "Leila is not 'one of my women' as you so crudely phrased it, and I'm damned if I'll force her to keep out of sight, as if she were. As to Julia being mistress here one day, that is open to doubt, as I have suggested to you before."

Charles flushed. "Very well. As a neighbour and friend, she took the trouble to ride across to enquire after Brancliffe. I hope I may invite as an overnight guest whom I like, without censure from you, of all people."

It touched Vivian on the raw. "You're only the heir-apparent, Charles. Shenstone is no more yours, at the present moment, than it is mine. I hope I may invite to my family home whom I like without *your* censure."

With uncharacteristic pugnaciousness, his brother took the disagreement further. "Certainly you may, providing that neither you nor your guests offend others with your behaviour. You surely don't imagine that one visit to your old home, plus complete control over dressing her, will turn a chorus-girl into a lady."

Abandoning the tie, Vivian walked across to where Charles stood with his feet planted aggressively apart. "We have already had one sharp exchange over my bringing Leila here, and you know damn well it wasn't with any idea of turning her into a lady. That girl of Lampton's had just committed suicide. They were close friends, so it was a terrible shock. On top of that, the police then put the poor girl through an unpleasant interrogation which made the situation a hellish sight worse for her, finally bringing about her collapse on the stage at Lindley's. Her doctor advised her to get away from London and the theatre. She knows no one but me, and I was on my way to Cornwall in response to a telegram from you stating that Brancliffe was dying. I had no choice but to bring her with me, where there would be no question of compromise. Leila is not my mistress. I told you that last night."

"Then why are you doing all this for her, for God's sake?"

The question caught him unawares, his usual eloquence deserting him. For some seconds he merely gazed back at his brother in a state of contemplation, unable to reply.

"You haven't lost your head over the girl, surely."

Tugging the bow tie from his shirt, Vivian said absently, "Must I remind you that I am three years your senior, and do not require a cross-examination on a subject about which you know practically nothing?"

"I know that Lampton was pelted with eggs outside the Foreign Office, and has been forced to lie low because his discarded mistress did away with herself," Charles said forcefully. "There are rumours that Falkwith's daughter is returning his ring."

"When a marriage of convenience turns into one of inconvenience, it's the usual pattern to call it a day. The Heywood girl killed herself because she was dying of cancer. It had nothing to do with Lampton's callous behaviour toward her."

"Of course it had! He's being blamed for it, isn't he? See how easily these affairs turn into scandals of unpleasant proportions? Men of standing should be extremely careful over sexual intrigues, and maintain impeccable standards of behaviour in public," his brother recited pompously.

His anger growing, Vivian cried, "Bravo brother! Our late father set us a damned fine example of that, wouldn't you say?"

"That's no excuse for you to follow it."

It was snapped out so sharply, Vivian was taken aback at the extent to which the quarrel had gone. He had never before known his brother in such a mood.

"All right, Charles," he said quietly, "you've done your duty as the future Lord Brancliffe. Let me just tell you something before we take this any further. When Father broke his neck on the hunting-field, a great many cuckolded husbands breathed a sigh of relief. I have never tampered with other men's wives, neither do I have any wish to do so. I do not have a very lovely wife of my own, whom I neglect along with my two small sons, in order to satisfy my indiscriminate lust. Now, either you apologise for your last remark, or I'll pack my bag and leave Shenstone for the last time."

Charles was visibly shocked at such an ultimatum. "Perhaps it was somewhat unjust," he allowed reluctantly. "I'm sorry, Viv."

"There's more behind this than Leila," Vivian said. "You have never lashed out like that at anyone, least of all me."

"All this female nonsense caused by Miss Duncan's presence here has made me edgy, that's all. Brancliffe wants to see you both tomorrow morning." Seeing Vivian's expression, he went on hastily, "Julia did mention the subject . . . but he already knew. She is making an issue of the whole thing, and I have been hard put to defend your decision to bring the girl here. Julia has very real notions of propriety. Dash it all, I summoned you to Brancliffe's death-bed, and you turned up with one of your . . . with an actress in tow. You must see how a girl like Julia would view that, to say nothing of that incident this morning."

Vivian sighed. "I suspect that the 'incident' this morning gave Julia the most pleasure she has had in a long while and she is making an issue of it in order to prolong the pleasure. Charles, you don't know that girl as well as you should if you still dream of making a match with her . . . and if you also imagine that she has very real notions of propriety. Believe me, the last thing she wants is for Leila to remain in her own room this evening. Julia's claws are out, and fur will fly in every direction. I guarantee that she is relishing the coming hours."

His brother grew irate once more. "Now look, Viv, I have been very tolerant over all this, so far . . ."

"No, you haven't," Vivian countered swiftly. "You've been making a damn fool of yourself. Nothing improper occurred this morning, despite what Julia hinted, and my relationship with Leila is really none of your concern. Charles, you've always been a transparent kind of fellow, and I know exactly what's behind this ridiculous pose of yours. Brancliffe's recovery has dashed all your hopes. Like me, you relished the prospect of his departure from our lives, and the fact that he is still with us is very hard for you to swallow." His brother's deep flush gave him away, so Vivian added, "I once suggested that you have him certified, then take over before the estate is totally ruined."

"You know my views on that," came the stiff reply.

"I do, but it's my guess that he'll live forever rather than relinquish his power over you," Vivian told him grimly. "If he ever does, he'll merely hand it to Julia in the safe knowledge that his reign will continue by proxy. Now, let me tie my tie, then we'll go down to witness her first tentative attempts."

"I can't allow you to speak of Julia that way," Charles said immediately.

"Then kindly remain silent on the subject of Leila," Vivian retaliated, "and on your way downstairs ponder the fact that we have never quarrelled over anything in our lives, until Julia Marchbanks came upon the scene. That girl will drive a wedge between us, if we are not careful."

Vivian viewed the coming evening with much apprehension. The return to Shenstone that morning, with Julia riding alongside the carriage, had been a great strain for Leila, who had been caught in a passionate situation which had developed before he knew it. She had retired to her room and remained there all afternoon, refusing to answer his frequent raps on her door in the hope of easing the awkwardness between them. Her present emotional state over the suicide of Rose Heywood, in addition to the demolition of her sexual barriers this morning, might make her unpredictable during the coming intimate foursome. He knew that she was still highly sensitive to the affair of Julia's earrings, and confrontation with the owner of them could produce the kind of female sparring over which men rarely had any control.

In truth, he was not sure what to expect from either girl. After Leila had gone upstairs on reaching the house, Julia had walked beside him through the Long Room, swishing her riding-whip into her gloved palm in a gesture of anger, as she had said, "Even down here in Cornwall we have heard of your reputation, Vivian, but I never hoped to see you in action. I admit to being impressed. Whilst I'm certain that you use more finesse in elegant surroundings, I really thought you captured the earthy flavour very well. The local peasants could learn from you, I'm sure." Her huge eyes had flashed fire. "How are you in a haystack?"

"Very good," he had returned swiftly. "How are you?"

After a second or two, she had laughed and raked him with a glance that had left him in no doubt of her thoughts. "The rapier thrust, eh? We must fence together one day soon. You are always at your most superb in physical pursuits . . . as I saw just now."

That exchange had confirmed his suspicion that her interest in the Veasey-Hunter family had more to do with him than with his sober brother. That being so, he had been torn with indecision all the afternoon. To persuade Leila to remain in her room while Julia reigned downstairs would not only be insulting to her, it would be seen as unconditional surrender by the other girl. On the other hand, the battle that evening would be subtle, in the extreme. Leila might be cruelly routed by a woman who would enjoy setting all three at each other's throats. All in all, Vivian would be glad when the evening was over.

When they had all assembled, he could not help being struck by the contrast presented by the two females. Julia's splendid curves were displayed in a dress of dark-red silk, low at the neck, full in the sleeves, with a skirt hanging in folds that made the material appear almost black. It was a bold colour for an auburn-haired woman to wear, but she won the challenge hands down. Rubies around her throat gave an added touch of opulence to an appearance that commanded attention, however reluctant he might be to give it. In contrast, Leila's willowy show-girl figure looked utterly desirable and feminine in pale-lilac satin, her tiny waist emphasised by a sickle of embroidery and beads, her graceful arms enhanced by gauzy sleeves. She had arranged her hair in the style used in the famous "stroll", and Vivian thought she had never looked more beautiful than then, surrounded by the treasures of an old house.

He was not best pleased, however, when he noticed that the only jewellery that she was wearing was the seed-pearl and amethyst bracelet given to her by another man. Julia fired her first shot almost immediately, by admiring the unpretentious piece and asking if it was a present from him.

"Gracious, no," Leila answered quietly. "It's part of a set that belonged to my grandmama."

Vivian's heart sank. When he had collected Leila to bring her downstairs for dinner, she had given him no opportunity to speak privately with her, by leaving her room at his knock, and questioning him on all the pictures and ornaments they had passed along their way. She continued to deny him any kind of intimate contact by taking his arm when dinner was then announced, and walking beside him in the haughty manner of the Lindley Stroll, refusing to meet his eyes. Wondering how he could best prevent a disaster that evening, he mentally ran through the list of cavalry tactics. There did not appear to be a single one for would-be warriors forced to stand aside whilst two other foes crossed swords. One glance at his brother's expression showed him that Charles would be of no help.

That Julia played hostess was unavoidable. Leila could hardly do so, yet Vivian felt that it gave an overwhelming impression of the other girl's status as future mistress at Shenstone. They settled at the long polished table set with gleaming silver and flashing crystal glasses enhanced by several branches of long ivory-coloured candles. With Charles and Julia at opposite ends, he and Leila seemed almost to be marooned in the middle of that length of mellow wood, and conversation therefore had to be conducted in appropriate volume before the servants. He tried smiling at Leila, but she merely looked back at him gravely, her eyes dark with her secret thoughts.

As the soup was served to the accompaniment of footfalls on the polished wood floor scattered with several large gold and blue rugs, Vivian studied the girl whom he had brought to his home so impulsively. For some months now, he had watched her deal with situations foreign to her background and, in view of the story she had told him that morning, she had handled them with commendable aplomb. The only time her roots had betrayed her had been over the earrings. This evening, however, she looked perfectly poised in these surroundings.

As an actress, she should be able to play a part, of course, but on stage she would know every movement, every word that would be spoken. He had witnessed her behaviour in unexpected circumstances, and had never been embarrassed by her. Could he have taught her so much in such a short time? Suddenly, he wondered if she had once been a wealthy man's mistress, like Rose Heywood. If so, had the affair left her hurt and bitter, too? Could that be why she was so adamant about not becoming his? Sharp, savage jealousy cut into him, leaving him shaken by its implications. No other girl had ever driven him to such lengths to console her unhappiness; no girl, especially one who consistently rebuffed his advances, had ever inspired him to defend her name and honour as he had to Charles earlier that evening.

He was shaken from his thoughts by Julia, who revealed that she knew Leila's identity by saying, "My condolences on the death of your friend, Miss Duncan. Suicide is very tragic, especially when the victim is so young."

Leila was visibly taken aback. "Has Vivian told you?"

"He had no need. The story has been in all the newspapers. I calculated that there could not be two Leila Duncans who were tall, dark-haired, and lovely enough to be one of the admired Lindley Girls."

She went on to ask, with apparent interest, all about life in the theatre. Leila answered civilly and frankly in what appeared to be an innocent conversation, until the experienced fencer slipped beneath her opponent's guard.

"How very fascinating! Now that you have told me of the new show, and your rôle of a Belgian peasant, I understand the little rehearsal this morning. Vivian was portraying the licentious soldiery, I take it. A little surprising in view of the fact that Charles told me you were here for a complete rest, Miss Duncan."

Leila seemed perfectly controlled as she replied, "Then you have the advantage of me, Miss Marchbanks. No one has yet told me why you are here."

Charles hastily signalled for the fish course to be served, then embarked on a long discourse concerning the increase in poaching during the past year.

"It really is too bad," he complained. "The occasional lost hare or partridge is only to be expected on an estate of this size, but wholesale thieving is intolerable. Our tenants are treated quite generously enough as it is."

Julia put down her knife and fork, to take up her wine-glass, smiling faintly. "You don't protect what you own well enough, Charles. Your gamekeeping staff is ludicrously small for an estate like Shenstone. Since acquiring Maxted's Farm and the surrounding acres, my father has taken on three more men. I doubt you have as many as three to protect your full acreage."

"Brancliffe is cutting numbers, not increasing them," Charles explained awkwardly.

"More fool you to allow it," came her brisk retort, increasing his discomfiture. "You run the estate on his behalf: when he dies, it will be yours outright. Tell him you *must* have more hands. If you haven't the pluck to demand the freedom to make decisions of your own, make them without his knowledge." She turned to Vivian. "Isn't that what you would do, if you were all set to inherit Shenstone?"

Narrowing his eyes at her sly thrust, he replied, "I'm not a man of the land, but a man of the sword. In military terms, anyone seizing what does not belong to him—like a poacher—usually provokes a war. It falls to our lot, as soldiers, to fight to get it back."

Julia's smile widened. "Exactly my point. *You* are a fighter, Vivian. Someone after my own heart."

"No, my dear Julia," he said, with a sly thrust of his own, "someone else is after that, not me."

"Are you enjoying the fish, Miss Duncan?" asked his brother. "We have it brought daily from the coast."

They all spoke then of the impressive coastline of Cornwall, Charles telling Leila the history of places such as Tintagel and Penzance so that she would not feel excluded from a conversation concerning an area unfamiliar to her. Julia enthused over the wild seas that pounded a coast that was tortured and indented, clearly delighting in the suggestion of untamed water cascading over the sharp rocky coves and inlets. Vivian watched her evident relish in talk of the power of the elements, and likened her once again to the women of ancient Rome. His gaze then passed to Leila, a girl with whom a man could surely find peace and great happiness.

She appeared to sense his scrutiny, and turned her head to meet his gaze fully for the first time since they had been discovered that morning in each other's arms. As their mutual acknowledgement of that moment returned in full, Vivian felt his pulse leap at the evidence in her eyes of an awareness of the manner in which their relationship had suddenly changed. She now knew, as he did, that there was no turning back.

The intimate contact between them was broken by the removal of the fish plates, which were replaced by others containing lamb cutlets. Encountering a sharp, icy glance from Julia, Vivian realised that he had fuelled her fire of battle with that speaking exchange with Leila. He could expect renewed attacks now. Well able to counter them himself, he hoped that she would not choose Leila as her victim, instead.

His own girl looked up at him reproachfully then. "This cutlet isn't one of your own lambs, I hope. Vivian."

Thinking of that delightful scene when he had placed the black lamb in her arms, he replied softly, "None of them is mine, my dear. I am simply a captain of Lancers, as I swore to you yesterday."

Faint colour crept into her cheeks at his reminder of her confusion on their way across the moor, and Julia's sharp eyes did not miss the exchange.

"It's probably one of ours, Vivian. We lose a number that way."

He shrugged. "If you allow them to stray onto this estate, you must expect to lose them."

"Until Brancliffe repairs his boundary walls, there is little we can do."

"I'll see to it shortly," put in Charles with an attempt at authority, plainly resenting the persistent interest in his brother from a girl he regarded as his chosen partner, not only for that evening, but for life.

"You have been saying that for months, Charles,' she told him dismissively, "and I have yet to see actions replace your words on the subject." Turning back to Vivian, she said, "The only course left open to us is to take something of yours, in return. Wouldn't you regard that as perfectly acceptable?"

"Acceptable, but most unlikely," he responded, well aware of her subtle play with words. "We guard what we have too well."

Fixing him with her bold luminous gaze, she said, "Really? I received the impression this morning that you gave it freely, to all and sundry."

"A false impression, my dear Julia," he countered calmly, conscious

138

of Leila growing very still on the other side of the table. "I heard somewhere that even Maxted's Farm and its surrounding acres were surrendered with definite conditions attached."

"You *heard* somewhere? My dear Vivian, you were standing beside me when the land changed hands. You cannot have forgotten that visit to Shenstone. I never shall," she finished with meaning.

"Of course he hasn't forgotten it," put in Charles irritably. "He was snowed in suffering from fever. That spell in Ashanti weakened his constitution—amongst other things, I understand."

Vivian felt a sense of shock at his brother's words, which plainly referred to something he had revealed in total confidence. Glancing quickly at Charles, never one to indulge in wounding taunts, he encountered belligerence to a surprising degree. It suggested that he had underestimated the situation regarding marriage to Julia. Charles must be more set on it than he had thought. Yet, surely he was not so besotted with the girl that he could not see that she did not share his enthusiasm, or that she had an iron will which would not be thwarted.

"I do not believe Vivian was weakened by the war in Ashanti," she declared then, "and I have proof of my case. I saw him battle to master a rogue stallion in driving snow, and I assure you I have never witnessed power and strength to match his. There is certainly nothing wrong with his constitution, Charles." Turning swiftly to Leila, she asked, "Is yours delicate, Miss Duncan? I have never known Vivian to drive a female in a carriage across the moors, so I must suppose that your health forbids you to ride."

"You suppose wrongly, Miss Marchbanks," Leila said quietly, "The demands of my profession are such that only robust health allows me to meet them."

"Ah yes, of course . . . I had forgotten the demands of your profession."

It was said with insulting innuendo, and Leila flushed with the shock of such rudeness in the midst of a civilised dinner-party, with servants standing within earshot of their conversation. Vivian burned with anger at Julia's behaviour, and spoke up immediately.

"The demands of Miss Duncan's profession have not only gained her my deepest admiration and respect, but also that of the entire population of London. Like Mama, she can enchant people with her musical talent, and send them home enriched by what they have seen and heard. It is a rare gift, and one that I find totally irresistible in a world full of poseurs and shams."

"No one could accuse you of being either, Vivian," Julia inserted swiftly. "Your status has been clear to everyone from the start, has it not?"

"I thank God for it, when I see the obligations from which I have been freed," he put in pointedly. "My life is my own, and so is my destiny. I would not surrender them for any number of acres, believe me."

An uneasy truce was declared then, and conversation was stilted but harmless as they finished their meal, then left the table to walk to the drawing-room. The men dispensed with port and cigars in order to remain with the two ladies, who gave their permission for the drinking of brandy whilst they had their coffee. Around a glowing fire, Charles embarked on the safe topic of the coming county show. In an obvious attempt to compensate for the fracas at the dinner-table, Charles was extremely attentive to Leila whilst explaining details of the annual event which all landowners relished.

Vivian was preoccupied by his ready defence of the girl sitting so erectly in the neighbouring chair. What had begun as "an exercise in tactics" had developed into a relationship he had not foreseen. Bringing her to his home had made the facts clear. At Shenstone, he was her protector and champion, her accepted partner in a foursome with his brother and Julia. He wanted the right to continue in that rôle but she had made it clear that a passionate liaison was out of the question. There was only one alternative, and Vivian realised that the truth had been lying dormant in him for some weeks. He had told Julia just now that his life and destiny were his own to follow; that he would not exchange that freedom for any number of acres. Yet he suddenly knew that the inheritance that should have been his had never seemed so beckoning.

Glancing around the room he had known since childhood, he saw the graceful furniture and works of art collected by past Veasey-Hunters. He also saw the porcelain, the jade, the ivory pieces everywhere; the antique clock standing in the corner with a pendulum swinging hypnotically; the carpet especially woven for that room—saw all those familiar things bathed in the seductive light of low lamps and flickering flame-glow, and seemed to be seeing them for the first time.

It was then that he realised Shenstone could be beautiful. Filled with love, the whole atmosphere would change. With flowers everywhere in summer, and leaping log fires in each room to give gaiety and warmth in winter, it could become a real home. Small boys could run through its corridors joyfully, could fill the vast rooms with the sound of youthful laughter, could chase across the moorland on ponies from the stables, carefree and confident. Small boys, and their beautiful artistic mother, could find life good and deeply worthwhile in this part of England, which boasted such splendours of nature. This place did not have to be repressive and cold, as he had always known it. His gaze then rested on Leila as she listened to Charles's account of livestock auctions, and he was swept with an alien sense of longing. All this was his by legacy of birth, yet he could offer her none of it. In that moment, he felt the cruelty of fate as a pain stronger than he could bear.

"I think there has been enough sentimentality around the fire," said Julia strongly, drawing his gaze from Leila with the interruption. "It appears that Miss Duncan has not yet been conducted around the ancestral home, Vivian. Shame on you! Did you think that she would not wish to see it? I cannot believe that a life spent amongst plaster antiques, simulated old masters, and glass diamonds has dulled her appreciation of the real thing." Her bold smile swept over Leila as she prepared to resume hostilities. "There is a Holbein here on which I should value your opinion."

Leila smiled back. "How flattering . . . but if Vivian has not been driven to show it to me, it cannot be worth my opinion."

Delighted by the quickness of her reply, Vivian said, "Holbein is not to Miss Duncan's taste."

"Not interested in old masters, Miss Duncan?" mused Julia. "You do not ride, and have rarely travelled outside the capital. Vivian has all too plainly instructed you in one subject only."

Masking his anger, Vivian got to his feet. "I shall redeem myself by showing Miss Duncan all that Charles will shortly inherit. Excuse us both, if you please."

Julia was ready for that. "It is too long since I saw some of my favourite pieces. As it is to be your brother's eventually, I feel he should do the honours this evening."

All four began strolling through the corridors and salons of Shenstone Hall, discussing the various heirlooms and rarities as they passed. In some places, it was necessary to proceed in pairs, so Vivian ensured that he always partnered Leila. Although she managed to hold her own in conversation that was skilfully engineered by Julia, there was a disturbing droop to her shoulders now, and an air of contemplation that suggested to Vivian a return of her distrust. He vowed to end the evening as soon as possible.

In consequence, when they reached the door of the armoury, he said, "We'll not bother with this, Charles. It can hold little of interest to ladies."

"On the contrary," cried Julia, swinging round in the dark panelled corridor, "it is one of the most exciting rooms in the house. Surely Miss Duncan will find more interest in weaponry and armour, than in all those things which have so far lamentably failed to please her. The theatrical profession frequently makes use of the gentlemanly art, does it not? The hero fighting the villain who has stolen his birthright," she quoted with meaning. "The crossing of swords to defend name and honour is surely something that she will appreciate."

"As a matter of fact, Viv, there is something I should like to show you," said his brother, pushing open the door. "Cousin Gerard thought it should be displayed here rather than at Hesketh Court."

There was an unpleasant chilliness in the atmosphere of that great gallery filled with suits of armour, shields, pikes, and ancient weaponry; sets of chain-mail, horse armour, helmets and brassards; breastplates, halberds, crossbows, and cruel flighted darts. Leila shivered, and Vivian lifted her cobwebby shawl higher around her shoulders. She seemed not to notice the small attention as she gazed around, absorbing the sombre implications of the exhibits.

On Vivian they had a more significant effect. In the low lamplight, the ghosts of past warriors appeared to flit in the dark shadowy corners, bringing him a return of disturbing memories of Ashanti. The faces of those two he had shot were suddenly as clear as if he were seeing them again. For as long as he lived, he would remember the utter terror etched upon them in the seconds before he had fired. That same terror had been in his own mind as he had knowingly betrayed his presence with those two shots. It had remained there as he had raced away from the scene, anticipating a spear in his back at any moment. The unforeseen consequences had produced doubts and recriminations that had dogged him, until fever had struck him down to put him in the hospital when the regiment was due to sail home. The doubts returned now, as he was reminded of pagan ritual, black eyes full of wildness, and tribal massacre of captives. He broke into a sweat of guilt. This room was too suggestive of martial savagery. It made him strangely uneasy.

Charles had reached the short wall at the far end of the long, narrow gallery, where swords, rapiers, sabres, scimitars and all manner of side-arms hung in impressive display.

"Here you are. It was used in battle by Father's great-great-uncle at Waterloo, if you remember," he said to Vivian, as he took a sword down from the brackets. "Feel the weight of it, and see how you'd like to enter battle with a weapon like that."

The sensation of holding the great heavy blade, plus the atmosphere of a room that had witnessed many a childhood humiliation, was so repressive, he said in clipped tones, "Our ancestors must have been men indeed, to wield such things with any accuracy."

A low voice behind him said, as he was about to hand the weapon back to his brother, "Are you saying that you are not man enough to handle it?"

He turned to find Julia challenging him with the same look in her eyes that had been there one evening just before Christmas. It reflected the sensation of basic emotions that the atmosphere in the room had aroused in him and, as he stood temporarily bemused, she took from the wall a slim rapier, adopting her stance with assurance.

"On guard, sir," she demanded.

Sensing subtle danger ahead, he murmured, "Very amusing, Julia."

"Do you care to defend yourself in a short demonstration of the gentlemanly art for Miss Duncan? She will have witnessed staged duels, where each thrust and parry is rehearsed. How much more she would enjoy a contest which is completely spontaneous, and which will display the *other* form of combat in which you excel." Over her shoulder, she asked, "What do you say, Miss Duncan?"

"It is for Vivian to decide what he wishes to do," came the quiet reply containing a hint of sadness.

Well aware of Julia's motives, Vivian said in matter-of-fact tones, "To give a demonstration, we should be armed with matching weapons."

"The advantage would be with you from the start," she countered smoothly. "Superior height, weight and strength, plus the fact that you are a professional warrior. Do you tell me that a cavalry officer declines to display his skill at the *arme blanche*?"

"No, really, Julia, this is hardly the time for it," protested Charles ineffectively.

Vivian seized the opportunity presented by his brother's intervention, however, and angled away to hang the sword back in place, saying, "A cavalry officer, even more than any other gentleman, never accepts a challenge to arms from a lady. It is a point of honour."

As he turned back, he found the tip of her rapier against his throat, and on her face the clear message that, if she had ever been teasing, she certainly was not now. Her real challenge had just begun, because he knew that he dared not move until she allowed him to by lowering that blade.

"Never accepts a challenge to arms from a lady?" she echoed with apparent relish. "Could it be because one is never offered?"

With the point of her blade gently pricking his skin, and the complete stillness of the other two telling him that they knew he was being held to some kind of strange ransom, he said as casually as he could, "Ladies offer a perpetual challenge, but they usually do so with gentler weapons."

"Which you know all too well how to successfully overcome—as I witnessed this morning," she breathed, betraying the real reason behind her behaviour. "Do you never tire of unequal odds and long for an opponent worthy of you, Captain Veasey-Hunter?"

It was said in light enough manner, but everyone in that room knew that her point held him immobile. He was being tormented in the most subtle manner, in front of a chorus-girl whom she regarded as an upstart. The longer the cat-and-mouse situation continued, the greater his humiliation before Leila. He had to end it quickly, and there was only one way of doing that.

"I found a great number of worthy opponents in Ashanti, Miss Marchbanks," he said quietly, putting up his hand in a swift movement to seize the blade and turn it away from his body.

He had underestimated her. Ready for such a move on his part, she stepped back, withdrawing the weapon in one lightning action. The blade cut across his palm, drawing blood, and he had to smother the gasp of pain it brought. For a suspended moment, their glances locked, and he saw in hers a blaze of passion that confirmed all his suspicions. Charles was living in a fool's paradise where this woman was concerned.

"*Touché*, sir," she remarked lightly, as she handed the rapier back to a white-faced Charles. "Another time, perhaps."

Putting his hand into his pocket, Vivian clutched his handkerchief inside it to staunch the blood. He kept it there as he moved across to Leila, standing like a slim ghost in her pale-lilac dress. He knew immediately that Julia had won hands down: Leila looked at him in the dim light of that room, and there was a goodbye in her eyes.

The evening could not recover after that. Julia had reduced the other three to an awareness of their mutual distrust of each other, and Leila chose to retire when they reached the foot of the main staircase. Vivian escorted her to her room, leaving his brother visibly shattered by the behaviour of the girl he accompanied back to the drawing-room. Still shaken by what had developed so unexpectedly, Vivian continued to clutch the handkerchief in his pocket as it grew wet with his blood. The stinging pain of the open cut was as great a restraint on him as Julia's actual presence there would have been. The symbolism of what she had done had resurrected all the humiliation of his childhood, and paraded it before the girl he had grown to love so much he could not risk losing her. Leila had just witnessed something she would never understand, any more than she had understood the wager for the earrings. Would he be able to explain it away . . . and would she give him the opportunity to do so?

They reached the door of the sitting-room adjacent to Leila's bedroom, without having exchanged a word. He stood aside after opening it for her, then followed her in as she turned to deny him entry. Totally hampered by the injured hand, which had to remain hidden, he had to let her walk the length of the room away from him before she turned to face him. She seemed unbearably remote; a shadow of the girl who had responded to his passion on the moor that morning.

"I should like to return to London tomorrow," she said quietly.

"Leila, please," he began, moving forward and cursing the wound that prevented his holding her in his arms.

"You promised to take me if I wished to go," she reminded him, before he could continue.

"That was yesterday, before you decided that Rose would come with me like a shot."

"Even Rose would decide that she had no place here, after what happened this evening."

They gazed at each other, searching for some way to pretend that nothing had changed between them. Finally, he said, "Sometimes, there is no choice but to accept the odds and do one's best in a situation one has not foreseen. I'll admit that I did not emerge with much credit, but you . . . my dearest girl, I was immensely proud of you tonight."

"For not letting you down? For using the right knives and forks, for not flattening my vowels, and for struggling to hold my own like any chorus-girl in a lord's mansion?"

He drew in his breath at her wounding words. "That's below the belt, Leila."

"Was it?" she cried in sudden passion. "I wouldn't know that. The peculiar rules of behaviour adopted by what we chorus-girls know as 'the nobs' are a complete mystery to me. Thank heaven they are, for it seems to me they are all designed to hurt and humiliate."

Moving nearer, he said huskily, "You're hurting me with every word right now. Is that what you really want to do?" At her silence, he went on, "I was proud of you tonight, because you showed me how wonderful Shenstone could be with the right people beside me. Please, *please* stay a little longer."

She turned away with a little shake of her head, and walked to gaze at the embers in the fireplace. "It's all make-believe, Vivian, as Mr Gilbert says. I am not really the glamorous creature Lindley's has made me. I'm an orphan with little education. You said this morning that it was only a matter of time. Well, time has now run out. You made it plain out on the moor that you can't forget that I'm a beautiful young woman . . . and Julia went out of her way to remind me this evening that there *is* only one thing men like you can have from girls like me. Take me back where I belong, Vivian. Please, oh *please*, take me home.''

His grandfather gave Vivian a cold look the following morning as he entered the sickroom. It was not in response to the old man's command, but to say goodbye. It remained dark on that side of the house, despite the warmth of the sunshine outside. Lord Brancliffe lay in his bed near the window, wrapped in rugs, his face even more hawk-like than usual.

"My instructions were that you were to bring that girl," he said, with a vigour that belied his illness.

Vivian ignored that, saying, "Good morning, sir. How are you today?"

"Damned loose living," the old man snarled. "I will not have you serving your mares under my roof."

"Is that why my father served his under the roofs of other men?"

With unexpected swiftness, the gnarled hand seized the walking-cane on the bed, and swished it through the air. It caught the back of Vivian's unbandaged left hand as it hung at his side.

"If you dare to speak to me again in that manner, boy, I'll have you horsewhipped off my property. I shall take great pleasure in doing it myself."

"You could not do it personally," he retorted with a bite in his tone. "It is time you came to terms with the truth that you are no longer the man you were, and that my brother and I are no longer small boys to be caned."

"Then do not deceive me like a small boy! You said nothing on your arrival of this affair. It was left to Bates to inform me that you had brought one of your lightskirts with you."

"On my arrival, you were being dosed and settled for the night by Dr Simms. We exchanged no more than several sentences, at his request, if you recall," Vivian said, with an effort to remain calm. "Bates informed you incorrectly, if it really was he who referred to my guest in such terms. Miss Duncan is a virtuous and valued friend, who has recently suffered a tragic bereavement. I brought her to Shenstone in an attempt to help her to recover from her shock."

"Why is she not in decent black, if that is the case?" charged his grandfather, pointing through the window with the cane.

Vivian looked out and saw Leila, dressed in a pretty blue costume, strolling the paths in the sunshine. The storm that had arisen at her rebuff last night was gathering in force, and the sight of this girl he loved, ready and impatient to leave, brought a return of his inner vision of how different Shenstone would be with her living there.

146

Suddenly, he was aware of the penalty of his birth as never before. What could he offer a woman? A nomadic life travelling from one garrison town to another, an income that was due to his mother's generosity, a name tarnished by a past scandal, a military career with a shadow already hanging over it. If Shenstone were his, he would open its doors and windows, let in fresh air to blow away the ghosts of unhappiness trapped here. He would set the servants washing porcelain and glass, polishing the beautiful mellow wood, cleaning the antique carpets so that the subtle colour of their patterns glowed once more. The corridors would echo with laughter as he chased her through them, to catch her, breathless and eager for his kisses, in his arms. The formal gardens would be a constant blaze of blooms, and they would wander the many paths, arms around each other, dazed by happiness. He would teach her to ride, and they would canter across the moor with the wind in their hair and exhilaration in their breasts. He would catch lambs for her to hold, and tell her that she held his life in her hands, also. If Shenstone were his . . .

"You will bring her here to me," came the cracked command that shattered the summer images in his mind, leaving only the dark storm clouds.

Turning back to the bed, he said, "No, sir."

The cane thumped the bed. "Dammit, she is staying in *my* house. You will do as I say."

"If you wish to insult her, you must come downstairs to do it. I will not bring her up here."

The old man considered him for a moment or two suspiciously. "Gallantry, eh? Who is this young woman? What is her pedigree?"

Losing his control, he said, "She is not a mare. I told you that just now."

"Your tongue has grown a damn sight too smooth, of late. You will curb it, or I'll do it for you," threatened the man who believed he still wielded power. "You refuse to tell me about this creature? Then I was right. She is a trollop of yours. Get her out of my house, d'ye hear? A room in an inn is the place for tumble-wenching. I will not countenance the presence of whores here."

"We are both leaving, "Vivian snapped, unable to control his temper any longer. "You never understood my mother, so you would certainly not appreciate the qualities of a girl who brought beauty to this grim old place for a while." Thrusting his bandaged right hand into his pocket, he spoke his mind to a man he no longer feared. "You imagine that you have chosen your sure successor for my brother, but you have under-estimated her badly. You ruled this household when it contained a bewildered, ill-used young woman, and two little boys. All three were defenceless and easy to dominate. Julia Marchbanks yearns to rule those who are strong and independent, longs for power more subtle and rare than yours. Charles provides insufficient challenge to her sadistic nature. She will never become mistress here, I swear. You will be thwarted, at last, and I regret that I shall not be responsible for it.

"You have made Shenstone a place of repression and misery; you have neglected the estate to the extent that it may well die with you. My poor brother is shackled to it, but I am free to leave. I have had enough of the ghosts waiting to take possession here. You are welcome to them. They make excellent companions for you. Goodbye, sir."

Collecting his coat and hat from his room, Vivian then made his way to the main staircase at the foot of which the suitcases stood ready. Charles was talking to Leila, who had come indoors at the approach of the carriage, and helping her to don the coat that matched the blue costume. They both glanced up at the sound of his descent, and his brother frowned.

"Good Lord, Viv, you look as if you've seen a ghost."

"A ghost is something from the past," he said heavily, noticing the dust that lay on high ledges in the panelling. "I was thinking of the spirits of the future."

Casting him a curious glance, Charles then led Leila outside to assist her into the sprung carriage, tucking a rug across her knees before coming back into the hall.

"I'm sorry that Miss Duncan found herself unable to stay a little longer," he said as Vivian shrugged into his overcoat. "It was a mistake to bring her here, however. I told you that at the outset."

"Yes, it was," he agreed forcefully, "but not nearly so big a mistake as you are making in imagining a future with Julia. You had a glimpse last night of the kind of woman she is. For God's sake be warned, and start looking elsewhere for a bride."

Charles stiffened. "I believe we have already thrashed that out. The affair is quite settled."

"Because Brancliffe has set his heart on it? It is growing increasingly clear to me, Charles, that you'll accept anything to ensure youself a peaceful life. If you are to take over all this before long, I suggest that you try standing on your own two feet. They are quite large enough to support you, and I'm growing a little tired of hearing your complaints whilst you stand by allowing yourself to be cheated by an old man with one foot in the grave. This is your inheritance. Try fighting for it, instead of wringing your hands and continuing to regard Brancliffe as the Almighty. He is not." Picking up his hat, he added, "Next time you have an emergency over land or horses, don't expect me to come down here in an attempt to help extricate you from something you haven't the courage to prevent."

With that, he went out to the waiting carriage, leaving Charles open-mouthed with mild shock. He had one more comment, however, as Dobbins gathered the reins.

"Don't send a telegram summoning me here again. Just inform me of the date of the funeral. Neither Brancliffe nor I wish to be together when he breathes his last." Nodding at Dobbins, he said, "We are ready to leave."

His brother still appeared thunderstruck, when the carriage rounded the curve in the driveway and headed for the ornamental arch across the main entrance. As they passed beneath it, Vivian had a strange conviction that he would never see Shenstone again.

They were both quiet during the first part of the long train journey. Leila appeared absorbed in the passing scene; Vivian was introspective. He could still see that harsh face on the pillows, see it twisting into an expression of contempt as he had called Leila a whore. He could see Julia's derision as she had gazed down at the open-air love-making, her air of superiority toward a girl she condemned as a wanton because of her profession, her undisguised triumph as she had humiliated them both with the point of a rapier. He realised then the similarity between Leila and his mother. Her colouring was entirely different, but she was also delicate and graceful, generous with praise, utterly feminine, and as painfully vulnerable as Margaret Veasey-Hunter had been. They shared a passion for music and singing, artistic talent that produced a vibrant and beguiling personality. Leila had brought Shenstone to life for a while, but she had been crushed last night by a stronger will. Even in that, the two were linked.

As the train crossed into Devon, then Wiltshire on its way to London, Leila fell asleep. Vivian studied her, lost in a maze of thoughts and emotions, a sense of impending loss invading him with every mile. The steward came to announce the serving of luncheon, and Vivian shook the sleeping girl awake. She ate very little, just sat watching the green countryside slipping away behind the window of the carriage, while he worked his way through an entrée and some pork chops. When he poured some wine for her, she mentioned the bandages on his hand for the first time.

"It must have been a deep cut. Is it very painful?"

Unhappy at her perception, he replied gently, "Not half as painful as your silence. Leila, you really don't have to return yet. Gilbert gave you an entire week in which to recover. Will you let me take you to a hotel—somewhere in peaceful surroundings, where you will be fussed over and allowed to rest?" At her expression, he sighed. "I'll return to Brighton, if you say that I must."

"No, Vivian," she told him, with a small shake of her head. "The shock of Rose's death has faded a little. I'm very grateful for all you have done for me, but I should like to get back to work now. I miss it, believe it or not."

He had to accept her decision yet, when they reached her basement and he went in to light the lamps for her, she seemed as daunted by the place as he. Everything within him protested at what he was doing. She should be surrounded by pretty things, by comfort and luxury. The storm within him began to rage once more, as he looked at the cheap furniture, the thin curtains, the bric-à-brac from pawnshops, and the ugly kitchen range that had to be blackened daily and filled with coal from a heavy iron hod. Then he looked at the tiny yard outside the open front door, where he had once stood with Oscar. The wall rose up a mere few feet from the sole window, blocking most of the light. He thought of this same girl sitting in the graceful rooms of his old home. He thought of Charles treating her civilly, under protest, and Julia snapping her sensual fingers in that lovely face which now looked so bleak. He thought of his grandfather accusing him of bringing a lightskirt into his house, and the storm broke, releasing a force he could no longer control.

Walking up behind her as she stood at the table unpinning her hat, he pulled her back against his chest and held her close, as he said against her temple, "It's no use. I can't leave you here and just walk away. I admit that I once expected to make you my mistress and set you up in an apartment—like Lampton and Rose Heywood. That was before I discovered the real Leila Duncan. You're wrong, darling. It isn't the glamorous creature created by Lester Gilbert that I have grown to love, but a girl who so possesses me I am nothing when she is not there. I want you, Leila. I want what girls like you can give to men like me—sunshine and laughter, a sense of proportion, and eternal devotion."

He began kissing her hair, her temple, her neck, tightening his arms around her slender body to show his yearning to protect her.

"You wouldn't have to live at Shenstone, you know that, and I wouldn't ask you to go anywhere where you felt you couldn't be happy. It would mean leaving Lindley's, of course, but you could continue your singing lessons, if you wished. I'll make you happy, darling, give you anything you want. There would never be anyone but you, I swear, because you have captured my heart, my senses and my future. For

God's sake, let me take you away from here and look after you as I long to do."

He then realised that she was unnaturally still, as if she had not heard or understood what he was telling her. Turning her swiftly to face him, he said urgently, "I'm asking you to marry me, my darling girl; to become my wife as soon as possible."

Shock silenced him. Her eyes were full of a wildness bordering on fear; tears stood on her chalk-white cheeks. In the grip of something frighteningly incomprehensible to him, she seemed incapable of speaking, staring at his face as if he were one of the ghosts they had left behind in Cornwall.

# CHAPTER EIGHT

April and May were the most difficult months of Leila's life. She hardly knew how she got through them. The evenings were occupied with performances which mercifully deadened her unhappiness. Even then, she was reminded strongly of Rose the moment she entered by the stage-door. It was fortunate that *Felicity May* was a new show with few memories of playing it with her friend, and her promotion to a sextet of singing girls meant her work fulfilled her more than it ever had before.

All the same, there was a terrible sense of aloneness in her life once more. On stage she felt the magic. When she came off it quickly died. She still chaffed with the other girls, still joined in the cheerful complaints and never-ending theatrical gossip, but the ghost of Rose was always there beside her to put an ache of loss in her throat and breast. Miles Lampton had managed to hang on to his wealthy fiancée, and married her at the end of May. Leila felt it was the final betrayal of the dead girl, and wept over press pictures of the wedding. The scandal had been put aside; the columns gushed admiration and respect for the influential couple. Rose was buried and forgotten.

Leila was tormented by an even greater unhappiness that could not be buried and forgotten. She did not know what to do, how to handle it. Vivian's proposal of marriage had shattered her—more so than his less honourable one had done. She had been expecting that. Now, having made her an offer she would have given up *anything* to accept, he would not take no for an answer. Her desperate protestations that it would not work because of the difference in their backgrounds, or because his family and friends would never accept her, were airily brushed aside by him. Even her dramatically noble assertion that marriage to her would ruin not only his social standing but his military career, was countered by assurances that his regiment would be honoured and delighted to accept a Lindley Girl into its ranks.

Although she could always hold out against his arguments, his love-making weakened her every time, and he knew it. He would not stay away, and she was unable to summon enough resolution to refuse to see him. After a few weeks, she had wildly offered to become his mistress; the very thing she had violently resisted before. Vivian, equally contrary, refused her offer. Tight-lipped, he had told her he would have no one calling her his lightskirt, and would take her as his wife, or not at all. In desperation, she had cried that it would have to be the latter. He had stayed away for an entire week. Then, one evening, he had been at the stage-door with an armful of flowers, and they were soon back where they had started.

Not the least part of Leila's anguish during that terrible period had been the thought of another woman becoming his wife. Knowing she could never tell him about Frank Duncan, she also knew the affair would have to end somehow. They were making each other desperately unhappy, and the responsibility for causing the break was undeniably hers. Yet she shied from the burden, unable to bear the prospect of his finding another woman to whom he would pledge his life and love—a woman who was free to marry. Julia Marchbanks had shown an intense interest in him, despite the suggestion that she was to marry the staid Charles. Leila could not forget that rapier held at Vivian's throat; a symbolic act of possession, without doubt. If a woman like Julia ever won him, he would have to sacrifice his soul along with his heart.

Saving her from complete despair were her singing lessons. Professor Halstein was a small undemonstrative man who believed in hard work. Leila did it willingly. The fulfilment she derived from hearing herself produce sounds more exciting than she had believed possible made the effort very rewarding. Her scales were improving weekly, and her teacher, who was normally very sparing of compliments, told her that he thought he detected the makings of a soprano beneath her warbling.

He had told her she should have a piano at home, in order to practise each day. When she had mentioned it to Vivian, a piano had arrived the following day on a delivery dray. She accepted this, as she also accepted the payment for her lessons, because she believed the money came from the sale of Julia's earrings. Having met the girl, that thought gave her an even sharper pleasure. In any case, Vivian gave her so many presents now which he would not allow her to refuse.

Her promotion to the sextet which, together with Franz Mittel-heiter's great popularity, was bringing the crowds to see *Felicity May*, was also bringing Leila more and more admirers. Wealthy men-about-town, who were delighted by her figure in the tight-fitting uniform she wore on stage, were even further dazzled by the female version who greeted them at the stage-door. Jewels, flowers and other extravagant gifts were showered on her by this growing bevy of beaux. She accepted it all as part of the performance, as instructed by Lester Gilbert, and it was rare for her to return to her basement immediately after the final curtain.

Her inclusion in the sextet had also meant an increase in salary, most of which had to be spent on clothes. Some of her escorts she quickly discouraged; others she saw regularly and liked for their wit and gaiety. Those suppers after the show meant only two things to her, however: good food that was essential to her health and, therefore, her voice; and delay in returning to her basement where unhappiness could no longer be held at bay.

To her dismay, Vivian revealed wild jealousy over every invitation she accepted, every man she knew, every present she received. With the approach of summer, military manoeuvres and parades increased. Cavalry regiments were much in demand as escorts to those visiting statesmen and rulers whose status commanded an official procession through the streets. Tied by his professional duties, Vivian saw less of Leila than before, and he bitterly resented the time she spent with other men. Finding him equally passionate in love and anger, she felt helpless to placate him. They quarrelled frequently, until he finally accused her of being incapable of genuine feelings.

"What is it you really want from me?" he demanded savagely as they walked together in the park one Sunday. "When I intended to become your lover, you flew into a virtuous rage and ejected me from the cab. Now I long to be your husband, you suggest becoming my mistress. Is it so that you would remain free, to play mistress to all those presently tempting you with the sparkling incitements to surrender? You underestimate me. I never share a woman's favours with all and sundry."

His words hurt her so much she could not speak for the thickness of tears in her throat. When he saw her distress he drew her to the seclusion of some trees, holding her close against him in his own distress.

"Darling, you know the thought of you with other men tears me apart," he murmured in desperation. "For God's sake, be my wife. Let's have an end to all this."

Desperate herself, she had answered against his coat, "Let's have an end to it, by all means. Stay away from me, Vivian."

He was back two days later at the stage-door. She told her escort for the evening that she was indisposed, then went with Vivian. The meeting only ended in another quarrel, and she did not see him for two weeks after that. She was just at the uttermost depths of misery, believing she had finally lost him, when she walked from Professor Halstein's house one afternoon to find a captain of lancers in full regalia, on Oscar, beside a waiting hansom. She was shocked by the naked unhappiness in his eyes which usually danced with lively amusement.

"I've been taking part in a military extravaganza in Hyde Park," he told her hollowly. "Lester Gilbert would have been impressed."

He rode beside the cab all the way to her basement, and she sat composing a stern speech to recite to him on arrival. Instead, she flew joyfully into his arms and agreed, with fervour, to forget all he had said to her in his unreasonable jealousy. They spent an hour together with a tray of tea, then it was time for her to prepare for the theatre.

He kissed her lingeringly, then confessed that he should have been at a royal garden-party rather than with her. "I shall have to go there now and trust I have not been missed," he said with a smile. "But Sunday is all mine. Come down to Brighton on the milk train, and I'll hire a carriage to drive you out through the orchards where the blossom is now at its best." He took both her hands to his lips, and looked at her significantly over the top of them to say, "There's an inn I know of where we can stay overnight if it grows too late, or if the weather breaks."

Knowing only too well that he was telling her he had surrendered, and meant to take her as a mistress that weekend, she could not bring herself to answer for a moment. It was almost certain he had used the inn before with other women. She felt deep resentment that he should take her there. Yet she had refused his pleas to treat her with honour, so she could hardly condemn this.

When she agreed to be on the train, he picked up his helmet ready to leave, turning at the door to ask casually if she had a supper engagement that evening. She answered cautiously that she was engaged to meet Billy Middleton, one of her regular escorts.

"Well . . . have a nice time," he returned with a nonchalance that failed to suggest he did not care. "You can always tell him about *Cyril* Rhodes."

Reminder of their special intimate joke hurt her unbearably. "I still think it suits him better than *Cecil*," she said quietly.

There was a multitude of words behind the look he gave her across the room. "I'm sure he'd willingly change it, if you told him that. You seem able to make a man do anything you wish, in the end."

On the following day Nellie came round from Clivedon Place. Leila was in the midst of vocal exercises, but the interruption came as a welcome relief. Seeing Vivian the day before had upset her, and she was worried about Sunday. It would make neither of them happy, in the long run, yet they could not continue as they were. Desire for each other was growing uncontainable, and her constant feeble excuses for not marrying him could only be construed by him in one way. Becoming his mistress might satisfy their longings, but it would certainly increase his jealousy of every other man she knew. With that on her mind her singing was suffering, and she thankfully abandoned her scales, despite Nellie's wish to listen.

"Not when you are paying me one of your rare visits. That would be awfully rude," she said with a smile, warming the teapot with water from the hissing kettle on the hob.

The young servant-girl gazed at her. "You are awful grand, these days, Lily. The way you speak is like them toffs as come to visit Sir Frederick and 'er Ladyship. Look at these cups'n that. Real china wiv a pattern on! You must 'ave ever so much money now."

"The tea-set was a present from Viv . . . from a friend."

"A *gentleman* friend?" came the awed question.

Leila measured tea from the caddy. "Yes, Nellie, I have a great many gentlemen friends, who show their appreciation of my performance by giving me gifts. They are so wealthy, it's no different from giving a cabbie or a waiter a tip for good service."

"Oooh!" uttered the girl uncomprehendingly. "A tea-set, though. Aren't you afraid you'll break it?"

Leila returned to the table, bearing the elegant pot belonging to the set. "Not really. Treat it like an old chipped cup and there's no problem. It's when you start being extra careful that breakages occur."

"Oooh!" uttered the girl again, overwhelmed by something beyond her sphere of understanding.

"Will you have a biscuit . . . or there's a Dundee cake in the pantry. I'll cut you a slice, if you'd prefer that."

A flush covered Nellie's plain face. "I wouldn't say no."

The cake was fetched, a generous slice cut and put on a plate with a cake fork. Nellie sat staring at it.

"What's the fork for?"

It was Leila's turn to colour slightly. She had forgotten how Lily Lowe and all those like her lived. "I'll cut it into smaller pieces for you," she said, slicing the cake into fingers before Nellie could take the whole piece in her hand and bury her face in it.

While she poured tea, she listened to Nellie's account of all the tittle-tattle of belowstairs at Clivedon Place. It sounded to Leila like another world, of which she could never have been a part. Then she heard the latest news of Nellie's Joe, who still could not marry her because he had not yet been promoted to checker at the brewery. When asked gently if she was being good, Nellie blushed. Leila concluded that Joe would never propose, because he was getting all he wanted already. That train of thought reminded her painfully of the coming Sunday, and the inn to which Vivian meant to take her. How would she know whether or not they occupied the same room in which he had taken his pleasure of countless others before her? How would the affair ever end, if she allowed this stage to be reached?

"Take care, Nellie," she warned sadly. "It's quite all right for the Joes of this world . . . or the Miles Lamptons. They relinquish all responsibility as soon as things become difficult."

"Oooh!" breathed Nellie, admiring Leila's big words more than she heeded them.

Ten minutes and another slice of cake later, Nellie pulled an envelope from her pocket. "Oh, this come two weeks ago. It's from another funny place, but the writin's different . . . Cook says," she added, being illiterate herself.

Leila looked at the letter curiously. It had been sent from a place called Hyderabad, but the handwriting was not Frank's, and the letter had an official stamp on it. Curiosity turned to apprehension as she took it up in her hand. Something must have happened to Frank. An educated hand had addressed the envelope, and the postage had been paid by the army. Her pulse began to thud and she was appalled at the joyous leap of her heart. Oh, dear God, if Frank had been killed there would be no obstacle to her becoming Mrs Veasey-Hunter; no need for that inn on Sunday. There would be no more distressing quarrels, unconquerable jealousy, or lies between them. With shaking hands she slit the envelope and read the headed sheet inside.

Dear Miss Lowe,

I am writing on behalf of one of the men in my company who is unable to pen this letter himself. I regret to inform you that Trooper Frank Duncan was engaged in a tribal skirmish in which he conducted himself bravely, but received wounds that necessitated the amputation of his right arm. He has been granted a medical discharge and is returning to England on the S.S. Marktown, docking at Tilbury on June 8th. He is most anxious that you should be acquainted with these facts and, as I understand you are a close friend and he has no family, I am very sorry to have to impart such sad news to you.

Assuring you of my . . .

The rest of the words blurred as she stared at that piece of paper, Nellie and her Joe totally forgotten.

Instead of going to see the orchard blossoms, Vivian received a letter from Leila that weekend. The shock of its contents affected him drastically in the days that followed. Every word of that letter was printed on his mind, every cruel phrase haunted him. On a single page she had stated that her career meant more to her than anything; that his constant pestering and immature jealousy was upsetting her concentration on vocal training. He must, therefore, accept that any kind of liaison with him, now or in the future, was out of the question. She had ended by stating that she would pay for future lessons by selling the presents he had given her.

Unable to accept the savage rupture, he spent his off-duty time in drinking heavily, or thundering across the Sussex downs on Oscar, hoping to exorcise the demons which had taken possession of him. To no one could he admit that he was broken apart by love for a woman he could not win. He had a reputation for dalliance with those whose honour was long forgotten, or who were not averse to abandoning it for his sake. He had thought himself a man with a good balance of virtues and vices, and had the freedom to give a little of himself to as many of his fellow-creatures as he wished, in compensation for a lonely childhood. Then he had encountered an elusive, enigmatic girl, who had swept aside all he had believed he knew of the female sex, to catch him in a trap from which he could not now escape.

These days, he saw in everything an echo of what she would say on the subject, how she would feel about it. Leila had opened his eyes to fresh points of view. She had shown him the other side of *affaires* like that between Lampton and the Heywood girl; she had revealed a surprising sense of honour based on personal pride rather than pride of ancestry or social position. Through her he had learned of the determination to succeed, and the actor's permanent struggle against being out of work and on the streets. Very often he had been humbled by her, mostly unintentionally, but had found the experience not unpleasant. He was haunted by her changing spontaneous expressions, her immense enthusiasms, her delightful confusion when teased, the sound of her voice and her fiery defence of the quality produced by Franz Mittelheiter against the mediocrity advocated by Lester Gilbert.

Night after night, he lay in bed racked with jealousy, torturing himself further by imagining her at Romano's, wearing some other man's jewels and telling him about the performance, or Lester Gilbert's latest innovation. Worse, he imagined her relating the details of her visit to a "lord's mansion", where a past admirer had raced over a meadow to catch a black lamb for her. Worst of all, he knew he would do it again, if she would only let him.

Finally, into the darkness of each night, he acknowledged that he had been challenged in a manner far exceeding anything Julia had instigated. Leila, however, had revelled in his weakness rather than his strength. She had been playing an exquisitely clever game ever since that evening when she had thrown him from the cab in a righteous rage. Acting a part, she had induced him to beg her friendship, promising to treat her only as such. Next, she had cleverly contrived free singing lessons by playing on his conscience over the earrings. By then, he had been so captivated he had taken her to his home, obliged Charles and Julia to entertain her as his guest, and defended her in the face of their contempt, as well as that of his grandfather.

Leila had played cat and mouse with him, until he had been prepared to do anything she asked. Revenge must have been very sweet indeed. For all his sophistication and sexual experience, he had been brought right to his knees by a virgin-faced little nobody of a showgirl.

For several weeks he went around like a man possessed, snapping at his fellows, bellowing at his men, and lashing his horses. His commanding officer took him aside for a man-to-man talk, but learned little from a subordinate who had always been something of a problem because of his curious background. The other officers of the 49th fell into the usual two camps. Vivian's friends excused him to a man; those who had always regarded him as less than a true gentleman, saw his behaviour as reverting to type with a vengeance.

The leader of this set of blue-bloods, Major Theodore Maule Redfern Fennimoore, had never socially accepted the man he sneeringly termed "Veasey-Hunter's by-blow", and exchanged words with Vivian only when military duties demanded that he must. With antecedents traceable to the first Tudor king of England, and boasting personal acquaintance with the Prince of Wales, Theo Fennimoore regarded himself as the pride of the regiment. His cronies tended to agree with him, and shunned Vivian more in support of their hero than because of his illegitimate status. Although it had been a little awkward, at times, their attitude had never caused serious trouble, until one afternoon several weeks after Vivian's receipt of Leila's letter.

The 49th was "At Home" to the British public on a midsummer Saturday, when temperatures soared to record heights. Men and beasts alike were bedevilled by the heat as they performed demonstrations of horsemanship, regimental drill, and all-out cavalry charges. Children were given rides on staid, retired chargers, young women were thrilled by brawny troopers in uniforms suggestive of heroism, who winked at them when no officers were near by, and the elderly were reassured of the might of their nation when they saw the gleaming lances and clear-cut features of these soldiers of the ageing Queen Victoria. The warlike aspect was softened by sporting events to show the British soldier as basically fair-minded and generous. The tent-pegging team, which included Vivian, demonstrated that the lance was not simply a lethal weapon, and a cricket match between the regiment's eleven and a team of gentlemen of Sussex proved that the Lancers were virile healthy youngsters, who would display the same sporting spirit in war as they did in the battle with the willow.

The highlight of the day, so far as the officers were concerned, was the attendance of Edward, Prince of Wales, to present a chalice to their Mess in recognition of their achievements in Ashanti. Due to evening commitments, the heir to the throne was to make the presentation during a light tea to be served at four o'clock. Accordingly, apart from those on duty, the officers gathered at three-thirty in the ante-room, sweltering in their full regalia, and longing for the cups of tea they would not be allowed until "Teddy" had been served with his on arrival. A message informing them that their royal guest was almost an hour behind his schedule was greeted with dark significant optical exchanges, since groans of protest would have been considered very bad form from officers and gentlemen. However, as the commanding officer was himself dying of thirst, he ordered the staff to serve glasses of chilled lime-juice to his subordinates standing around spurred, and wearing clothes that enclosed them like a second skin.

The babble of conversation was on one subject alone: the Committee of Inquiry into the disastrous Jameson Raid eighteen months ago, which had failed to secure British control over the Transvaal and its gold-fields. The affair had caused world-wide protest and, although the leaders of the rebel army had been imprisoned, Cecil Rhodes had tardily been summoned to London to explain his part in the warlike action and, it was hoped, to clear the British Government of complicity. The findings had that morning been released, and all those in opposition to the present government were calling it a "whitewash". The enemies of Cecil Rhodes, who were many, were furious because he had suffered no penalty despite admitting master-minding the attack.

Vivian stood within a group of his friends, his mind elsewhere. He was in a black mood after another restless night that had left him with a pounding head. In consequence, his performance at tent-pegging had been deplorable for a man who rarely missed a pick-up on the end of his lance. He had roared imprecations at the corporal who had set the pegs, snapped at his team-mates when they had tried to commiserate, and jumped from his charger, Merlin, to hand the animal to his groom without a word. He was going to pieces. Acknowledgement of the fact merely increased his self-disgust, blackening his mood further. How much longer would it take to ride out the humiliating blow of that letter, with its astounding implications? How much longer would it be before he felt free and full of confidence again?

"Some of your people went out there, didn't they, V.V.H.?" asked a voice beside him, bringing him back to the present.

"Went where?" he queried in flat tones.

"The Transvaal."

Frowning at John Kinson, who was a close associate, he tried to collect his thoughts.

"Come on, old fellow, pull yourself together," advised Gerald Piper in a friendly manner. "We've all had bad days. I once missed every damn peg there was."

"You always miss every damn peg," John commented frankly, turning his attention back to Vivian. "I recall that you told me some of Brancliffe's miners went out to the gold-fields when the tin slump came."

Through the muzziness in his head came temporary clarity. "Yes. A large number of men from all over Cornwall sailed out there to seek their fortunes. I doubt any one of them succeeded, with Kruger bleeding them white with taxes and levies."

"Just my point," enthused John, embracing the group with his glance. "Rhodes was right to instigate the raid. He deserves our admiration for his attempt to improve conditions for our countrymen."

"I can't agree," argued a young lieutenant named Jeffries. "He risked starting a fresh war with the Boers. After the humiliating trouncing they gave us last time I, for one, would not relish embarking on a long campaign in South Africa. Ashanti was enough for me. I'm very happy to remain here for a few years in peacetime garrison duties."

"South Africa can't be compared with Ashanti," said another of the group. "My sister and her husband have settled there, and write that it is a splendid and beautiful country."

"Which is why Rhodes wants *all* of it," pointed out Gerald Piper. "Dash it all, the Boers are farmers, who show little interest in digging up the gold. Why should they be allowed to penalise our countrymen who do? Think, though, if the Jameson Raid had been successful."

"It would have started a war," insisted the youthful Jeffries.

"It would also have brought down the government," put in Vivian, trying to concentrate on the subject. "Although Chamberlain has been cleared of complicity, the enemies of the Empire will remain convinced of it. Rhodes nobly shouldered full responsibility, and has been allowed to return freely to Cape Town as his reward."

"Rhodes won't give up because of one set-back. We'll have a war with the Boers over that gold before long," swore Gerald Piper. "He has scooped the diamond bounty into his own coffers without bloodshed, but Paul Kruger is determined to fight for the Transvaal. We'll be out there with guns yet, take my word for it."

"He won't risk a full-scale war," reasoned Vivian, all the talk of Cecil Rhodes reminding him of a blue-eyed girl who could never remember his name. "Rhodes is no military tactician, that much is obvious from the failure of the raid."

"What about that Matabele business?" charged Gerald Piper.

"What about it?"

"He put down the rebellion, didn't he?"

"*Soldiers* put down the rebellion," Vivian declared with a touch of belligerence. "It would never have arisen if Rhodes hadn't taken his troops from Rhodesia for Jameson's use. I went there *en route* from Ashanti, don't forget, and heard the opinions of those close to Rhodes. A great man, there is no doubt, but he would never make a general. Impetuous, single-minded, unwilling to take advice, he seems to chase his ambitions in the manner of a man watching the sand running through an hour-glass." Tossing back the last of his chilled lime-juice, Vivian placed his empty glass onto the tray being carried between the grouped officers by a steward. "Even his most stalwart friends admit that Rhodes is contemptuous of the military men he uses to gain his ends, and refuses to see that the ruthless approach that he has toward gaining power cannot be used in warfare."

"So you are not one of the man's admirers, V.V.H.?" asked John.

"Quite the contrary," he said, wishing his head would stop thudding as hard as it was. "My mother, who lives in Rhodesia and knows him well, speaks very highly of his unique qualities. I have every respect for her opinions and judgement. In any case, he must be one of my heroes," he went on forcibly. "Rhodes is a man with no title or fortune, who has climbed above many who have both—proof enough that a man is what he is, not what his ancestry or bank balance makes him."

"We'd all agree with that," put in Jeffries hastily.

"God, I wish H.R.H. would dig in his spurs," commented a captain named Christianson, in an attempt to change the subject. "The scent of smoked salmon and cut cucumber is tormenting my taste-buds."

John Kinson glanced down the room at the tempting array of tea-time fare set out beneath the protection of fly-netting. "A nice breeze would help. The smell of the food would then be carried out through the window, instead of lingering invitingly."

They all fell silent momentarily, contemplating the delayed tea, and into that silence came a loud drawling voice from the nearby group.

"I say the fellow's a dyed-in-the-wool scoundrel. Empire-builder, be damned! His public patriotism cloaks his private ambitions. A country named after him, Prime Minister of Cape Colony, uncrowned king of Kimberley, nominal emperor of the Matabeles, and premier Rand-lord, his thoughts are more of his own power than that of his mother-land and her people."

"Come, that's a trifle stiff, Theo," protested a titled captain standing beside Major Fennimoore. "Rhodes has increased the Empire's territories no end."

"Went to some damned obscure grammar school," came the fierce rejoinder from the senior man. "Comes from yeoman stock. Made his reputation through double-dealing, treachery, and the sycophantic courting of those who could help him. Found myself in the same company as Rhodes, once. Cut him completely. H.R.H. only tolerates him because Her Majesty feels that his achievements must be acknowledged by the Crown. The Queen, God bless her, is forced to do many unpleasant things for the good of the nation as a whole, but there are numerous foolish females who openly worship at Rhodes' shrine. I would not name anyone in such a connection, of course, but one cannot credit that the ladies who form part of his coterie have any claim to intelligence."

That remark, clearly audible to those around Vivian who had just heard him claim that Margaret Veasey-Hunter was one of Rhodes' circle of acquaintances, could not have come at a worse moment. Already roused to belligerence by thoughts of Leila and her *Cyril* Rhodes, he was all set to hit out after such provocation.

Swinging round, he demanded in furious tones, "If you cut the man whenever he is in your vicinity, I challenge your right to any knowledge whatsoever of those close to him."

Silence fell in the room as Theo Fennimoore fitted his monocle to his eye to study the man alongside him. "Did someone speak, Miles?" he drawled.

Glancing awkwardly over his shoulder, then back, the Honourable Miles Gosthorpe murmured, "Better to drop the subject, eh?"

Vivian was in no mood to suffer the patronising attitude of these men, who had been latent enemies for some years. "Why drop it when it has just become interesting? I am waiting for an explanation of a sweeping statement made by someone with no more intelligence than those he condemns."

As if Vivian had not spoken, Fennimoore complained to those in his own group, "The Committee of Inquiry found Rhodes guilty, then allowed him to go off scot-free. That practice is being followed with disgusting frequency lately, as we in this regiment are too well aware. As a result, society is becoming riddled with bounders and opportunists, who masquerade as gentlemen and get away with it."

The obvious reference to something regimental honour demanded should be a closed book brought those concerned in the growing drama under the intense scrutiny of every man in the room. To Vivian, it was the match to ignite his present explosive temper. Pushing free of his friends' restraining hands, he was hardly aware of the tenseness amongst men who lived by a code of behaviour peculiar to their profession and rank.

Confronting Fennimoore, he challenged through tight lips, "No gentleman would have said what you just said, so which are you, Fennimoore—a bounder or an opportunist?"

In an atmosphere in which a pin would have been heard dropping, the blue-blooded major cast a derisory glance over Vivian, then began to turn away without deigning to reply.

Heart thudding as sickeningly as his head, Vivian seized the man's arm to drag him back, face to face. "Which are you, Fennimoore? I'll have an answer from you," he swore.

"You'll have nothing from me," came the icy retort. "I do not deal with those of your cut."

Knowing that he could not let his adversary go unpunished for referring to something everyone present knew was a touchy subject, Vivian roared, "You'll deal with me now, or I shall be obliged to teach you a lesson you'll not easily forget."

Shaking off Vivian's grip on his sleeve, and flushing darkly, Fennimoore said with a sneer, "There is nothing a bastard could teach me, unless it is how to fire at the enemy and manage to kill my own men instead."

Beyond control, Vivian struck the man across the face, so hard the blow left a white hand-print that slowly darkened to red as his victim grew pale with shock.

"You'll regret that," choked Fennimoore against the sound of general consternation from those around, who knew he had gone too far. "By God, you'll regret that!"

Still consumed with the mixture of inflammable emotions, Vivian stood ready to fly at the other man's throat if he made a single move toward him. Several men laid hands on his shoulders restrainingly, but he shrugged them off, lost to all thought but revenge. Then John Kinson came between the two, a wild look on his face.

164

"For God's sake, man, he's here," he said with low-voiced urgency. "Pull yourself together, it's the Prince of Wales."

Seeing those near by stiffening to attention, Vivian's scattered fiery senses told him that something else had become the focal point of their interest. Allowing himself to be dragged round to face the main entrance, he slowly grew chill, with the reaction after violence, as the senior members of the 49th entered with a middle-aged portly man destined to be their next monarch.

The mark of Vivian's hand was still on Theo Fennimoore's cheek while he was being genially greeted as a friend by the royal visitor. Vivian received no such amiable treatment, of course, and he endured the several hours of that visit, fighting the sensation of standing with a heavy board strapped to his back as a punishment, knowing that he had awoken a dangerous sleeping enemy that day.

"Go away," advised Professor Halstein. "You are wasting my time and your own money. Go away, and come back only when you decide that you really wish to learn how to sing. This you do now is like a . . . like a fish in a bowl. You open and close your mouth like a fish in a bowl, and have as much effect on the world as he." He flapped his hands in a gesture of annoyance. "Go away! I do not wish to associate myself with such sounds."

Leila left his house without protest. Her scales had been purely automatic; the songs had been meaningless. Her top notes had wobbled, then petered out. A fish in a bowl had the consolation of pretending that his voice would be magnificent, if he had one. She had just heard her own, and could no longer pretend.

She walked slowly in the early September sunshine, until she reached St James's Park, where she turned into the afternoon tranquillity of rose-beds, sun-dappled lawns, and cool water. Allowing herself the luxury of abandoning her thoughts in favour of her senses, for once, she followed the many paths between the smooth stretches of grass. All around her were the sounds of children's laughter as they played ball, or made daisy-chains; the quacking of ducks and their splashes as they glided in to land with their webbed feet feathering the water. From the distant bandstand came the sound of music.

She admired the massed roses: yellow, flame, white, or velvety-red. There were some as pink as seaside rock, others the colour of shrimps, still more the delicate pale shade of the inside of a shell. There were bushes covered in small open blooms that were a riot of colours; others bearing huge curled layers of petals with hearts richer in hue than the rest.

She watched the water-birds as they upended suddenly to reach particles of food below the surface, then came up again into sunshine which sparkled the drops of water left on downy feathers. She smiled as they waddled ashore, to preen themselves beneath the long trailing willow-fronds touching the water. Her stroll took her past high-born ladies in lace, with matching parasols, and their grey-coated escorts; young girls in muslin, arm-in-arm with undergraduates in blazers and straw boaters sporting their college colours; nursemaids in blue uniforms and white starched aprons, pushing perambulators containing the next generation of England's peerage; scarlet-coated soldiers walking out with their sweethearts, or on the look out for new ones. There were small boys in sailor-suits, and girls in frilly dresses with coloured sashes, all wearing straw or linen hats to protect them from the sun. There were dogs on long leashes, a little boy bowling a hoop, a girl pulling a wooden chicken whose head jerked and whose wings flapped as it rolled along on fat brightly-coloured wheels at the end of her string. Then two dogs met and had a scrap, the hoop hit a grey-bearded gentleman on a seat, and the chicken fell over. There were yaps, strong words on disciplining children, and tears over the chicken. Everything was put to rights, and peace returned.

Leila strolled like a Lindley Girl, and drew many glances. She enjoyed the attention created by her cream organdie high-necked blouse, tailored cream skirt, with its lilac silk sash fastened with a huge cream gauze tea-rose on the left side of her waist, and the large cream hat with lilac gauze ruching. For a while she allowed herself to be anyone she wished, for no one could spoil her illusions. She was Franz Mittelheiter's partner in Lindley's most successful show; she was Dame Leila Duncan, the celebrated operatic soprano. Then, the dreams were swept aside as she became, for a few aching moments, Leila Veasey-Hunter, adored and adoring wife of a man she could not put from her heart and mind.

In the midst of crossing the bridge, she paused and gazed down the full length of the lake as it lay in silver and dark patches, broken only by the arrow-head ripples left by gliding birds. Her senses had been given their moment of freedom. Cruel reality now returned. The elegant young woman at whom these people glanced was Lily Duncan, wife of a one-armed uncouth trooper, who was out of work and likely to stay that way. She was the legal spouse of a bitter, jealous man who had been robbed of his pride by an Indian tribesman . . . and by a lady's maid who had become a cultured, much-fêted actress.

Frank had been home three months, and had turned her life into a nightmare of ugly emotions and even uglier thoughts. Up until the day he had arrived, she had been tempted to lie low and hope he would never trace her. She had gone to Tilbury to meet his ship because she could not allow him to go to Clivedon Place demanding his wife's new address. Nor could she risk his going to the theatre, with even more disastrous results.

They had met as two strangers. She had known him because he was the only passenger with dark curly hair and just one arm. He had not known her at all. The memory of those first few hours was now mercifully confused; there had been no alternative but to take him back to the basement. That was when the real nightmare had begun. It could be compared with taking in any disabled man from the street and being compelled to live with him. It was *her* home, *her* things paid for with *her* money . . . and there was only one bedroom. Frank had been stunned, ill at ease, angry. She had been resentful, defensive, repulsed. Nothing had changed in the following months.

She frowned as she gazed down at the water gliding slowly beneath the bridge on which she stood. When she had lived with Miss Bates, the retired governess, she had been taken to church twice every Sunday and taught to recite passages from the bible. With the departure of Miss Bates, her religious timetable had increased to rectory proportions. Yet Leila had never prayed of her own accord, never thought that there was really anyone there to hear her words. The only legacy had been a set of morals that ensured she had a conscience. That conscience was now ruining her life.

The stranger who shared her basement was a deformed outcast, who had no more idea what to do about the situation than she had. He had once been a robust, self-confident man living a Spartan but manly life amongst others of his kind. He had been handsome, stocky, and as lusty as a young man could be. He had married a pretty servant-girl who had given herself to him enough times for there to be a possibility of pregnancy, then sailed away for four years leaving her with thirty shillings and the address of his mother, in case he had put her in the family way. He had seen the wonders and horrors of India, frequented the brothels and drinking-hells, and experienced the savagery of battle. Then, he had been chloroformed one day, and awoken to find his right arm in a basket beneath the table on which he lay.

He was no longer any use to the army, so they had sent him home with a small pension to compensate for the arm, and crossed him from their records. He had sought the pretty maid and found instead a plum-in-the-mouth actress called Leila, who lived in a place where he was expected to take off his boots on entering, eat with half a dozen different sets of cutlery, put his ash in a china dish with flowers on, say "excuse me" when he belched, and keep out of sight of any callers. What he must *not* do was sit around in his braces, mop up his gravy with a hunk of bread, call her Lil, use coarse army language, or take off any of his clothes in front of her. Above all, he must not expect to use the bed when she was in it.

Leila's conscience told her Frank must be broken enough in spirit without all that, but she could not bear his rough manners, his uncouth habits, or his filthy language. She could not bear his calling her Lil, or making vulgar remarks about her figure. Mostly, she could not face the thought of any kind of intimacy with him. She avoided all physical contact, even when handing him things. It bothered her that he would naturally believe it was because of his disability, but it would have been the same if he had returned from India whole. Her husband now totally repulsed her.

Vivian had always smelt faintly of perfumed soap, clean linen, freshly washed hair, and warm healthy skin; Frank smelled of stale sweat, beer and badly digested food. Vivian's teeth were very white, his smile so full of instant gaiety; when Frank smiled it was more of a leer, and his teeth showed yellow with gaps where some had been drawn by the army doctor. Vivian always wore silk shirts, or starched linen; Frank had the rough flannel he had known all his life. Vivian's manners had been designed to turn even a dressmaker into a temporary duchess; Frank had no manners at all. When Vivian spoke to her he made the most complicated words flow with ease over his tongue, and when he spoke her name he caressed the sound. Frank stumbled over his words, and when he said "'ere, Lil" something inside her shrivelled up.

Although her wretched conscience told her it must be terrible for Frank, it was just as terrible for her . . . and it was getting worse. Once he had recovered from the shock of her changed circumstances, Frank had tried to assert himself by saying she must give up the theatre. She had countered that by pointing out that they had to live, and it was her work that brought in the only money. He had amended his ultimatum to be effective from the day he started work. But no one wanted to employ a one-armed ex-trooper—a breed many still believed to be the scum of the earth. So Leila continued at Lindley's, but guessed it must be difficult for a man to live by his wife's earnings. It was even more difficult for him to accept the existence of her admirers.

They had argued loud and long over it, Leila insisting that it was part of her job and meant nothing, also that Lester Gilbert was likely to end her contract if she persistently refused invitations. Frank had threatened to go to "Bloody big-arse Gilbert" and tell him his "beautiful bitch of a bawdy-queen" was *Mrs* Duncan. Frightened and angry,

Leila had declared she would be thrown out, and challenged him to find work that would give them a life as good as her money gave them. Frank had struck her around the face, and she had run from the basement in despair.

The supper invitations had continued, and Frank had begun drinking heavily. On several nights Leila had arrived home to find him occupying the bed, drunk and snoring, and had had to make one for herself on the floor by the range. The worst aspect of the present situation was the question of conjugal rights. Leila understood what Frank was suffering, and her heart ached for any person who had lost an arm and, with it, his sense of pride and self-respect. She also knew all about men's sexual demands, which overcame all other considerations, and appreciated that it must be difficult for him to live in close proximity with a ripe young female he had the legal right to take whenever he wished. Yet she could not bring herself to be a sexual partner to him. Now, she was growing afraid that he would take her by force, and stayed away from her basement for as long as she could. When drunk he was capable of doing anything. That was the extent to which the situation had declined by that afternoon in September.

Many times she had thought of never going back to her home, but all she owned was in that basement, and Frank would surely pursue her to Lindley's and end her career. Even changing her name and auditioning for another show in the West End would do no good. Her face was too well-known in theatrical circles, and any other manager would want to bill her as Leila Duncan. She thought up many wild plans, methods of escaping the dilemma and misery, but they all came to grief one way or another, and constantly at the back of her mind were Frank's words at Tilbury. "Well, Lil, I stood by you when you was in trouble, and married you. Now it's your turn to stand by me."

She pitied him, agonised over his plight, but felt the same for herself. How, in God's name, would it all end? Standing there on that bridge in the park, she wondered if there really was someone who listened to prayers. Vivian would know.

She began walking again, speaking his name under her breath and silently asking him once more to forgive her for what she had had to do to him that day. Unless she had made him truly hate her, she knew he would have come back to her again. Fighting back the tears, she walked on beneath the shade of trees, remembering every line of his face, his smile, those laughing eyes, that voice. *The sort to get a girl into a bedroom quicker than anything.*

Oh, Rose, she cried inwardly, if only you were here to tell me what I should do. Three people are being destroyed by my weakness one summer afternoon three years ago. Is the only way out to follow your example?

Blinded by tears, she stumbled on through the park. She could no longer go to Professor Halstein. He had told her to go away, and he had been right to do so. To sing, a person had to have joy within, a total sense of dedication, and an untroubled spirit. It was pointless to go on. With the love of her life gone, and her ambition ruined, all she could see ahead was the slow, inevitable slide to degradation and marital rape by a man she could neither love nor desert. How well she now understood why Rose had done what she had done. When it came to a choice between slow destruction, or instant peace, there was only one answer, surely. Lester Gilbert believed in ending the run of a show before audiences began to decline. Leave them wanting more, was his maxim. But who would want more of Leila Duncan now? Frank would be less tormented without her; Vivian would be in the arms of too many others to care. There was no one else in her life. Turning to grip the nearby rail in despair she stared at the cool peace of the lake and found it irresistibly beckoning.

"Are you all right, ma'am? Can I be of assistance to you?"

Swinging round in startled fashion, Leila found a tall, spare man in correct morning-attire regarding her with concern.

"Is there some way I can help?" he repeated in kindly manner. "You appear to be in distress. Perhaps I could secure you a cab."

"Yes . . . yes, that would be very kind," she managed, taking the arm he offered, to walk with him through the nearby gates into the Mall. "Some bad news, you know."

"How very unfortunate. Best to get home where you may rest and recover, dear lady."

Her courtly rescuer waved his cane, and a hansom drew into the kerb. She thanked him sincerely, and sank back in the privacy of the interior as the horse moved off. The passing scene went unnoticed as she pondered the strange coincidence. The elderly gentleman had been Sir Frederick Clivedon, her former employer. She thought of his courtesy, his gentle manner, his complete ignorance of the fact that he was speaking to his daughter's previous maid, and could almost hear Rose's voice saying, "Oh Lei, what a laugh!"

If her own laughter sounded more like weeping, there was no one there to notice.

It was two a.m. before they left Romano's, and the early October mist was hanging like a veil over the London streets to give them a suggestion of ghostliness. Leila willed the carriage to go faster. Billy

Middleton was showing all the signs of growing too ardent, and she was uncertain how he would behave. Either way, it would have to be her last engagement with him, because she had vowed never to let any other man get to the point Vivian had done. It was a great pity. Billy was an amusing and uncomplicated companion, a young man with boyish enthusiasm for everything he did and a great propensity for having fun. She had grown fond of him, too fond not to put an end to their friendship before he was hurt. She had already hurt two men deeply. There would be no others on her conscience.

As she had feared, the young politician produced a huge rope of magnificent pearls as a prelude to his declaration of love, and she had to hurt him, after all. As gently as she could, she refused both his gift and his adoration before he could make a proposal of dishonourable or honourable nature. She told him that she valued her theatrical career above personal relationships, and would always do so. It was a difficult and upsetting scene, and she finally let herself into the basement telling herself young Nellie was a fool to envy her. Beauty was a weapon of power she would gladly relinquish.

Her heart sank the minute she stepped inside the door. Frank was in the bed, sitting up against the iron bed-head, watching for her arrival. He did not look drunk—far from it. There was a sense of purpose about him that was far more disturbing, and the bed she always made up for him in the corner of the main room before leaving for the theatre had been put away again. Wondering what approach she should adopt, she slid the big bolt on the door and went across to the range to warm herself after the chill of the night. Frank could not see her there, and she stood with a hammering heart, playing for time.

"Bit late, aren't yer?" came the rough accusation. "Don't take this long ter eat a bit of gobbler and wash it down with what you calls 'bubbly', I know."

"It's misty out. The cabbie had to drive slowly."

"Oh yer? On the orders of 'is nibs, I s'pose. Slow enough fer a bit of 'ow's yer father on the way."

She stayed silent and, a moment later, he asked loudly, "You still there, Lil?"

"Yes . . . and I'm very tired."

"Come ter bed, then."

Gripping her hands tightly together she stayed by the range, filled with apprehension and wondering what on earth to do. If she left again and managed to find a cab at that hour in Mirtle Street, where could she go?

The voice came again from the bedroom. "Don't tell me you don't fancy a bit, after the warm up on the way 'ome. A young 'ealthy girl like you ought ter be able to ter take more'n one poke in a night."

She put her hands up over her ears to blot out what he was saying. Then he was there in the room with her, in his long baggy underpants and flannel vest with the right sleeve hanging loose. The neck of the vest was open, and she could see the dark matt of hair on his chest. Three years ago, on a summer afternoon, the sight had excited her. Dear God, how she had changed!

"I've told you before, there is nothing in the least immoral about my engagements after the show," she said, trying to edge away to put a chair between them. "My escorts are gentlemen."

He laughed harshly, and told her that *gentlemen* had the same twitchy organs as the common man in the street and needed to use them the same way and just as often. "And it don't matter if it's a bloody cab or a terrace basement, mine's as good as a gentleman's any day. It's time you found that out, Lil."

She backed as he moved toward her. "I can't, Frank. It's the wrong time of the month."

"No, it bloody isn't," he snapped, his strong-featured face working with anger. "That was last week—or so you told me."

"I'm tired, and I have a terrible headache."

He smiled sourly. "You didn't 'ave one three years ago, Lil. If I remembers, you was only too eager for it. If it wasn't fer me 'aving such a job first time, I'd 'ave thought you'd bin at it since you was old enough."

Leila's pride began to curl up and shrivel at his coarse references to something beyond her present comprehension. She tried to explain it to him, and to herself; tried to excuse something that now filled her with shame.

"I was alone—had been for most of my life. The string of people who brought me up did so for charitable reasons, not through love. When I met you, Frank, I felt I had found someone of my own, at last. That was all I wanted; someone to be interested in me as a special person. That day . . . out in the country . . . it wasn't planned. You know it wasn't. You know how I cried afterward. It was you who made me continue doing something I knew was wrong. I was afraid you'd go off and leave me as lonely as I was before, if I didn't give you what you wanted."

Frank's expression did not change. "You're wringing me 'eart, Lil, straight y'are. *I made you do it.* I remembers very well 'ow yer rolled around in delight. Don't tell *me*, gal. I'm not one of yer milksop *gentlemen*. I knows when a little tart's enjoying 'erself under me. And you're going to again, Lil."

Unable to stand any more, Leila took her chance and fled for the bedroom door, which had a key. But he had anticipated her. His left arm shot out to grab the full sleeve of her midnight-blue dress. The silk ripped, leaving her shoulder bare to the lacy camisole beneath. At the same time, his foot hooked around her ankles to send her to the floor, face downward. He was on her instantly, a great weight that pinned her to the carpet, with no chance to move.

She lay sobbing for breath as he sat astride her, tugging at the fastenings of her dress and camisole, until her back to the base of her spine was bared. Then he ripped the skirt of the dress down to the hem, and tried to pull her silk drawers off until he realised that he was in the worst position to do so. He moved to sit on the back of her knees but, with his weight now removed from her body, Leila made a desperate bid for survival. Once he had taken her it would be the beginning of the end. Leila Duncan would have been destroyed.

She was young, physically fit, and stronger than her slender frame suggested. Twisting round, she began clawing and kicking without discrimination, careless of how naked she became during the struggle. Frank was unprepared for such savage opposition, and it was his physical handicap that finally prevented his conquest of her. Even so, he was as desperate as she, probably also realising that the outcome would decide the issue, once and for all. In consequence, Leila was covered in bruises and bites before she managed to drag herself to her feet. Stumbling frantically into the bedroom, she slammed the door and locked it with hands that could hardly turn the key. Almost demented, she lay against the wall in no more than the tatters of her petticoat, while Frank hammered on the door with equal dementia, shouting obscenities and calling her the vilest things imaginable.

She remained against that wall, shaking uncontrollably and feeling degraded by the girl she had once been, until it grew quiet outside. Then for some time after that. A prisoner in her own home, she wondered wildly how she would find the courage to unlock that door.

It was almost dawn before she relaxed enough to close her eyes. She slept well into the next afternoon. On waking, she lay silent, trying to come to terms with this latest crisis in her short life. Then, dressed in her most severe blouse and skirt, she tiptoed to the door. Turning the key as silently as she could, she stepped fearfully into the room where she had once been so happy.

Frank was sitting in his braces, with a bottle of beer and a great doorstep of a sandwich on the table beside him. There were several empty beer-bottles on the draining-board. The blankets and pillows he had used were still on the floor in the corner. Swallowing nervously, she walked past him to make herself some tea. The thought of eating was repugnant, but she knew it was essential to have something before the performance. Putting an egg on to boil, she cut thin bread-and-butter to have with it. When it was all ready, she carried it to the table on a tray and sat facing her husband. The egg stayed untouched, while she sipped tea and worked herself up to what she was determined to say.

"My body is black and blue this morning," she told him quietly.

"That's yer own fault, silly bitch," was his savage reply.

Getting to her feet, she clasped her hands tightly together. "That is never going to happen again, Frank. Leila Duncan or Lily Lowe, no woman deserves to be treated that way by any man, much less her husband. You are in an appalling situation, I understand that. But so am I—which you *don't* understand. In three years I have become an entirely different person, with an entirely different set of values. I have been trained to speak correctly, wear elegant clothes, and move in the same circles as those who once employed me. I am no longer Lily Lowe, and can no longer accept the things a lady's-maid could. I cannot, and will not, go back to being that girl. Let us get that quite clear. I would sooner die."

She moved closer to him when he showed no signs of violence. "You have often quoted to me that you stood by me, therefore I must stand by you. I believed it, until a little while ago in that bedroom, when I analysed it. Three years ago I thought I was pregnant, and I was frightened. But, you know, there was very little by way of "standing by" me, Frank. You went through a marriage ceremony in which you lied about your profession, then you sailed off to India for four years to live as a bachelor. You gave me thirty shillings, and the address of someone in Scotland whom you said was your mother. But I was only to write to her if there was a baby and I was subsequently thrown out by the Clivedons. She was not told of your marriage, the army authorities were not told, and I was instructed by you to keep it secret from the Clivedons. I could stay with them, you said, and you wouldn't have to send me anything from your pay. You were going to save it for our future, instead. So, apart from a marriage certificate, thirty shillings, and the address of a stranger at the other end of the country, I was left to fend for myself. That is precisely how you "stood by" me, Frank.

"Luckily, I wasn't pregnant, but the Clivedons told me to leave for a reason I could never have forseen. I spent your thirty shillings trying not to starve while I tramped the streets looking for work. I did not write to your mother in Scotland, nor did I write to you for help that would lessen those savings for our future. I had to keep my marriage a secret in order to gain and keep the job at Lindley's. But I never forgot that I had a husband, and have been totally faithful.

"You, on the other hand, have done very well since that wedding, because you were in constant work, with food and lodgings paid for, plenty of company, and travel in a foreign country. Were you thrown into the street in favour of a hoity-toity trained nurse? Did you wonder desperately where the rent or your next meal would come from? Did you remain totally faithful to Lily Lowe? Yet, when you lost an arm, and they no longer wanted you, you came straight to the wife you wished no one to know about. You have been here four months, Frank. You've had comfortable accommodation, excellent food, heating when it's cold, a generous supply of beer and tobacco . . . and a companion who pays for it all." She gripped the back of the wooden chair. "Don't speak to me of 'standing by' any more."

"Lil . . . I got . . ."

"Be quiet," she told him sharply. "I haven't finished yet. I was prepared to give you all this for as long as necessary. All I asked in return was that you tried to behave decently, and that you continued to keep our marriage a secret for the sake of my job, which is essential to us both. As for not being a wife to you, it has nothing to do with your losing an arm. If I loved you, *nothing* would make any difference. But I don't, Frank. I never did. I was lonely, and you were too determined. That's all there was to it . . . and it's three years too late now."

As he made to move, she repeated quickly, 'Too late, Frank, and last night was the deciding factor. If I owe you any debt from three years ago, I'm going to settle it. Before I leave for the theatre today, I'll give you thirty shillings and the address of a charitable organisation. I shall be away for a lifetime longer than four years, but you must tell no one about our marriage, because I might then have to share some of my salary with you." She picked up her tea-tray. "I'll send someone for my things in the morning. The rent is due on Saturday, so you can stay here until then."

He stared at her, shaken. "You don't mean that. You can't walk out on me, Lil!"

A rat-a-tat on the door broke into the moment, and Frank swore loudly as he got to his feet, roaring at the caller to "shut that row". He strode across to the door and pulled it open angrily.

"Well?"

There was a low murmur, and Frank put his arm out across the doorway to bar entry.

"It's not *Miss* Duncan, it's *Mrs*, and what would you want wiv my wife? If you're another of them scented bastards as takes 'er to the Savoy

175

bloody Grill, you can 'op it quick. You might look impressive, matey, but I could make mincemeat of you, and 'ave the law on me side."

Leila thought the world had stopped at the sound of that voice, a voice she knew so well in all its moods. Turning in disbelief, every breath, every muscle, every blink of her lashes seemed suspended as she gazed at him across the width of the room. Still holding the tray, she was immobilised in a shocked limbo that left her feeling so naked he must surely see the bruises and bites from last night; see Lily Lowe lying beneath a heaving soldier in the corner of a field; see a tearful frightened girl gratefully giving away the rest of her life for thirty shillings and an address in Scotland.

The pain in Vivian's eyes, his anguished, questioning expression, brought the final destruction of what had been between them. He appeared as unable to break the terrible moment as she, and they continued to gaze at each other over Frank's head while strong bastions crumpled like paper, victorious armies fell to a man, and eternity finally ceased.

Eventually, he stammered in a voice grown thin, "Forgive me. I . . . I have made . . . a mistake. A great mistake."

She had to watch him turn and climb the area steps, until there was nothing of him but the ringing footfall on the pavement above. All that was left to her was the memory of a beloved face hollowed by suffering, a mouth tugged down by bitterness, and eyes that had been full of damning questions she could never now answer.

Someone tried to prise her fingers from the tray, but she clung to it still. If she did not hold on to something, she would surely dissolve into a pile of ashes, like a fire that can never be relit.

# CHAPTER NINE

Vivian walked blindly through the streets of London for some hours, with no awareness of passing traffic or people around him. Twice he stepped from the pavement into the path of oncoming carriages, but walked on oblivious to the danger he had so narrowly missed. Late afternoon turned toward evening, and the lamps in the street began to glow yellow through the swirling October mist. The numbers of those on foot decreased. It was only the working-class, the needy, or the desperate who walked after dark on nights when the shrouded streets made crime easy.

A rich man had a fat wallet, a gold watch, rings or cuff-links of precious stones, cigar-case of tortoise-shell or silver, maybe a snuffbox, or an ebony walking-cane with gold or silver knob. No matter how large or strong the victim, a slight brush in passing, a brief pause to enquire the time, or a young girl "accidentally" tripping in his path was enough to relieve him of one or more of those things before vanishing quickly into the obscurity. In certain areas of London, a group of villains could surround a man in an instant and take the lot, including boots and hat, then disperse as quickly as they had gathered.

Strangely, Vivian walked that evening unmolested, even the prostitutes recognising a deaf ear when they saw one. Perhaps the people of the night sensed a desperation as great as their own, an anger against circumstance that bred untamed aggression, a point reached where a man would let himself be humbled no further.

Gradually it grew brighter, more noisy. There was much more movement around him. Something dark rushed at him: voices shouted, a hand took a grip on his arm.

"My word, sir, you practically walked straight into those horses!"

Vivian stared at the full red face with protuberant eyes and thick white moustache. "My thanks," he murmured.

"Yes . . . well, damned careless on a night like this," came the bluff comment. "Get yourself safely inside, my dear young fellow, or get a cabbie to drive you home. You look a bit cut up."

Vivian stayed where he was as the elderly man walked off up some steps. All he could see were the words *Felicity May* in lights that danced before his eyes. He stood staring at them for a long time. If Julia had not been staying with her aunt for six weeks, if she had not expressed a desire to see the show everyone was talking about, if he had not accepted her challenge knowing she had made it because Leila was in the cast, he would never have seen how pale and strained she had grown, how much sadness her lovely blue eyes now held. He would never have been forced to compare the lifeless automatic creature she had become with the vital glowing girl he had allowed to rule him.

Seeing her again after nearly five months, and in such a state, had been fatal. At the first opportunity, he had travelled up from Brighton determined on a show-down. Even so, he had walked the length of Mirtle Street several times before going down the steps to her basement.

Believing himself to be the victim of a virtuous woman's revenge was better than the truth. Another man's wife! A great bargee of a man in baggy trousers, woollen vest and braces; a rough brute of a man with one arm and the language of a trooper. He saw again the coarsely handsome face, the thick black hair that also rioted on his chest, the yellowing teeth. *What would you want wiv my wife?* Then Leila, standing white-faced and clutching a tray, in a familiar room that now had beer-bottles everywhere; a bread-board, chunk of cheese, pickled onions in a stone jar, all on a table without a cloth; and rumpled bedding still in a corner at four in the afternoon.

He stood outside Lindley's Theatre, the battle inside him continuing to rage. Another man's wife! It was almost obscene to think of that beautiful, fastidious and essentially feminine girl being possessed by a rough, foul-mouthed creature in vest and braces; to think of her sweet-smelling softness being crushed beneath an oaf who smelled of beer and pickled onions. Every sense urged him to go back and snatch her away, save her from the degradation of such a liaison. That was inflamed emotion speaking with urgent persuasion to his pride. Cold reason had other things to say to him.

Leila Duncan was an artificial creation of Lester Gilbert's fertile talent. In reality, the girl was an orphan from the lower classes. She would certainly be better matched with a man of her own kind, than with a "scented bastard", as that ruffian had described him. She was no gentle virtuous virgin, but a calculating married woman who had played him for all she could get. It had been more than a few presents she had wanted from him. God, how she must have revelled in his offer of heart and noble name! How exquisitely comic he must have appeared to her on his numerous returns, after her humiliating rebuffs. Even after receipt of that cruelly destructive letter, he had gone back once more. Her clever scheme had taken no account of such self-demeaning foolishness; she had plainly been totally disconcerted by his visit after what she had intended as irrevocable rejection. There had been no time to hide the husband away.

The lights at the theatre entrance, the colourful dresses of the women entering, the elegant cloaks and opera-hats of their escorts, the flurry as carriage after carriage arrived then drove off, were all part of the turmoil inside him as he cried out against cold reason. Had there been anguish, not fury, in her eyes as she had gazed at him? Was she trapped, not the entrapper? He would never know the answers, because he must not see her again. He stood there riding out the pain of knowing that, even now, his love for her was not dead.

Lindley's Theatre had swallowed all its patrons now. It would be quiet outside until eleven o'clock, when they would all be disgorged. Young men would then flock to the stage-door with bouquets or baubles, as he had done. Turning blindly, he wandered off into thickening fog, seeking escape from the shock of something he could not accept.

Kitson greeted his arrival at the house with the news that Dr and Miss Marchbanks had agreed to have dinner, after waiting more than an hour for him. Declining the offer of food, Vivian walked into the drawing-room just as he was. He supposed he greeted Rupert and Julia, apologised for his lateness and the manner in which he was dressed. If he did, he was hardly aware of it. They both said things at him, and he must have replied sensibly. Rupert then departed, saying something about a medical emergency that had been telephoned to him from their aunt's house, adding that he would join them at the reception as soon as he was free.

The room was quiet after Rupert's departure. Vivian stared into the fire, seeing only that basement apartment with beer-bottles all over the place, pickled onions in jars, rumpled bedding still on the floor. Dear God, could she really be married to that brute? How could he bear to leave her there? How could he possibly take her away? She was another man's wife, and she had told him in that unforgettable letter than he was to stay out of her life.

The sensations of shock began to return. He knew of only one sure way to dull them. Reaching for the decanter with automatic movements, he poured himself a stiff drink and downed it swiftly.

"Don't you think you've already had enough?" asked a cool voice beside him.

He turned to gaze at the woman in a low-cut dress, who was studying him with assessing eyes. Having forgotten her presence, her reminder of it with a remark that smacked of reprimand touched him on the raw.

Julia Marchbanks could have been the source of his rift with Leila: the girl he loved had changed dramatically after that visit to Shenstone.

"Don't you think you should hold your tongue?" he responded. "I am not one of your brothers to be kept in line, thank God."

"Amen to that," she agreed softly. "I take it we shall not be going to the Earl of Maw's reception tonight."

"Reception?"

A faint smile touched her mouth. "Perhaps it's just as well, under the circumstances."

"What circumstances?" he demanded aggressively.

"The circumstances of your being well on the way to total inebriation. I always thought you could hold your liquor, Vivian. My brothers all can."

"Damned paragons, the lot of them," he swore, keeping quiet about the real reason for the state he was in. Let her think he was drunk. "You beat them all into a cocked hat," he went on as if he were. "Do you know that?" He poured another drink defiantly. "Is there anything at all at which you are a failure?"

She sank gracefully onto a settee facing him, apparently unwilling to continue that line of conversation. "I shall have to return to Cornwall at the end of the week. Father writes that he cannot entertain unless I am there to play hostess, and my brothers complain that no one comes to call when I am away. It is very amusing how men cannot do without females around them."

"Ha," he growled. "There you are wrong. You have never been with a regiment on the march. There is nothing so enjoyable or satisfying as the company of other men. They are undemanding, understanding, and play straight with you. There is loyalty, trust, high personal regard, even a willingness to die for you, if necessary. Give me a female comparison if you can," he challenged, waving the decanter at her.

She smiled. "I admit I cannot. There is nothing so dull as a parcel of women, who can talk of nothing but hemming and water-colours, or the cunning of their cook. They will smile and flatter to your face, then go behind your back at the first opportunity to criticise and denigrate. A person cannot have faith in anything they say, they will break promises without the least compunction, and their single desire appears to be to pursue their selfish ends without regard for the feelings of those they trample along the way. I will own, they are poor creatures."

Her words rubbed salt in his open wounds. "Does that mean you do not count yourself amongst their number?"

"You think I should?"

He raked her with deliberately bold scrutiny. "A poor creature . . . no! But most decidedly feminine."

She laughed softly. "So I should hope. You are most decidedly masculine, Vivian," she declared, matching his boldness in the way she studied every inch of him. "I understand your father was an immensely virile man, to whom few women could say no. You are the same."

Anger and humiliation washed over him anew, as he turned away to put the decanter back on the table. A blue-eyed girl in ostrich feathers had said no to him time and time again. This afternoon, her uncouth husband had said it, whilst she had stood watching.

"Few women are given the opportunity to say no to me," he said savagely.

She was suddenly there facing him, her eyes glowing with green lights. "You fool!" she cried. "You are like a wild stallion racing aimlessly, wasting his strength and heedless of his own power. With a little schooling, and the right hand on the rein, that same creature could be magnificent." Her hand rested persuasively on his arm. "You don't need Shenstone, my dear, or a title passed to you merely because you are next in line. You are one of those rare men to whom the world is an oyster."

He stared at her, feeling incredible tiredness overtaking him as he tried to concentrate on what she was saying. Then he realised that he was looking at the necklace of sapphires which matched those fatal earrings. It lay against her throat to taunt him with memories.

She drew even nearer, putting her other hand on his arm. "Your blood is as blue as your brother's, but you are not shackled to tradition, as he is. Yours is the freedom to do as you wish with your life. You have a superb body, and a rebellious spirit. With those two attributes, you could acquire a home so splendid it would make Shenstone appear a hamlet in comparison. You could win a title of your own, bestowed on you as a reward for achievements that would be recorded for posterity and your sons."

Her hands gripped his arms tighter. "Vivian, you are an exciting mixture of aristocrat and rebel, with a glittering future beckoning. So far, you have chosen to ignore what I immediately saw when you returned to Cornwall last December. You have tried to annul the circumstances of your birth by dulling your excellent brain with brandy, and expending the power of that wonderful physique on a series of loose-living women who go from you to a dustman in the course of one afternoon. Can't you see that your unusual past makes you unique? Rather than attempt to compensate for what you imagine you have lost, you should use the advantages to the full. You are a temperamental thoroughbred, fighting shy of fences you don't want to take. Handled with skill and judgement, you'd take them effortlessly."

His head was beginning to pound, as the fiery brandy melted the ice in his veins. "Not all thoroughbreds are high-flyers," he murmured, almost mesmerised by the flashing sapphires against her creamy skin.

"You are," she insisted fervently. "You could fly higher than them all, with the right hand on the bridle. A woman who was your match, someone who would complement your fine virility and the breeding that is undeniable, a female who is not 'a poor creature but who is decidedly feminine' would help you to reach heights few men achieve. In *every* sense," she finished, with exciting innuendo.

With a strange feeling of a sword at his throat, once more, he said warningly, "You are treading dangerous ground with a man of my reputation, I hope you realise."

"A reputation even more bizarre than I suspected," she retaliated, her large eyes widening further with some dark emotion. "I heard something today which more than confirmed my beliefs. The story is being whispered in drawing-rooms and salons. London is agog with it."

Shrugging off her hold on his arms, he was already crying an inward protest as he demanded, "What is being whispered? Come on, Julia, out with it."

"You killed two of your own men," she charged, looking him straight in the eyes. "In the face of hostile natives, you risked capture and subsequent torture to remain behind and shoot them down in cold blood. The official version states that you did it to save them from ritual slaughter by their captors, but rumour has it that it was over some woman."

It was what he had feared since returning to England, and it came as a final blow on a day when life was hammering him into the ground like one of the pegs he collected with his lance. Turning away from her, he walked to the fireplace, where he gripped the mantelshelf and bowed his head between his outstretched arms. Fennimoore had acted out his threat; his own reputation would ensure that society believed the more scandalous version of the affair. Closing his eyes in mental anguish he relived that moment when he had acted instinctively. His boyhood trials at the hands of his grandfather had ensured that he was an excellent marksman. The two white men had died instantly, shot through the head.

Hands seized him and turned him around. Julia was looking at him with an expression that was almost one of triumph.

"Can you still not see the obvious?" she asked urgently. "I don't care about the truth of the affair. All I see is the evidence of courage and raw passions that turn a man into a giant. Take off that blindfold, Vivian, and look at me hard. Can you deny that I am the perfect partner for you? Do you doubt that I could tame you, and turn you into the high-flyer you really are?"

As he stood in the dazed aftermath of shock, she reached up to unfasten the sapphires from her neck. Dangling them from one hand, she said, "I am prepared to lose these if I fail to convince you."

"What would I want with a necklace?"

"It matches the earrings you won from me on a previous wager. You still have them, I trust?"

He nodded. Now, more than ever, they were associated with defeat.

"Good. I want them back rather badly," she told him in silken tones. "The set would then be complete again."

"You sound remarkably sure of yourself," he commented, finding her confidence irritating against the lack of his own.

"I am. What's more, you know it, my dear Vivian. Do you dare to accept my challenge?"

The desire to hit out, to retaliate in some way was manifested in a swift surge of recklessness. "The odds are heavily against you, my dear Julia."

Her laugh was low and seductive. "Are they? We shall see. However, if I should lose, you will have the complete set to give to one of your earthy chorus-girls, as a reward for rolling in the hay with you."

Her words increased his recklessness. "I'll roll you in the hay, one of these days."

"Oh no, you won't," came her crisp response. "I wouldn't settle for as little as that whore Leila Duncan."

Losing the last of his control, he reached for her. "You'll settle for what you damn well get!"

Everything about her was more generous than Leila—her curves, her full mouth, her uninhibited response. Desire for her overwhelmed him, and he had to exorcise that basement room, the beer-bottles, the black-haired husband who would certainly know how to roll a conquest in the hay. Most of all, he had to exorcise the memory of a girl holding a tray, who had finally destroyed him that afternoon.

Julia was still in his bed when his valet walked in, without ceremony, accompanied by Rupert Marchbanks, who was worried as to the whereabouts of his sister.

In another week it would be Christmas. As Leila neared the theatre that evening, she thought of the previous one which she had spent with Rose. She had not shared that kind of loving closeness with anyone else, and she still missed her friend badly. Grief had changed to wistful sadness now that she understood what could drive a person to suicide. It had been a feeling of betrayal, of having been shut out from her friend's total despair, that had caused initial anguish. Now that she had experienced similar despair, Leila knew that it was a very private feeling. The knowledge drew her closer to Rose, and lessened her sense of loss.

She had left Frank that day, and had not seen him since then. A new basement apartment, in which she lived alone, made little difference to her basic problem, however. Still tied to a loutish husband with little hope of breaking free, she was haunted by what she had done to Vivian. Two days after that unforgettable afternoon, when he had appeared unannounced after five months' absence, the newspapers had been full of sensational news concerning the Veasey-Hunter who could never inherit the family title and estate.

Appalled, she had read details of the Ashanti affair, which had been represented in conflicting lights by various publications. Not for a moment had she believed that he would shoot a man over a woman—or over anything else. Nor did she believe that he would have taken such drastic action if he had thought there was the remotest chance of rescue. The Court of Inquiry had been satisfied on all counts. Why drag the affair through the columns of rival newspapers?

Also in the accounts were the reasons why Charles Veasey-Hunter, the younger son, was heir to the Brancliffe inheritance. For days, she had been consumed with misery, which had plunged to depths beyond bearing when the newspapers reported that Vivian had been assaulted by the demented mother of one of the men he had killed, that he had been pelted with eggs by abusive crowds waiting outside the barrack gates, and that one of London's more free-and-easy military clubs had terminated his membership, leaving him now unable to enter any establishment exclusive to army officers.

Over and over again, she asked herself why he had not confessed these things to her. She answered every time by reminding herself that she had been unable to reveal to him the secret in her own life. If she had been honest with him right from the start, her conscience would not now be bleeding and her heart would not be in hibernation. Finally, numbness had relieved the pain. It allowed her to immerse herself in her career. Although her singing lessons had ceased, she still had the piano Vivian had bought her. Concentrated practice at scales and vocal exercises gave her a sense of purpose; determination to fill her life with activity which gave little time for introspection gave her a reason for going on.

As she passed Monty at the stage-door that evening and stood brushing the snow from her fur collar, Jack Spratt greeted her cheerily, then added, "Mr Gilbert wants to see you most particular. Soon as you came in, he said."

Leila immediately altered direction. Past experience had dimmed optimism at such summonses. Instead, she felt apprehensive. She always felt apprehensive, these days.

Lester Gilbert rose from behind his massive desk at her entry, and smiled. That was nothing to go by. He invariably broke unpleasant news with a smile.

"Miss Duncan, how charming you look! A Russian princess from out of the snows; a Swedish noblewoman come to address her warriors; a phantom of Christmas goodwill!" It was his usual mode of greeting, and she stood, hands still inside her muff, waiting for him to come to the point.

"You are looking a bit peaky of late, my dear. Nothing amiss, I trust? No family troubles; surely no financial worries? You are also losing a little too much weight. My patrons like to see . . . er . . . *healthy* girls on my stage, you know."

"I'll try to eat more, Mr Gilbert," she promised, on the point of turning away.

"Good! Splendid! You are becoming quite a favourite with my gentlemen. The ladies, also, of course," he added quickly. "You have developed very nicely under my guidance. I am more than satisfied. Did I not once tell you I rewarded diligence?"

"Yes, I believe you did," she murmured dutifully, wishing he would let her go and change for her first number. She had arrived late, as it was.

"I am giving you the rôle of Lola, the gypsy, for the present. Megan is ill with bronchitis, and likely to be incapacitated for some time. Now run along and prove that I have not been mistaken in you." He laughed boisterously. "You will dispense with the dark wig, my dear. A natural gypsy, I deem."

She smiled obediently. Just now she had been a Scandinavian Amazon. "Thank you, Mr Gilbert. I'll do my best."

It was what he expected her to say, and it brought another beaming smile as he led her across the plush drawing-room interior of his office to the door. The truth only hit her as she walked through the ant-like activity of stage-hands, putting the finishing touches to the first set after the matinée. There was always a frantic hurry between houses, because the first and last scenes of *Felicity May* demanded very elaborate full sets. There was a crash, an oath, a dive to save a wing falling as she threaded her way through it all, trying to recall the sequence of the gypsy scene. She found she could not remember any word of it, much less the song. Suddenly, the entire plot and musical score of *Felicity May* was a mystery to her. Fright gripped her stomach. Megan had been all right at the matinée. How could she have become ill so quickly?

Jack Spratt crossed her path and she grabbed his arm. "Where can I get a copy of the script? I have to play Lola and must learn the lines. I *must*, otherwise I shall go on stage and stand mute."

He patted her hand. "No, you won't. The minute you get out there it'll come to you."

"Yes, I'm sure it will," she murmured, convinced that it would not. "But I must have a copy of the script, just the same. Where does the prompter sit? Do I start first, or the orchestra? Oh lord, I think the song is in the wrong key for me."

He laughed. "You're so terrified, you're sure to be marvellous. Come with me and I'll find you a copy of Lola's part. You don't need the whole play, my dear."

Clutching the sheets of paper he gave her she went to the dressing-room where the news was already known.

"Make way for the gypsy, girls!"

"Left your caravan outside, have you, Lola?"

"Read my palm, dearie, but leave out the naughty bits."

They all carried on with the normal frenzied scrum of preparations before curtain-up, but several said it was about time the part was given to someone who could really sing. They were all pleased for her in the throw-away style they all adopted, but she was busy scanning lines she was sure Lola had never said before, as she took off her dress and applied make-up. It was only when she reached for her military costume and found it missing that the girl beside her said she was not expected to take both parts, and that Maisie had been chosen for the sextet.

Feeling more terrified by the minute, she put on the gypsy outfit which hung on her a little. Someone pinned it tighter around her waist, and she took down her dark hair so that it hung loose to her waist, threading flowers through it as she recited the lines over and over again under her breath. Once she was ready, she squeezed into a corner out of everyone's way, and prepared to wait all through Act One and halfway through the second, until she had to go out and face those unseen people in the crimson tiers. She had wanted this for so long; now she was petrified. If only she had continued her singing lessons. *You are like a fish in a bowl and have as much effect on the outside world as he does.*

She should have gone back to Professor Halstein and tried again. She had given up too easily. To wait for the right time meant waiting forever. Franz Mittelheiter had said that she must give up everything for singing, yet she had given up singing. For what? Convinced that she was about to walk on stage tonight and put an end to all her hopes, she sat through Act One in misery, staring at her script without seeing it.

During the interval bustle she huddled in her corner. Those around her chatted and laughed, as they changed costumes with expert swiftness in the cramped space. She envied them; longed to be one of their number again. Being the gypsy was terrible. She remembered Rose once saying: *Anything that goes wrong will be blamed on the gypsy, that's quite obvious.*

"My, my, they get away with it every time," cried a blonde who was scanning a newspaper open on the bench. "First that Lampton brute, now this one. Saved by a woman, who gives him back his respectability." She glanced across at Leila. "Have you seen this yet? One of yours for a while, wasn't he?"

The numbness began to wear off, as she got to her feet and walked to look at the page. The wedding had been a military one, with bridegroom and guard of honour in full regalia. Julia Marchbanks looked serenely unblushing in antique lace. Her father, along with her brothers, wore thundercloud expressions. Charles Veasey-Hunter looked as haggard as Vivian. The report beneath the photograph stated that the Honourable Margaret Veasey-Hunter had been unable to travel from her home in Rhodesia for her elder son's wedding, and Lord Brancliffe had been too ill to attend. There was a brief inevitable reference to the incident in Ashanti, in which Captain Veasey-Hunter had shot two Englishmen in curious circumstances. The journalist expressed his hope that a man who had always been surrounded by unfortunate bizarre events had broken his jinx by marrying one of the West Country's most captivating and accomplished young women of pedigree. The item concluded with the fact that, after a three-month honeymoon in Europe, the happy couple would occupy a country mansion near Brighton, where the 49th Lancers were presently stationed.

Leila lowered the paper slowly, unaware that the dressing-room had emptied again. So Julia had won! He had surrendered his soul to a woman who would not rest until she controlled him utterly. Was that what he had come to tell her, that day three months ago? If Frank had not been there, could she have stopped him? How? A Lindley Girl married to an ex-trooper could do nothing to help him. Even if she had been free, as his wife she would have been of little effect in his present social trials. Although he did not love Julia, he had acquired a wife of his own class, who would soon silence the tongues of scandalmongers with her powerful personality. She would manage and protect his military career, ensure that he was accepted on equal terms with the other officers in his regiment. Julia would also give him sons; a woman as strong as she would surely only produce male children. On reflection, perhaps he was getting a good return for the surrender of his soul; better than the return he had received for the surrender of his heart.

So it was finally, irrevocably over! She had not taken her own life, yet she was lifeless without him. At the end of a deep, hopelessly impossible attraction, Vivian had found salvation. What was left for her? An absent oaf of a husband, a job as a chorus-girl, and years of loneliness ahead. That was her reward for heeding Lester Gilbert's advice to maintain the magic at all times. What did a girl do when the magic ran out?

"Two minutes, Miss Duncan," carolled the call-boy around the door, and she let the newspaper slide to her feet as she stood up.

In the wings she felt numb, her heart like lead. Corporal Standabout, the comedy lead, joked and chaffed her to make her relax before he took her on to tell the regiment a gypsy had come to reveal the truth about where Felicity May's affections lay. She was tugged on stage by his hand gripping hers, and she then saw a familiar scene from a new angle. She had never been at the front of the entire company before. It felt immensely lonely. The footlights dazzled her, and beyond them was darkness. It was a listening, warm, human darkness.

The cue line was spoken, and her own voice said what it should. Then she was drawn into the group of chorus-men in smart uniforms, who reminded her of a tall officer walking across the barrack square with an impudent smile on his sun-browned face. Playing cards were put into her hands, and she quoted obediently, "The Queen of Hearts is much in evidence."

All those around her gasped in anticipation. "Here is the King," she went on in a voice that rang around the darkness ahead of her. There were more gasps from people she had seen every evening, yet who somehow appeared as strangers now. "There is also a knave—a black knave, who comes between them," she warned, holding up the cards for them all to inspect. Then she closed her eyes. "I see a dark man who comes between the Queen and her true love; a dark man in uniform, standing before the fluttering tricolour."

The members of the regiment, and the group of peasants all reacted noisily. Their dashing lieutenant was dark-haired. Was he a Frenchman in disguise: a traitor? Was their darling Felicity May harbouring a black knave in her affections? They begged the gypsy to tell them more.

The music began, and Leila walked to the very footlights, further than she was meant to go, because she had to reach those people out there; had to share her feeling of deep betrayal with them. The words and music echoed the pain reawoken that evening. The sound of her voice swelled to reach those unseen tiers, as she sang of her heartbreak to each and every person out there. Next minute, the cast had slowly moved forward to cluster around her. Strong male voices joined in on cue, but she found herself easily able to sing above them. Soon, the entire auditorium was filled with the haunting song of love's treachery, and it created total silence from the other side of the dazzling footlights.

Leila's cheeks grew wet, as the words she sang expressed her emotions too well. Nothing could hide from her the fact that her voice had never sounded like this before. She was no fish in a bowl, but a girl who had loved too well, and lost. The song rose to its climax. The strong harmony of a full chorus swelled around her to match her effortless top notes, but the anguish wrought by the picture of a wedding that should have been hers grew too much. Before the sound had died away to silence, she fled from the stage. In the wings, she clung to the curtains with hands that shook. In the auditorium, the audience went wild.

"My dear Miss Duncan, you have my congratulations." Franz Mittelheiter, waiting for his entrance dressed as a French officer, was there at her side. "You must continue your lessons."

"She must certainly have lessons, and I shall meet the cost," boomed Lester Gilbert. "That exit was pure magic, my dear, *pure magic*. There cannot be a heart that is unmoved, an eye that does not have a tear glistening at the corner. Do you hear that applause? I have been in this most privileged of professions long enough to know what that means. You have touched them, my dear," he raved, in complete contradiction of all he had said previously about the dangers of making an audience at a musical comedy feel too deeply. "You have reached across that most difficult of barriers between the footlights and the front rows. You have won their hearts, without a doubt. You will play the gypsy for the remainder of the run."

Leila still clung to the curtains as if they were a lifeline. The one person she had longed to reach had not been out there—would never be out there again.

It was Christmas Eve, and the stage-door at Lindley's was as busy as a toyshop. Young men, and some not so young, were gathering in a regiment of cloak-swinging, opera-hatted admirers bearing hothouse roses or orchids, small velvet boxes, or large beribboned parcels with names of furriers or couturiers stamped on the sides. Hansoms stood in a long line awaiting the appearance of the ladies in their satins and silks, their diamond ornaments, and their rich cloaks trimmed with soft expensive fur. Fifty yards away in the main street, there was all the noise and bustle of a departing theatre audience. Coachmen called up private carriages, commissionaires hailed passing cabs, large parties of people noisily arranged to meet up again at so-and-so's to continue the festive jollity. Those from the gallery shouted "Merry Christmas" to each other, before running to catch their trams.

Lights flooded out from the main entrance of Lindley's, but the narrow lane leading to the stage-door was shadowy. The wind whistled up from the main road. Snow flurries stung the cheeks of those who waited there, and settled in small drifts against walls.

Inside Lindley's, there was as much colour and activity as there had been during the performance. The girls were all dressed to kill, and bubbling with excitement as they exchanged presents, kisses, or caustic comments, according to the recipient. Lester Gilbert had bestowed a gift, along with a glass of champagne, on every employee, and his own personal coterie had gathered in the opulent room he called his office to tell each other alcoholically how wonderful they were. Adeline Tait and Franz Mittelheiter were carefully avoiding each other, as they always did off-stage these days, but each had an armful of expensively wrapped presents, and the open doors of their dressing-rooms showed a miniature Covent Garden of flowers inside.

Leila used the gaiety to keep at bay thoughts of the previous Christmas with Rose, when they had laughingly pretended to read the tea-leaves that predicted every dream would come true. How different reality! The doomed Rose had said goodbye to the world, holding on to her dreams. Leila had carried on to see them all shattered. She was still taking the rôle of the gypsy, and gaining rapturous responses from audiences nightly.

After that first emotional performance, she had pulled herself together. The distress caused by reading of Vivian's marriage had hardened into determination to make her career her only love, in future. She had remained as Lola, the gypsy, accepting Lester Gilbert's offer to pay for her singing lessons. Professor Halstein had welcomed her back cautiously, but had soon recognised a new, hard-edged sense of purpose in her response to his tuition.

Amidst the backstage revellers that night, Leila was probably the only one who would be glad when the Christmas break was over. She was joining a large group of girls and their escorts, who had been invited to a party being given by her own most consistent escort. Robin Gaye, eldest son of a prominent advocate, had hired a boat laden with presents, to take them all down the Thames to his riverside lodge, where they intended to dance the night away. Robin was eccentric, but

Leila favoured him because he was interested more in having fun than in making demands she could not fulfil.

At last, someone made a move to leave, and the backstage party broke up. Leila put on a dark hooded cloak, as did most of the girls, then made her way to the stage-door where Monty Monkton had made a fortune in tips that evening. She shivered with the cold as she stood in the entrance, looking for Robin, who had probably emulated the other escorts by waiting in the hired cabs. It took a moment or two for her eyes to become accustomed to the darkness outside. When they did, her knees turned weak with fright. A short distance down the narrow alleyway, huddling against the wall in an angle that offered slight protection from the snow flurries, was Frank.

He spotted her simultaneously, and started forward. Instinct led her to draw back, turning to fight against the outward surge of people. She stayed several feet from the entrance, trembling and irresolute, feeling trapped. What was he doing here? He had looked desperate enough for anything. She dared not go out to face him. He could rob her of the only thing left in her life, if he chose to reveal the truth. Dear God, what could she do?

There was only one means of leaving Lindley's without using that door. The main entrance to the theatre opened to the busy street, and was situated fifty yards from that alleyway where he lay in wait for her. If she could reach home safely, there would be time to think; time to plan against this new threat. On the point of turning toward the auditorium, there was a commotion outside followed by a woman's cry of fear. A rush of actors swept her along with them to the stage-door, then into the snowy night outside. There, in a cloak similar to Leila's, Adeline Tait was struggling with a one-armed man who was trying not to loose his hold on her purse.

"You got ter give me money, Lil, or I'll spill the bloody beans good and proper," Frank was shouting in a hoarse desperate voice. "Give it me, you whoring bitch!"

Two top-hatted men lunged toward him. He swung round to evade them, slipped on the snow, and grabbed Adeline Tait's shoulder near her neck to save himself from falling. The girl screamed in the belief that he was about to choke her to death, and let go of the bag he had been after.

Flinging it to the ground, she shrilled, "Take it, take it," before pulling free of him, and rushing hysterically down the dim lane toward the bright lights of the street. Frank started after her, but was brought down by a group of waiting escorts, and lay sobbing for breath in the snow. Leila had turned as cold as that white covering, but her blood seemed to totally freeze when she took her gaze from Frank's prone figure just in time to see the girl, who had been mistaken for her, rush headlong into the path of a passing carriage. Adeline Tait was tossed into the air like a rag-doll, then fell to lie twisted and still in the gutter.

Women screamed, men shouted and ran forward. All traffic was halted by a huge gathering crowd. All those clustering by the stage-door rushed to join it, leaving Leila to walk slowly after them. Frank had been jerked to his feet, and was being frog-marched to the scene by those men who had tripped him. He seemed stunned by the fall, and by the turn of events. People were rounding on him. Mature men shook their fists furiously; some hysterical youths had to be restrained by their friends. Women were shouting abuse, carried away by the shock of what they had just seen. A policeman appeared, and Frank was handed over to him.

"He tried to steal Miss Tait's bag."

"He seized her around the throat."

"I heard him threaten to kill her, if she did not hand over her money."

"No one is safe at night with beasts like that around."

"Hanging is too good for monsters like him."

"Murderer! Foul murderer!" sobbed an aristocratic youth hardly past his school-days. "You've killed an *angel*."

Those who had witnessed the drama, and those who had not, all gave their opinions to the policeman holding Frank by his collar and threatening him with his truncheon.

They were carrying Adeline Tait from the road now. Her face and head were a mass of blood, one arm hung useless, her legs that had twinkled in dance steps around the stage so many times were crushed. Their darling, the girl who had put light and joy into so many lives with her pertness and vivacity, had been extinguished like a candle. Leila felt completely frozen as she stared at the body, which had been lain reverently upon the spread cloaks of her admirers. Then she raised her eyes, to see Frank looking back at her as if he saw a ghost.

The girl beside her took her arm. "Come on, Leila, there's nothing we can do, and it's terrible just to stand and look at her like this." She coaxed further. "Come on! It's all over, and they've got the man who did it."

Still she stood there, hypnotised by Frank's look of despair, until a tall young man with a monocle arrived to take her hand.

"Do come away, my dear," said Robin Gaye. "It's a most frightful affair."

Frank found his voice then, and appealed to her. "Lil, I never meant this. I thought it was you. I wouldn't do what they say I did. Tell them . . . tell them I . . ."

She let Robin turn her away, as if she were a stranger who had never set eyes on him before. She let her wealthy friend lead her to a waiting cab and help her in. As it drove past she saw Frank's white face momentarily. Then he was left behind in the midst of a hostile crowd.

Adeline Tait's dramatic death hit the headlines everywhere. Following on the suicide of Rose Heywood, Lindley's Theatre was again at the centre of a story that aroused public feeling in conflicting ways. The cynical old-stagers declared the drama would bring capacity houses to Lindley's for weeks to come. For once, they were wrong. Where Adeline Tait had managed to survive the advent of Franz Mittelheiter because of her long-standing popularity with so many of Lindley's patrons, her poor little-known understudy was completely over-shadowed by his voice, and by his dashing personality. She failed miserably right from the start, and *Felicity May* was as dead as the effervescent girl who had played her. The show closed on New Year's Day 1898.

Journalists had been delving into the background of the man arrested on a charge of assault with attempted robbery. There was column upon column about his chequered childhood, following his father's desertion of his mother soon after his birth. Ethel Duncan had been traced to an address in Scotland, but it appeared that she had run off with a travelling salesman seven years ago, leaving four months' rent owing and no forwarding address. No one knew her present whereabouts, least of all her son.

There was a great deal about Frank Duncan's service in India, much being made of the wound which had necessitated amputation of his arm. The more crusading publications highlighted his plight, and that of all those servicemen like him, on being discharged by the army after such a sacrifice for Queen and Country. Unable to find work, rejected by society, what other course was there for such men but to turn to a life of crime, they asked their readers. Public opinion was swayed into believing Frank Duncan to be a victim of lack of government concern for serious social problems.

A few days later, he was again dubbed a vicious criminal threat to law-abiding citizens, when a woman calling herself Mary Duncan walked into a newspaper office, armed with a marriage certificate, demanding money for her story. She claimed to have married Frank Duncan six years before, when he had been working as a stable-hand in York. He had spent all her savings, then vanished leaving her with a babe in arms, and another on the way. Revenge was what she wanted; on him and on the army recruiting-officers who gave men the opportunity to dodge their responsibilities by parading as heroes in scarlet jackets.

On the night that Leila learned from a newspaper that there had been no mother in Scotland to whom she could have gone in a time of trouble, that she had never been legally married to Frank Duncan, and that she could have been Vivian's wife all along, she went to bed with a bottle of cheap gin and drank herself insensible. It had been the only way of getting through the tormenting hours of darkness. In the morning, she felt sick and ill, but full of an anger so great it fostered an unshakeable resolution. Never again would she risk being used by men. From that moment on, she would use each and every man who came her way. They would help her achieve all she wanted, and not one of them would touch her heart.

*Part Two*

# CHAPTER TEN

Vivian crested the rise and reined in, remaining in the saddle as he gazed at the panorama of which he never tired. The blue-green of the Atlantic lay to his right; the deep indigo of the Indian Ocean far to his left. Where the seas thundered landward there were vast golden beaches, playgrounds of migrating flocks and the occasional frolicking seals. The surrounding hills, green at the base, grew rocky at the point where they met the wide beautiful sky in craggy outlines that reminded him of the stark tors of Cornwall. Everywhere, wild flowers formed vivid rainbow gardens on rock face, grassland, and seashore. Orange and lemon trees were a riot of blossoms, which mingled with the purple jacarandas and giant bridal magnolias down in the sheltered vales. Amongst their branches, birds of every hue formed a moving rainbow of their own, as their bright plumage flashed momentarily in the sun.

Running his gaze from the pale golden rock, clear cut against the sky, down to the emerald bars of trees shading avenues of white houses of graceful proportions, Vivian sighed with an emotion not unlike yearning. Springtime at the Cape was a stunning mixture of colour, warm scents, and gentle breezes, which could seduce a man's senses into making him captive forever. A magnificent land, yet there were prizes beneath its surface that were driving men headlong into war.

Swinging his leg over the back of the horse, Vivian dismounted and slowly walked the few yards to where a flat-topped rock provided a seat, with an uninterrupted view of the area in which the house he had rented could clearly be seen. The stone struck warm through his breeches as he perched on that rocky outcrop, where he was often to be found before returning to that house . . . and to his wife.

For a while he simply gazed downward, lost in a procession of remembered incidents that had led to the present intolerable situation. If the regiment had been posted to an area like Ashanti, where women could not accompany their husbands, there might never have been a fatal deterioration in a marriage forced by circumstances. As it was, the move to a country with a seductive climate and every excessive delight of colonial society had given Julia the very weapons she had craved. Those weapons had been used against him by the most subtle of minds, until he had been rendered almost powerless. Now he realised the moment had come to make a bid for freedom, or go under forever. So he sat on in isolation, knowing that up there he was his own man rather than the one Julia was driving him to be.

Leaning forward with his arms along his thighs, he fought against the sensation of having returned to the trials of his childhood. Yet there was the same drive to rule in Julia as there had been in his grandfather, the only difference being that his wife was motivated by a strange form of love, rather than by hatred.

The marriage had caused dramatic rifts in both their families. Sir Kinsley and his sons would have preferred to individually horsewhip Vivian for his violation of Julia, then marry her off very hastily to Charles. Only Julia's calm, cold insistence on a showy society wedding, with everyone in attendance, had forced her family to accept something so unpalatable to them all. They were totally unforgiving of the loss of a title and an estate bordering on their own, and they would never recover from the joining of the only female in their family to a bastard, however aristocratic.

Vivian frowned as he recalled his brother's reaction to the affair. After thirty years of a relationship that had survived all their grandfather had done to differentiate between them, they had quarrelled so bitterly that there was no longer any contact between them. Charles had been shocked to the core, outraged, unwilling to believe such fraternal treachery. He had managed to coat everything Vivian had done since returning from Ashanti with the veneer of guilt—his warnings about marrying Julia had been made to disguise his own lust in that direction, his dallying with the chorus-girl, whose name Charles had forgotten, had been one of his military diversions to detract attention from his real objective. Charles had then declared that Vivian had always hated and resented him, and the theft of Julia was plainly his revenge motivated by jealousy harboured for too long.

The revelation had killed Lord Brancliffe. Collapsing on hearing the news which had been kept from him for as long as possible, the old man had died two days after the wedding. The honeymoon pair had declined to leave the Swiss Alps in order to attend the funeral, and the new youthful Lord Brancliffe had heaped further coals onto the fire of his brother's treachery.

The most bizarre result of the marriage had been Vivian's legal acquisition of that area of land designated as Julia's dowry, if she married anyone other than Shenstone's heir. Sir Kinsley, who had bought it after years of frustration, was forced to surrender it to his unwelcome son-in-law. It had been an action only slightly less galling than giving up his only daughter. Vivian had immediately written to tell Charles he could again count it as part of the Shenstone estate, only to receive an official communiqué from the family solicitor declining the gift of land. Without hesitation, Vivian had then closed off the road running through the area from east to west, thereby denying both his brother and his father-in-law access to their own estates from those directions. He had then reinstated the original tenant of Maxted's Farm, who had been ousted by Sir Kinsley in favour of one of his own men. It had only been after several months of marriage that Vivian had realised that he had wreaked the most acute vengeance on his grandfather, who had made no allowance for Julia having a will as strong as his own.

Shifting his position on the rock, Vivian wiped his damp brow with the back of his hand. The strength of Julia's will was the root of the trouble between them, and he could see no way of ending it without creating the kind of drama neither of them wanted. How could a man be actively virile, gain professional acclaim and social popularity yet, at the same time, feel emasculated? How could he? Yet he did.

On returning from their honeymoon, Julia had quickly won the admiration and devotion of the regiment's officers, from its colonel down to the newest cornet. To the members of a cavalry regiment, a female's equestrian skill counted more highly than her beauty. When she rode almost as well as any man amongst them, conversed frankly and boldly in their presence, yet still delighted them with her excellent taste in dress which perfectly set off her statuesque attraction, there was not a man who could resist her. Within six months she had had Vivian's fellow officers eating out of her hand, including Theo Fennimoore, who felt that she had somehow legalised the 49th's bastard by marrying him.

In her inimitable manner Julia had managed to sail through the first days of the Ashanti scandal, when it had been headlined in the newspapers and discussed over the length and breadth of the country. During the days leading up to that unhappy wedding, Vivian had lived a nightmare of doubts when angry crowds awaited him outside the barrack gates, and old acquaintances cold-shouldered him in clubs and restaurants. Worst of all, he had been physically assaulted outside his lodgings by the hysterical mother of the Engineer captain he had shot. Her words of abuse haunted him for weeks, until those three months in Europe gave him respite from the affair. By the time the honeymoon had ended, there had been a fresh scandal in the newspapers and in the minds of the British public.

Through his wife's connivance, and due to his regiment's desire to publicly defend their confidence in one of their officers cleared of guilt by an official Court of Inquiry, he had been promoted to major one month before the 49th had sailed to Cape Town on the first day of January in that year of 1899. He had rented a large mansion considered by Julia to be worthy of their social and military standing, and from that time on a marriage that had been tolerable had grown intolerable.

Quickly establishing herself as a premier hostess, Julia had seized every opportunity to further her husband's military career and social popularity. Devoting herself wholly to the task, she had accepted and extended invitations without consulting Vivian. She had offered his services to committees; she had volunteered, on his behalf, to serve as adjudicator, assist with the organisation of open-air shows and displays, and perform in military tattoos. Worst of all, she had taken any opportunity that offered to commit him to contests of the sporting variety, claiming with complete confidence that her husband could perform almost impossible feats with ease.

The result had been that Vivian had found himself forced to attend a constant round of balls and parties, which invariably continued well into the night. He had served on all manner of committees that took up much of his off-duty periods. He had spent long hours organising events in which he had no real interest, and had been obliged to practise regularly for public performance of military skills such as tent-pegging, and the slicing of turnips with a sword at the gallop. In addition, he had had no alternative but to engage in feats of strength and stamina with any fool who boasted to Julia of his own skill.

At the beginning, he had resisted, lost his temper with her. She held all the aces, however. Due to her enormous popularity with the civilian and military elements, it had proved impossible for him to refuse to accompany her to social events without appearing churlish and ill-mannered. It had been difficult to avoid accepting the places on committees without offending influential bodies, with whom the military desired good relations. Participation in displays had been obligatory, once his prowess had been so highly extolled by his wife in every parlour in Cape Town. Even more impossible, was a refusal to uphold wagers made on his behalf by her. To call off such contests would have humiliated his wife, reflected badly on the regiment, and cast doubts on his own standing as a gentleman.

Leaning forward, he put his head in his hands, closing his eyes in despair. At a time when he had been shattered by the only woman he had learned to love, and by public condemnation of an act that would go hand in hand with doubts for the rest of his life. Julia had promised a remedy. For that he had been deeply grateful, but gratitude had blinded him to the truth that her aim had been to take over his life lock,

200

stock and barrel. He was now exhausted, physically and emotionally. His wife even turned passion into a marathon that challenged him not to flag before she did. Her peculiar trait of revelling in extremes of masculine strength was receiving full rein, in a carefree, indulgent colonial society that regarded the military as no more than a colourful addition to the round of pleasant diversions.

He realised the danger point had been reached. Last night he had been forced to fence with John Kinson, as a result of Julia's boast of his skill with foils. His opponent had been his inferior, yet he had only marginally won. His movements had been sluggish, his eye had deceived him, his brain had refused to work fast enough. It had made him face the fact that his life had come full circle. The penalty of failure was worse than it had been in his boyhood. Then, there had been just one elderly bigoted man to deride and denigrate him. Now . . . !

Getting to his feet restlessly, he gazed down onto the house he had come to hate, to regard almost as a prison. Walking away from Julia would mean abandoning his military career, creating yet another scandal, becoming a drifter in one of the distant colonies as yet underdeveloped. Hell hath no fury, he told himself. Julia would hound him unmercifully. There was only one hope of escape—the war everyone said the Boers would never dare to precipitate. He had experienced war in Ashanti, and it had been terrible. Yet he longed for it now as his only chance for freedom.

The number of horses in the stables told Vivian that his wife was entertaining, as usual. His home was almost an unofficial officers' mess. The fact might have raised a few eyebrows in some quarters, save for the fact that Mrs V.V.H., as Julia was known in the 49th, had made it crystal clear that she was passionately devoted to her husband. What might have been considered suspect in a flighty woman was viewed as commendable adherence to the duties of an officer's lady in her.

Vivian saw it as yet another facet of her command over his life, and the urge to escape grew even stronger in him as he wearily mounted the stone steps leading to the verandah running around the pale stuccoed walls. Exotic creepers rioted along the verandah, but he saw nothing of the colour, smelt none of the heavy scents of the blooms as he entered with reluctance, and made his way to the salon decorated in cream and grey, with rich blue furnishings. Inside, he found four officers of his own regiment, and two strangers in the uniform of an artillery regiment. They all had glasses in their hands, as they lounged at ease in chairs clustered around their vivacious hostess.

The laughter slowly petered out as they rose to their feet at his entry, but the gesture was no more than casual acknowledgement of his rank.

Julia turned, left her seat, and made her way to him quickly; an arresting sight in a gown of shaded amber silk that he had not seen before.

"Darling, I have been quite distracted!" she exclaimed as she neared and, before he guessed her intention, reached up to kiss him full on the mouth before the interested gaze of six pairs of eyes. "John says you left barracks shortly before he did, yet you arrive so late. Whatever has delayed you?"

Resenting her public embrace and the tone of censure, he replied with deliberation. "Perhaps it was reluctance to see John again quite so soon."

Her eyes widened in speculation as she recognised his mood, but she laughed lightly as she linked her arm through his and drew him further into the room.

"I should think it more likely to be the reverse, after proving you were the better fencer last night. I am surprised, John, that you are not now in fear and trembling," she teased, giving a smile to the officer in question.

He smiled back. "Not with you present, Mrs V.V.H. I have never known a man so tractable as your husband becomes when you are with him."

The coloured boy appeared at Vivian's side with his customary glass of iced lime-juice and soda. He took it with a nod, then looked across at the two strangers, saying, "Perhaps you would present your new acquaintances, Julia."

Introductions were made, the artillery-men revealing that they were *en route* for Kimberley to advise on defences. The older of the two, a tall sandy-haired man called Sinclair, smiled at Julia.

"Now I have seen the cut of your husband, ma'am, I agree with you that I may well live to regret my boast."

"I trust you have not become too faint-hearted to defend it, sir," she replied challengingly.

Feeling himself growing tense, Vivian said, "Would someone kindly explain this conversation, which apparently concerns me in some way?"

Sinclair turned back to face him. "Your wife, Major Veasey-Hunter, counters my claim to own the fastest grey over a long distance. I am too much of a gentleman to question the veracity of a lady, but I believed she might be swayed by marital admiration when she vowed that you could outride me, on a grey called Mountfoot St George. We have provisionally agreed on a circular course from the Law Courts to the base of Signal Hill, on this coming Sunday morning at eight. Do you find that satisfactory?"

Still in the mood that had overtaken him in the hills, Vivian heard himself say, "Perfectly satisfactory, save for the fact that such a race is out of the question. Mountfoot St George does not meet the rules by virtue of being owned, not by me, but by my wife." He forced a smile. "Your boast looks set to stand, Sinclair. I have no grey to match against yours."

Julia's reaction to his refusal to accept the challenge was not lost on any man in the room, and Sinclair tried to cover the moment by laughingly declaring that he was probably being let off the hook, since his horses were not really at their best after the long voyage from England. The other men began talking energetically then, drawing Julia into a conversation about a present the 49th intended to purchase as an engagement gift for one of their junior officers. Left in the proximity of the two men on their way up-country, Vivian took the opportunity to question them.

"Am I wrong in surmising that your professional advice is being sought because of the present emergency?" he asked Sinclair. "There seems to be no other reason to send artillery experts to a city in the middle of scrubland."

Both men nodded, and the other, called Blaise, said in a low voice, "You are the umpteenth man to describe Kimberley in that manner. It does not fill us with confidence. The damnable place sounds to us like a perfect sitting duck. Of what use will a few obsolete cannon be against scattered horsemen advancing on all sides?"

"You think it will come to that?" asked Vivian with interest.

"Surely you are in a better position to know that, Major," countered Sinclair. "You have been stationed at the Cape for nine months, and must have assessed the situation."

"There you are wrong," Vivian told him, signalling the boy to bring more drinks across to them. "The general view in South Africa, is that the Boers are no more than a bunch of aggressive farmers who would not dare to take on the strength of the British, who have the might of an empire behind them. You are probably more *au fait* with the situation, in England. Down here in the toe of the country, so to speak, it is possible that we are more divorced from what is happening in the northern states than the government at home."

Captain Blaise frowned as he took a glass from the tray offered by the servant. "I'm afraid it's much the same story there. A head-in-the-sand attitude that pays no heed to men like my eldest brother, who fought against these 'aggressive farmers' in eighty-one. Anyone who was present at Majuba will tell you the kind of foe the Boer can be. That hillside was thick with our dead and dying. To risk a repetition of that humiliation at the hands of these Dutchmen would be madness. It needs more than Sinclair and I to advise on non-existent artillery, to prevent what I believe to be inevitable."

Excited by a view that matched his own, Vivian strolled across to the french windows standing open to the verandah. The two men followed, recognising his wish to speak more privately. Once outside, he looked at them shrewdly.

"Rhodes swears there is no danger."

"The man is a fool," declared Blaise immediately.

Vivian wagged his head. "I have heard him called a great many things, but never that."

"He lives in a fools' paradise, which amounts to the same thing. Not content with establishing a country named after him, he truly believes Southern Africa is his for the taking."

"It is the spoils beneath the surface that interest him so much, at present," Vivian pointed out.

"Therein lies the crux of the situation," interpolated Sinclair. "The Boers wish to farm the land; we desire to dig it up for the diamonds and gold beneath it."

"A number of British people also wish to farm it, Sinclair. In fact, they do. I have been a guest of those of my countrymen who have settled here very happily."

"There are also a number of foreign prospectors seeking to make a fortune by delving below the surface," said Blaise dryly, "yet I doubt they'll join us in the bloody business of protecting their rights."

"What are their rights?" mused Vivian, his gaze straying to the spectacular vista backed by the great flat-topped mountain. "My brother has put his wealth into gold; my mother has large investments in diamonds. He lives on his Cornish estate. Mama makes her home in Rhodesia."

Captain Blaise eyed him curiously. "I am not certain what point you are making, Major."

He shrugged. "No more am I . . . except, perhaps, that we might very well soon be taking up arms in defence of a great many people who have never set foot in South Africa."

"Surely that is beside the point," reasoned Sinclair. "We shall take up arms in defence of Britain and her empire. A parcel of farmers with long flowing beards cannot be allowed to undermine it."

Vivian nodded. "I agree. Would it not be pleasant, however, if the sacrifices made by our fellows in high-buttoned tunics were sometimes appreciated by those who benefit from them?"

The two men smiled. "The riff-raff of society in red coats," quoted

Sinclair. "The soldier has been reviled from time immemorial. I think we must accept that we shall always be regarded as society's most hated necessity. If we were the kind of men who looked for rewards, surely we should have our hands in the soil of this country groping for rich prizes, instead of patrolling it with rifles."

Vivian smiled back at them. "It's good to talk with men of sense and vision. Down here in demi-paradise too many succumb to the drug of pleasures that neutralise a sharp brain."

"Well, sir, I imagine that would be all too easy," put in the youthful Blaise smoothly. "With a charming and beautiful wife like Mrs Veasey-Hunter, what man would relish a war that would tear him from her side?" Finishing his drink, he went on. "I think you need have no fear of that. If war does come, it will be in the Transvaal and the Orange Free State, where garrisons have been receiving reinforcements for the past few months. Down here in demi-paradise, you will hardly feel any change." Turning to his companion he said, "Come, Sinclair, we should take our leave of our hostess. We are committed to dine with the Elsworthy-Smythes whom, we have been warned, are intolerant of late-comers to the extent of going to the table without them. I don't relish a few scraps in the servants' quarters in place of a good dinner."

Sinclair laughed. "If we are to be living off field rations shortly, by all means let's have as many good dinners as we are offered. You will excuse us, Major?"

"Naturally," said Vivian, chilled by the thought of the war offering no escape for him. "Perhaps I will challenge your grey sometime, Sinclair."

"Come up to Kimberley," the visitor invited. "I'll be there for the next three months, unless Kruger is not bluffing and sets his farmer-army at us within that time."

The departure of the two artillerymen broke up the social gathering, and the others made their reluctant farewells. No sooner had the door closed behind the last of them than Julia turned on Vivian, her pent-up anger bursting from her in a torrent.

"How *dared* you humiliate me in that manner? To decline a challenge which I had instigated in order to prick the conceit of that man Sinclair suggested that I exaggerated, that I had lied about your skill and the stamina of Mountfoot St George. How dared you do it in the presence of so many of our friends?"

"On the same impulse that prompted you to display such generous affection for me in the presence of so many of our friends, no doubt," he replied.

"I did not know then that you were going through some kind of ridiculous rebellion," she told him furiously. "To say that you could not accept because the grey was owned by your wife was infamous! You inferred that I was to be compared with that low Mrs Quincy, who holds the purse-strings in that marriage and is proud to advertise the fact. Worse, it paints you as a poor creature ruled by your wife."

His mouth twisted. "I beg your pardon. You should have told me that you wished no one to be made aware of the truth."

It silenced her for a moment, and she stood on the expensive blue-and-grey carpet assessing the situation that had taken her unawares. From her gleaming auburn curls to the hem of her rich silk dress she presented a picture of voluptuous self-confidence, and the slight shock of his aggression did little more to it than cause her to consider the quickest way to bring him back to heel. Sitting gracefully in one of the cream brocade chairs, she looked up at him with an air of tolerance.

"I suppose you had better reveal the reason for your late home-coming. Presumably, this mood of yours has been engendered by something or someone you encountered *en route*. Come, confess!"

Anger ignited and raced through him like wildfire. "By God, you speak as if to a recalcitrant child! All I have to confess to you, Julia, is that I intend to decline any challenge, race, match, contest or wager you instigate on my behalf from this moment on. If you feel it will humiliate you, the wisest course of action is to refrain from a practice which suggests to me that you will only consider this marriage fully consummated when I breathe my last."

She sat very still as she looked him over from head to foot, with her own brand of sexual assessment. Then she smiled.

"Very well, darling, throw away all I have worked for over the past eighteen months. Earn yourself a reputation for faint-heartedness. Toss away all notion of regimental obligation, and allow society to tell itself that 'Veasey-Hunter's by-blow' is reverting to type." The smile vanished. "Oh yes, Vivian, I know what Theo Fennimoore used to call you. Have you any idea what it cost me to flatter and cajole that well-connected fool into accepting you as an equal? *Have you?*" she demanded, as she rose to her feet again. "Have you any notion of the depths to which I had to lower myself in order to survive, unscathed, the scandal of what you did in Ashanti?"

He stood silently, noting the sheen of perspiration on her brow, and the quickened movement of her breasts that showed the extent of her agitation, despite her fight for composure.

"You are a senior officer today, because I did my utmost to ensure that you were given promotion. You are respected, admired, trusted, and generally liked by all those whose opinions count, only because I engineered the opportunities for you to win such popularity. The details of your birth have been forgotten; you are accepted everywhere. Why do you think that is so, Vivian?," she demanded icily. "I have given you status and dignity. I have put an end to your wild ways, your succession of mistresses, your extravagances so often compared with those of your disreputable father. The world now sees you as a steady, responsible and devoted husband; a pillar of society and a dauntless upholder of regimental honour."

"How do you see me, Julia?" he asked coldly. "Still as a thoroughbred you mean to school?"

"I have," she claimed fervently, moving toward him. "Haven't I taken you over fences you never dreamed of jumping?"

"Where do you propose that this thoroughbred should end? In the knacker's yard?" he snapped. "You have enough experience of horses to know that the best partnerships between rider and mount are when complete understanding lies between them. You have no understanding of me whatever, and the course you have set for our marriage takes no account of whether or not I wish to follow it." Roused to such an extent that he could no longer stand still, Vivian walked to the fireplace where silver cups bearing his name adorned the mantelshelf.

"Look at those. They're not sporting trophies; they are the gleaming evidence of your self-indulgence. Have you any idea of what it cost *me* to win those for you?" he demanded, using her earlier approach. "Have you any notion of the depths to which *I* had to lower myself in order to support your well-nigh sadistic determination to make me prove that I was bigger, stronger, more skilful, more virile than any other man you encountered?" With a movement of his hand he swept the collection of silver onto the floor, then found he was shaking as he confronted her. "You claim to have given me status and dignity. You . . . a mere Marchbanks! The law might dub me a bastard, but my forebears on both sides were some of the noblest in Europe, I'll remind you."

He began to walk across to where she stood, pale but still outwardly composed. "You have been doing all this for yourself, Julia, but this is where your self-indulgence ends. From now on, I shall attend social gatherings only if I choose to. I shall decline to sit on committees or any similar body, and I shall make it clear that I have lost interest in sporting competition of any kind. It will cause talk, but it will be a nine days' wonder."

Julia glanced pointedly at the jumble of trophies on the floor near his feet, then back at him. "Very impressive, my dear. You are always at your most splendid when your self-control slips, and I have enjoyed this little display of aggression enormously. Has the storm yet blown itself out?"

Still in the grips of his anger, he said, "You can be more insufferably superior than any woman I have ever known, Julia."

"I am not surprised at that," she riposted acidly. "The women you have known, my dear Vivian, have been courtesans, whores, and trollops masquerading as ladies . . . like Leila Duncan." Her eyes narrowed. "It is very plain that that affair still troubles you, for every time I mention her name you react quite visibly. She was a little upstart who appealed to your baser instincts, that is all. I not only more than satisfy *all* your instincts, I also devote myself to your advancement in every sphere. She could only have taken you down. There is only one thing creatures like that can give to men like you."

Even after two years, that reminder of Leila's words threatened to open a wound he had believed healed. "*Give* is the operative word," he emphasised harshly. "You don't give me anything, Julia. The devotion to my advancement is relentless and obsessive. I have no choice but to take it."

A satisfied smile touched her strong features. "So you have regained your senses, and admitted the truth. Now that your little rebellion has ended, we will go up to prepare for the dinner party being given by Lord and Lady Claude." Slipping her arm through his, she looked up at him with relish in her large eyes. "There will be time enough, however, for me to match the storm clouds still in your eyes with some physical thunder and lightning that will dispel them completely, darling."

Breaking free of her, he cried, "You still don't understand! I meant what I said about bringing to an end this intolerable struggle for excellence. I am sick to death of flattering the influential, and performing tricks that will satisfy your need to drive me to the limits of endurance. Up in the hills this afternoon the notion of being a contented failure was irresistibly appealing. That is what I intend to be from now on. You see, I no longer care what the world thinks of me."

She stood outlined against the french windows framed by rioting yellow blossoms, suggesting an expensive cameo, and her next words put an end to his glimpse of freedom.

"What of your son who will be born in March? Do you not care what *he* will think of you?"

Life continued as before during that month of September. Vivian felt only regret at his part in the creation of life within his wife. If the child should be the son she confidently predicted, he would never satisfy her impossible standards. If it should be a girl, the little creature would be

208

reared as a boy in skirts. Knowing the pain and humiliation of an unhappy childhood, he realised the chances of his preventing a repeat experience for his own child were very slim. Julia would have unformed clay to model just as she wished. His depression deepened further, and when he passed the railway station one day to see troops of the Loyal North Lancashire Regiment entraining for Kimberley, he knew he would give anything to be going up-country with them. If war came, the 49th Lancers looked set to remain in Cape Town, carrying out normal garrison duties.

Reining in, he dismounted to stand watching the bustle of khaki-clad troops noisily piling their rifles and kit into the waiting train. The men were laughing and eager, shouting to each other that "Johnny Boer" would soon return to his plough when they swaggered through the streets of the diamond city. The officers were engaged in seeing their horses established in straw-lined trucks, supervising the loading of their excess of baggage, or bidding farewell to wives and sweethearts, who stood aside in civilised sadness at parting from the moustached stalwarts eager to prove their skill at arms.

Watching that scene unfolding before the breathtaking backdrop of Table Mountain against indigo sky, Vivian's sensation of envy grew so great it formed a lump in his throat. He well remembered once telling Julia that there was nothing to compare with being part of a regiment on the march. It was all there before his aching eyes: the cameraderie of those who knew their lives were dependent upon the staunchness of the ranks surrounding them, the easy conversation between men of similar bent who could speak their minds without the curb of female presence, the general acceptance of a man's right to shape his own destiny within the confines of duty. Best of all, there was a sense of identity, of purpose, of being vital to a cause.

Forcing himself to turn away, he mounted again and rode slowly through the tree-lined streets, automatically acknowledging the salutes and bows of those who found Mrs Veasey-Hunter's husband so tireless and obliging. Little did they know that Mrs Veasey-Hunter's husband felt desperately trapped. He could never walk away from Julia now and leave his child, as he had been left by his own father, to the misery of domination by a will that refused to be thwarted. By his own actions, he had cut off all hope of retreat.

There were guests' horses in the stables of his house, so Vivian entered quietly and went along to the library, telling the boy to bring his lime-juice and soda there as he wished to deal with some correspondence. It was cool in the lofty room shaded by a large flame-of-the-forest tree, the atmosphere of dark wood, leather-bound books and silence suiting his mood very well. He sipped the chilled drink appreciatively as he thought of that scene at the railway station, interpreting it only one way. His countrymen were mounting a show of strength designed to force Kruger to back down. The Boer leader did not appear to be the kind of man to do so.

The Boers were Dutch settlers with extreme religious beliefs, hardy constitutions, and an unshakeable conviction that the vast southern tracts of Africa constituted their "promised land". Evolving from the nucleus of traders established by the arrival of the Dutch East India Company in the eighteenth century, the Boers had never been easy partners of the British traders who had arrived practically on their heels. The former were idealists; the latter imperialists. The Dutch were Calvinistic, austere and dogmatic. To them, even the strictly moral Victorian British had appeared decadent.

The rush to claim the beautiful country of burning sun and awesome landscapes had increased animosity between the two races and, as the Boers had advanced northward to conquer the unknown, so the British had followed. Animosity had deepened into hostility when the British, who had established themselves as governors of Cape Province, banned the keeping of black slaves. The Dutch had refused to free theirs, and had trekked further north searching for peace, and the freedom to establish their own nation in the continent designated by their teachings as theirs by divine right.

It was at that point that a third contender for land had come upon the scene. Successive droughts and the wholesale slaughter of wild game to the point of extinction in central and eastern Africa had driven nomadic tribes further and further south into the lusher areas inhabited only by a race of pygmy people. These shy creatures had retired into the bush to live out their simple lives, but the southward flowing masses had eventually come face to face with the northward flowing Boers. The confrontation had been bloody, before a frail peace had been negotiated. Tragically, the native leader had betrayed his word, and the trusting Boers had been hacked to pieces in a horrendous attack that had instilled in the Dutch a permanent mistrust. The native tribes had finally been forced to agree territorial rights after yet another war, in which the British had sacrificed thousands of troops in defence of the Boers. Such sacrifice had mollified the two European races, for a time, and they had lived in grudging harmony having divided South Africa into four states, of which they controlled two each.

All might have continued that way save for the discovery of gold in one Boer state, and diamonds in the other. The gold area of the Transvaal had received a flood of prospectors of all nationalities, known to the Boers as uitlanders, who had soon outnumbered the ruling Dutch. Extorting huge sums from those who were recovering the underground riches with no help from them, the Boers had refused to give these uitlanders any rights of citizenship in return for their crippling taxes. When the same situation had developed in the diamond area of the Orange Free State, Cecil Rhodes, with the monopoly in the sparkling trade, had soon contrived the annexation of the area dominated by Kimberley, and added it to the British-ruled Cape Colony.

However, the gleam of gold still dazzled British eyes. The annexation of the gold-fields would be impossible, so deep into Boer territory were they. Pressure of a military kind had seemed the answer. A short war in 1881 and the foolhardy Jameson Raid in 1895 by an army of British patriots had failed to achieve either control of the rich Transvaal, or the gaining of rights of citizenship for foreign prospectors. Never a nation to give up easily, Britain was presently preparing to throw the might of an entire empire against her intractable old enemy, if all else failed.

Vivian stood at the open window of the library, yet saw nothing of the extended gardens beyond as he thought of his two years in Ashanti. The enemy there had been a breed of men with primitive ways and primitive weapons, yet with knowledge of a terrain so deadly to white men that it had made them into formidable adversaries. In this more southerly, civilised part of the great African continent, the Boers were educated, armed with modern rifles which they handled with excellence, superb horsemen, and strengthened by the conviction that God was on their side. Something told Vivian those men hastening up to Kimberley would be taking on rather more than aggressive farmers, if Paul Kruger mobilised his people.

Finishing his drink, Vivian turned away to his desk, reflecting that his own countrymen always began with one great disadvantage. Their wars were always fought in the country of enemies. It would be the same this time. The Boers knew their land like the backs of their hands; the British did not even possess maps charting the huge areas of open country between cities. Military authorities had always used the railways to move their troops, but a short stretch of track had only to be blown by the Boers and isolated garrisons could be completely cut off. Small wonder Sinclair and Blaise had worried about the defences of Kimberley.

It was almost like a continuation of his thoughts when Vivian put the empty glass on the desk and noticed the postmark on the letter topping the pile awaiting him. The handwriting was that of his mother, and surprise was mixed with alarm as he opened it with the small silver knife. How could she be writing to him from Kimberley, when he had believed her to be at her Rhodesian mansion safely distant from the rumblings of war? He read the two sheets rapidly, then lowered them to the desk as he sank into the leather chair. The Honourable Margaret Veasey-Hunter was staying in Kimberley with friends, and begged her dearest son to obtain leave of absence in order to visit her on a vital matter. She knew he would not fail her, and awaited news of his arrival with great impatience.

Vivian sat trying to control the excitement arising within him. His colonel would not refuse leave requested on the dual grounds of his duty to respond to such an urgent request, in addition to the wish to escort his mother from a prospective danger area. He saw his chance of freedom. It might be for only a short while, but it would be all the sweeter because of it. Putting back his head, he closed his eyes in relief. The city of diamonds had never seemed as dazzling as it did at that moment.

# CHAPTER ELEVEN

Vivian boarded the train for Kimberley on the following evening, taking with him some surprising items of baggage for a man supposedly going on leave. Besides loading into trucks his best two chargers, Oscar and a sandy-coloured gelding called Tintagel, there were in his trunk his pistol, sword and field glasses. A long tiring journey lay ahead of him but, before he turned in that night, he sat with a brandy and soda thinking about his mother whom he had not seen for three years. Whatever had prompted her visit to Kimberley, it could not have been more providential. With every mile he travelled along the railway Cecil Rhodes dreamed of building from the Cape to Cairo, Vivian's spirit grew lighter and his sense of excitement increased.

Naturally, his first duty would be to persuade his mother to leave the diamond city for somewhere safer, but the freedom to be himself plus the opportunity to be in the thick of a growing crisis, could only be due to the machinations of fate. Rhodes was presently assuring everyone in Cape Town that Kruger had been rattling his sabre for most of the year, and the fact that large commandos of Boers had been spotted moving around the veld simply meant an extension of his great bluff. However, Vivian's colonel had granted his request for leave with the proviso that he assess the true situation in Kimberley, and send reports back. It appeared that the army had less than total faith in Mr Cecil Rhodes.

Vivian was suddenly swept by memories of a dark-haired girl confessing shyly to him that all his brother had spoken of was a man called *Cyril* Rhodes. That had become one of their private jokes later, when he had fallen into the trap she had baited with what must surely rank as her finest histrionic performance. Strange that fate had sent his regiment to the very place where Rhodes was pursuing his policy to paint the whole of Africa pink on the map, even if the earth were stained blood-red in the process. However, it was not of the relentless empire-builder that he continued to think as the wheels clattered over iron rails, taking him across a darkened coveted land, it was of Leila Duncan. She could have owned him more totally than Julia, but she had chosen instead to force him to his knees then walk away. Even after two years, the sensation of shock at finding her living in sluttish manner with a coarse brute claiming her as his wife, was still only just beneath the surface. Yet the trap she had set remained in his memory as irresistibly sweet while it had lasted.

During the next day, the train snaked its way steadily northward, passing through contrasts of landscapes, each equally awesome in its own way. Great walls of grey rock, split here and there by sparse growth and falls of water that frothed and sparkled in the sun, gave passengers a sight of mountain ranges crossed by the early Boer trekkers in their waggons pulled by teams of oxen. Here and there, small deer could be spotted leaping from ledge to ledge in those isolated heights and, above the crests, birds of prey circled spread-winged against the stunning blue of the cloudless sky. Then the track left the grandeur of the ravines. As far as the eye could see in every direction stretched arid sandy soil, dotted with stunted growth and apparently devoid of life. Known as the Great Karoo, the plain shifted and shimmered in the mid-afternoon temperature that neared one hundred degrees, and Vivian's eyes ached from gazing through the open window.

He left his compartment to make his way to the open-air platform at the rear of the carriage to smoke a cigar, and it was whilst he stood there in conversation with another passenger that he spotted a large group of horsemen some way off. His companion, a Swedish merchant, appeared not to see them, so Vivian remained silent on the subject, but he was conscious of that moving mass on a sun-baked basin broken only by the shining iron track ahead and behind them. He saw all too clearly how easy it would be to stop all movements of troops. A few yards of broken track, in the middle of terrain such as this, would bring the might of any empire to a halt.

By the time the sun dipped to flood everything with crimson, it was possible to make out a distant series of flat-topped hills known as kopjes. Beyond those hills lay Kimberley, but they were further off than they appeared. Familiar with the tales of men who had crossed the veld and found distances tragically deceptive, Vivian turned in, knowing that it would be some hours yet before he arrived at his destination.

Kimberley had begun as a prospectors' settlement, and then progressed through all the stages of shanty slum, miners' boom town and financiers' centre. From a solitary farm owned by the brothers De Beer, the discovery of diamonds had set men digging, brawling, drinking, whoring and speculating, until the wealth brought up so laboriously from the soil had sorted the men from the giants. After the battle of those giants just three had remained, headed by Cecil Rhodes. He had formed a monopoly company named De Beers. The ugly earthworks, that had pitted the area with enormous holes in the diamond-bearing soil, had been filled in, and shafts had been sunk so that the digging could be done below the surface. The old unsightly earthworks had been replaced by new unsightly headgear, but the canteens, brothels, gambling-dens and prize-fighting booths had vanished along with the legion of hopeful prospectors.

Kimberley had become emminently respectable, with stately colonnaded buildings, race-course, botanical gardens, mansions of style and graceful architecture, a public library, a grand theatre, a tram service, and electric street-lighting. There was the Kimberley Club, run along the lines of the most illustrious of London's establishments for gentlemen of means and status, setting the standard for the citizens of that diamond centre of the world. If the ghosts of the old rip-roaring, exciting pioneering days were sometimes heard sighing in the wind, the sound was drowned by orchestral concerts, ballads sung by genteel guests at genteel parties, quadrilles and waltzes in elegant ball-rooms, and the ever-present rumble of machinery. Progress had come to that city in the middle of the veld.

Vivian's first sight of it came as something of a surprise. A pleasantly green area of high civilisation appeared to have sprung out of the surrounding dusty desolation like a mirage. Yet, as he stood at the railway siding supervising the unloading of his horses, he found himself thinking that Captain Blaise had been right. From the military viewpoint, Kimberley was a sitting duck. In the centre of a huge arid plain, with no city walls, sturdy gates, or areas of high ground within the city, any large attacking force could surely overwhelm it easily. As the second richest city in South Africa, and the mainstay of the British-ruled areas, it was ridiculously unprotected. When one also took into account its proximity to the borders of both Boer strongholds, such neglect of its safety smacked of madness.

Shaking off the thought as he stood in the springtime sunshine, Vivian told himself that a man of Rhodes' calibre would hardly be absent from his diamond company headquarters at such a time if there really was danger of war. Yet a small inner voice reminded him that Rhodes was not a soldier, and many a war had been fought because of the mistaken confidence of great men.

When the horses had been offloaded, he paid a porter to take his trunk to the Grand Hotel, before mounting to ride into the city with his spare horse on a leading-rein. As he rode, he realised that his first impression had been slightly erroneous. The British troops he had watched entrain earlier in the week were in evidence as he neared the picturesque wrought-iron market, where a riot of colourful fruit and vegetables, rolls of cloth, beadwork, ostrich feathers and all manner of foodstuffs were selling well. Selling so well, it seemed as if the towns-people were stocking up in preparation for an emergency. The North Lancashires in their khaki pith helmets mingled with men of the locally-raised Diamond Fields Horse—brilliant equestrian part-time soldiers in uniforms with the familiar bush-hats turned up on one side—and members of the Kimberley Police, who had infinitely more *élan* than their calm, painstaking British counterparts.

It was not a mere market-square scene, Vivian realised. Waggons loaded with sand-filled bags were following one after the other eastward through the city; the men in uniform were all armed and purposeful. His pulse-rate accelerated. Someone in this city appeared to be taking Kruger seriously. Vowing to seek out Sinclair and Blaise at the first opportunity, he reminded himself that his first duty was to call on his mother at the home of her hosts Sir Mayne and Lady Weldon. Only when he had discovered why she had sent for him could he pursue his military interests. All the same, as he entered the old staging-post inn on its corner site overlooking the square, his heart was singing a sweeter song than it had sung for many, many months. Since leaving Cape Town he had given no thought to his wife, or to the child who would bind them inexorably together when autumn came to South Africa.

When he trod up the wide staircase of the Weldons' home at four that afternoon, Vivian realised that the elegance of London, the chic of Paris, and the grandeur of Vienna had moved into Kimberley with the lords of finance. Her hosts had left Margaret Veasey-Hunter to greet her son in private, but echoes of their English country-house roots were evident in the cream and gilt decor and Regency furnishings of a room filled with knick-knacks, hung landscapes and bowls of hothouse flowers.

His mother rose from a *chaise-longue* as he was announced by the manservant. The first-floor sitting-room opened onto the inevitable verandah, which let in the soporific scents of blooms drenched by sunshine. After an absence of three years, Vivian was struck by the radiance of a woman who looked too young to have a son of his age. With her silver-fair hair upswept into shining swathes that accentuated the lines of breeding in her narrow face, eyes of a blue verging on grey added to an initial impression of remoteness. Her elaborate chiffon gown in love-in-a-mist blue, beaded with tiny grey pearls, heightened that impression. In spite of that, she beckoned in an indefinable manner that gave Vivian a vivid recollection of a girl in ostrich feathers, swaying haughtily about the stage and beckoning him in much the same way, as he had watched through his opera-glasses. He strode forward to take his mother's outstretched hands, and kiss her cheek. French perfume filled his nostrils as he straightened up to greet her.

"Can it really be so long ago that we said goodbye? Those three years have surely passed in reverse for you."

Gripping his hands tightly, she looked up at him in dismay. "My dear, have you been ill? I would never have wished you to undertake the journey in such circumstances."

Taken aback, he was uncharacteristically lost for words. "Your letter stated . . . I could not think why you had chosen to come here at such a time. Naturally I travelled up at once, in concern for you."

Still treating him to unhappy scrutiny, his mother continued her theme. "You have grown so thin, and your face is full of signs of stress. I confess that I was not happy when you came to me from Ashanti, but you had been ill with fever after an exhausting campaign. I made allowance for that, and you had recovered your old wicked charm before you left me. Whatever has happened to take the sunshine from you so completely? Can it be that you are still being hounded over the tragic shooting of two of your colleagues?"

Still off-balance from her unexpected greeting, he shook his head. "Other scandals have occupied the tongues of the world since then."

'So where has it gone, that self-possession and air of defiance? I used to believe you would one day take on the whole world and emerge the victor. What has happened to the son I remember?"

"I have grown older, Mama, whereas you appear to be younger," he said in an effort to change the subject. "Now, perhaps you will tell me why you have come here at such an uncertain time, and what it is that you wish me to do for you."

"How long can you remain in Kimberley?" she asked, still avoiding a direct answer.

Releasing his hands from her grip he said, "Colonel Messenger granted me three weeks' leave, but I daresay it could be extended, if necessary."

His mother nodded, and returned to sit on the *chaise-longue* striped in claret and gold, patting the empty space beside her. When he did not immediately accept the invitation, she looked at him pleadingly.

"Vivian, do sit here while we talk. I have seen so little of the man who has developed from the little boy I tried so feebly to protect. Do not deny me the pleasure of your proximity for this short while that we are quite alone together."

Sighing, he sat beside her. "Mama, you are well aware that I can deny you nothing."

217

"You deny me the truth, my dear."

"I . . . I am not sure I understand that charge," he said warily.

"Are you happy in your marriage?" she asked, out of the blue. At his silence she continued. "You say you have not been ill; you demolish my fears over that Ashanti affair. There is only one other explanation for the distressing change in you; something I have suspected all along." Putting her hand on his as it lay on his knee, she frowned. "Soon after we parted in Rhodesia, Charles wrote to me that it was his hope that I would return to England for his marriage to Julia Marchbanks, shortly after his twenty-eighth birthday. I next heard that you were to wed the girl, in such haste that it was impossible for me to be present on the occasion. Then, the rumour that Brancliffe had expired through shock reached me. You know how fast such snippets of malice travel . . . and how far."

Her faint sigh held an echo of a long-ago scandal that had affected them both so cruelly. "It does not take an exceptional intelligence to deduce that you stole your brother's bride, picked especially for him by that indomitable old man. There was one aspect I did not understand, however. My memories of Julia are of a plump hoyden of a child—the type of female Brancliffe would probably admire, but not you, Vivian. Until you walked in just now, I was forced to believe that Julia must have altered quite remarkably to have captured a man like you so completely that you would take her, at all costs."

"Now that you have seen me?" he prompted, knowing the subject had to be pursued to its conclusion.

"I believe that it was your brother's bride who stole you. My dear, however did you come to let such a thing happen?"

He was spared an answer to that by the entry of the manservant and a coloured girl. They brought in tea in a silver service, delicate china patterned in peacock-blue and gold, a sandwich-stand containing tiny triangles of bread with expensive fillings, and a frosted cake. By the time the pair had set out china and starched napkins with fussy perfection on the low table, and the man had poured tea to hand to them both, Vivian felt that the need to acknowledge the probing question had passed.

"I trust Charles is still in regular correspondence with you, Mama," he said, taking several of the minute sandwiches from the stand offered by the girl.

His mother gave a dismissive wave of her hand to indicate that the servants should leave them, and told Vivian that his brother was meticulous over his monthly letter.

"Poor boy, he is so very earnest," she complained with a wry expression. "Your letters have always been so vivid, so full of your extrovert personality, and so *spasmodic*, I have to add," she finished in chiding maternal fashion. "Charles sends me a concise account of all that I have no wish to know, but tells me nothing of his feelings or expectations. Brancliffe stamped out all vivacity from him years ago. What is to become of him, Vivian?"

"Nothing, until he recognises his great good fortune and uses it to his advantage," he replied vigorously. "Good God, he has complete freedom to make anything he wishes of his life. It is a sin to throw that freedom away. Shenstone does not have to be bleak and repressive. He should fling open the doors and windows, set an army of servants cleaning and polishing, then fill it with beautiful woman and men of intellect every weekend. Out there in the midst of spectacular moorland, galloping over that springy turf, flying over ice-blue streams and chasing between rearing craggy tors, a man can feel the sheer vitality of life. With the right woman beside him he could win happiness and fulfilment second to none."

There was a short silence when he finished speaking, and he saw naked sadness on his mother's face. Then she said, "You care so deeply, even after all these years. I am so desperately sorry."

Aware that he had spoken from the heart in describing his former home, he tried to cover the moment of weakness. "It is I who should be sorry, Mama. We have spoken of nothing but my brother and me, when I have come here expressly to be of some help to you." Shifting forward in his seat, he added, "Allow me to cut for you a slice of this confection that was plainly produced for your especial enjoyment, then please tell me what I am so anxious to know."

She watched as he cut a dainty portion of the cake, seeming hesitant to comply with his request. When she did speak, it was of something he had least expected.

"I wish you to attend an evening party tonight, Vivian."

"Mama!" he remonstrated. "Can we please discuss the point of my journey to visit you?"

"The party is being given to mark your arrival in Kimberley," she told him quietly. "Our host will be Baron Von Grossladen, who has asked me to become his wife."

Vivian was completely shaken by such news. Fortunately, she did not appear to expect a comment from him, and continued calmly, "If I marry Gunther, all monies I presently receive under the terms of James's will are forfeit. I shall not suffer. Gunther is a wealthy man. I cannot expect him to maintain payment of the allowance I have made you all these years, in compensation for your father's unjust treatment.

I wish to do nothing that will hurt you, however, so I brought you here in order to meet him and help me with my decision."

No more than a mile away from that elegant sitting-room, in a hotel apartment close to the theatre, Leila stood surrounded by the beautiful clothes necessary for a grand tour of South Africa. Evening gowns hung on the walls in a riot of pale and vivid shades. On the bed lay a scatter of shawls, scarves, wraps, lacy handkerchiefs, and delicate underwear designed for men to appreciate. The dressing-table sparkled with an assortment of bracelets, clips, earrings and necklaces lying carelessly amongst silk fans with jewel-encrusted sticks, several long ropes of milky pearls, and open boxes containing evening gloves. On a table behind her were boxes of chocolates and crystalised fruits, flanked by baskets of exotic flowers.

The show had been running in Kimberley for two weeks, and her popularity had been instantaneous. As elsewhere, men in this city of gems were only too eager to shower her with gifts. It had been the same in Durban—lavish persuasion; universal disappointment. Her hands stilled momentarily as she selected items bought from only the most famous houses of fashion. How far along the road of fame she had travelled! It had been a harsh and painful road, each step made alone until Franz Mittelheiter had offered a helping hand when she had been almost there.

After *Felicity May* had closed, Lester Gilbert had lost his magic touch. Knowing it would have been madness to dispense with Franz, the tenor had nevertheless constituted the impressario's major problem. After a succession of flops, it had been apparent that unless he could find a leading lady with a voice to match that of London's latest darling, there might never be another success at Lindley's. Mittelheiter had known this, and stormed into the great man's office after yet another show had closed, to declare that he had the obvious solution to their combined difficulties.

Immediately, after a year of short solo rôles or duets that had never done justice to her talent, Leila had begun rehearsing with the Austrian in the title-rôle of a new musical drama written by a brilliant, little known, Viennese friend of Franz Mittelheiter. *The Hungarian Heiress* had brought crowds back to Lindley's, and had established an exciting vocal partnership of a kind unknown in popular theatres. At Lindley's, Leila had occupied the coveted single dressing-room; off-stage she had occupied an attractive apartment decorated in blue and white, which she had paid for herself. Men had been permitted to pay for everything else she owned, but none had a key to her front door. Success had been wonderfully sweet: the power it brought sweeter still. She had used it to the full, and there was no resemblance between the *soigneé*, self-possessed leading lady and that simple trusting little fool, Lily Lowe.

Two attractive people who conducted a stage romance of riveting power each night could easily have made the mistake of believing there was more than professional rapport between them, but Leila and Franz were in love with success to the extent that they created it with eagerness and total dedication. She had questioned him on the subject once.

"How do we manage to be so romantically convincing when we are both so cynical, Franz?"

"*You* are cynical," he had protested. "I am merely a tenor playing a part on a stage. Then, I am the dashing handsome archduke who is madly passionate for you."

"But not when you leave it?" she had teased.

Shaking his head, he had remonstrated with her. "Have I not always told you that the first rule for success is to remove passion with the grease paint? Do you always obey this?"

"I follow all your advice, you know that."

"What of the man who once made you sing the gypsy with such heartbreak?"

She had turned away. "That was a lifetime ago. I have forgotten him."

She had believed that then; she still believed it. The last she had heard of Vivian was a brief reference to the fact that he had not returned from his honeymoon in Europe to attend Lord Brancliffe's funeral. Feeling sure Julia would see that scandal never remotely touched her husband again, Leila was not surprised at the apparent withdrawal from the London social scene of the Veasey-Hunters. After several months of dreading a meeting at popular supper-rooms, or in one of a dozen parks frequented by those in carriages or on horses, she began to relax and think herself cured. It was easier to put him and those bittersweet months out of her mind, if they were unlikely to come face to face, and if her companions made no mention of him in conversation. Love was too painful: fame brought fulfilment.

Young Nellie Wilkins had not been forgotten, however. When the pregnant girl had arrived at Leila's basement three days after Frank Duncan had caused the death of Adeline Tait, the former lady's-maid who had just discovered the treachery of men had taken her in without hesitation. Leila had also paid for the doctor. He had delivered a daughter who would never know her father working in a brewery. Vowing that she would have thrown herself under a train but for Leila's kindness, Nellie's gratitude took the form of undying loyalty.

As time had passed, Leila had taught the girl all she knew about waiting on a lady. When they had moved to the blue-and-white apartment, Nellie had worn dresses of stiff silk, with a cap and apron, and had been shown the correct way to admit and announce visitors. The girl called her new mistress "madam" in company. When they were alone she called her Leila. Never, *never* Lily. In return for a small wage and a roof over the heads of herself and little Sally, Nellie gave Leila a form of love she had never before experienced. A strange relationship, perhaps, but one that had given both girls what they had most needed at a time when their lives had seemed bleak.

Nellie stood beside Leila now as she selected her gown and accessories. After the evening performance she was to attend a party, ostensibly as a guest but almost certainly to sing to them, solo and in duet with Franz. Leila's most persistent admirer, to date, in this city was an artillery captain called Sutton Blaise, and he would escort her to the home of Baron Von Grossladen in Kimberley's most exclusive residential area. It would be her first encounter with the high society of this city of gems but, if she carried it off as well as she had in other towns on this South African tour, it would be another citadel demolished.

"How about the dark red?" suggested Nellie helpfully. "You always look ever so nice in that."

"No," declared Leila reaching her decision, "the yellow satin is more suited to the occasion. I suspect that the more stiff-necked members of local society will be at the party, and they would be sure to look down their noses if I arrived resembling the ladies of the diamond-boom music-hall. I'll save the red for those who will appreciate it. We must hurry. The curtain rises in fifty minutes. While you pack the dress and this shawl into the box, I'll make a start on my hair."

Sitting at the dressing-table, Leila began unpinning the dark tresses before brushing them into one long flow of hair. "Put in those white gloves with bead embroidery on the backs . . . and that ivory comb with peacock feathers," she instructed Nellie over her shoulder.

"What about shoes?"

"The yellow satin ones to match, of course."

"Jewellery?"

Her hands stilled their brushing, and she looked her image in the mirror right in the eye as she said, "I feel sure that Captain Blaise will send more than a corsage this evening, but put in the collar of aquamarines, just in case I'm mistaken."

"A week's a bit quick, isn't it?" commented Nellie, busy with the packing.

"Yes," Leila mused, still confronting her reflection, "but that man is consumed with impatience for action—of any kind."

With her head deep in the wardrobe in her search for shoes, Nellie mumbled, "He'll get it quick enough if them Boers do start a war, like they all say."

"What do you know of the Boers, Nellie?" Leila asked in slight amusement.

The girl emerged, her face flushed with exertion. "The troops down at the market are full of tales. One told me that last night he was operating that big light they've put up on the tower, and it showed up ever so many of them riding up and down and looking this way. I don't like the sound of it, Leila. They frighten me."

Leila wagged the hairbrush at her. "It's the soldiers you should be afraid of, my girl, not the Boers. Once bitten, twice shy you should be. You should never believe all the soldiers say."

"It's not only them," the girl persisted, growing pinker than ever. "Old Mr Loftus at the theatre said his son saw lots of them with guns, on our side of the border, when he came through with supplies last week. What have you to say to that?"

She continued putting her hair into the braided peasant style required for the first act. "Franz has received an assurance from Mr Chewton that civilians would not be affected by any fighting, and that if it continued for more than two or three weeks – which is highly unlikely—he would cancel the tour and send us home. Goodness knows what would happen then. The redecoration of Lindley's will take at least six months, which is why we came on this tour. With the show every bit as successful here as it was in London, and with Lindley's nowhere near finished and ready for a second season, sending us back now would be a disaster Mr Gilbert would not contemplate. Think how disappointing it would be for us, too. I love it here, and long to see the rest of the country. Anyway, I can't believe there will be a war," she finished, deftly pinning a braid around her head. "Captain Blaise, and all the officers I've met, have assured me that it is no more than a bluff by that dreadful man Kruger."

"Huh!" cried Nellie. "You've just told me not to believe all the soldiers say, but them officers are soldiers, when all's said and done."

It was no more than a short distance to the theatre, and Leila would have walked had it not been for the express command of Meredith Chewton, their manager for the tour, that she should travel by carriage because it gave a better impression to members of her public. As she sat beside Franz that evening, Nellie's talk of war kept her silent. Her most fanciful dreams had never included a journey to a country such as this. To a simple girl raised in London, Cornwall had seemed vast and uninhabited. South Africa overawed her, and the thought of having to leave it so soon was too disappointing to contemplate.

They had docked at Durban and had an initial wildly successful run in what she considered to be one of the most beautiful places she had ever seen. They had stayed in accommodation near the beach, and the sound of crystal-clear breakers crashing onto the shore as she had lain in bed was something she would remember all her life. That city of rioting flowers and golden coast had captured her heart, so that, at first, she had found Kimberley a disappointment. Yet she had soon discovered the fascination of unearthing diamonds, during a visit to the mines, and realised that beauty had many faces. The animal life was varied and colourful, but she still had to see her first wild lion. That treat had been promised her when they moved on to Johannesburg, where the cast was due to spend a weekend at the home of a wealthy hunter. Their final venue, Cape Town, would provide the thrill of seeing the famous flat-topped mountain. If war came, forcing them to return to England, she might never have the opportunity to come back to this land of natural wonders.

"You are extremely quiet, Leila," Franz said, bringing her from her thoughts.

She smiled at him. "Could there be a greater contrast than that between the bustle, noise and grime of London's streets, and this wide avenue full of perfume from such unusual blooms? Just look at those birds. Bright red starlings! Can you imagine them in London?"

He shook his head. "Nor in Vienna. Each place has its own charm, you know, like women."

That brought a soft laugh from her, as the carriage began to slow towards its destination at the rear of the theatre. "I beg you not to break too many hearts at the party," Leila said. "The husbands of your victims will refuse to attend the show. It's only a small community, and we need all the patrons we can get."

He gave her the flashing smile which caused most of the heartbreak. "The husbands will come to see you, my dear. That is why we are so successful together."

There was every proof of it that evening. The theatre was full. The élite of both Kimberley and its suburbs occupied the boxes, while the stalls and circle were filled with traders and the military. The story of *The Hungarian Heiress* was simple enough. It concerned the love of an archduke for an impoverished daughter of a vintner, a girl deemed unsuitable to be his bride until she goes to Paris, becomes a renowned opera-singer, and is left a fortune by a royal admirer. However, the costumes were more than usually lavish, and the musical score so hauntingly melodious, it had captured even hardened theatre-goers in London from the first night. To the citizens of a city in the heart of an open plain, such sights and sounds were truly stunning, and their roars of approval must have raised the ghosts of past entertainers.

Leila possessed the quality of passionate purity needed for the rôle of Kati, and Franz was utterly believable as the archduke. When they appeared in the finale, he in elaborate uniform with honours sparkling at his breast, and she in a vivid Hungarian creation of blue and green with a circular head-dress smothered in dazzling mock jewels, the fervour of their reception should rightly have lifted the roof from the building. Leila stood smiling into that tumultuous darkness with her heart singing. *This* was rapture, total enslavement, ecstasy beyond price. This could be gained from no man on earth.

Leila's dresser moved around with practised speed to help her remove the stage costume, then don her clothes for the party. During this period, the call-boy was delivering a succession of posies and baskets of flowers, which were placed around the room so that the recipient could read the cards attached to them. It was not until the boy delivered into the hands of the black-gowned dresser a jeweller's box with a white hibiscus attached to the lid, that the woman took it directly to her mistress.

Leila merely nodded, impressing on Mrs Finch to make haste with the arrangement of her hair. Sutton Blaise was of medium height, with a swarthy complexion and brooding eyes, so she decided on the high-piled *coiffure* she had worn for the Lindley Stroll. It made her look tall and remote, which she felt would cause her escort to pause before acting impetuously tonight. Only when she was quite ready, with the peacock-feather hair-ornament in place to accentuate her height even further, did she open the velvet box. He had good taste, and Leila was charmed in spite of herself. The pendant, on a fine silver chain, represented a hibiscus wrought in tiny diamonds. On the card, in thick aggressive writing which typified the man, was a simple message: "Wear this tonight and make me the happiest man in Kimberley."

Fastening it around her neck, Leila put the aquamarines into the box Nellie would collect shortly. Then she draped the silk shawl over her shoulders, took up a beaded bag and went out to meet her escort. He was dressed in the smart evening kit of his regiment, and saluted before taking her hand to kiss it. His gaze had gone straight to his pendant around her neck, and confidence was in his voice and smile as he said, "My tribute pleased you. Baron Von Grossladen has no idea how inconvenient his party has suddenly become." Handing her into the waiting carriage he added, "Once he meets you, my dear, he will certainly understand why we do not remain until the end."

"Do parties have an end?" she asked lightly, settling herself in the corner of the carriage. "It seems to me that guests stay until dawn breaks, but that the party has slipped away somewhere during the early hours."

He laughed, sitting closer to her than was necessary in the roomy interior. "I confess, to my disgrace, that I am rarely sober enough to witness the phenomenon, although I suspect that you may be right." Leaning closer he murmured, "You were magnificent on stage tonight. Who would have believed you capable of such fire and passion?"

"It is Franz who cultivates that," she responded, retaining her light tone. "I feel altogether different once the curtain drops." Drawing her shawl up to cover the shoulder nearest him, she continued deliberately, "Captain Blaise, I do beg you to put my mind at rest. My maid returned to me today with fearsome stories told to her by the soldiers. Is it true that the Boers have crossed the border in large numbers, and appear to be gathering together in armed bands?"

He gave a sigh of irritation at her change of subject. "The troops exaggerate. It is their stock-in-trade."

"You are also a soldier, sir. Do you always give the truth of a situation?"

His teeth showed white in the darkness as he smiled. "The truth of this situation is that I am with a lovely young woman who has shown me that she is not averse to my attentions, and I have no intention of discussing anything other than the pleasures of the night to come." Putting a hand up to her chin, he said challengingly, "You will now do away with 'Captain Blaise' and 'sir'. My name is Sutton, as you know very well, my sweet Leila."

Tilting her head away from his finger, she told herself that she had not mistaken the man's impatience. She would have to end the relationship before he got out of hand. In a small place like this, it could be damaging if he were allowed to grow too aggrieved.

"That is an uncommon name, I should guess," she said. "I have met only one other gentleman called Sutton. Do you know your namesake, the Duke of Dornmead? A quite delightful personality."

"No, I regret I have never encountered the fellow," was the disgruntled reply, as he shifted back in his seat. Mention of such exalted acquaintanceship had plainly taken some wind out of his sails.

By then, the avenue around them had filled with carriages, all making their way to the grand house laid back in extensive grounds, and their driver was obliged to join a queue along the curving driveway leading to the front door. Leila was impressed. Her host for the evening must be someone of considerable standing.

Once inside the house, her escort behaved in exemplary manner as they mounted the wide staircase rising from a hall that was a-dazzle with the finest crystal chandeliers. They moved slowly forward, with other guests, to be welcomed by their host. The Baron proved to be a tall well-built man with silver hair, a proud face that seemed remarkably pink amongst all those tanned by the sun, and ice-blue eyes. He greeted Leila with courtesy, saying how honoured he was that she had accepted his invitation.

"My dear lady, dare I beg from you the infinite privilege of a song for myself and my guests after you have taken some refreshment?"

"I shall be pleased to sing for you, Baron," she replied pleasantly. "There is nothing I enjoy more than my music."

With a bow of acknowledgement, he then turned to a striking woman standing beside him, whom Leila supposed was the Baroness.

"Allow me to introduce a very dear friend who has agreed to act as hostess for me this evening. The Honourable Mrs Veasey-Hunter."

Leila offered her hand automatically, because the sound of that name rendered her incapable of straight thought. He had claimed that his mother lived in Rhodesia, yet there could be no doubt of this woman's relationship to him. Fairer even than Vivian, there was something in her smile that echoed his in the most haunting way. Leila supposed that she said all she should, but her one thought was that she was looking at the woman who had stood by and allowed her sons to be browbeaten by a cruel old man. The press of guests behind them meant that they had to move on into the crowded salon, where the women outdazzled the chandeliers with the gems around their throats, and the men wore shirts with diamond studs.

Leila was still in a turmoil as Sutton Blaise presented some of his military colleagues, and Franz waved to her from the centre of a group of admiring ladies. Margaret Veasey-Hunter had appeared composed and self-assured. Could she ever have been a neglected young creature, afraid of her father-in-law to the extent that she could not defend her children? Had that striking woman, who was "a very dear friend" of the Baron, ever been a child bride in that great stone mansion in Cornwall?

It was as well that Franz took command of the situation when the moment came for them to entertain the guests, because she had given no thought to it since her arrival. He came to her to report that the small orchestra playing in the adjoining salon had been provided with the music from *The Hungarian Heiress*, and he had arranged with the

227

conductor that they would sing their main duet, followed by his solo: "Where is your heart?"

"You will then conclude the performance with 'My Faraway Love'," he said with a smile, "just to capture the husbands of the ladies whose hearts I have just broken."

An announcement from the Baron set all the gentlemen seeking chairs for their partners, and it was almost five minutes before Leila walked into the centre of the room with Franz to sing the lilting love-duet that ran through the show. It was always difficult adjusting the volume of their voices to the size of the room, but it came more easily than usual because the windows all stood open to the warmth of the evening, lessening the echo thrown back from the enclosing walls. It was also difficult to conjure up the emotional depths when performing off-stage. Thinking herself into the part of Kati took longer when the audience was visible, she found. But Franz was the dashing hero on- or off-stage, and his quick response to the music always helped her own.

She stood to one side while he weakened the knees of every female present with his plea: "Where is your heart?" Allowing him every moment of his well-deserved applause, Leila then let him draw her out for her own solo. Well into character by now, she began the verse with the same emotion it aroused in her on a darkened stage, leading straight into the chorus that invariably brought a tense hush in those listening to her. It did so then but, instead of losing herself in the song, that silence made her aware of a late arrival appearing in the small adjoining room. Only her expert training kept her singing as she recognised him, even from a distance and in dimmed lights.

In her heart she had known the moment was bound to come, but not here, not now. When he stopped abruptly and stood so still in the doorway, it was clear that he was as stunned as she at the encounter. The music played on, and she sang with it as that moment of confrontation sizzled between them like an electric current. Every glance, every word, every memory of their lost love rushed headlong through her as their glances held, and could not break away. Because of it, she found that she was singing just to him as the reprise of that chorus unfolded.

"My faraway love I long just for you.
These lips, still unkissed, whisper my sighs.
I wait and I dream, to hope I am true
Till you come to me here with love in your eyes."

As applause filled the crowded salon, Leila was aware only of that tall figure in the doorway. But when he moved slowly forward, and the lights played over that familiar uniform and the pale shining hair, she grew cold. Could he be the Vivian she had loved so deeply two years ago? Gone was the devil-may-care look, the laughing eyes, the aura of supreme self-confidence. His face had grown thin and watchful; the green eyes looked haunted as they gazed at her down the length of that room in shocked disbelief. Dear God, she thought. Julia has extracted a high price from him in return for her devotion.

Knowing that she had to get away, knowing that every moment ticking past as they gazed at each other was destroying what she had become, she turned blindly from the group of enthusiastic people approaching her and Franz. Sutton Blaise came to her immediately, full of his own brand of admiration, and appeared only too glad to respond to her plea to retire from the crowded room. With his arm around her, the dark-haired captain led her along a corridor and into a deserted room lined with bookshelves.

Once there, she turned to him in explanation. "Forgive me. The atmosphere was very close and humid."

"That was not all," he said, watching her closely. "That song brought out all the fire and passion I mentioned on our way here. Herr Mittelheiter must be highly skilled at arousing it, if he can do so in a crowded room." He smiled confidently. "However, there are other men who are equally skilled, especially under the perfect conditions." Tilting her chin up with a strong finger, he asked, "Shall I give the Baron our excuses? You have sung for your supper, and thus fulfilled all that was expected of you this evening. The rest of the night is ours, my dear."

Emerging from her moment of panic, his words began to make sense. So did the look in his eyes. Breaking from him she backed several paces.

"You may certainly make our excuses to the Baron, Captain Blaise, but I then wish to be escorted to my rooms."

He advanced on her. "My own wishes exactly. Your rooms will serve our purpose admirably."

Backing still further, she realised how badly she had underestimated this particular man. "You have made a very great mistake, I fear."

Smiling wickedly, he shook his head. "No mistake, sweetheart. You read the message I sent with the diamonds, and you gave your answer by wearing them tonight. The time has come for you to honour your side of the bargain."

Feeling more and more disgusted, Leila said in cutting tones, "There is no *bargain*. I don't sell myself for a few diamonds—or for anything else. A gift is merely that. It buys you nothing."

His mouth tightened. "Oh no, miss, you are a little late for that stage of the game. You were very well aware of where my attentions were heading. I am not a man to indulge in dalliance for long. I want you, and this is where you give me the reward for my very open admiration."

Before he could move nearer, she reached up to unfasten the pendant with trembling fingers. Holding it out to him, she said, "I believed this to be a gift from you. You apparently meant it as an advance payment for something I never give. Now honour is satisfied on both sides."

"Honour!" he repeated contemptuously. "That's rich coming from a female of your kind."

Stepping forward, she slipped the diamonds into the pocket of his high-buttoned tunic, saying with a composure she did not feel, "You evidently misjudged the kind of female I am, Captain Blaise. It's a mistake men often make."

His lips curled. "You must expect that. What else are they to think, when you accept the kind of expensive presents they have no need to give to their wives?"

Not trusting herself to continue the scene in her present shaken state, she informed him icily, "Your expensive present has been returned. Now please go, before your claim to be a gentleman is negated by your appalling behaviour."

Giving her a final contemptuous glance, he left the room rattling the double doors as he slammed them behind him. Left alone, Leila gripped a nearby chair as she strove to regain the cold determination she had believed no man would ever penetrate. That belief had been shattered during the singing of a love-song. Somehow, she must reinforce it.

It was a moment or two before she grew aware of the sound of soft clapping behind her. Spinning round, her heart still thudding, she saw Vivian lounging in the doorway from the verandah. His applause was slow and mocking as he gazed at her with an echo of the way he had looked on that terrible October afternoon.

"Bravo, my dear. The man no longer has his jewels flung back at him as he is pitched from the cab. This version is much more civilised and, since the gallant Captain Blaise seems unlikely to persist in pestering you, as some fools do, I suppose it won't be necessary for you to introduce the brutish foul-mouthed husband. Or have you also refined that part of your act?"

# CHAPTER TWELVE

For the remainder of that evening, Vivian spoke and acted like a man at the end of a long tiring journey. Only he knew that the journey had been into the past, and not the one from Cape Town to Kimberley. How *could* Leila be here? With an entire world populated by millions, what cruel stroke of fate had brought them simultaneously into a room, in a house, in a city on a plain, in a vast continent so far from their homeland?

Walking deliberately late into that party, he had already been a man deeply disturbed by the news his mother had broken some hours earlier. Then, a voice from an upstairs room had chilled his spine, and he had followed it to discover that the haunting sound had come from lips he had kissed with such desperation. In pale yellow, with her hair piled high, she had looked the same girl who had walked out to him on that first evening, in response to a bouquet she had believed to be from his respectable brother.

There was no doubt that she had been as shocked as he, yet she had controlled herself to the extent that he must have been the only one in the room to recognise the fact. That could not have demonstrated more clearly the truth of what she had written to him. He had been an impossible obstacle to what she had now successfully become. Retreating to the verandah whilst he pulled himself together, he had heard her speaking to someone in a nearby room. He should never have gone in search of that conversation. She had walked away from his words which were intended to wound, leaving him to suffer the pain of them instead.

He had still been in that state when his mother had sought him out, her silence on the lateness of his arrival being somehow worse than a lecture. When introduced to his host and possible future stepfather, Vivian had taken an instant dislike to the man. He was trying very hard to cover the fact now that the guests had departed, and they sat together in the mansion built especially for the man who had invested heavily in diamonds, and made a second fortune. His first had been accumulated by the family porcelain business in his native Germany.

Gunther Von Grossladen was imperious, a stickler for protocol and immensely shrewd. In growing dismay, Vivian saw a number of similarities between the man his mother appeared to find so fascinating and old Lord Brancliffe. Admittedly, the German's iron fist was velvet-gloved, but there was no doubt of his intention to have his way in every aspect of his life. Margaret Veasey-Hunter was either blinded to the fact by his obvious charm, or she was the type of woman who accepted domination as inevitable—maybe even enjoyed it. Vivian had grown up believing his mother had been a helpless victim of Veasey-Hunter men. Was that assumption wrong? He caught himself wondering, as he watched his mother's behaviour toward the same type of male arrogance.

On a night when confusion prevented clear thought, and he was finding the heat of Kimberley very trying, Vivian participated in the conversation with no more than stilted comments. Sitting in a small salon that gave the impression of rising and falling like the train in which he had spent several days, the Baron had quickly dispensed with the niceties regarding Vivian's career and marriage. Then, he approached the vital matter with a confident smile.

"Margaret has seen little of you since you departed the family home for university, Major, and I suspect that she still thinks of you as the boy you were then. Such touching concern for you, but such foolishness. A man of thirty-two, with a flourishing military career and a devoted wife, should not be regarded as a consideration in this matter. Would you not agree?"

"What we two agree upon, sir, is immaterial," he replied with caution. "It is Mama who must make a decision, and make it with the confidence that it is the right one."

The ice-blue eyes narrowed. "You mean to retain your hold on the apron-strings?"

"I think I have never held them," he responded stiffly, trying to maintain cohesive thought in that stifling atmosphere. "What I certainly intend to retain is the relationship with my mother, which entitles me to speak on her behalf when she has brought me across a continent in order to do so."

The Baron turned to Margaret with a slight frown. "You have asked your son to speak on your behalf, in a matter that surely concerns only we two?"

"No, my dear, of course not," she contradicted gently, destroying Vivian's defence of her at a stroke, and leaving him even more confused over her behaviour. "Vivian has always been conscious of his duty toward me since the death of his father, and I made him aware this afternoon of how much I wished you two to like each other."

With a satisfied smile, the other man turned back to Vivian. "Ah, you see the misapprehension under which you have been labouring?" Leaning back at ease with the crystal brandy-goblet in his hands, he went on, "Margaret has acquainted me with the unfortunate circumstances which have burdened her all these years with a maternal compulsion to compensate you for something no one could help. I appreciate that affection for your mother has led you to stifle your repugnance to the notion of being financially supported by a widowed female, for fear of upsetting her foolish, but possibly natural, feelings of remorse over your legal illegitimacy. However, your forebears cannot be denied and, as a gentleman of such distinction, I am persuaded that you will be greatly relieved to have this uncomfortable obligation removed in so happy a manner. It must also be a comfort to you, to know that this will be the last occasion on which you are brought across a continent to do your filial duty," he continued smoothly. "Your mother will have a doting husband on whom to rely for all she might need."

Fighting lethargy, reaction from the meeting with Leila, and an instinctive dislike for this man who constituted the second shock of this strange day, Vivian heard himself say, "My understanding of the situation is that Mama has not yet reached a decision that will gain her a doting husband. However, if she does decide to become Baroness Von Grossladen, it will in no way affect my filial duty toward her. I will cross any distance to reach her, if she sends for me."

His mother leant forward, a small frown on her face. "You foolish boy, Gunther was not suggesting that there would be any change in our relationship. You will always be my beloved first-born, whatever happens, but you have a wife now, and there will doubtless be sons of your own demanding your advice and support. They will rightly have first claim on you."

He stared at her, a slender gentle woman with a fragile kind of beauty, whom he had loved and hotly defended for as long as he remembered. She was handing him back his devotion, to give to a wife who wanted blind obedience rather than affection, and a child who would be taught to expect no more than reflected glory from his father. Did no one need his *love*?

The Baron, who was watching Vivian with shrewd interest, seemed irritated when a manservant approached with a letter on a silver tray, announcing that the messenger who had brought it had insisted that the matter was urgent. Asking their pardon whilst he read it, their host rose to his feet and walked out onto the verandah. Almost immediately, Margaret spoke in a chiding undertone.

"Vivian, what strange mood has overtaken you? I was prepared to

233

overlook your bad manners in arriving so late, on the grounds that you had undertaken a long journey and needed to rest, but you are being uncharacteristically pugnacious.''

The room appeared to be shifting and heaving in the most peculiar manner, and he felt the tight, high collar of his tunic practically choking him on an evening when the air was undisturbed by even the slightest breeze.

"Forgive me, Mama," he mumbled, "but I had not realised that your decision to marry Von Grossladen had already been reached. From your words to me this afternoon, I imagined that you had sent for me to . . . to seek my advice and approval before reaching your conclusions.''

"I do not have either, that much is plain." She sank back in her seat with a sigh. "I had hoped so fervently that you two would become friends, that Gunther would be to you the father of whom you were virtually deprived.''

Wiping, with his handkerchief, the beading of perspiration that had risen on his forehead, Vivian marvelled that she could see the arrogant German as a willing, kindly stepfather to himself and his brother.

"I am rather mature to require a substitute for someone I have never missed," he pointed out, wishing his mother's vision would stand still before his eyes.

"I confess I do not understand you," came her voice from one of the figures in the chair next to his. "There is something extremely peculiar about your behaviour tonight. I accept that my news was rather more of a shock to you this afternoon than I had imagined, and it was apparent from the moment you greeted me that you had undergone a drastic change since our last meeting. There is more, surely. Something has happened since you left Lady Mayne's house which has put bitterness in your voice and in your expression. If you are not careful, you will make an enemy of the man for whom I care deeply. If you love me, as you claim, you will prevent that, at all costs. The consequences would be tragic, Vivian." Her hand fell on his knee. "Whatever is behind this inexplicable attitude?''

By that time, he had recognised the signs of something he had experienced before. He tried to tell her dancing figure that he must get to bed as soon as possible, but the words refused to be said as the heat of his body increased even further, drenching him with sweat.

"Vivian. *Vivian.* Dear heaven, he is ill," exclaimed a faraway feminine voice.

A bell rang, then he was being assisted from the chair as the familiar shakes began. Voices came to him as if through a blanket, and his legs buckled so that he had to be supported by a strong shoulder beneath each arm.

"*It must be that wretched fever. Poor boy, it takes such toll of him.*"

"*This could not have come at a worse time.* Liebling, *I have serious news. Colonel Kekewich, who commands the military in Kimberley, writes to me that Paul Kruger has issued an ultimatum which your countrymen cannot, without humiliation, meet. There will be war within the next few days. Rhodes is on his way from Cape Town to help defend his interests and friends here. We have no resident garrison, and the fall of the diamond city would be unthinkable.*"

"*Gunther, no!*"

"*There is no cause for alarm, I promise you. Once he arrives, we shall form a committee to direct operations regarding this city. The British troops in South Africa will be mobilised at once, of course, but it seems unlikely that your son will be fit to rejoin his regiment, as all men on leave are being asked to do. He will doubtless chafe at the delay when he recovers.*"

Those were the last words Vivian heard, before succumbing to a particularly severe bout of fever. When he emerged from it, he discovered that it was impossible for him to rejoin his regiment. Within four days of their ultimatum, the Boers had crossed their borders to surround both Kimberley and a small town called Mafeking two hundred miles northward. They had moved with such swiftness, the British had been totally unprepared. However, the enemy were in force around the "sitting duck", and appeared content to starve the city into submission rather than lose men's lives whilst rushing to capture a large population they would, somehow, have to guard and feed. All roads leading to Kimberley were held by the enemy; the railway had been cut. Any person moving out onto that plain was clearly visible, a perfect target for men of the land who were expert shots. No one could pass in or out of the diamond city.

Vivian could only wonder at the machinations of fate. Trapped in that city with him was a girl who had caused such a storm within him it had never blown itself out. In the days to come, he could not avoid her. He had come to Kimberley seeking escape, but had found no more than a captive freedom.

As soon as he was able, Vivian sought out the man who had been placed in command of all cavalry troops in Kimberley, to offer his services. From Major Scott-Turner he learned the facts of the situation. The Boers had been gathering their forces during the winter period when the veld was an inhospitable place, waiting for springtime to provide adequate forage for their horses as they moved from place to place.

Then, they had presented the British with an ultimatum: withdraw all troops from border areas, return to Britain all reinforcements that had arrived in recent months as a show of strength, and turn back all those ships presently bringing huge numbers of crack soldiers from Britain and India. These impossible demands had guaranteed a refusal, and provided the Boers with the opportunity to launch the war they dearly wanted. Overconfidence had lulled the British into refusing to take Paul Kruger seriously, and they had been stunned by the swiftness with which the two sieges had been achieved. All available troops were being mobilised, but priorities were hard to assess, as yet.

Martial law had been declared in Kimberley, and outlying stations had been successfully evacuated to boost the strength within the city. Several train-loads of supplies had been brought in from depots down the line before bridges had been blown by the Boers, so hardship was unlikely to be experienced by the population whilst waiting to be relieved. As a precaution, shelters were being swiftly created for the civilians in case the enemy should advance near enough to shell the city itself.

Amongst the population were several Boer families, who posed a problem. An invitation from the man commanding the besieging force to all these families to join him had been accepted by only one. The rest could not be forced to go: they were legal citizens in the British province. There were many such people who had settled happily in territory ruled by their national enemy, but they chose to play no part in the present struggle for power. What they might do if their countrymen overran the whole of South Africa was a matter for speculation, but they showed no more aggression, at present, than their normal disinclination to mix with their British neighbours. In Kimberley, they were tolerated, but a watch was maintained to ensure that they made no atttempt to slip out with information, or send signals of any kind.

Major Scott-Turner accepted Vivian's offer gratefully, glad to have a regular cavalry officer who had seen active service in the war against the Ashantis. If he had views regarding the shooting of two Englishmen by this volunteer, he made no mention of them. With only the locally-raised horsed regiments to fulfil the vital cavalry rôle, any man capable of leading untried troops in combat was welcomed with heartfelt relief. Arrangements were speedily made for Vivian to occupy a tent in one of the camps that had been set up near the perimeter of the city, and he shook the man's hand as if sealing a bargain, before departing for the Grand Hotel to collect his horses and equipment.

On his way back into the centre of the city he encountered a man riding a showy grey horse, and recognised Captain Sinclair.

"Great Scott!" exclaimed the stocky, sandy-haired artillery-man riding across to him. "I sincerely trust you are not here in response to my invitation, Major."

Vivian smiled and shook his head. "In view of the state of war, which you predicted would come, I hope your boast regarding your mount was not exaggerated. You may have need of fast flying hooves before long."

They fell in alongside each other, apparently both heading in the same direction, and Vivian asked, "What success did you have with the 'few obsolete cannon' you suspected comprised this city's defences?"

"Success?" Sinclair scowled. "Blaise and I made surveys of the surrounding countryside—flat, my dear fellow, for miles and miles —then estimated the potential of the city for artillery emplacements. Having done that, we listed the number of guns, the range and capacity of each which, in our dual opinions, would give adequate defence of this place." He scowled again. "Our report is probably halfway down the line in some isolated station run by a dim-witted settler, who will have no idea of the extreme non-importance now of the envelope we had marked URGENT."

Vivian sighed, shifting his pith helmet so that it better shaded his eyes. They still ached in the bright light of day.

"I suppose it hardly matters, since the Boers are evidently intending to sit out there hoping to starve us into surrender."

"Good artillery could have blasted them from their positions, and reduced their capacity to counter a break-out by our troops."

"Which troops?" asked Vivian dryly. "Our present strength suggests that any attempt to break the siege would have to be made in a circular attack in ranks one man deep."

"I know, I know," agreed Sinclair gloomily, guiding his horse around a pothole in the road. "We have enough food and water to sit this out for a prolonged period, and our army outside has enough to do trying to contain the huge Boer commandos crossing the veld with ease, whilst they try to repair the railway track each time a new breach is made. Take my word for it, Major, we shall be trapped in this damned place for weeks while our colleagues gain all the glory in battles to free us."

"There's not much glory in repairing railway track, surely," put in Vivian.

Ignoring that, Sinclair went on with his grousing. "The only excitement we shall experience will be the battle between the military and civilians in Kimberley. Rhodes can't stomach soldiers, at any price. Add that fact to these, and reach your conclusion. Kekewich has proclaimed martial law; Rhodes is declaring himself leader of siege operations. Kekewich has forbidden the sending of any messages other than military despatches; Rhodes is in constant communication with Cape Town in an exchange of information he keeps secret from the military commander. Kekewich is putting into practice the normal controls on food, water and freedom of movement, in a garrison which may have to survive investment for some time; Rhodes is asking—nay, *demanding*—that troops come to our aid immediately, as we are in danger of being overrun."

He reined in and turned to face Vivian. "Our greatest enemy may well be inside the city, and I do not envy Kekewich his command. Rhodes is uncrowned king of Kimberley by virtue of his mining concerns. He controls De Beers, and De Beers controls the city. Those citizens who are not employed by him are mostly his wealthy friends who do not care to cross him. I have heard that he has set up a committee of his own to deal with the crisis, and all leading residents have been appointed to serve on it. What appears to some military men as the final insult, is the confidence Rhodes shares with Baron Von Grossladen, when it is well known that Germany has been providing the Boers with arms and openly supporting their cause, along with most of Europe. Von Grossladen, whose family is reputed to have been kicked out of a proud Prussian regiment two generations back, hates soldiers even more than Rhodes does."

Saluting Vivian with his whip against the rim of his pith helmet, Sinclair prepared to ride off. "We may have that race yet, Major, in our haste to depart from internal strife to the peace of the veld."

Vivian rode on alone, deep in thought. Sinclair's revelations did nothing to lighten his depression, although one of them explained the attitude of his future stepfather. There seemed little doubt that his mother would marry the man, although the crisis had naturally delayed a final decision on where and when. Vivian had been aware that Germany supported their present enemy, going so far as to provide troops to swell their numbers. Did the Baron's financial interests in Kimberley overrule his obligation to support his fatherland? Rhodes apparently had every confidence in the man, but Vivian decided it would be unwise to tell his mother anything of a military nature which she might repeat in his presence. Moving down to the tented camp would make that vow easier. With the Weldons acting as her fond hosts, and the suave Baron making all her decisions for her, it was apparent that his mother had no need of her son's protection. From now on, he must ensure that he had no need of his mother's money. With the prospect of a child to support before long, it was a problem he could well do without, in the midst of all else.

Sinclair's other observation that the siege would be protracted was probably sound enough. An armoured train had gone out whilst Vivian had been ill, but the strength of the Boers at outlying stations had driven it back. Scott-Turner, in command of the cavalry, had told Vivian that there would be a great deal to occupy them, as he had orders to prevent the enemy from closing in to positions that would allow them to shell the city itself. To that end, the mounted troops would be on permanent stand-by to repulse any forward rushes, and observers would be posted on all earthworks to watch the enemy positions through telescopes, and signal any signs of movement. That was the only news that cheered Vivian slightly. He intended to seize any chance of action, any opportunity to break from the city and those encircled within it.

With her own nerves in a ragged state, the theatre closed, and the situation so uncertain and frightening, Leila found it hard to stay calm in the face of Nellie's hysteria. Dabbing her forehead once more with the scented handkerchief, she tried to forget the trying heat, and reason with her companion.

"Do stop crying," she implored. "You're working yourself up to an unnecessary degree of panic. I warned you before not to heed things told to you by the soldiers."

"T'weren't the soldiers," came the muffled response.

"Then who told you this riduclous story?"

The girl lifted her tear-stained face, and gulped back her sobs. "A pair of women in the market-place."

"They were probably Boer women," said Leila firmly. "Trying to scare us all would be one way they could help their people without aggression. Silly creatures like you make their task easier. Is that what you want, Nellie?"

Shaking her head furiously, which sent her untidy hair tumbling further from the pins, she declared, "It was little Sally I was frightened for. Poor little mite."

"Yes, of course," agreed Leila, relenting a little as her gaze rested on the skinny toddler Nellie was clutching protectively. The child was hardly appealing, with her pointed face, mousy hair and dark, closely-set eyes, yet she had a merry personality that Leila could not resist. Having been present at the child's birth and watched her grow to her present stage of walking and talking, she felt closer to Sally than an aunt. In her more introspective moments, she wondered sadly what the future held for the illegitimate Sally Wilkins. Would she one day be seduced by a soldier, who then sailed away leaving her with thirty shillings and an obsolete address?

239

"Don't you think it's right, then?" asked Nellie, recapturing her attention.

Leila smiled and shook her head. "Whoever put that story around credits us with very little commonsense, if they think we would believe that British women and children are to be handed over to the black people when Kimberley falls. It's pure nonsense!" she declared, mopping her damp brow again and cursing the heat that seemed to be growing worse with each day. "The black people here all work for us, whether in the mines or as domestic servants. They rely upon us for their livelihood. Look, Nellie," she continued, searching for a form of reassurance the girl would understand. "You once worked for the Clivedons. Can you imagine Sir Frederick and his family being afraid, if someone threatened to hand them over to you and cook, for instance?" Pausing to allow that absurdity to sink in, she continued. "That's the equivalent of this tale. If I still haven't convinced you of its silliness, remember that the black tribes have far more reason to hate the Boers than they have to hate us."

Nellie's tears had stopped, and she was merely sniffing as she regarded Leila with red-rimmed eyes. "I don't know what I'd do without you, honest I don't."

"You don't have to do without me, so don't start worrying about that now," Leila put in hastily, feeling she could stand no more misery for the moment. "Did you buy the cloth for Sally's new dress?"

Diverted, Nellie brought out the piece of sprigged cotton she had chosen. "There was a real hullabaloo at the market," the girl said then. "Seems all the shopkeepers have put up their prices something dreadful, because they know everyone's anxious to stock up while there's the chance. The women are real mad. One said it's not right to make profits from people's predicaments—whatever that means—and some are talking about going to see the colonel or somebody about it. You should've seen the prices what have been put on tea, biscuits and things like that—just ordinary things."

"It's inevitable, I suppose," sighed Leila. "I'm sure food will have to be allocated fairly before long. Colonel Kekewich must be occupied with military defence, at the moment. It all happened so quickly, nothing is properly organised."

Nellie sat down, taking Sally onto her lap automatically. "Has Mr Chewton sorted out anything yet?"

"I'm going to the theatre shortly. The cast is gathering to hear what he plans to do. Poor man, I really can't see any way of making money, with the situation as it is. The curfew at night puts paid to normal performances, and I cannot see the military allowing us to give daytime shows—if anyone was prepared to come, that is. I imagine every pair of eyes in Kimberley is watching for movement out on that plain, except for poor Mr Chewton, whose eyes are studying the losses on the balance-sheet. He has cut expenses as far as he can—like moving us to this cottage, and the chorus into cheaper rooms—and I expect him to tell us all today that he can't pay any wages while the show is closed. We shall be able to manage, but some of the chorus will have a hard time of it."

"No more than anyone else, so Bill says."

Leila frowned. "Bill?"

"Bill Sedgewick. He's a sergeant I've got to know," confessed Nellie, her cheeks flushing.

"Oh, Nellie!"

"He's nice," came the swift defence. "Bill's a gentleman, Leila. He wouldn't do nothing like that."

"I hope you wouldn't give him the chance," countered Leila force-fully. "Don't let this emergency soften you, my girl. There's something about soldiers preparing to risk their lives for others' sakes that endows them with qualities they don't possess. It's easy for a girl to get stars in her eyes that dazzle the truth. Men are all the same, Nellie. They are *not* noble, courageous creatures whom we should reward with our undying blind devotion . . . or with anything else."

A broad smile crossed Nellie's face as she stroked the hair of her illegitimate child. "You've made that speech about men so many times, I could do it word for word for you. I never thought Jim was a noble, courageous creature, Leila, and *you* was the one married to a soldier . . . at least, you thought you was."

Setting Sally onto her feet again, she crossed to Leila and squatted beside her chair. "I know I made a mistake with Jim, but there's others who aren't like that at all. I know I'm a silly girl who believes most of what I'm told, but there's one thing I can see better'n you. Getting all those necklaces and bracelets can't undo what Frank did to you. What's more, they won't keep you company when you're lonely, nor look after you when you're sick and old. They don't even make you happy. I've not seen a longer face than yours since the siege began. It's not just the Boers, is it? Was you really fond of that Captain Blaise? Your misery-face seems to date from the night of that party, and he's not been round since then."

"He knows better than to do so," Leila said, feeling the pain of that evening gathering inside her once more. "No, Nellie dear, I'm fond of no one save you and Sally." Forcing a smile, she added, "Those necklaces and bracelets might stand us in good stead, if this siege lasts long. I can sell them in order to live in the style required of a leading lady. As Lester Gilbert would say, 'The magic must be maintained at all times.' Even when soldiers are preparing to risk their lives for our sakes," she murmured, lost in thoughts she should not have.

The cast of *The Hungarian Heiress* met backstage that afternoon. There was something infinitely depressing about the deserted theatre that was soon transferred to the members of the touring company caught up in a war. Meredith Chewton had spoken to Colonel Kekewich who, understandably, had more important considerations than a cast of actors and musicians who merely represented mouths to feed and persons to safeguard. From the military point of view, it was out of the question to allow large numbers of residents to gather in the theatre, even during daylight hours. A couple of shells on the building and the casualties could be serious.

The manager had next gone to Cecil Rhodes. The great man had assured him that the authorities in Cape Town, plus the British Government in London, had been made aware of the imperative need to relieve Kimberley at once. That being the case, it would be no more than a matter of days before life returned to normal. In the meantime, Mr Rhodes would be pleased with some small entertainments at garden parties in the homes of his friends, given to relieve the stress of the present situation and to show that all was well in his city of diamonds. Mr Rhodes had everything under control, he insisted.

The prospect of "prancing and warbling in the gardens of nobs for sweet Fanny Adams", as one member of the chorus put it, did little to help the general gloom of the cast. They remained in small disconsolate groups in that atmosphere of grease paint and artificial scenes, when Meredith Chewton departed, a worried, unhappy man. Leila and Franz wandered onto the stage itself, still set with the backcloth and flats representing a vineyard where the archduke discovers Kati at the start of the operetta. Their footsteps echoed in the auditorium filled with the familiar smell of perfume and cigar smoke, left by those who had sat enthralled with make-believe.

"An empty theatre is as sad as a room no longer visited by a loved one," commented Franz quietly. "The sense of yearning is the same."

Leila turned to him questioningly. "Have you ever loved someone that much, Franz?"

His dark gaze rested on her with unusual seriousness. "How else do you suppose that I can persuade an audience that I love Kati—or any other heroine of the boards?"

242

"*Discard passion with the grease paint.*" She quoted his words with gentle teasing. "What went wrong?"

He put a hand on her shoulder. "*Leibchen*, in those days I discarded passion when I *donned* the grease paint. She could not accept that, could not help turning every woman I knew into my mistress. We had so many quarrels . . . yet that room, without her, was unbearable."

Fascinated by this revelation from a man she had believed untouched by depths of feeling, she asked, "Did you never consider giving it all up for her sake?"

"Giving it up?" he echoed in astonishment. "My voice is my divine gift; the theatre is my fulfilment in life. Would *you* give it all up for love?"

*Yes, yes,* an inner voice cried. *For him I would have given up anything.* "No, of course not," she said firmly. "Franz, we shall have to make arrangements for our daily rehearsals. If we are forbidden to use the theatre, I suggest that we ask for the piano to be moved to my cottage. We can run through our vocal exercises and songs far better there than in your hotel room. Do you agree?"

He nodded. "Vocal exercises in a veld cottage. Gilbert's senses would be outraged."

She laughed. "He will be outraged by the Boers' lack of consideration in surrounding us in mid-tour; pained by their lack of aesthetic appreciation." Sobering, she asked, "Do you think it will last long?"

He shrugged. "I have been speaking this morning with our recent host, Baron Von Grossladen. He thought we were compatriots. I soon assured him that I was not." His smile broke through, giving a reminder of his on-stage fascination. "I have no wish to be a cold arrogant Prussian, when I have the warm heart of the true Viennese."

"He struck me as a man of intense self-assurance," Leila commented, remembering that slender silver-fair woman beside him, whom he regarded as a close friend.

"Who would not be? This baron is one of Rhodes' close associates, with wealth almost to match his. What he told me proved, I think, the saying that Rhodes owns Kimberley. The De Beers company has great herds of cattle, and warehouses full of tinned foods and other supplies. It maintains its own regiment, with an arsenal of rifles and ammunition. The main stocks of coal are within the mines' compounds. The city cannot survive without De Beers and, since Rhodes controls the company, he controls the city and everyone in it. Although the military commander is at loggerheads with the man, he must depend on him for almost everything. The diamond company has given a quantity of land-mines, which have been placed around the perimeter of the city and connected with exploders at the works. The employees of the company have been set to digging deep trenches to accommodate men with rifles, and fortified posts have been erected on the earthworks at each mine. Barbed-wire has been unrolled around us, and searchlights sweep the plain all night. We are perfectly safe, the Baron says."

"Do you believe that?" asked Leila.

"No . . . and neither does anyone else. Why would Rhodes be signalling desperately for help from all his friends in high official places, if there is no danger?"

Leila looked at him in concern. "What shall we do if the Boers do break in?"

"I know what I shall do," he replied immediately. "I shall allow them to believe, like the Baron, that I am German and sympathetic with their cause." Giving another swift smile, he added, "You can pretend to be my Frau, if you wish. They will then treat you with great respect."

Unable to copy his light-heartedness, she said, "You'd have to take on my maid on her child. Nellie would never pretend to be German. She was terrified this morning by a story about handing over the women and children to the tribes for sport."

Franz put his arm behind her back, and began leading her away from that vast silent auditorium toward the back regions. "I also heard that story, put around by the Boers in the city. Their women are hardworking, with little humour, and suspicious of uitlanders. They must regard *us* as sinful and godless—especially you, my dear Leila, in clothes that emphasise your charms and set all civilised men clamouring to meet you."

"All civilised men will be occupied with defending the people within this city, including the humourless hardworking Boers. They will have little time to admire me, or any other female," she said, passing a group of chorus-girls still discussing the dismal situation.

"Nonsense! It is at times like this that people need beauty and gentleness. This war could be the means of giving you your greatest opportunity, my dear Leila."

"Which is?" she prompted.

"To capture a titled husband, who will ensure that you eclipse every other leading lady, past or present. That surely is your greatest desire."

She shook her head. "Right now, Franz, my greatest desire is to leave Kimberley. No one can grant that wish save the Boer commander presently surrounding us with his men."

She walked back alone to the cottage in a quiet tree-lined road, feeling that even Lester Gilbert would see that preserving the mystique of a leading lady was less than vital in the midst of a siege. She strolled, in the late-afternoon sunshine, through streets filled with those wishing to make the most of the opportunity to be out and about before the curfew, at dusk. Her progress was slowed by numerous men, who saluted or doffed their hats before offering to escort her. Answering every time that she would not dream of taking them from their vital errands, she moved on before they could insist.

Most of the women she encountered smiled at her, although the attitude of some of the plainly-dressed wives of Dutch settlers made her dwell on Franz's words a short time before. Actresses were still often regarded as creatures of the *demi-monde*, and the majority of the men behaving courteously toward her probably shared that view, as did Sutton Blaise. None of them mattered, save the one who had voiced his opinion in tones that had betrayed his need to hurt as he had been hurt.

Then, as if thoughts had become reality, she saw a lone rider approaching. Her heart-beat quickened. With all military men now dressed in khaki, it was not easy to tell them apart. She knew this one so well, even distance could not deceive her. They could not avoid passing, and each instinctively slowed as the space between them grew less and less. She had run from Vivian at the party. Her silent departure after his cruel destructive words had been at a dignified walking pace, but she had been running, just the same. Afterward, she had heard that he had succumbed to fever later that evening, and she had then believed that onsetting illness had been responsible for his appearance. Now, as he drew Oscar to a halt and sat looking at her the way he had two weeks before, she realised that a mere bout of fever could never have wrought such a change in him. The khaki tunic and breeches were a warlike contrast to the colourful uniform he had worn in England, and the deep brim of the pith helmet cast shadows over his face. He could have been a stranger, yet her heart and body knew him as they had known no other man.

The moment lengthened between them, and he seemed as powerless as she to break it, until he asked, at last, "Do you still regard riding as a skill you could not master?"

What had happened to that deep caressing voice? *The kind of voice to get a girl into a bedroom quicker than anything.* That memory of words spoken by Rose so long ago, broke through her suspended self-control to lead her to ask, "Does Oscar still perform tricks at your command?"

It was clearly not a day for answers. He ignored that, instead saying in his new brusque manner, "It appears that you achieved your goal, once you rid yourself of encumbrances."

"I still have some way to go yet," she said, sensing that all they were going to do was hurt each other further.

He gave an assessing nod as his gaze flicked over her rose-pink skirt with goffered hem, and the sheer blouse in pale mint-green embroidered with a delicate pattern of apple-blossoms.

"I think you'll get there without much difficulty. Is fame as sweet as you imagined it would be?"

"Is marriage as sweet as you imagined it would be?" she countered.

"You should know all about the sweetness of marriage—unless that obnoxious brute was lying when he claimed that you were his wife."

She gazed at him feeling raw pain at the recollection of a man who could not give her up, standing in a doorway whilst he was destroyed by a truth that had been a lie. It was impossible, now, to tell him the story of a simple girl who had sold her future for thirty shillings, so she took refuge in yet another lie.

"As you said, he was simply part of my old act."

The darkening of his eyes told her that every word was touching the old wound. "Now, it is Mittelheiter who steps in when all else fails, I take it."

"Franz stepped in to give advice, encouragement, and recommendations to Mr Gilbert to give me the lead in the show. That is the root of our friendship," she said quietly. "It is to him that I owe the extent of my success."

"Aren't you forgetting men like Sutton Blaise? Mittelheiter might shower you with advice and encouragement, but it must have been a battalion of besotted fools who provided you with the expensive trappings of a leading lady." He raked her from head to foot with a bitter scrutiny. "I imagine that you allow men to dress you, these days."

"Vivian, please stop," she begged, feeling unable to take much more, yet unable to walk away from him.

"Take some advice from someone who can speak with the voice of experience in such matters," he went on relentlessly. "It won't do to price yourself too highly, at this stage. I would have thought Blaise's pendant sufficient payment for a few hours in your arms."

Her self-control vanished completely. All she wanted was to hurt him as much as he was hurting her, when she cried, "You have paid an unbelievably high price for a few hours in *her* arms, and the whole world must be aware of the fact. It was obvious all along that she would be content with nothing less than domination of your body and soul. She is destroying you, Vivian."

He studied her with all the hunger of the past, as he said, "I paid a far higher price for a girl who wanted even more from me. It was she who destroyed me."

Robbed of the power of speech or movement by those words, Leila

246

could only stand and watch as he set Oscar in motion. Soon, he was no more than a distant figure blurred by the heat rising from the dusty road—a man who had just confessed that he still loved her. The confinement in a city containing him no longer seemed insupportable, as she realised that his life was as likely to be lost in the defence of Kimberley as that of any soldier.

# CHAPTER THIRTEEN

By the middle of November, everyone was aware of the grim penalties of being under siege. With insufficient troops to effect a breakthrough, Kekewich could only use his men for two purposes. By mounting frequent sorties in varying directions, he kept the Boers concentrated in large numbers around Kimberley. This prevented them from leaving just a token force watching the city, then advancing toward the strategic Modder River. Also, by sending out the cavalry, supported by the infantry in the armoured train, he hoped to prevent the surrounding force from advancing to secure positions dangerously close to the perimeter. In his first objective, he succeeded. He did not keep the enemy at a distance, however.

After an offer to give all women and children forty-eight hours in which to accept safe passage from Kimberley, which was ignored, plus a demand for a subsequent surrender, which was also ignored, the Boer commander, Wessels, began his bombardment. Panic ensued amongst the women and children during the first few days, so frightened were they by the distant guns, the whine of shells flying overhead, and the smell of cordite which filled the air. War had become more than just a word to them, and the prospect of death too real.

Soon, however, they realised the shells were of such poor quality that the bombardment was an interesting way of passing the time, with the added prospect of making a little extra money. Quite a lot failed to explode, and those that did caused very little damage. The daily bombardment then became a fearless routine. Observers with flags were posted on earthworks to watch for spurts of smoke signifying the firing of Boer guns. Residents saw the flag go up, then hurried into a shelter for a few moments while the shell flew overhead. When a dull thud announced the landing of it, there was a rush to pick up souvenirs, often still hot, which fetched as much as five pounds in the market. It became a common sight for children to the running around during a bombardment, unconcerned by the danger they were in. Warnings issued by Colonel Kekewich went unheeded, and he had more to worry him than youngsters unchecked by their mothers.

Even so, the daily shelling added to the stresses of those imprisoned in Kimberley. Prices of supplies had been fixed by military edict, so those who had been making swift profits at the start of the siege were thwarted. Restrictions had also been placed on meat and flour, to prevent hoarding by those wealthy enough to buy huge consignments at one time. It could not be called rationing, but it was a measure taken with thoughts of future difficulties in mind. The daytime whine and thud of the shelling, the confinement in their homes during the night-time curfew, the sense of captivity within a specified area, and ignorance of outside news due to the cutting of telegraph lines by the enemy, soon made people irritable and complaining. The little news that did reach the community, brought through enemy lines by runners, was black.

At the end of October, they heard that huge numbers of British troops had been forced to retreat after disastrous battles with the farmer-army, and were now besieged in the important rail-junction town of Ladysmith, along with those already garrisoned there. Because the surrender of this vital place and those trapped within it was unthinkable, Ladysmith became the first priority of any relief column. The residents of Kimberley and Mafeking were told to "sit tight". As they were given no indication of how long they were expected to do this, morale plunged. The civilians were told one thing by the uncrowned king of the diamond city, and another by military proclamations. As many of them were employees of De Beers, the general bias was toward Rhodes. The local troops were torn by dual loyalties, which added another burden to the stress of military duties from which they were free only on Sundays, when the Boers stopped fighting on religious grounds.

By one member of Kimberley's defenders, the heavy demands were welcomed. Vivian relished each mounted sortie; each flirtation with danger. In that tented camp housing only military men, he found an element of strange peace in the midst of war. His companions expected him to do only what every other man did. There was no compulsion to excel, to prove that he was superior. Those members of Kimberley's mounted regiments accepted him at face value, unknowing and uncaring of his past but recognising that he had been blooded in battle in Ashanti. For that alone, his opinion was respected and his leadership welcomed. In turn, he put his trust in the advice of those men who knew the terrain around their native city, especially when riding out beyond the defences onto that exposed plain. There was no more avid volunteer than Major Veasey-Hunter of the 49th Lancers, and the cavalry commander took advantage of it, little knowing the reasons behind this eagerness from a man forcibly separated from his own regiment.

Finding that whenever he ventured into the city to visit his mother there was no escaping Baron Von Grossladen, in person or in conversation centred on him, Vivian used the call of military duty to excuse him from the filial one. A regular exchange of notes between mother and son was apparently satisfactory to Margaret Veasey-Hunter, who seemed to have made up her mind about marriage now that she had told her elder son the facts.

Apart from the cessation of a very generous allowance Vivian would somehow have to bear, his mother's devotion to the German led him to reach a dismaying conclusion as the days turned into weeks. His youthful ideas concerning his mother had been erroneous. The victim of his grandfather's indomitable will she might have been, but a passive one. He realised now that it had been at his own insistence that she had accepted the invitation to visit her cousins in Rhodesia, and thus escape the misery of Shenstone Hall. Having settled happily within their guiding influence, she had remained because it had been the easiest thing to do. Now that Gunther Von Grossladen had taken command of all her decisions, his mother was perfectly happy to relinquish protective guidance from her son.

With new and painful insight, he then realised another error in his youthful thinking. Heredity had mixed looks and personalities to produce a fair-haired boy with his father's traits, followed by a true dark-haired Veasey-Hunter in looks, with the traits of his mother. Of the two sons, he was himself a truer heir to a line of vigorous men than his hesitant, meek brother Charles. With that thought haunting him for several days, his insight then took him a stage further to make him realise that his grandfather's animosity toward him had been more complex than he had ever guessed. His ability to confront the old man would normally have earned Brancliffe's respect. Charles's placid disposition would naturally be despised by someone of his grandfather's ilk, not admired, hence his fierce determination to marry him off to Julia in order to put a strong will back into the line.

In growing astonishment, Vivian realised that his grandfather's cruel, merciless approach had been born of the need to punish fate for robbing the family of the rightful robust heir, and leaving a quiet, sober younger son whom the old man could not like. Denigrating, attempting to destroy the independent will of the boy who could not inherit, had been Brancliffe's way of dealing with one of the few things in life he could not control. Small wonder he had set such exacting standards, driven him so hard, lambasted him with such a cruel tongue. It had been the only way a shattered old man could pretend that the grandson he admired was a disgrace to the family, a slur on a distinguished name, and totally unfit, for the rôle of heir. At that point in his amazing conclusions, Vivian realised the true extent of the blow he had dealt his grandfather by marrying Julia. He had received just punishment for his actions, however.

That punishment was intensified every time he thought of the girl who was a fellow captive in the diamond city. Since that meeting in the street, they had passed several times when duty had taken him away from the camp. No word had been exchanged—he had simply saluted with his whip—but the desire to dismount and walk with her, to be seen as her accepted escort, had been dangerously strong in him each time. Along with the unwelcome conclusions about his mother and grandfather, there had been another, even more unwelcome. Deeply jealous of every man in Kimberley who knew or spoke of her, constantly anxious for her safety during the shelling, and plagued by memories of those bittersweet six months together, he could not deceive himself that love for her had died. If she once crooked her finger at him, once showed that she cared, he knew he would be unable to resist.

Knowing that, he avoided the city streets, and walked away from conversations with his fellows who spoke of her singing in the De Beers compound, and at various residences at the request of Cecil Rhodes. Already a great favourite with the troops, arrangements were under way for Leila Duncan to sing at camp concerts, to raise morale. Vivian could only raise his own, by volunteering for every action that would allow him to escape a city containing a mother who no longer needed him, and a girl he dared not see.

By mid-November, Vivian was familiar with the sensation of riding Oscar or Tintagel alongside the huge, chugging, armour-plated train filled with infantrymen, who peered through loopholes ready to fire at the enemy, and watching, himself, for the chance to give chase. At other times, he would ride out with a large body of cavalry, drawing the Boers out to attack whilst another horsed contingent charged their weakened positions. It was routine siege activity, which did no more than reduce numbers on both sides and relieve the shelling on the beleaguered community. The garrison was too small to attempt to break out; the enemy appeared unwilling to attempt to break in. The only hope for Kimberley was the arrival of a relief column before being starved into submission.

On November 27th, in the sixth week of investment, low spirits were dramatically raised when the continuous signals from the searchlight atop one of the mines were answered. From the distant darkness came a series of flashes, establishing contact with British forces advancing from the Cape. Although the exchange consisted of no more than basic identification, it established the relief column at the Modder River, little more than twenty miles away. Kimberley went wild with excitement. In a matter of hours, they would see the rising dust of a huge rescue force. Impromptu parties were held, despite the curfew, and residents produced luxury foods which had been hidden in cupboards ready for the celebrations. After six weeks of shelling, and silence from the outside world that had suggested they were abandoned to their fate, they could not wait for the moment of actual liberation. Twenty miles was "almost there", so far as the residents were concerned.

So far as the military commander was concerned, twenty miles was one day's march. When, on the following morning, the regular bombardment stopped abruptly shortly after commencement, Colonel Kekewich deduced that the encircling enemies had spotted the relief column and were about to attack it in force. In consultation with his senior commanders, he devised a plan to hamper the Boers and aid his countrymen in their advance. Accordingly, orders raced through the tented camps, setting men on their feet and snatching up rifles with excitement. At last, action against the enemy which would be decisive to the war.

Vivian shared the general excitement as he rolled from his camp-bed and reached for his tunic, shouting to his groom to saddle Oscar immediately. Buckling on his gun belt, he then rammed the pith helmet onto his head as he dipped it beneath the open flap of his tent. The sun blazed down from an afternoon sky, as he rode to the point where around two thousand troops were assembling with the normal organised pandemonium. It was an exhilarating sight, and most of the city's population appeared to have turned out to watch the spectacle. In something approaching a holiday mood, they saw the soldiers as the best of fellows, noble heroes full of daring. Vivian's smile in response to their enthusiasm was twisted. Until now, encouraged by Cecil Rhodes, the populace had considered them to be blundering, complacent fools.

Joining the large contingent of mounted men—around six hundred, he would estimate—Vivian then heard the plan from Scott-Turner. A combined attack was to be made on the Boer positions to the south, between the city and the Modder River. This would keep enemy attention on them, rather than on the relief troops advancing northward, and dispossess them of key positions on two ridges from which they presently commanded large areas in both directions. A force consisting of practically the entire infantry strength, was to attack one ridge under cover of strong artillery fire from six field guns; the cavalry were to support them on the right flank, and attempt to seize three

redoubts on the other ridge if and when the Boers retreated, demoralised by defeat on the first ridge. At the same time, the armoured train
would be sent out to the point where track had been recently blown up
by the enemy, the troops within it engaging those along the railway to
prevent their reinforcing their comrades on the ridges.

It was a splendid plan, and confidence was high despite the fact that
they were preparing to sally forth onto an open plain during the
pounding heat of afternoon, without advantage of stealth or surprise. If
their comrades were doing so in order to reach them, the least they
could do was show matching grit and courage.

Vivian was given command of some local men he had come to know,
in military terms, from earlier sorties. One or two were hotheads,
several had more enthusiasm than skill, but most were men whose
excellent horsemanship compensated for their lack of battle experience.
They trusted him, and obeyed any order he gave. He smiled at them
now, privately wishing that he had his own lancers for this decisive
attack. It was then that he realised he would be free to return to them
shortly, and the excitement left him. Garrison duties in Cape Town did
not appeal to him, nor did the thought of a pregnant wife awaiting, to
whom he must explain a drastic drop in income on his mother's
marriage. He had no idea, as yet, how he would compensate for that.

The order was given; forward movement began. The rhythmic thud
of boots, the jumble of hoof-beats and squeak of leather saddles, the
rumbling of artillery wheels, sounded impressive as the khaki ranks
passed through the perimeter defences in a long winding column. Once
out on that sun-baked plain, however, the uncanny silence of such vast
stretches of barren land swallowed the warlike noises. Then the feeling
of vulnerability set in. Vivian experienced a prickling at the nape of the
neck as he rode Oscar alongside the infantrymen, whose sunburned
faces were growing wary now they were so unprotected. It was always
the same during those moments just before a battle. Nerves were tense,
eyes ached from scanning innocent-looking territory for the enemy
known to be there, ears practically burst with the anticipation of sudden
uproar all around. Mouths grew dry, throats tightened, bodies were
held rigid. Once shots rang out, identifying the enemy, there was no
time for thoughts or emotions. Those came afterward, when reaction
set in and a man buried his friends—or shot them to save them
appalling agony during dismemberment.

Vivian swallowed nervously and fingered the strap of his pith helmet.
He was sweating profusely already, like all those with him. The
infantrymen had beads of it on their faces as they tramped across the
dust-dry plain toward the stony ridges hiding the Boers. The air of

tension practically sizzled now. Away in the distance, the armoured train betrayed its presence with baritone coughs as it emitted smoke, and by the dazzle of sun on metal as it advanced cumbersomely along the track. There was something comforting about its distant presence; it looked so invulnerable.

A sudden series of staccato bangs made Vivian jump, along with most others on that exposed plain. Oscar sidled nervously; other horses reacted more violently. Then, shells began exploding around them, creating further panic amidst the animals. Calming Oscar, Vivian twisted in the saddle to look for their own artillery. Something appeared to have gone wrong, for the guns were not in their specified positions to provide the cover they needed. In dismay, he saw that some had halted too soon, the gunners replying to the Boer fire with shells that fell short, far too close to their own advancing men.

Once begun, a battle invariably proceeds under its own momentum, no matter what the initial plan, and so it was now. The open plain became a hell of cries, shouts and neighs as bullets and shells flew around stirring up a pall of choking dust, which filled men's throats and settled on their faces as a gritty coating to prick their eyeballs. Much too soon, the infantry were letting fly a hail of rifle fire that landed harmlessly yards from the enemy positions. They, themselves, were pinned down by Boer bullets, with no more protection than sparse scrub.

It soon became apparent that the cavalry were the main target for the Boers, who knew that a man without a horse in such terrain was virtually helpless. Vivian looked urgently across the surging sea of khaki and horseflesh, trying the spot Scott-Turner through the dust-filled air. Instead of prancing ineffectively, they should be attacking, drawing fire to allow the infantry to advance. What was the man thinking of ? Almost immediately, the order to advance came, but it was not what Vivian was expecting. They were directed to attack the second ridge, to storm and capture the redoubts—a move supposedly only to be made if there was evidence of an enemy retreat. At present, there was heavy firing from that direction, with no sign of a withdrawal on either front. It smacked of madness, but they all obediently wheeled and headed off at the gallop, leaving the infantry virtually unsupported.

Vivian set Oscar flying across the open stretch, sensing that he was in a situation which would have to play itself out. The afternoon turned into a thundering, roaring suspension of time, beneath a relentless sun. His tunic was sticking to his back, his face was coated with grit as he raced at the head of his men toward the fortified rocky sections behind which the enemy must be sheltering in some strength. Once within range, they were met with a hail of fire. The earth around Vivian began to dance with the impact of bullets. He drew his own revolver, shouting hoarsely to those he led to fire only when they sighted their target. Bullets whistled past his ears, and he remembered that these men of the country were superb shots. Men began falling around him; horses screamed with pain. Oscar did not check his stride, however, and Vivian was soon near enough to spot bearded faces peering over rocks and side-tipped waggons. Firing at specific targets, he bent low over Oscar's back as the animal gallantly charged the redoubt.

When no more than several yards away, Vivian was hit in the thigh. Gasping with the burning pain of the wound, he took Oscar on toward the barricades, firing at the stranger-enemies until a thud against his helmet knocked him so badly off-balance he could not adjust to Oscar's sudden swerve to the left. Toppling from his saddle, his foot jammed in the stirrup. Crying out with pain, he was bumped and jerked over the uneven ground parallel to the redoubt as Oscar raced onward. Eventually, his agony grew too great to bear, and a sharp crack from a stone against his bared head gave him blessed relief in unconsciousness.

The mass funeral of the overzealous Scott-Turner, and nineteen others killed in the attack, was attended by a huge crowd of mourners, mostly military. The long line of waggons bearing flag-draped coffins, had been a sombre and depressing sight for those who had been so full of rejoicing the previous day. The sound of rifle volleys in salutes to the dead seemed to fill the silence over the city, reminding the citizens that the war was still with them. The assault had failed. The Boers were still in the redoubts, and there was no sign of the relief column.

In the little tree-shaded cottage in one of the quieter streets of the city, Nellie carried out her tasks mechanically, her eyes red from weeping. The sergeant with whom she had struck up such a happy friendship was in one of the coffins being lowered into the earth. Leila respected the girl's grief and left her alone, fervently thankful that Vivian's name had not been on the list of dead posted on the notice-board. She had watched them all depart, and knew then the anguish of wives and sweethearts of soldiers off to do battle.

Day after day, she had feared for his safety. The many officers she had come to know had spoken of frequent cavalry actions, small groups of mounted men sallying forth beside the armoured train, and scouting parties attempting to discover positions and strengths of the enemy. Mention had often been made of the Lancer officer who volunteered so readily. The news that he was treating his life with scant regard worried her even more than his obviously deliberate absence from the city. In a small captive community which received no news from outside, the encircled area became the whole world, and no one within it could speak or act without news of it reaching all ears.

Leila knew that Margaret Veasey-Hunter was to marry Gunther Von Grossladen when the relief column arrived, and that her son had ceased visiting her, communicating by letter only from the military camp. Convinced that she, herself, was more probably the cause of his self-imposed absence from the centre of Kimberley, Leila longed for the chance to talk to him, to reassure him that it was possible for a civilised relationship to exist between them all the while they were trapped there, with no possibility of escaping each other. He could not remain in his tent for week after week. Even with certain restrictions in force, there were social functions and recreational activities to ease the tension. No man could deny himself the opportunity to relax a little from the danger to which he seemed so eager to expose himself. Vivian had looked to be on the verge of cracking up when they had met in the street over a month ago. He would surely do so unless he released some of the tension.

If she received constant news of him, then so must he be aware that she was engaging in many activities designed to help morale. Although the theatre remained closed—indeed, it had been hit by a shell already —the cast of *The Hungarian Heiress* were taking part in entertainments of various kinds. Aside from singing to guests in the houses of the influential residents, they appeared at afternoon gatherings within the De Beers compound, where they provided a little respite from the concentrated work of producing shells and smaller ammunition in the mines' workshops. On several occasions, they had taken part in open-air concerts with the regimental band—all by arrangement with Cecil Rhodes. Leila had been introduced to someone she had never thought to meet, and experienced great disappointment. Lacking any obvious charm, and with a strange squeaky voice, the man had been nowhere as sensational as his reputation. With thoughts of Rose, she had mentally dubbed him Curious Cecil.

Apart from entertaining at concerts—including plans for a grand one which had been postponed on contacting the relief column—Leila had a constant stream of visitors to her cottage. Although some of the men of the chorus had found employment in De Beers' many projects, the girls were finding life very difficult and stressful. Living in cheap lodgings paid for by the worried Meredith Chewton, they received no wages and had nothing to do all day. Inactivity being the worst aspect of a siege, Leila tried to cheer them by allowing them to gather in the pleasant rambling wooden bungalow with its delightful shady garden full of sweet-smelling shrubs. It soon became a favourite rendezvous for troops off-duty, who would sit in the garden chatting to the girls. The men of the local regiments, who comprised the bulk of the defence force, had homes and families in Kimberley, but the British troops were far from home and appreciated the chance to forget war for a while in the company of pretty girls.

A great favourite with them all was little Sally Wilkins. Those of the men who were fathers loved to teach her nursery rhymes, or take her onto their knees to relate a story. Some made toys for her from anything they could find, or brought a precious egg for her tea. The theatre girls also received presents, now and again, and one received a proposal of marriage. Siege gifts could be very strange compared with normal times, and a lively, flirtatious girl would be thrown into transports of delight over a packet of tea or a wedge of cheese saved from a soldier's rations.

The officers soon heard the news, and began arriving on Leila's doorstep, also. To make things easier amidst the ranks, she entertained them indoors, with Nellie as a chaperone, or in company with Franz. The presents she received were the more usual ones of flowers, a fan, a stole, or jewellery—something which the diamond city had in abundance during that emergency.

It became a regular thing for happy laughter to be heard coming from the young people in the cottage or its garden, where pretty girls cheered the spirits of men risking their lives to defend them. Although Leila was aware of the disapproval of some of the more prudish of the city's womenfolk, and was consequently publicly snubbed by them when she walked or drove through the streets, she did not let their attitude put an end to something she felt was of great value in stressful circumstances. She was far more worried over the attitude of just one man in Kimberley.

On that day of general mourning, no one visited her save Franz, at his usual hour. In view of Nellie's unhappiness, and the sombreness of the occasion, Leila told her friend that she had no heart for practising scales.

"It seems a little insensitive to pretend that nothing has happened," she continued. "In any case, we shall be abandoning the tour and returning to England shortly. They say the relief column is sure to be here by the end of the week, and the whole company will be packing ready to leave the minute Mr Chewton arranges transport for us."

"I think not, Leila," he told her with a shake of his head. "Von Grossladen, who persists in his attempt to pronounce me one of his countrymen, revealed to me just an hour ago that his great friend

Rhodes is determined that Kimberley will be restored to normal, immediately the siege is lifted. The theatre will reopen, with business as usual. The shell caused little damage, it seems."

The hand waving the fan to cool her face stilled, as she looked at him in disbelief. "What of the war?"

Franz shrugged his wide shoulders nonchalantly. "Rhodes desires only to remove the war from his city and his mines, then wash his hands of it."

"He can say that when they are out there burying twenty men who died defending his city and his mines?" she cried.

"The great man did not approve the plan for the assault, and feels that they made a vainglorious attempt to justify themselves when relief is on our doorstep. I believe I am inclined to agree with him."

*"Franz!"*

*"Liebchen*, they are out there burying twenty men, and the situation is unchanged," he pointed out.

"But . . . but surely it might now be worse, if they had not attacked," she protested, unwilling to dismiss twenty deaths in such prosaic terms. "I can't credit the suggestion that you are not grateful for their sacrifice on your behalf."

He gave her a persuasive smile, all his charm in evidence as he said, "I think they did not go out rashly to face the Boers on behalf of one Austrian tenor, you know. Perhaps it was for the sake of Leila Duncan. That I could understand."

Still unhappy over his flippant approach to a disaster, she said rather sharply, "There is only one woman who could inspire such noble sacrifice. Queen Victoria of England."

He sat regarding her for a short while, then asked, "What has happened to the cool Miss Duncan, who allows no man to touch her heart?"

"Whatever do you mean?" she parried, knowing too well the answer to his question.

"You are back in the fictional romance of *Felicity May*, with an entire regiment in love with their darling on the eve of Waterloo. This is reality, Leila."

"No, Franz . . . no, it isn't," she contradicted. "Reality is everyone going safely through the streets, men being safely at home with their wives and families, us giving pleasure and excitement to crowds in a theatre. This isn't reality. Yesterday, twenty men were alive: now they're being buried to the sound of rifle-shots. *For our sakes, Franz.*"

"For the sake of gold, *liebchen*," he argued firmly. "This war is for possession of a gleaming substance, beneath the soil of a country which surely has enough beauty above it. Those soldiers died so that men like Rhodes can gain wealth and power before some other man does." Fixing her with a stern eye, he added, "You have forgotten my advice to remove passion with the grease paint, and allowed the romance of war to weaken you."

"Romance!" she exclaimed hotly. "What is romantic about war?"

He smiled. "The moment a villain dons an impressive uniform and sallies off to battle, he becomes a hero. When a hero dons one, he becomes adored by every foolish female he encounters. Villain or hero, someone in Kimberley has broken through that protective barrier, Leila. Already, you cannot sing scales because men are being buried. Soon, you will refuse to perform because there is always someone being buried, somewhere. Are you a dedicated actress, or a foolish female?"

Knowing that there was truth in all he said, she tried to end the subject quickly. "How can an actress be dedicated when she is prevented from performing?"

"You are performing . . . daily," he reminded her. "You have forgotten that that is all you are doing, because you can now see your audience. Close your eyes when you sing, and rid yourself of the dangerous notion that the men gazing at you are about to go out to die for your sake. If that does not work, think instead that they are going out to *kill*; that they have chosen to do that, as surely as we have chosen to entertain, as a means of earning a living. That should banish any romantic notions presently filling your very beautiful head."

She gazed at him, strangely disappointed in a man she had always admired. "You are very cynical."

"So, once, were you. It enabled you to create magic with me. Take care, Leila. Success is a fragile substance, which disappears quickly."

She was silenced by his inference and, after a moment or two, he rose to his feet with decisive movements. "Very well, if you still feel unable to practise your vocal exercises, I have a proposal more in keeping with your mood. Come with me to visit the wounded in the hospital. There were many yesterday, including the son of the gentle lady Von Grossladen intends to marry."

"*Vivian?*" she breathed, before she could stop herself. "Is he badly hurt?"

Franz studied her face. "So, it is Major Veasey-Hunter who has inspired such fervent support for our khaki-clad defenders! I do not know details of his wounds; only of his distinguished wife in Cape Town."

"You're wrong, Franz," she told him, in as controlled a tone as possible. "He inspires nothing more in me than any man in khaki."

They walked through a long ward in the one-storey hospital, which had never been intended for war casualties. Warned by the nurse who greeted them that her patients were in low spirits, Leila was much affected by the gladness their own appearance created. In a dress of white spotted muslin, fitting tightly in the bodice, and embroidered with a diagonal flight of blue birds across the skirt which dragged the ground behind her, she reduced some of the men to a state of such shyness, they blushed when she spoke to them. They treated her as a lady, and enough of her former resolution remained to prevent her thinking how differently one of their number had once treated a lady's-maid called Lily Lowe.

Throughout that tour of the men's ward, half her mind was on the meeting to come. How badly wounded was he? Suppose he was dreadfully maimed. It would surely be cruel to confront him without warning, at a time when he could not walk away from her. She should not have come. He had made it plain enough that he wished to avoid meeting, and she should respect that wish. When they left the ward and crossed the verandah to the smaller room housing the officers, she detained Franz with a hand on his arm. He turned to her questioningly.

"It is so hot," she said faintly. "I think I cannot face any more today."

"Um, so soon your gratitude fades?" he asked dryly. "It must have been very much hotter on that plain yesterday, while they were defending you, eh?" Eyes narrowing shrewdly, he took her elbow in his hand. "You cannot face *him*? The danger is worse than I imagined. Come, *liebchen*, you are an actress. Perform your rôle as fully as he performed his yesterday."

Pushing open a fly-screen door, he led her inside. Vivian was on a chair beside the first bed, and he saw her at once. In that initial unguarded moment, the mixture of strong emotions in his expression weakened her immediately. She halted involuntarily as he struggled to his feet with the aid of a crutch and a hand on the bed. Their glances held, conveying messages they could not speak, until Leila's attention was taken by Franz speaking.

*"Küss die Hand, gnädige Frau."*

Turning swiftly, she saw Vivian's mother there on a second chair. In a gown of silk-embroidered lace, enhanced by a collar of antique amethysts she wore around her neck, Margaret Veasey-Hunter appeared very composed as Franz greeted her in true Viennese style. Then she glanced past him to Leila, including her in her warm smile.

"Miss Duncan, how very commendable of you. On so hot a

day, anyone might be excused for remaining at home behind drawn curtains."

Moving further into the room, rejoicing that Vivian's leg wound did not seem severe, Leila replied, "The nurses here are surely more to be commended, Mrs Veasey-Hunter. A bandage and a cool hand on a brow are worth more than a smile to wounded men."

"There is no bandage for wounded spirits, however," pointed out the older woman. "Perhaps a smile is the only remedy then." Glancing back toward the bed, she asked, "Do you know my son?"

"No," said Vivian immediately.

With Franz there beside her, Leila had to amend that flat denial. "We met once in England, Major. You have apparently forgotten the occasion."

"I imagine no man could forget meeting you, Miss Duncan," he responded, leaving her to invent further.

"I am told by your friends that you have a particularly bad memory, sir." Seeing the dark shadows like bruises beneath his eyes, and the obvious pain he was in, she added gently, "They also say that you compensate for that with impeccable manners—which are presently obliging you to stand when you ought to be resting. Please sit down again."

Margaret Veasey-Hunter indicated his vacated chair. "If you sit here beside me, Miss Duncan, Vivian can settle comfortably on the bed while we chat."

Encountering no more from Franz than an enigmatic look in response to her optical plea for a way out of the situation, she took the empty seat which placed her no more than two feet from Vivian. Their knees almost touched, as he lowered himself onto the white counterpane and set the crutch at an angle against the wall. He was silent as his mother embarked on a conversation concerning the great popularity Franz and Leila had aroused in the residents of the captive city.

"Mr Rhodes has many times expressed his gladness at the good fortune of having such a distinguished company in the city when disaster fell. He works extremely hard to keep spirits high in these exceptionally trying times, as you are well aware, Miss Duncan, and applauds anyone assisting him in the task. Your willingness to entertain, to say nothing of the open house I hear you maintain, all helps to cheer those less resilient than yourself."

Conscious of how such words would be translated by the silent man on the bed, Leila said, "If I am resilient, it is only because the heavy responsibilities faced by many people here are not on my shoulders."

The other woman smiled. "You are a woman, my dear, and not expected to shoulder heavy responsibilities. Gentlemen do that."

Before she could stop herself, Leila asked, "What *is* expected of us?"

"Exactly what you are doing, *liebchen*," inserted Franz smoothly. "Although it is not appreciated in every quarter, Mrs Veasey-Hunter. Miss Duncan has met with some fierce resentment in the market-place, and elsewhere, mostly from the Boer families here and from the wives of settlers from the poorer end of the city. They appear to hold strong views on our honourable, much-lauded profession."

"Perhaps they know little about it," said the voice that had haunted many of Leila's days and nights. "They are simple people, who believe what they see on the surface. It's easily done."

Leila looked up at him quickly. "They see what they want to see. It has nothing to do with simplicity, and everything to do with prejudice." As he gazed at her with wary questioning in his eyes, she added, "In my profession, things are often not what they seem. People play a part for good reasons; they speak of feelings which are not truly theirs. Situations develop to confuse people. A change of costume turns a person into someone else. To convince others of something which is not true, is the basis of our art."

Too late, she realised that her words were open to conflicting interpretations. He nodded, saying carefully, "I am told by *your* friends, Miss Duncan, that you are a mistress of your craft."

"I think you should not concern yourself with the opinions of a few ill-bred creatures," put in Vivian's mother, apparently unaware of the undercurrents in the room. "They are doing little in this emergency save grumble and criticise." Angling her head upward to Franz standing beside her, she went on, "I heard from Gunther that you once studied engineering, at your father's command, and have expressed an interest in Mr Labram's work at De Beers. Have you arranged an appointment to visit the workshop?"

They embarked upon a discussion of the attempt by George Labram, the American chief engineer of the mining corporation, to cast a great cannon to aid the defence of the city. Leila took advantage of the opportunity to speak to Vivian under cover of their conversation.

"Were you very badly hurt?" she asked urgently. Then, seeing his expression, she added softly, "Please don't look at me that way. I'm referring to the reason why you are here in hospital."

"I see. A bullet in the leg, that's all."

His very resistance increased her determination to reach him, to ease the atmosphere still between them. "You could have been killed. It could have been your funeral today," she pointed out with meaning.

He shook his head. "I have a tendency to keep going back for more, whatever happens."

Looking him steadily in the eyes, she said, "I appear to have that same tendency. You have insulted me twice in this city, and are well on the way to doing so again now. I came here today knowing that we would meet, and that you would behave this way. Vivian, I am not standing at your door with a huge horse, putting you at an impossible disadvantage, but you are in the similar position of being unable to force me to go. You asked me, on that unforgettable occasion, to put aside your first insult and become your true friend—just a friend. I am asking you to do the same now."

He made to speak, then remained silent instead, studying her as if seeing her again for the first time since that day with Frank. Finally, he said thickly, "When I made that request, we didn't know each other. It's too late for friendship, isn't it?"

"It's too late for what we have now," she pleaded. "We are captive here, and time may be running out, Vivian. Can't you see?"

"What do we have now, Leila?"

It caught her off-balance. She did not know. Or, knowing, she dared not say. His question was still unanswered when Franz concluded his conversation with Margaret Veasey-Hunter, and turned to remind Leila that there were other patients to see. They moved on with a brief farewell, and spent a further half-hour speaking to men Leila knew quite well. She was conscious of being watched the whole time. Yet, when she gave a final general farewell to those in the room, it was Margaret Veasey-Hunter, rather than her son, who was watching her so intently.

Franz called a cab for the return ride, and Leila sank back thankfully against the squabs. Had a truce been established between them? Could there ever be anything as lukewarm as the feeling between them now? In the streets, people were standing around discussing the relief column. What else was there to discuss after six weeks of isolation from the world?

Thinking of what Franz had told her of the theatre being reopened with business as usual, she felt no thrill at the prospect of resuming nightly performances. The troops coming up from Cape Town would be here by the weekend, and the danger would be over for the residents of Kimberley. What of the army, however? The soldiers would move on in pursuit of the enemy. The danger would not be over for them. Had her olive branch today been offered too late? Next week he could be gone—gone until they came face to face again someday, somewhere, and pretended to be strangers. Or gone from the world completely.

"You sang the gypsy song to him that first time?" asked Franz, revealing the direction his thoughts had been pursuing.

She nodded listlessly. "I had just seen the photograph of his wedding in the newspaper. I suppose I was singing my farewell."

He seemed relieved. "Soon, you will be Kati again to my archduke. Think of him while you sing 'My Faraway Love', then forget him when the song ends. In the meantime, capture as many hearts as you wish, so long as your own remains free. The army will be marching on next week. I beg you not to be one of those silly creatures in tears for a soldier who loved then left her."

"Don't worry, Franz," she told him hollowly. "I will never be one of *those* silly creatures."

He helped her to alight from the carriage at her cottage gate, then kissed her on the cheek before climbing back to continue to his own destination. She walked up the path to the stoep running around the outside of her rented home, and along the wooden way to the open door of the main parlour, lost in thought. It was very quiet. Sally would be having her afternoon nap, but Nellie was usually in the kitchen singing an off-key song. Perhaps she was still upset over the funerals, and staying with Sally.

Hot and depressed, Leila crossed to her own room, intending to splash herself down and change into a loose wrapper. Passing the table, an envelope caught her eye. Guessing that it contained an invitation or a request to sing, she left the letter lying there until she emerged once more, feeling refreshed. Then she settled in a cane chair near the open doors, slitting the letter open with a tiny silver knife. In the humidity of pre-dusk, she read the few words on one plain sheet of paper. There was no address, and no signature.

> You and your harlots led them into vile ways. They gave in to temptation when you offered them the sins of the flesh, and the bottle that contains the juice of the Devil. They thought only of lust and liquor. The Lord took His vengeance on them yesterday. He upheld the righteous, and punished the weak sinners. YOU KILLED THEM. Pray to the Lord for redemption, and cease this corruption of men before they all die.

It grew unbearably cold on that hot, airless evening, as Leila stared at the words on that page. She thought of Lily Lowe in a field with a persuasive soldier. She thought of that same soldier tearing her clothes off in a frenzy of lust in a basement room. She thought of a sophisticated

264

officer attempting to buy her with another woman's earrings. She thought of that same officer advising her not to price herself too high, and saying that he felt the diamond pendant was quite enough to pay for a few hours in her arms. Her body began to shake convulsively, and waves of nausea swept over her. Unaware of the onset of darkness, she finally had to rush to the bathroom.

# CHAPTER FOURTEEN

Within a week it would be Christmas; the last one of the nineteenth century. Although Cecil Rhodes had set a team of volunteers making Christmas puddings for the troops, there was little seasonal cheer for the captives of Kimberley. The relief column could be heard but not seen. Everyone, save the official look-outs, had abandoned the eager scanning of the horizon for rising dust which would signify imminent relief. After so many frustrated hopes, so many days of speculation, depression had driven away all interest in the army just over the distant hills.

On December 11th the thunder of battle had shaken the city outskirts, bringing people into the streets to rejoice again. The sound of gunfire had ceased; when the horizon remained bare, so had the rejoicing. A brief message relayed to Colonel Kekewich had informed him that the advance had been halted at Magersfontein. Only a taunting signal flashed by the encircling Boers had given the hint of a major defeat of British troops. Deciding not to reduce morale by releasing the news to the civilian population, the military commander had instead earned an increase in their distrust in him. One of the worst aspects of siege was the lack of knowledge of events outside, and Kekewich had underestimated the effect of withheld news on those he was defending. With nerves stretched tightly after nine weeks of uncertainty and fear, with shells falling daily except Sundays, each person trapped in the diamond city preferred to know the truth, even if it was unpalatable. Left prey to their imaginings, they quickly felt that they had been abandoned. Resentment soon ignited into anger; anger into violence.

When the *Diamond Fields Advertiser* published a protest against "secret military orders", which could only have been leaked to the editor of the newspaper by Rhodes, there was well-nigh a mutiny against the military element. Kekewich unfortunately could not deny that he had received a directive that all civilians would be required to leave when relief came, because troops could not be spared to provide continual defence of so large a community. With thoughts of financial ruin, loss of homes and property, privation for children and old people while soldiers ran riot to loot the city in which they had such pride, there

266

was more than a suggestion that it would be preferable to surrender to the Boers. So much for Rhodes' confidence that it would be "business as usual" once the investment was broken.

When a military decree instigated rationing of tea, coffee, vegetables and most other foodstuffs, civilian disillusionment with those in uniform was complete. It was as well that they were unaware of a series of messages brought in by native runners, who had evaded enemy positions between Kimberley and the relief column. Kekewich was faced with the news that staggering losses had been sustained at Magersfontein, resulting in the column being pinned down indefinitely. Reinforcements and revised plans were being sought, but the military commander of Kimberley was asked to be prepared to hold out until the end of January. That request was superceded by another changing the date to the end of February. With Rhodes opposing his every move and the populace very solidly against him, Kekewich was almost at his wits' end. Not only was he suffering equally with every captive, he had a disgruntled force to feed and keep in a state of fitness to fight when the moment came.

Not unnaturally, the troops resented the animosity of the civilians. They were not being asked to risk their lives for the sake of a city which, in the case of the British troops present, was neither their home nor part of their own country. However, *not* being asked to risk their lives was an even greater source of resentment to the soldiers than the people's hostility. Knowing that the encircling enemy was pinning down those coming to their aid, knowing that British troops were dying in droves on the other side of those hills, made them burn to strike a blow of their own. Common sense had to prevail, no matter what. If the ponderous relief column could not defeat the Boers from outside Kimberley, a small, tired, underfed force from within would never succeed. With enemy attention now on Magersfontein, there were no rushes on the city to repulse, and there seemed little point in sorties that resulted in temporary tenure of redoubts at the cost of further lives. The soldiers were frustrated by inactivity and the taunts of the civilians; the officers were depressed by a sense of impotence, and by the lies they were ordered to tell those who were getting the truth from Cecil Rhodes.

Then there were the heat, dust and flies; the lack of mail and major newspapers; the curfew which imprisoned people in their homes after dusk; the daily queuing for food; the regular shelling; the fear of an uprising among the black workers, who were being penalised in a war which did not immediately concern them; and there was the boredom of meeting the same people day after day and having nothing fresh to say to them. To compensate for lack of news, attention turned to siege gossip.

After two Boer residents were caught wandering outside the defences, and subsequently adjudged to be passing information to their country-men, all those of Dutch origin in Kimberley were tarred with the same brush and ostracised. A woman who had been widowed during the big assault which had failed was labelled a Jezebel because she was seen accepting milk for her baby from another soldier. A rush of malingerers when the butter ration was restricted to children and invalids, led to several genuinely sick people being insulted with charges of lies and greed.

Some British troops were accused by local soldiers of trying to seduce their wives; some British troops did seduce local wives. Members of Queen Victoria's army fought those of the diamond city's force, the former claiming that Kimberley was a second-rate settlement, the latter that their opponents were part of a second-rate army unable to defeat a parcel of farmers. In the higher echelons of society the strain was similarly being felt. Personalities clashed; jealousies erupted. Rifts opened between those who were presently in favour with Rhodes, and those who had fallen foul of him or become disillusioned with the man. Whispers began concerning the loyalties of Baron Von Grossladen, whose fatherland was supplying arms and men to the Boers, and speaking in open support of their cause at international meetings. His close association with Franz Mittelheiter—another German, near enough—was questioned. Could the tenor be passing messages to the Boers with his songs? Why would a singer go so often to the engineering works at De Beers, if not to count the number of shells being produced and transmit the information to the enemy?

A Swedish countess had been seen at her window with a hand-mirror. Admittedly, she had apparently been inspecting her *coiffure*, but the sun had been deflected from the glass, and signals could well have been transmitted to her son who was known to be with a medical team tending prisoners of the Boers. Situations which would have been considered ridiculous in normal times, were tinted with fierce patriotic conviction as the days turned into weeks, then weeks into months, with no sign of their ordeal ending.

Leila was now receiving frequent anonymous letters. All were in similar vein, although written in various hands, accusing her of running an establishment at which her "troupe of painted harlots" lured men into indulgence in "those sins which the Lord shall drive from them with His wrath". They still upset her, although not as drastically as the first had done. Who delivered them was a mystery, but it was always when she was away from the cottage, and Nellie was either queuing for their rations in the market, or in the lower garden pegging out the washing. That someone was close enough to see all that happened at that tree-shaded bungalow, gave Leila an uncomfortable feeling, yet none of those women living near by appeared to be religious bigots, or even frustrated spinsters. Why she was so certain that women were behind the campaign of hate she did not know, except that it seemed possible that those who had lived hard and frugal lives, with the type of men who were natural tamers of wild lands, would react this way against the entertaining of soldiers by actresses—both breeds having been long condemned by society.

Nellie had been left in ignorance of the letters, and Leila was glad of her decision when the emphasis switched to little Sally—"the misbegotten fruit of your sins". For the first time since the child's birth, Leila wondered if anyone else imagined that the child was hers. That led to the daunting question of whether it was generally believed in the city that she was running a brothel. The soldiers who came would surely heartily dispute it, and the officers that she personally entertained would soon silence any talk of impropriety. Even Sutton Blaise, who now refused to acknowledge her existence, could not claim success in that direction.

All the same, the sensation that unseen eyes were watching her, put a strange prickly sensation down her spine whenever she walked through the streets. To demonstrate her defiance, and because she felt that it was essential to maintain what little beauty could be found in their prolonged ordeal, she continued to wear elaborate gowns that proclaimed her a leading lady in fashion as well as talent. The bulk of the townswomen dressed in homespun frocks with small bonnets, but Leila brightened the streets with apricot, eau-de-Nil, lavender, chartreuse and blush-rose gowns, topped with huge stylish hats of ribbons, gauze, feathers and artificial flowers. Others protected themselves from the sun with dark umbrellas; Leila's face was always enhanced by the delicate shade from a lacy parasol when she walked out. Perhaps she deliberately chose to present a picture of extreme femininity in public. A man called Frank Duncan had brought her down once. She would not allow a parcel of spiteful women to repeat his success.

On that morning one week before Christmas, Leila rode in a cab to Baron Von Grossladen's residence, where she had been invited to discuss plans for a special concert on Christmas Eve. Certain that the Boers would respect the significance of that religious festival with a halt in hostilities, those with influence determined to ease tension and raise low spirits during the short respite. Because of his close alliance with Rhodes, because his home was set in spacious grounds, and possibly because he knew his German nationality was causing suspicion, Von

Grossladen was prepared to stage an open-air concert on his property for any adult resident who wished to come. A neighbouring diamond-merchant was willing to arrange a party for the children of the city, utilising the varying talents of the cast of *The Hungarian Heiress* to entertain with tricks, comedy and dancing.

Wearing an elaborate swathed gown of lemon voile, trimmed with black and white striped ribbon, and a matching hat, Leila was announced by the manservant at the door of the first-floor salon. After greeting Margaret Veasey-Hunter, then her host, she went on to explain the note of apology Franz had sent him earlier that morning.

"For a singer, even the slightest trouble with one's throat must be treated seriously," she said, accepting the offer of a chair beside Vivian's mother. "The intense heat in Kimberley is trying enough, without the flying dust when the wind rises. Franz knows that it is important to rest his voice now, so that he might be able to sing on Christmas Eve."

The Baron, in an impeccable grey morning suit, sat gracefully after ensuring that his female guest was settled. His smile was smoothly confident, and Leila asked herself why she distrusted him when there was no obvious reason for her to do so. Her feelings for his bride-to-be were based on her original opinion of any mother who could allow her sons to be so cruelly dominated by their grandfather. Although gently charming whenever they met, Margaret Veasey-Hunter had not re-deemed that opinion. Beneath the well-bred courtesy, Vivian's mother still gave Leila the impression of being placidly self-centred. How was it that her son had apparently never recognised it?

"Mittelheiter will not let us down," the Baron decided. "He knows that we are all presently making greater efforts than are normally required of us, and will react accordingly. So, Miss Duncan, in his absence we are left only with the delightful business of discussing your own participation in what I am determined will be an event spoken of for years to come." His ice-blue eyes lit with momentary warmth. "History books will record the undaunted spirit of the people of Kimberley in their time of greatest peril."

"I am not sure that I wish to be mentioned in history books," mused Leila, "although men like yourself and Mr Rhodes undoubtedly will."

"We shall see, we shall see," he responded with total confidence.

"In company with Colonel Kekewich," she added.

His smiling affability vanished in a moment. "One hopes that historians will be kind to the man; that they will gloss over some of the more . . . er . . . *unattractive* aspects of his command here."

"Come, Gunther, he is not too much of a villain, surely," chided

Margaret, managing to match her fiancé's air of remote civility with the coolness of her blue-grey eyes, and a morning gown of natural shantung. "Cecil paints him black, I know, but it cannot be easy for a man to cover himself with glory in a static situation."

He patted her hand indulgently. "Cecil deals with him, *liebling*, which gives him unique insight into the conduct of a man faced with a task to which he is disastrously unequal. You may rest assured, however, that your safety does not lie entirely in his hands."

Leila seemed possessed by a demon of defiance that morning, for she heard herself say, "As it is Colonel Kekewich who spends his days and nights cooped up in his perimeter watch-tower, while the remainder of us are free to enjoy morning meetings such as this, surely it is he who holds our safety in his hands—his and those of the men he commands."

Margaret studied Leila with sharp interest, while Von Grossladen managed a thin smile. "*Lieber Gott*, such fervent defence of the military, Miss Duncan. Ah, of course, you are a great favourite with them, I hear."

Leila's uneasy speculation on the full meaning of that comment ended abruptly, when the voice of the manservant at the door behind her announced, "Major Veasey-Hunter."

Fighting the urge to turn, Leila sat with her thoughts and composure scattered as Margaret smiled a greeting at her son.

"Vivian, I am so glad that tiresome duties did not prevent your joining us, as they so often appear to do."

Leila knew his voice well enough to recognise the wariness in it, as he replied, "Your note suggested that the affair was of some importance, Mama."

As Von Grossladen showed little satisfaction at his arrival, Leila guessed that the gentle Margaret had not consulted him on the subject. As she watched the older woman accept her son's kiss on the cheek, a small stab of awareness made Leila wonder if she had underestimated a second Veasey-Hunter.

"I trust you are well," said Vivian then, "and you, sir." Turning to Leila with a telling glance that denied the formality of his manner, he murmured, "You have me once more at a disadvantage, Miss Duncan. I was unaware that I would have the privilege of meeting you today."

Seeing, in one comprehensive glance, that he looked surprisingly less strained than before, and that there was evidence of a return of something approaching the old assurance in his bearing, she smiled her gladness into his eyes.

"We share surprise at each other's company, Major. I see you are quite recovered from your wound."

"Recovery can take a very long time, and leave a man deeply scarred," he said with deliberation. "I must count myself fortunate."

"Gunther, I knew you would approve of my sudden inspiration this morning in sending for Vivian," Margaret said with an air of sweet femininity. "I have not seen him since he quit the hospital, you know, and it seemed emminently sensible to have a gentleman to substitute for Herr Mittelheiter this morning, in addition to obtaining the military view of your plans."

Struggling to maintain his Prussian punctiliousness in the face of growing annoyance, the Baron signalled instructions to the hovering manservant, saying curtly, "That you wished to see your son is perfectly understandable, Margaret. My plans, however, are in no way dependent on the military view. Let us all take coffee together now, in social manner. There seems little point in continuing the meeting: with Mittelheiter absent and the emphasis on the progress of healing wounds sustained in an unnecessary and fruitless confrontation, I fear we should settle very few of the questions I had intended to raise." Baring his teeth in a smile in Leila's direction, he continued, "You may confidently leave things in my hands. Together with Mittelheiter, I shall plan the programme to suit your capabilities, rest assured."

Vivian lowered himself into a chair, his left leg clearly still hampering easy movement. "Are you fully aware of Miss Duncan's capabilities, sir?" he asked with deceptive innocence.

"I have heard her sing on enough occasions to know that she has a voice of great power and beauty," came the clipped response. "I think I do not need the military view on *that*, Major."

"Ah, but have you seen her 'stroll' when dressed entirely in white ostrich feathers?" He looked at Leila, as her heart began to hammer, and there was evidence that his other wound was healing when he smiled. "My memory has returned, you see. I now recall that occasion in London when we met before."

"My dear Miss Duncan, white ostrich feathers!" exclaimed Margaret softly. "I am surprised that any gentlemen, in particular my son, whose memory has always been excellent, could forget a sight which must have been excessively attractive."

Well aware, by now, that the woman had invited Vivian there for reasons of her own, Leila replied with feigned calmness, "When I explain that I was one of thirty girls chosen for their matching looks, you will understand how someone, even with Major Veasey-Hunter's excellent memory, might not recall the meeting with clarity. Had he been with an entire company of Lancers, I doubt I would have remembered him."

The manservant arrived with coffee in exquisite Von Grossladen porcelain, ending a line of conversation which everyone present knew was merely a sharpening of wits, and not to be believed.

"I have another son, Miss Duncan," said Margaret confidingly. "He runs the family estate in Cornwall. The poor boy will be so distressed over our predicament: his mother and brother captive."

"Charles probably does not know, Mama," put in Vivian after sipping his coffee. "He doubtless believes you to be still in Rhodesia. If he cares to discover news of the 49th, he will assume that I am with them."

"Unless Julia has written to enlighten him." Margaret turned swiftly to Leila. "Do you know my son's wife?"

Sensing Vivian's sudden stillness, she said carefully, "I know few people outside the world of theatre, I'm afraid."

"She is in Cape Town, and must be quite distracted over the dangers Vivian might encounter here."

"Julia is not a women to become distracted," Vivian put in firmly. "It seems to me that Miss Duncan will not wish to hear about a succession of people she does not know, when she has been invited here to discuss how she will entertain us all at a concert. I hear the full military band is to play, in addition to the orchestra from the theatre, sir," he said to the Baron. "As Miss Duncan is so distinguished a performer—even in London's West End, where talent abounds—she really should be accorded the courtesy of arranging her own programme. In the theatrical profession, a leading lady is not told by anyone else, including her leading man, what she will sing or how she will perform. She is consulted about her wishes and desires, then given every consideration in the performance of them."

Von Grossladen flicked him with a cool glance. "You know a great deal about the Thespian art, Major. Perhaps you have mistaken your vocation and should, instead, be treading the boards." He nodded a bow in Leila's direction. "I am clearly uninformed concerning your exalted standing within the profession, Miss Duncan. Forgive me if I have treated you peremptorily."

Leila nodded back, unable to resist adding, "No one in Kimberley is exalted, sir. We are all equal in captivity, surely?" Allowing a short pause for that comment to be digested, she continued. "Major Veasey-Hunter is correct in his surmise that I would prefer to decide my own programme, which I will then offer for your perusal. An artist, Baron, is a creature of moods and fancies, someone to be indulged—as Mrs Veasey-Hunter will confirm, being of musical inclination herself."

"How wonderfully discerning of you, my dear," marvelled the older

273

woman. "I believe you have never heard me play the pianoforte, nor have we ever discussed music together."

Realising her serious slip, Leila covered herself as best she could. "Your sensitive interpretation of classical pieces is spoken of by everyone who has had the pleasure of hearing you play. The word is, that you would rival some of our greatest pianists if you ever became a concert performer."

Her smile was an acknowledgement of a compliment, but Margaret's blue-grey eyes held more than a hint of speculation now. "Perhaps you should include me in your concert, Gunther," she teased lightly, turning to him.

"No, *liebling*, I would not permit my future wife to perform before the general public like a . . . like a . . ."

"Like Miss Duncan, who has been doing so for ten weeks under extremely trying conditions, in a commendable desire to ease the many trials being suffered by those in Kimberley," said Vivian pointedly. "Mama can hold a room full of people captive with the beauty of her performance, but we all know to our cost, that many a drawing-room entertainer holds an audience captive only through their good manners. Leila . . . Duncan," he added swiftly, to cover the suggestion of familiarity, "can hold a theatre full of people captive—people who are even willing to pay for such captivation."

After a moment's silence, Margaret said softly, "Your fervour suggests that you have experienced such captivation, Vivian. One might imagine Miss Duncan herself to have caused it, except that you appear to have forgotten the white ostrich feathers until coincidentally reminded of them."

He seemed ready for that, for his answer was very smooth, with just the right amount of nonchalance in his tone. "You left England so long ago, Mama, you have never been made aware of my great fondness for musical shows. The atmosphere on a first-night is indescribable. Even the sanest go mad with excitement."

"Indeed, yes. I recall that your father was exceptionally fond of first-nights . . . and all the excitement that accompanies them," she ended with delicate deliberation, looking full at her son for a moment or two. Then she turned to the Baron with a gentle smile. "Would it not be wonderful, Gunther, if your Christmas concert could go into history as just such an event?"

The manservant brought more coffee, and conversation turned to serious concentration on arrangements for the concert. Throughout the discussion, Leila was aware of Margaret's speculative gaze on both herself and Vivian. She grew increasingly afraid of making a fatal slip of the tongue. In consequence, she began her leave-taking the moment it became possible to do so. Then, Vivian appeared to undermine all the good she was attempting to do. When the manservant announced the arrival of the cab at the door, he rose with their host, then crossed the floor, saying that he would see her into the carriage. Feeling that protests would only highlight the incident, Leila said her farewells, then descended the stairs beside him, not knowing what to expect when they reached the foot of them.

With the manservant standing respectfully aside, she turned to Vivian to say, "Thank you for your defence of my talent."

"I was invited as a substitute for Mittelheiter. That impossible fellow would surely have defended you."

As they stood together beneath that sun-washed portico, with the exotic sensual perfume of recently watered shrubs wafting on the faintly stirring air, it was suddenly as if three years had never passed and she was again a hesitant, confused girl in a yellow dress, confronting a tall officer she had not expected to find awaiting her. His eyes told her animosity had flown; his searching expression made nonsense of any resistance to her. Making no attempt to walk away, or break that moment of awareness, Vivian was silently telling her something she could scarcely believe. It was dangerous, but it beckoned unbearably as she gazed at his clean shining hair, square sun-browned face, crisply-starched warlike khaki with polished leather straps, and tall boots filmed with fine dust. Her senses remembered the smell of soap and clean linen, the caresses from hands that were well-kept, a mouth that felt sweet and firm on her own, a smile which lit the entire day, and a passion that had refused to die. Her senses remembered, and her body responded.

"Have you accepted my request that we should be friends?" she asked cautiously.

"It's essential to be backed by a very large horse and a crowd of curious spectators, to bring that off successfully," he replied, all the old fire back in his eyes.

"So we are not to be friends?"

"As I told you, it's too late for that."

Against every inclination, she had to say, "As your mother has been at great pains to point out this morning, it is too late for anything else."

"Is it?" he asked quietly. "Is it, Leila? The world outside this perimeter is temporarily denied us. While this siege lasts, we are divorced from all ties and obligations save those demanded of us here. In our present situation, priorities have changed. Strangers have been brought together and become interdependent. I have ridden out with men of this city, who have accepted my leadership even knowing that their lives may depend on it. Those who make a living bringing from the ground diamonds designed to adorn women, are now making shells designed to kill Boers. There are relationships being swiftly forged, which will be just as swiftly put aside when relief comes. Until it does, can't we two make the most of this little enclosed world we have? Can't we enjoy our captive freedom for the short time that it lasts?"

Not entirely certain what he was asking, she hesitated for some moments before saying, "You don't appear to need a very large horse and a crowd of spectators to court success."

"I'm not asking a very angry girl if we can just be friends. That's when the large horse becomes necessary."

Longing to give him the answer he wanted, yet still confused, she said, "Rose would agree without hesitation."

"You are the one I am asking."

"You know the answer," she cried softly. "You knew before you put the question."

"No, Leila. I shall never again take anything for granted where you are concerned."

There were rugs from every room in the place draped over the fence, when Leila arrived back in a state of continuing confusion. Puzzled, and slightly irritated, by this evidence of Nellie's thoughtlessness in allowing the black girl to beat carpets at the front of the cottage, in full view of those passing, she climbed from the cab and went straight along the wooden stoep leading to the rear of the house. There, she found Nellie sitting on the back steps, clutching her small child against her, rocking back and forth. Realising that there was something wrong with this girl who was a friend as well as a maid, Leila sat down beside her on the top step. It was then she realised that Nellie was white-faced with anger—so angry, in fact, that it robbed her of speech until Leila repeated her solicitous questioning and shook her shoulder gently.

In a peculiar strained tone, Nellie said against the top of her child's head, "Them rugs was the only way of coverin' it up. I didn't know what else to do when it wouldn't come off. Lor' knows how many others see it afore I did." Reverting to her inbred way of speaking due to her agitation, she turned her head suddenly to demand of Leila, "'Oo would've done sich a thing? Little Sal's never done nothin' to 'urt anyone, pore mite, and I've be'aved meself since I bin wiv you, you know that. Why put that on the fence for everyone to see . . . and why after all this time? If I find out 'oo done it, I'll wring 'is neck," she cried in a crescendo of fury. "I'll wring 'is neck, good and proper!"

276

With her own emotions presently in a volatile state, Leila could make no sense of the girl's outburst. Her attempt to coax Nellie indoors, away from the dusty steps where ants crossed industriously back and forth between dying leaves from an overhanging tree, met with the kind of fierce resistance induced by shock.

"Nellie, please tell me what this is all about," she demanded, feeling the heat of noon filtering through the overhead branches to make her uncomfortable in the fashionable dress and hat. "Why did you allow Mim to drape rugs all over the fence by the street? What kind of impression does that give to the neighbourhood?"

"A better one than seein' *that* writ in large letters."

"Seeing what written in large letters?" asked Leila warily, an unwelcome suspicion entering her mind.

Tears came swiftly, to roll down the girl's cheeks as her voice shook. "I know I done wrong wiv Jim, and I s'pose I weren't never punished, cos I got a life I never dreamed of wiv you . . . and I got little Sal to love. I can't never thank you for what you done for me, Leila," she continued with difficulty, "so I can't never forgive 'ooever writ that on your fence about me."

Already suspecting the answer, Leila asked quietly, "What is written on my fence, Nellie?"

After a few distressed moments, the girl confessed in a broken whisper. "Someone's writ *whore*. I'm not that—reely I'm not."

Even half-suspecting it did not lessen the impact of that confession, and the confused delight of her recent minutes with Vivian shrivelled up and died, as the basic truth of what he had been asking became all too clear.

Staring out across the parched grass, where she had encouraged her friends from the theatre to relieve their own boredom along with that of the British troops so far from home, she said tonelessly, "You're quite wrong, Nellie. That word was intended to describe me."

Christmas Eve dawned, and the inhabitants of Kimberley no longer joked about the arrival of the relief column bearing sacks of presents, as a surprise. Everyone now knew that serious reverses were being suffered by the British pinned down beyond the distant hills. There would be no merry Christmas for them, either. The military element knew that there was a chance that the diamond city might be left to its eventual fate, because troops were badly needed elsewhere in Natal. For the civilians, surrender might not be too different from the life they presently led, with the additional advantage of a cessation of shelling to recommend the idea to them. For the troops, however, the prospect was one of imprisonment, hardship and professional humiliation. Accordingly, the opportunity to relax and celebrate during the Christmas cease-fire was seized even more avidly by the soldiers than the settlers.

After a week of excessive entertaining, both at her cottage and at the various army camps, Leila faced another heavy programme on Christmas Eve. It began with an early rehearsal with Franz for the evening concert, followed by a trip to one of the camps to help distribute Cecil Rhodes' plum puddings to the troops. She then planned to rest in her room after a light luncheon, in readiness for the concert which was to form the early part of the evening. After it, they had both been invited to a grand dinner at the Von Grossladen residence. She viewed that dinner with more trepidation than the concert, because Vivian was to be there. In the seven days since her fence was daubed with paint, she had sent vague negative replies to his several notes, and had luckily been out on the one occasion that he had called at the cottage.

The word on her fence had been painted out, but it was still written on her mind too clearly to be put aside. It seemed to her that they had come full circle. He was a virile man, under stress, facing the possibility of death at the hands of the enemy each time he rode out beyond the perimeter. Denied his wife, he needed the release of a woman's company. Who, better than she, could provide the solace he sought? She had refused an offer of marriage from him; she had ejected him from the cab after his offer to become her protector. Now, he could no longer offer marriage, and she was seen to be entertaining the military *en masse*. There was only one thing he could think, and that was the old truth about what girls like her could give to men like him. It was that thought which shadowed the day as she carried out her engagements which led her inexorably toward evening.

Franz was filled with his usual self-confidence during their rehearsals, and remained with her to drink coffee whilst waiting for a carriage to take them both off to distribute puddings. In it, he spoke with enthusiasm of a massive gun being designed and cast at the De Beers workshop by George Labram, the American engineer.

"He is being eagerly encouraged by two Artillery officers named Blaise and Sinclair," he added with a chuckle.

"I am delighted to learn that Captain Blaise is now finding a satisfactory outlet for his eagerness," she responded dryly.

"There is another, Leila. She lives in the Wesselton district."

"Ah! I trust she displayed more gratitude for his diamond pendant than I did. What of this gun, Franz? Is it so fearsome, it will scare away the Boers and set us free?"

He looked at her pensively. "You should not treat such a subject with levity."

"Then speak of it to the Belligerent Baron, who will not accept your disclaimer to being his compatriot. I am tired of war, of hopes and promises; tired of being captive with no prospect of escape. I want to go home, Franz. Oh, how very much I long to go home."

Thoughts of London, Lindley's Theatre, and her attractive apartment filled her mind all the time she smiled automatically at the brown-faced men in khaki, to whom she handed puddings. They most likely imagined that she dealt out her sexual favours with the same smile on her face. Could it possibly be one of them who was conducting a campaign of hatred against her, rather than one of the devout wives of settlers? Maybe she should not be deceived by their suggestion of shy or awed admiration. It might be that they put her on a par with the Diamond Queens, who had entertained men on and off stage during the boom days.

She and Franz returned hot and tired to their respective lodgings, relishing the thought of resting for an hour or two in a dim room before the demands of the concert. All thoughts of that vanished for Leila, however, when she discovered Nellie on her bed, gripped by shaking fits and vomiting with distressing frequency. Guessing that the girl was in the first stages of some kind of fever, Leila dropped her parasol and bag on the floor and set to work. Sally was standing beside her mother, crying. There was no sign of Mim, the black girl, who had probably read the signs of the devil in Nellie's condition, and fled. Settling the child on her own bed with a cup of milk and some picture books, Leila then sponged Nellie's heated body, sprinkled cologne on a fresh pillow, and made her as comfortable as possible whilst reassuring her that she would fetch the doctor right away. Still in an elaborate shell-pink muslin gown, with a shady hat of strawberry-coloured silk and feathers, Leila left the bungalow to find a cab.

It was noon, the traditional time for resting indoors, and there was no cab on the streets in that area. Cursing the fact, she began to walk in the hope of finding a vehicle returning from a journey, the driver of which would surely recognise the urgency of her errand and turn back. Leila was full of fears. Nellie had been in a strange state since the defilement of the fence, which had forced Leila to reveal the truth about the anonymous letters. She hurried through the deserted streets, searching in vain for any kind of vehicle that would take her to the house of the doctor on the far side of the city. On the point of concluding that she would be obliged to walk there, she reached a junction and spotted two horsemen in uniform coming toward her. Certain that they would help, she waited for them to draw nearer. Both were men of Kimberley, with whom she had no personal friendship, but they responded to her plea without hesitation. One rode off at the gallop to fetch the doctor, the other offered to accompany her back to the cottage.

"There is no need for that," she told him gratefully. "Your own family will be waiting to see you, and I am well able to walk over the route I have just taken. Your companion is rendering me the most valuable service, and I am immensely thankful for that."

They parted, and Leila hurried back through the quiet city, glad to be spared such a long walk. Still, she was anxious as she covered the length of the dirt roads, growing hotter than ever due to her fast pace. Fever on top of malnutrition and an emotional week following that insult on the fence could be dangerous. In no way a replacement for Rose, Nellie nevertheless held that place in Leila's heart which had been a vacuum after the suicide of a girl who still occupied her memory. If Nellie should be lost, there would be no one save an endless procession of men who regarded her as anything but a friend. Without Nellie, her life would be lacking warmth, spontaneous affection, and a loyalty which made no demands. Rounding a corner of a crescent, from which there led a pathway connecting with the quiet street where she lived, Leila offered up a prayer. Once again, she wondered if anyone up above really heard all the words of supplication. She repeated them, in case it was true.

At the far end of the narrow lane, a woman was just leaving her garden gate to walk down it in the opposite direction. She appeared to be carrying a broom, but Leila was too worried to ponder the strangeness of that. Another woman entered the lane behind the first. She, too, was carrying a long stick which could have been a mop or broom. Something unusual about the way they walked a few steps apart, yet not falling in together to chat as they walked, made Leila first curious, then wary. Only then did the odd fact of the brooms really register. Faint unidentifiable alarm touched her.

Turning uncertainly, she wondered whether to retrace her steps and then take the longer route home. Her alarm increased at the sight of three more women, who had entered the lane behind her and were following slowly. They each held something which suggested a weapon of some kind. Deep inside her grew a sensation of terror, of anticipating danger of a kind she had never before imagined. Looking wildly for an escape from that lane, she spotted a slight thinning of the bushes on the left-hand side, which could provide passage through to the road beyond. Moving swiftly from the dappled light of the path into the shadowed gloom created by the crowding foliage, she made for the place where it appeared possible to push through to a more open area.

With her heart racing, she realised that it had been an illusion. An impenetrable wall of shrubs lay beyond the sparser growth. Spinning around in real fear, it became plain that she had placed herself in the worst possible danger by leaving the path. There might have been the chance of a passing soldier, a mine-worker, a friendly woman entering the lane, or even seeing the situation from the roadway at the end. Here, anything could happen within a few feet of the lane itself, yet not be witnessed by anyone passing through it. Swallowing to ease her dry throat, she stood like a hunted deer, casting around for some means of escaping those closing in on her.

They were leaving the path now—all five together—and she could see the hatred written on their faces lined by climate and the rigours of poverty. Each was in a plain dark gown, high at the neck and covering every part in their tough bodies. Each had hair tightly dragged back into a knot. The hands holding their weapons of wrath were brown and roughened by hard work, the veins standing along the backs of them. These were some women of the city of diamonds, who had never been adorned by the dazzling stones which had brought prospectors to overrun their simple settlement. These were women who lived by a strict puritanical code, which demanded a punishment to suit the sin.

They advanced in silence on Leila, and she pressed back into the undergrowth instinctively as she saw the selection of articles they held. Her hat was caught by a fine twig which pushed it forward over her right eye. Desperately jerking free, her hair was tugged at the roots as the hat, which was securely pinned in place, was caught anew, holding her immobile. The cry of pain she gave was like a signal to women whose rigid moral uprbringing taught them to see evil in beauty and gaiety of spirits. As they closed in, Leila pleaded with them in vain to let her speak, explain the truth of what she was. Blows from their sticks began raining on her head, back and shoulders, as they cursed her glorification of the female form to bring about the downfall of men.

Aggression was born of pain. Kicking, clawing, denouncing their bigotry, Leila fought back. Her retaliation merely served to increase their ferocity. Someone mercilessly dragged the pretty hat from her head, and it felt as if the hair was being torn from her scalp. Hands clawed at the neckline of her dress, ripping it from her body with a strength imbued by the conviction of righteous vengeance on a sinner. Frantically trying to protect her head from the punishment of flailing sticks by folding her arms across it, she had no means of counter-attack. Sinking to her knees beneath the assault, she felt a greater humiliation than when Frank had attempted marital rape. There had been faint justification for his actions, a sane explanation for his tragic desperation. This abuse by her own sex smacked of degradation so extreme, she felt their wrath turning her into the creature they accused her of being. Stripped, humiliated, cowering from their blows, she had become a slut, a wanton, a woman without pride.

Once on her knees, they knew she was completely at their mercy. She was pushed flat and held down, while revenge was completed. There was a mixture of blood and tears on her cheeks as she subconsciously echoed Nellie's words in broken tones.

*"I'm not a whore. Really, I'm not."*

As the place around her began to grow dark she realised that the cry was meant, not for her attackers, but for Frank Duncan, Sutton Blaise and a dozen others like him who had tried to buy her body with trinkets. Mostly, however, it was for Vivian Veasey-Hunter.

He told himself that he had to pass the bungalow, anyway, so it was not as if he had deliberately sought her out. Finding the place empty save for the odd little maid, and her odd little child, Vivian decided to wait until Leila returned with the doctor. There might be some way in which he could help her, some errand he could carry out on her behalf. Reassuring the sick girl that he was on hand, he went into the sitting-room, where a window gave a view of the road.

Since their last meeting, he had been on sorties designed to discover the enemy's strength—whether reinforcements had arrived to make a last stand to prevent final relief of the city, or whether the encircling force had been depleted in order to send more men to those at Magersfontein. The outcome had been depressing. They had lost two men whilst proving that there were as many Boers outside Kimberley as there had ever been. To counter the stress of such duties, he had approached Leila by letter, then called in person when her replies had implied that she was committed to an endless round of engagements. Knowing that they would meet that evening, he wanted to be alone with her first to put at rest his faint suspicion that she had once more been acting a part, when she had agreed to his overture last week.

Restless, knowing from Nellie that Leila had set out almost half an hour ago, Vivian wandered onto the stoep, anticipating her return. Almost immediately, he saw a carriage approaching from the distance. Why he should feel such relief he did not know, but it was so strong he went down to the gate to meet her.

The doctor was alone. Vivian's sense of relief reversed into one of alarm, which was intensified when the man told how Miss Duncan had apparently intended to return to the patient after Peter Van Kleef offered to ride for medical help. With some abstraction, Vivian ushered the doctor into Nellie's room, then returned to the stoep, the half-formed intention of going in search of Leila at the back of his mind. The midday sun burned down onto the empty dirt road stretching into the distance in both directions. The heat silenced even the birds in that noon period. The only sound, as he stood on that wooden verandah, was the pulsating song of cicadas and the far-off clatter of machinery at De Beers.

Would there ever been anything more than this present life? he wondered. Would death come to him during a last-stand defence of this alien city? If not, and he one day rode out beyond the perimeter to continue the fight elsewhere, part of him would remain here. Fate had brought them together again in circumstances of stress and need and, while he lived, Leila would occupy his heart and mind. If he had ever doubted it before, he knew it for certain now.

Awareness of movement in that still scene dawned on him slowly, and even then he did not fully recognise what he saw. Screwing up his eyes against the glare of the sun, he watched as something emerged sluggishly from the background and began moving forward. Walking the short distance to the far end of the stoep, Vivian gazed at a strange figure who had apparently materialised from the undergrowth. He frowned as he tried to make sense of the oddness of appearance and behaviour. It walked in lurching fashion, yet not exactly aimlessly, and looked to be a boy in some peculiar garb.

For several moments, Vivian stood there immobilised by curiosity. Then, some inner sense quickened his heart-beat, and drove him to vault the rail into the garden in his urgency to reach the road. He was breathing fast—painfully—when partial recognition slowed his running steps into a faltering walk. Appalled, he stopped some yards from her in a hiatus caused by shock. She came on in the same lurching manner, as if she saw or heard nothing. Her long white cambric drawers were stained by vegetation, red earth and blood. The laces of her bodice had been cut so that it hung open; her breasts beneath were smeared with horse dung and the dark juice of berries. Bruises were already darkening her arms, shoulders and face, where her skin was scratched and torn. One eye was swollen and almost closed over by bruised lids; her mouth was puffy and bleeding at the corner. The beautiful long dark hair had been shorn, so that no more than short spiky tufts stood like a satanic halo around her head. Leila Duncan had been destroyed.

Letting out a great sigh of distress and protest, Vivian moved toward her, arms outstretched. Her voice harsh, distorted, almost inhuman, halted him again.

*"Don't touch me!"*

That chilling command from a girl who had died, yet still lived, kept him frozen with horror as she slowly passed him, sustained only by an awesome brand of pride. Recognition of that pride, which he had also experienced, kept him immobile while she passed and continued along the centre of that dusty road, in a besieged city, at the heart of a country in conflict.

Pride proved to be stronger than flesh, however. Six yards beyond him she suddenly faltered, then collapsed to lie still, with her face in the dust. He went to her like a man possessed, picked her up in his arms, and began to carry her home. Burning inside him was that same instinct which had made him shoot two Englishmen. This time, he had been too late to prevent pain and suffering; this time, he would have shot the attackers, not the victim.

# CHAPTER FIFTEEN

Vivian stayed at the cottage for the rest of that day. After treating Leila's injuries, cleaning the dye and filth from her body, and giving her a sedative, the doctor hesitantly agreed to make no immediate report. He then departed, promising to send a nurse to care for both patients and tend the child, in addition to a reliable coloured girl to replace the one who had fled.

Looking into her room to check that Leila was still sleeping, Vivian then sat for a while trying to recover from the shock of what he had seen that morning and decide the best course of action he should take. It was essential to protect her from any gossip or scandal during this initial period. He sensed that it was also essential to keep people away from the girl whose beauty was a vital part of her professional success. No female would care to be seen in such a condition; more so, an actress dependent on maintaining an aura of physical perfection.

He could only guess at what had happened to her after her meeting with Peter Van Kleef and his companion. Leila either could not speak of it, or refused to do so. Apart from her spine-chilling command to him not to touch her, she had said no word to him or to the doctor. That she had been deliberately and brutally assaulted was certain, but by whom and under what conditions would remain a mystery until she chose to talk about it. Having done all he could to organise the situation at the cottage, he was now faced with the problem of the evening concert. As she was due to play a major part in it, the organisers must be told something. Unwilling to contact Von Grossladen personally, Vivian finally scribbled a note to Franz Mittelheiter, stopped one of the cabs back on the streets after the noon lull, and paid the driver to deliver it to the tenor's hotel. He then returned to the cottage, settling in a cane chair near the window while vengeful anger possessed him once more.

It was evidence of his shaken state that he was unprepared for the arrival of Franz, returning in the cab with which he had sent the note. In the course of his protective command of the affair, it had not occurred to him that the Austrian would rush to Leila's side on hearing that she was unfortunately indisposed and unable to perform that evening. Still angry, still filled with the desire to defend her, Vivian got to his feet as

Franz strode up the path with all the appearance of a man with the right to be there. He stopped short at the doorway, however, plainly unpleasantly surprised at Vivian's presence. Then he stepped inside, unsmiling and aggressive.

"Major Veasey-Hunter, what are you doing here?"

Taking exception to his attitude, Vivian responded swiftly. "I could ask the same of you. Shouldn't you be busily making alternative arrangements for this evening? Your great friend, Von Grossladen, will be extremely put out by this development. He was hoping the concert would be an event for history books to record, naming him as a siege hero."

"*You* sent the note to me?"

"Yes. It was a statement of fact, not an invitation to come here."

"Perhaps you would explain me the nature of Miss Duncan's indisposition, and why you have taken it upon yourself to act as her spokesman."

Resenting the attitude of this man, of whom he had often been jealous because of his ability to arouse fervent admiration in Leila, Vivian stood his ground grimly.

"The nature of Miss Duncan's indisposition is such that she will be unable to perform this evening. I told you that in the note. There is no reason whatever why I should explain my presence here to you."

Franz's eyes flashed with temper. "Would you prefer to explain to your gentle mother . . . or to your wife?"

"My God, Von Grossladen is certainly your friend," he snapped. "I suggest that you leave, Mittelheiter, before we come to blows."

"If you have any regard for Miss Duncan, you should leave," came the quietly furious response. "Her reputation is too much valuable to be damaged like this."

It was the first significant remark the other man had made, so Vivian controlled his urge to take him by the collar and physically eject him. It would not help Leila if two men were seen fighting on her premises. Much as he resented the Austrian, the man was her stage partner and, presumably, had a right to the truth.

Relaxing slightly, Vivian said in more reasonable tones, "I am doing my utmost to prevent her reputation being damaged. That's why I wrote to you and not to Von Grossladen. As an actor, you should be well able to deal with the problem of the concert without arousing undue curiosity. I am assuming that your friendship with Miss Duncan goes deeper than that with the Baron."

Wary of the change in approach, Franz hedged. "Your own connection with Von Grossladen is surely closer than mine could ever be. A future stepfather, I believe. Your connection with Leila, however, can only be a thing of the past." Frowning, he added, "Still I do not understand your presence here. Where is the maid Nellie? If it becomes known that you have been here alone with Leila, there will be talk of a kind to harm you both. Do you not care of that?"

Vivian shook his head. "I have been a subject for malicious gossip all my life. No one knows that I am here, save you and Dr Treeves. I have his promise of silence. Do I have yours?"

"*Lieber Gott*," exploded Franz. "What is happening here? I will see Leila before I have one more word with you."

"You'll not see her." Vivian stepped into his path as he started forward. "The doctor administered a sedative to both Leila and the maid. They're sleeping."

"They are *both* ill?" asked Franz with growing alarm. "This is like madness. I demand to know the truth of this."

Much as he disliked the idea, Vivian realised that he had no option but to reveal the truth to Leila's partner. Public knowledge of her condition would have to be concealed for some time, and this man would best know how to do that. Perching on the back of a chair, he embarked on an explanation which affected Franz to such an extent that Vivian's jealousy revived at the hint of a relationship which exceeded professional co-operation. He forced himself to say, in conclusion, "Until Leila tells me the details of the attack, I intend to hide the truth. If there should be a prosecution and subsequent trial, Dr Treeves will testify to her injuries, but I'll allow no one to see her unless she gives her permission—and that includes you."

Vivian was then treated to a stream of Viennese passion heightened by an artistic temperament, as Franz raged at him and at anyone else who came to his mind, demanding rhetorically why anyone would commit such a cruel and barbarous act.

"Is it not enough that we have no freedom, no food, no hope?" he cried. "Who are you to let these things happen? Are you so afraid of these farmers with rifles that you allow them to hold us here so long?"

Getting to his feet again, Vivian said heatedly, "Von Grossladen has recruited you into his anti-military ranks, that's plain. If you had ever wielded a sword in real battle, you would realise that there is a great difference from your gilded stage heroics, Mittelheiter. Our smart uniforms get dirty when we fight; our wounds aren't painted on with make-up. The best that we can hope for each day is a hot meal, a few hours' sleep before the next battle, and a live horse to ride. We aren't guaranteed a happy ending and the girl we love when the curtains close. Volunteer for the colours, man, and earn your applause the hard way."

There was a short pause, then the Austrian said, with a twist to his mouth, "You chose your profession, as I chose mine. Spare me, if you please, the heavy tragedy. You are free to resign from this so hard life of yours."

"Not in the middle of a war," Vivian countered savagely. "Soldiers are not permitted emotional outbursts, like actors. They can't storm out of a performance because they don't like the colour of the coat they are asked to wear . . . or because they are billed as Frank Mitten in case Englishmen can't pronounce a foreign name."

There was a longer pause, and Vivian realised that he had betrayed the existence of a long association with Leila: only she could have told him that piece of backstage information. The other man's handsome face registered a series of expressions as the confrontation continued. Then he nodded in satisfaction.

"This is not, I think, about warriors and players, after all. It is about passion for a woman you can never have, but I can, if I wish."

Vivian pushed down his jealousy resolutely. "What we are supposed to be discussing is the best way to preserve the dignity and reputation of a girl who has been viciously attacked and injured. As the person who was on the spot when it happened, I have done everything possible to ensure initial protection from public knowledge of the affair. I am a friend of Leila's, and have the advantage of being a member of the military force which presently governs this city. As such, I can control most aspects. What I cannot do is deal with the professional side of her life, so I am asking you to do that on my behalf."

"By what right?"

"By the right of humanity, Mittelheiter," he returned, losing his patience. "You have heard of it in your world of make-believe, I suppose?"

The other man stiffened in anger. "I dislike you greatly, Major."

"The feeling is mutual, I assure you," Vivian snapped. "Since Leila appears to find both of us to her liking, however, we shall have to make an effort to overcome our animosity if we are to be of any help to her now. Do I have your promise to do whatever is necessary to allay suspicion for a few days?"

"I promise you nothing. Anything that I shall do shall be for Leila, that is all. Now, I shall go to see her."

Barring his path once more, Vivian said, "You'll see her when she agrees that you may, not before."

Controlling himself with difficulty, the other man said through tight lips, "I believe that you would use force. I admit to be unwilling for a fight, like silly boys over a village *Mädchen* in a musical comedy. But I must say to you this one thing. Leila Duncan is a creature of great talent, who gives pleasure and delight to the world. You are a creature who kills for payment. You give sadness and loss to the world. She has some love for you—I will admit this much—but she has greater love for the theatre. You have a wife in Cape Town to whom you will return when the siege ends. All you can offer Leila is the sadness and loss you offer the world. You will do as much harm to her as these people today. Is that your desire? You have done what any man should for a person in trouble. Now go!"

As Vivian began to feel like Goliath facing David, the tenor added, "If you have true regard for her, any adulterous love, go from here and leave her free of the chance to return that feeling. I understand her; I have seen her struggle to achieve all she has today. I am the one man who will never ask her to give it up."

"Because you love her, or because she is the perfect partner to complement your own talent?" he asked, suddenly weary. "I recall that you were in a series of failures before Leila played opposite you. If she gave it up, where would you be?" Sighing heavily, he added, "We are all victims of our own desires, whatever they might be, Mittelheiter. I don't hold the monopoly in that. My only desire at present, however, is to protect Leila from further harm. I am just a soldier with nothing much to do until the Boers end their Christmas cease-fire. I mean to remain here until she is able to reveal what happened this morning. You, on the other hand, are committed to the limelight and applause tonight. For her sake, go off and lie as convincingly as you can to Von Grossladen. No doubt, he'll be upset about not going down in history as the presenter of both Duncan and Mittelheiter at his splendid concert, but if we paid killers continue to be afraid of the farmers with rifles, the siege might continue until next Christmas. Then he can have another shot at getting into the history books."

The nurse was extremely efficient. She knew exactly how to handle those who were ill, and those who were not. As Vivian sat in a reverie, gazing at the fading pink of dusk, a figure in white suddenly came between him and the view from the window.

"Major Veasey-Hunter, I shall be settling my patient for the night very shortly," said a brisk voice. "There will be no need for you to return after dinner. Miss Duncan should sleep until morning, and I shall be on duty all night to keep an eye on her maid. The fever is at its height."

"Dinner? I have no intention of going off to eat dinner," he said, getting to his feet.

"It is Christmas Eve, sir," she reminded him firmly. "Special rations have been brought out for the occasion. Of course you must eat dinner. You will help no one, least of all Miss Duncan, by refusing the opportunity of a very good meal, for once."

"You are," he pointed out.

"I am on duty."

"I know all about duty, Nurse Springfield. At times like these, even those at isolated outposts are not left on their own. I would not dream of deserting you so selfishly, just in order to eat a good dinner," he assured her, as determined as she.

"Please don't be difficult, Major."

"I am never difficult, Nurse."

"Sir, you surely don't have the notion of spending the night here."

"What if I have?"

"I should then be obliged to ask Dr Treeves to order you to leave. He has two small children, so I would regret taking him from his family on Christmas Eve . . . on this one, particularly."

"So would I," said Vivian quietly. "The best thing we two can do then is to negotiate a settlement of the situation. I will undertake to leave, if you will change your ruling and allow me to see Miss Duncan as soon as she awakens."

The girl's indecision lasted only momentarily. "Very well. Only because it is Christmas Eve, understand."

He nodded. "Certainly."

"She is awake now, as it happens. You must realise, however, that if she does not wish me to allow you in, you must honour her wishes."

"Of course."

"You will leave without fuss?"

"*Yes*, Nurse. Now will you please go to Miss Duncan and waste no further time?"

As the girl went off, Vivian asked himself if he should simply walk in, whatever Leila's answer. Something told him that if he allowed her to send him away, the chance fate had granted them by sending him there that morning would be lost. With the thought strong in him, he moved through the corridor leading to the main bedroom, and was standing by the door when it opened. The nurse never gave him Leila's answer, because he stepped in past her, all his attention on the girl lying in the lamplit room. On reaching the bedside, fresh horror and compassion flooded through him. The bruises looked darker, more damaging. The swollen eye was closed up completely. She gazed up at him with the other, but he could not divine her feelings because the face he had known so well could no longer register expressions. It could have been that of a stranger.

Words did not come easily now that he was there with her, he discovered. What could he say in such circumstances? Perhaps Mittelheiter was right, and he should stay away from her. Leila had asked the same thing of him two years ago.

"You are in excellent hands," he said eventually. "Nurse Springfield is extremely capable, and will be on duty here all through the night. I will arrange for two men to keep watch until morning. One will guard the rear, the other the front of this cottage. You'll be in no danger, I swear."

Hearing a click behind him, he turned to discover that the nurse had left them alone. Sitting on the edge of the bed, he thought how ironic it was that the intimacy he had yearned for in the past should finally come under these terrible circumstances.

"Mittelheiter came on receipt of my note, whilst you were sleeping," he told her then. "He was a great deal upset, but rose to the occasion by going off to fabricate a story to satisfy Von Grossladen. No one this evening will know the truth."

Although it was clear that she was absorbing all he said, Leila remained silent, making no gesture toward him. Anxious, upset by her injuries, he tried again to arouse some response in her.

"Leila, I'm not going to press you to tell me the details of what happened to you this morning, but whoever did it will be punished under martial law, whether they were soldiers or civilians. Can you name or identify them?"

Still there was no reply, even though he waited patiently for several minutes. Unwilling to accept her silence yet loath to leave her side, he gazed around at the room furnished with relics of the boom days, now shadowy in the low light. All at once, the depression of continued captivity in this alien city grew almost unbearable. Where had youth and happiness fled? For a while, he had believed both could be found with this girl. What was he hoping for now? Some sign that his belief in her was justified; some rekindling of a passion she had coldly and deliberately denied? He had tried to avoid her, and failed. He was now trying to help her, with as little success. Kekewich had secretly been asked to hold out until February. How would he get through two more months of confinement with a girl who held him in inexplicable thrall, knowing that he must see her, hear others speak of her, yet continue to hold aloof?

Turning back to her with the resigned intention of saying goodnight and leaving, he did neither. Feathering his fingers across her wet temples where tears were running to soak into the pillow, he said huskily, "I would have given a year of my life to have prevented this. Tell me who did it, and I will put them under guard personally."

When her head moved in a faint negative as the tears continued to flow, he added, "Does that mean you don't know, or that you refuse to tell me?"

For answer, she turned her face despairingly into the pillow. The gesture aroused such compassion in him, he gently cupped her bruised cheeks with his hands and made her look back at him.

"Darling, what you did in England makes no more sense to me now than it did then," he confessed softly, dropping all pretence or evasion. "Despite your evident success, the years which have wrought changes in us both, I still believe that you once came very near to loving me. Let me help you now. Give me your trust in this situation, if nothing else."

After a second or two, her bruised hand covered his as it curved around her cheek, but emotion still prevented her from speaking.

Knowing, without doubt, that this was the moment for honesty, Vivian took her hand up to his mouth and kissed it, carefully and gently.

"I told you last week that we are presently living in a world apart; a world in which it is possible for me to say this to you. I loved you then: I love you still. I think I shall always love you. For God's sake, let us finally have the truth between us."

"The truth?" she echoed through her swollen mouth. "Oh, Vivian . . . the truth is that I loved you then, I love you still, and I shall always love you."

Leaning forward until his face was no more than inches from hers, he asked desperately, "Why, in God's name, did you drive me away?"

A voice broke into that moment, shattering it forever. "Your time is up, Major. I must ask you to leave. Miss Duncan needs to rest."

He rode slowly through a city celebrating Christmas under siege. From the houses he passed came the sound of laughter and music, as the occupants found temporary escape from fear and privation. They were celebrating a season of peace and goodwill, yet the shells were piling up in De Beers' workshops ready to resume killing in a few days' time, when the Boers decided that the festivities had continued long enough.

The streets were quiet, stretching like long luminous corridors in the white moonlight. He appeared to be the only moving creature in sight. Tilting his head back, he gazed at the sky; dark, endless, filled with stars that were brilliant in the clarity of an African night. He thought of his countrymen at Magersfontein, lying in bivouac under this same sky and wondering how many more nights their eyes would witness. He thought of those encircled within this area of civilisation in the midst of wild, inhospitable veld. Would it really take two more months to reach Kimberley from Magersfontein? Would they be able to hold out that long? Would he be there to welcome them in, or would he be in a mass grave on the outskirts of this city thousands of miles from his home? Suddenly, he yearned for Shenstone, and the beautiful landscape of Cornwall. He yearned for a day when the sun had shone gently onto a rich green meadow, and he had handed to a pretty girl a black lamb and his undying love.

The camp was practically deserted. He ate a good meal in the Mess tent with the Duty Officer, who called to his attention the notice-board to which was pinned a message flashed to them from the relief column.

I wish you and all my brave soldiers a happy Christmas.
God protect and bless you all.
Victoria Regina

The Queen's message served to intensify his yearning for home, and the two officers talked of England and all its aspects which seemed so desirable that night. Returning to his tent, Vivian took off his boots and tunic, then lay on the camp-bed with only the light of the moon for company. It did not once occur to him that he should have been at Gunther Von Grossladen's concert and later dinner. He gave no thought to his mother, or Franz Mittelheiter, who would be present at both. His mind was totally occupied with a girl who had, tonight, whispered brokenly the proof that healed the wounds from two years ago.

The twentieth century dawned in Kimberley almost unmarked. New Year's Day 1900 found the besieged city more concerned with the drastic increase in the Boer bombardment, and the rumour that supplies of beef had almost run out making it necessary to slaughter horses for human consumption. The notion was so appalling to troops and civilians alike, the surge of public protest swamped interest in the advent of a new year, a new century. Christmas had come and gone. The celebrations which had fleetingly brightened their lives were now forgotten with the resumption of siege monotony, crushed hopes, and the fear of death from constant shelling. Those who had celebrated together no more than a week before were snappy and ready to fly at each other's throats over the slightest thing once again. Food rationing was beginning to have a serious effect on health. Disease and fever were spreading, particularly amongst children where fatalities were occurring daily. The regular interment of pathetically small coffins reduced the morale of the population further, and still the relief column was beyond the hills at Magersfontein.

One man, however, managed to find a happiness he had almost forgotten during those early days of the twentieth century. Vivian survived the hunger, the heat and threat of sudden death by living each day in the glow of recapturing a girl he had thought lost to him. Each time he rode out with small parties checking Boer positions, each time he cantered beside the great chugging armoured train filled with riflemen, each time he patrolled the cattle pens on the outskirts of the city, ready to drive off Boer attempts to seize the dwindling number of beasts, he was filled with a confidence and energy he had not known for several years. Self-possession had returned in full force. He was under no obligation to prove anything, either to himself or anyone else. Once more his own man, vitality flooded through him.

Leila earned not only his love but his admiration. It did not cross his mind that he, himself, might be responsible for the determined recovery she had made. All he saw was a girl with courage and resourcefulness. An expert with stage make-up, she had disguised the cuts and bruises on her face just as soon as the disfiguring swellings had subsided, and a dark wig from the company's properties covered her shorn head. Clothes which fastened at neck and wrist hid the discoloration of her beaten body, so that it was barely possible for him to believe that he had ever seen her as he had on Christmas Eve. Determination, however, could not overcome her inability to sing. Shock still affected her inwardly, robbing her of her voice. She spoke in no more than a husky whisper, which supported Franz's public lie concerning a lowering fever which had drastically attacked her vocal chords.

Vivian grudgingly accepted that the Austrian had done a wonderful job of allaying suspicion, and was also an obvious comfort to Leila during her recovery. There had necessarily been a truce between the two men, for her sake, but the professional jealousy of one and a lover's jealousy of the other would never make them compatible. It had also been inevitable that a stream of well-wishers had called at the cottage during the Christmas period, to leave gifts and flowers. Leila had grown so agitated when told, Dr Treeves had been obliged to ban all visitors save the two men his patient appeared to need beside her. Neither they, nor the doctor, could coax from her the details of the attack which had half killed her. Her refusal to speak of it meant that no action could be taken against those responsible, and the lies concerning her condition had to be maintained.

Although he longed to avenge her, Vivian's most urgent pleas would not change her attitude. The doctor had assured him there had been no evidence of rape, or any kind of sexual assault, so Vivian thought it unlikely to have been soldiers, drunken or sober. What puzzled him was the shearing of her hair; an act more usually associated with female vengeance. Yet he could not think of any cause for it against the girl he loved, and she would not even discuss the subject with him, despite her clear trust in him now.

During those strange suspended days in their world within a world, their love expanded and deepened beyond the passion they had known in England. When they kissed it was a salute inspired by understanding, gratitude and unhindered devotion. Subconsciously recognising that time, their most precious element, was inexorably running out, they spoke freely during those intimate sessions. Telling Vivian the facts of her bigamous marriage to Frank Duncan, Leila nevertheless could not bring herself to reveal the reason for entering into it. Shame still held her in its grip. Not so he. The truth of that night he had spent with Julia, which had sealed their future, led Leila to wonder at the complexities of fate which seemed determined to keep them apart. Was their love so wrong, that having been brought together, they must be kept apart, at all costs? What had fate in store for them now? Neither pretended that there was not danger in his forays outside the defensive perimeter, and he spoke to her of the sensations and emotions of battle, holding nothing back. On one particularly empathetic evening he told her of the Ashanti affair, explaining without drama or excuses why he had shot two of his comrades. In doing so, confidence in the rightness of his action returned to banish the doubts created by the subsequent scandal.

Leila, in turn, spoke freely of her experiences at Lindley's until Franz had demanded that Lester Gilbert should pair them in the new show. She admitted to using the adulation of her many admirers to further her career, adding that none had ever received from her more than detached friendship in return for the costly presents they, alone, chose to give her. Her feeling for Franz was deeper and more committed, she confessed, but their mutual passion was only for the theatre. In those days following Christmas, they retrieved from the past all that had been lost, and much more beside. Perhaps they were the only two people in Kimberley who never looked for the rising dust of a column on the march; never listened for the thunder of guns that would signify coming freedom from captivity.

On January 8th there was outcry from the residents when they were told, after queuing for several hours in the market-place, that the meat on sale was horseflesh. No one had believed that rumour would become fact. The horse was regarded with great respect by those who depended on it for life on the veld; it was practically revered by cavalrymen, who counted a charger a friend. The townspeople refused their ration of meat, and renewed their campaign of aggression against the distant British troops who appeared to be making no effort to rescue them. Infantrymen baulked at the thought of cooked horse, but experience of war had taught them to do many things in order to stay alive, and they resolutely accepted it so that they would be fit for action, when it finally came. In the cavalry camps, guile was used. The men were only told the nature of the meat they had eaten when the meal was over. Some promptly heaved, and vanished to a quiet spot, but most reluctantly resigned themselves to eating their faithful friends as their only hope of staying alive themselves.

When Vivian received a note from his mother asking him to see her on a matter of some urgency, he guessed the reason. He was slightly surprised that the Weldons, with whom she was staying, had not sufficient alternatives to horsemeat in their vast stores. They were friends of Rhodes, who controlled the herd of cattle within the De Beers compound. Slightly irritated at being summoned on such a matter —one with which the suave Baron could surely have dealt—he nevertheless rode up to the Weldons' elegant residence soon after dusk. Since the Boers now shelled during the night as well as day, there was a ban on the use of lights after nine-thirty in the evening. If he called on his mother before the city was compulsorily darkened, he could go to Leila afterward. They had often sat together in no more than moonlight, which enhanced even further their new harmony of spirits.

Margaret Veasey-Hunter was alone in the airy sitting-room when Vivian was conducted up to it by a servant in spotless white coat and trousers. She looked more fragile than usual in a dinner gown of mist-green silk under lace, and her collarette of fine diamonds flashed coldly beneath the impressive chandeliers. Crossing to the *chaise-longue* striped in claret and gold, he found his smile fading at the sight of her expression. Had he mistaken the reason for her summons?

"Mama, there is some emergency?" he asked. "I came as soon as I was able."

"Emergency? I suppose one might describe it as such," came her frosty comment. "Have you taken leave of your senses? Has there not been enough scandal connected with your name that you must invite more?"

Stiffening, he said, "I think you will have to explain that curious greeting. I have only two hours ago returned from a reconnaissance to Carter's Ridge, and my wits are not as sharp as they might be."

His mother rose to her feet, her pale eyes suggesting a rare anger as she looked up at him. "You may abandon that air of innocence, Vivian. You do me a great injustice if you imagine that I am taken in by it."

"You imply that I should instead adopt an air of guilt? You do me a great injustice by accusing me of inviting further scandal, when I have no idea of your charge."

"No idea! The whole of Kimberley is talking of little else."

"The main topic being discussed in Kimberley is the killing of horses for human consumption," he reminded her as levelly as he could.

Studying him silently for several moments as her anger increased, she finally said, "So you mean to brazen it out! Well, you have always possessed your father's weakness in that direction, but I believed you conducted your liaisons with more intelligence and delicacy. This is sheer madness. Not only are you surrounded here by men with the highest influential connections, who could wreck your career at a word, you are also confined in a community where scandal is presently being culled from the slightest evidence. It was apparent to me from the start that your marriage was little short of disaster, but Julia is, nevertheless, your wife. Have you no thought for her in this situation?"

"In which situation, Mama?" he asked carefully.

His mother resumed her seat with rigid grace, then said, "As you appear determined to avoid the issue, I suppose I must speak more directly. Your blatant intrigue with that . . . that *actress* exceeds all notions of propriety. I suspected—indeed, I could hardly not be certain—that there had been an earlier liaison between you, but I never imagined that you would resume it in so obvious a manner. Your conduct, Vivian, is not only deeply damaging to your wife, but also to me. Gunther is so incensed, it was only at my fervent entreaty that he allowed me to speak to you before doing so himself."

Vivian's careful control broke at that. Before he knew it, he was saying a number of things which had been no more than thoughts until then.

"Baron Von Grossladen, in company with any man, may speak to me on whatever subject he wishes, of course. But, as with any other man, I am under no obligation to listen to what he says. The only people in this community who have any right to question my conduct are military men holding any rank higher than mine. I am thirty-two, Mama. No one save a complete fool would imagine that you are in any way responsible for what I do."

He took a breath to steady his rising anger, then continued as calmly as he could. "During these three months of captivity I have had a great deal of time in which to think. It is surprisingly lonely out there on the veld, despite the company of others watching for the slightest dazzle of sun on a hidden rifle, or the puffing of the train filled with silent men who know they could be blown up at any moment. All my thinking has resulted in the recognition of two surprising truths. Firstly, it is now clear to me that Brancliffe's cruelty when I was a boy was to cover his love and approval of the heir he could not have, and his deep disappointment in the one he did not want. By pretending contempt for me and warmth for Charles, he hoped to turn pretence into reality. His failure to do so made him into an embittered eccentric, who finally punished himself more than any of us for what fate did over thirty years ago.

"The second truth, Mama, is that you were less the victim of Brancliffe's intolerance, as I always believed, and more the victim of your own need to be controlled by a will stronger than your own. That had never occurred to me until I saw how Von Grossladen so completely dominated your decisions and opinions, and how very content you were for him to do so. From there, I went on to explore an even more astonishing fact. My father was a lecherous fortune-seeker when you first married him. He was even more so when you married him for the second time. Why, Mama?" he demanded forcefully. "Why did you marry such a man again three years later, knowing what he was and knowing the life you would resume leading? It was certainly not for the sake of your infant son, because you knew very well that I would remain illegitimate."

Leaving a long enough pause for her to digest his inference, he then added, "I can, perhaps, understand a dutiful daughter of seventeen allowing herself to be forced into a marriage of convenience, but there can be only one reason why a woman of twenty with a child condemned to be a bastard, and with three years' experience of life with a libertine, should agree to do it all over again."

Sitting unhurriedly beside her, Vivian fixed his mother with a straight look. "I have loved you dearly, Mama. For years I have defended you to Brancliffe . . . even to Charles. The fact that I am now a little disillusioned does not mean that I would no longer defend you, or that my affection for you has ceased. I do, however, now see clearly enough to recognise that you summoned me here tonight on Von Grossladen's instructions, and that it is his own reputation about which he is so concerned. He gives not a tinker's cuss for my military career, or for Julia's feelings. It is merely because I am the son of the woman he has chosen to marry, that he concerns himself with what I do. His German nationality is already making him unpopular, in some quarters. He is desperately seeking respectability and passive heroism. If you cannot see that, Mama, it is a greaty pity. However, I shall be obliged if you will refrain from sending for me again on matters which are my concern only. I will not expect you to defend me, but a mother should not accuse her son on the word of someone known to be biased, no matter how willing she is to do his bidding."

After Franz had left, Leila was able to drop her pretence that she believed his assurance that her voice would return once the effects of her ordeal had diminished. She was full of fears, still, and when she was alone they rose to the surface. The lowering effects of prolonged captivity caused people to act in unpredictable fashion, so it was not surprising that her courage had vanished at a time when she most needed it. Day after day, she sat staring at the doorway knowing that the thought of passing through it into the street outside filled her with terror. In a way, she found that particular fear quite understandable. Worse, however, was the fear that she might never sing again. Whereas it simply required a physical effort to make herself go out into that street again—which she would do one day, she told herself comfortingly —she had no control over the voice which just would not come at her bidding.

Not all her yearning to sing, nor all her desperate efforts to practise with Franz beside her, brought the sounds which had once come from her throat. The more she tried, the more frightened she grew. Franz did not appear to understand, for once. As a singer himself, he surely should sympathise with her desperation, not brush it aside with bland assurances that time would resolve the problem. How much time? So long, that she would be replaced in the show by a girl who was not like a goldfish in a bowl, opening her mouth to find no notes pouring out? So long, that Leila Duncan had become old and grey? So long, that London's West End had forgotten the girl who had once created magic with the famous Franz Mittelheiter?

At that point in her feverish thoughts, panic always seized her by that very throat which now betrayed her. What if that creature created by Lester Gilbert, that girl who had fought for a place in the limelight, that glamorous woman for whose favours influential men vied, should cease to exist? Lily Lowe had been sold for thirty shillings; Leila Veasey-Hunter had been denied by a bigamist. Who would be left? A singer without a voice? A nobody whose beauty condemned her as an obvious whore?

Staring at the sunlit scene outside the cottage, Leila fought the demons that gripped her shaking body as identity became elusive. Who was she? If Lester Gilbert had truly created her, he had not revealed to her what she would be when that creation ceased to exist. She could never be Vivian's wife; she could not revive Lily Lowe. Those wonderful sounds that had first struck Rose, then an entire audience at Lindley's, were her only salvation. Yet how could she make them again, when all her vocal chords produced were cracked notes? The sense of isolation, of slowly fading away into a fleeting shadow took hold of her so strongly, she could stand the pain of it no longer. Tears came too easily these days.

"Oh, Leila!" exclaimed Nellie's voice behind her. "Every time one of them gentlemen comes, he upsets you. Best they don't come, if you ask me," she added, sinking down by the chair to take her hands.

"I didn't ask you, so kindly keep your comments to yourself."

"All right then, I'll tell Sally all the latest news. She likes my company, she does. 'Specially when I bring back something extra to eat, give me by Captain Peek. He said it was for 'the loveliest lady in Kimberley'. I was ever so surprised when he give me this big bag, Sal," she continued, ignoring Leila in favour of the narrow-faced toddler she drew onto her lap as she sank to the floor. "Do you know what was in it? Guess, lovey! Well, there was two eggs, a tin of ham, and an orange. Now, where that saucy gentleman laid his hands on such things you might well wonder, but he whispered in my ear that he'd been on a raid out by one of the farms yesterdee, and it were wonderful what was lying about. So he *said*, and I do believe him, Sal. He's an officer, and Miss Duncan give me permission to believe what *they* say. Seems to me she's a bit soft over one or two of them."

Leila dabbed at her eyes, taking a deep steadying breath. "All right, Nellie, you may cease that silly game and give Sally to me while you fetch us a cup of tea. Even if it is the last of our ration, there is nothing I want more, at this moment."

The child was placed on her lap as Nellie said dryly, "The way you've been lately, the tea was used up two days back. The Major brung us some extra last week, so I've been using that."

"How many times have I told you not to say 'brung'? Your daughter will copy you, ruining all my attempts to teach her to speak well," Leila pointed out. "So what's the latest news from the market-place?"

"There's still a big bother over the horsemeat," called Nellie from the adjacent room, where she was setting out china. "There's still half the people won't take it, and those as do gets called rude names by the others. One big fat woman with a face what looks like a horse, anyway, was there with a notice on a pole, saying they was sinners. 'GOD GIVE US CATTLE TO EAT, BUT HORSES TO WORK FOR US,' it said. I don't know much about God, but it seems to me if He's what parsons say He is, He'll have give us brains to think what's best when we're in trouble."

"Nellie, *you* haven't bought horsemeat!" cried Leila appalled.

"Course I haven't," she replied calmly, re-entering with a tray to put on the table beside Leila. "But I do see that the troops have to be fit and strong, so it's not fair to call them names for eating it. They don't want to." She looked at Leila with a frown. "I think siege is very cruel. There's babies and old people dying every day. They're not soldiers; they don't fight anybody. And here we are *all* hungry and miserable, yet *we* don't want their silly gold. Why've they done it, Leila?"

She sighed, hugging Sally against her in a subconscious gesture of protection which hurt her bruised ribs. "It's a matter of prestige, Nellie. The British are proud of Kimberley. It's a symbol of their endeavour and foresight, besides the diamonds being a source of great wealth. The fact that an Englishman heads De Beers and virtually owns the city itself, demonstrates to the world that we are a nation to be admired. It would be a tremendous humiliation if the Boers took the city, and captured Mr Rhodes. They have boasted that they will put him in a cage on display, if they get him."

"Ooh, they never would," cried Nellie in disbelief.

"No, I don't suppose they really would," she agreed, "but Colonel Kekewich is determined not to risk finding out. I feel dreadfully sorry for him. He's such a quiet, well-mannered man, it must be painful for him to know the people are suffering, yet be unable to put an end to it."

Pouring tea, Nellie revealed a new innovation. "They're starting a soup-kitchen for all those as want it. You have to get tickets and queue, of course, but I thought it would do Sal good—and us, too—as we've stopped eating meat. What d'you think?"

Leila took the cup and drank her tea thankfully. Food was of little concern to her, lately. Either her throat or her stomach seemed unable to accept it. Franz chided her on the subject, but only Vivian managed to persuade her to take some nourishment. He seemed able to persuade her to do many things, these days.

"I should certainly get tickets for you and Sally," she replied.

"You need it, too," Nellie insisted. "Please do what Mr Mittelheiter says. You must have good food if you want to start singing again."

"I don't think I ever shall," she confessed.

"Then they'll have won," cried the girl in strong protest. "Them wicked creatures who did that to you will've finished you off good and proper."

Leila shook her head. "It has nothing to do with them."

"Course it has! Because they writ that on the fence, you've stopped everyone coming here, just as if it was true. You won't eat, and I know you don't sleep much because I hear you walking about. If you've made up your mind you won't never sing again, they'll win. It's like this siege. The Boers shell us, starve us, frighten us, and keep us trapped here. We don't give in, though."

Knowing that there was much truth in what the girl said, Leila still tried to avoid acknowledgement of it. "You have no understanding of artistic inspiration."

"Mebbe not, but Mr Mittelheiter has. He says the same as me." taking the fidgeting Sally from Leila's lap, she went on sadly, "I feel it's my fault. If I hadn't taken to my bed, you wouldn't've gone for the doctor all by yourself like that."

Leila was instantly concerned. "That's very foolish, Nellie. Surely you realise that it's always easy to say 'if I hadn't done that' or 'if you hadn't been forced to go there' et cetera. Those women had generated such hatred for what they imagined I represented, they would have given vent to it sooner or later."

Nellie held a cup to Sally's mouth, watching carefully to ensure that her child spilt none of the precious milk. Then she looked frankly at Leila.

"Why won't you tell the Major who did it? He's driving himself nearly daft over not knowing, and he'd see to it they was locked up and punished."

Some long-ago shame revived within her, at the thought of telling the man she loved why the women of the city had done what they had. Her cracked voice grew sharp as she said, "Our friendship doesn't allow you to suggest what I should, or should not, tell my friends."

"Sorry, Leila. But if they was reported and put away somewhere, you wouldn't be afraid to go out any more."

"I'm not afraid," she responded swiftly. "I simply do not care to be seen in this condition by all and sundry."

"You look all right to me," came the caustic response. "There's no amount of make-up and wigs would turn me into a Lindley girl, but I wouldn't 'arf go out and show them what for if anyone done that to me. They must be pleased as punch with themselves right now. Got away with near murder, they have, and made you hide away like a mouse in an 'ole 'cos you're frightened to show yourself."

"That's quite enough, Nellie," she said, stabbed with guilt at the words. "I do not need my maid airing her opinions freely in my presence."

Unblushing, Nellie addressed herself to the small child once more. "You know, Sal, there's all them poor men risking their lives day after

302

day, and pining for a bit of cheer and sunshine from the prettiest lady in Kimberley. No, lovey, it's not your ma, but a girl wot used to be a maid herself before she turned into a kind of princess, like in story-books. But she's locked herself in the castle, and thinks she's the only one who's miserable. What do you think of that, Sal?" Wiping the child's mouth with the corner of her apron, she added softly, "What say we tell the Major what he wants to know? Then p'raps she'll come out of the castle."

Leila heard it all with growing guilt. The reference to her humble origins reminded her of the disasters she had overcome during the past five years, through sheer determination. Was she losing it? In past ages, women condemned as witches were thrown into the centre of the village pond by their accusers. If they drowned, punishment was considered to have been justly done. If they swam to the bank, their survival was attributed to their evil powers. They were then done to death by burning. Leila Duncan had not been destroyed by her accusers, neither had she bestowed martyrdom on her attackers by having them punished on a charge which would have caused everyone in Kimberley to speculate on the truth or falseness of it, to her further humiliation. Was she prepared to allow a group of bigoted women feel justification for their brutality, by hiding away as if guilty? Should she not swim for the bank, and confront them with the pride of knowing that they were wrong?

"All right, Nellie, you have made your point with your silly fairy-story," she rasped. "I'll go out with you this afternoon to get these soup tickets, but if you ever tell Major Veasey-Hunter what he wants to know, that will be the end of our relationship. Do you understand?"

Nellie looked up with a sly smile. "I wouldn't never tell him, Leila. He's that fond of you, he'd likely go out and shoot them all afore they could be arrested."

Leila discovered that it was not merely mental reluctance that had governed her confinement to the cottage. Carefully made-up, with wig in place, and dressed in an off-white skirt with a high-necked frilly blouse in palest lavender muslin, she then encountered a physical fear of stepping through the door into the wide unprotected area beyond. Resolution began to falter as she stared at the broad sun-washed street stretching into the distance. Unaccountably, she began to tremble, and perspiration stood on her brow as her limbs grew too leaden to move. It was almost as if she had turned into solid ice on that hot windy afternoon, like the snow figures made by London's children when dark winter whistled through the streets and commons.

There was a tug on her hand, and she looked down into the pinched face of Sally Wilkins. The child's mouth was moving, yet Leila heard nothing save the thundering in her own ears. Another face appeared, almost level with her own. The mouth in that was also moving, but no voice could drown the sound of terror. Staring wide-eyed at Nellie, Leila shook and shivered as if in a fever, until memorised words came clearly to her through the tumult riding her body. She heard Vivian's voice so clearly, he could have been speaking them there and then, rather than a week ago.

*It's the loneliest feeling in the world riding across that plain, even though there are others at your side. Out there lies the unknown. What will happen within the next hour or so may bring the end of life, or the beginning of a courage you did not know you possessed. It seems impossible to go forward, yet you do so because there is no choice. When you return, there is a sensation of great relief, of course, but also a strange inner peace with your conscience.*

"Leila, are you all right?"

The voice was beside her, and she found it was now possible to turn her head, the thunder in her ears fading fast. "Yes, Nellie, I'm all right," she managed in her husky voice. "Shall we get started?"

The streets were remarkably full of people now that the lateness of afternoon had brought slight relief from the great heat. Using the shade from her parasol to the greatest advantage, Leila walked through the centre of Kimberley as if it were that exposed plain beyond the perimeter defences. It *was* the loneliest feeling in the world, despite those who greeted her warmly, expressed a hope that she had recovered from her illness, and asked permission to call upon her once more. She went on because she knew she must, but fear walked with her, and she searched the crowds for those grim accusing faces, the tight mouths and expressions of hatred.

Kimberley had changed in the past three weeks, she discovered. Buildings were toppling; there were many more craters in the roads. Evidence of shortages was rife, with notice-boards covered in military advice and edicts, shop-windows plastered with apologies, and many stores closed for the remainder of the siege. Poverty was now pronounced in this city of wealth. Those walking through it looked exhausted and dispirited, the less affluent having grown gaunt. Many of the poorer white and the bewildered black people simply stood or sat around listlessly, having nothing to do with their time. Even wags had abandoned their practice of scrawling jokes referring to the relief column or the ineffectiveness of Boer shells. The relief column was no longer a joking matter, and Boer shells were now effective to the point of daily injury and destruction.

As if to prove the fact, the encircling enemy at that moment resumed their bombardment whilst it was still possible to see their targets in daylight. A faraway roar, followed by a series of thuds in the direction of the Premier Mine, alerted those in the streets to the coming danger. Familiarity had bred a certain contempt, however, and the concerted dash for shelter of the early days had changed to a resigned alteration in direction, with no quickening of pace. Nellie was more concerned than some, and swept her toddling child up to hurry with her to one of the holes dug in the roadside bank, and covered with corrugated iron topped with sandbags. Leila hurried beside her, filled afresh with an apprehension she had forgotten during three weeks confined in her cottage in a relatively safe area of the city.

The afternoon was now full of the sounds of aggression. Continuous thunder from enemy guns was like a distant echo in reverse, when louder roars betrayed the explosion of the shells they had disgorged. Crouching in the shelter, with the sour smell of earth filling her nostrils to remind her of that afternoon in the shrubbery, Leila gazed out and up at the magnificent sky. It was so blue, it gave credence to the idea of a paradise in Heaven. What if her life should end in this city? Would Lester Gilbert's maxim of closing a show before audiences began to tire of it apply to Leila Duncan? Was it the perfect time to die for a girl who might never sing again? Was it the perfect time to die for a girl who could not face parting from a man she loved and could not have? On the first occasion that she had faced both crises, she had dreamed of emulating Rose. What if the fatal hand should not be hers, and she never left Kimberley? Gazing up into the cerulean sky, the thought did not seem at all unattractive.

There came a loud swishing sound, and all those in the shelter ducked instinctively. The earth around them shook; the view ahead dissolved into a reddish-brown rising cloud as tremendous waves of sound assaulted their ears. There was movement all around her as shock caused a minor panic over the nearness of the missile. The dust cloud dispersed to reveal a gaping crater in the road they had just walked, and an array of shrapnel spread out in a wide circle around it, glittering in the sunshine as if diamonds had been unearthed and thrown up to the surface. Shaken by the notion of death arriving almost at her feet in answer to her thoughts, Leila hardly noticed the scrambling beside her. Then movement took the shape and form of little Sally, walking unsteadily on her thin legs toward the bright things on the ground ahead, caught by the fascination of glitter and sparkle, as the other children were. Mothers began shouting to them; some went out after the smaller children who were oblivious to commands for obedience.

Nellie uttered a dire threat, and started out along the road where Sally was heading for a large roundish piece of shell which resembled a gleaming silvery ball in the light from the lowering sun.

Leila did not hear the approach of the next shell. Her stunned senses merely registered the mushrooming of another red-brown cloud of dust containing solid fragments that flew in every direction. The whole scene appeared to act itself out in silence, which made it totally shattering. The earth walls around her trembled and sprung leaks of fine soil, the other occupants of that shelter flung up their arms to protect their heads, that magnificent sky vanished behind a veil of shifting, choking dust, all without identifiable sound. The darkening of the sun lasted for endless minutes, and Leila found herself back in an experience which had occurred on Christmas Eve. Thrown off-balance, she was suffering pain from blows as darkness descended. Then someone was helping her to her feet, speaking kindly to her, holding her steady as he coaxed her upward into an atmosphere brightening with every moment.

She had never seen the man before, but he had a trusty look about him which gave her a sense of thankfulness for his presence. With an arm supporting her, he led her forward across an uneven surface scattered with debris. There was a woman lying on the road in a twisted, grotesque position. Someone was covering her with a cloth—covering her face, as they did with the dead. Leila knew that face, and loved it. A little girl was sitting beside the body, patting one of its hands.

# CHAPTER SIXTEEN

The death of Nellie in so tragic a manner, after she had recovered from the fever at Christmas, brought home to Leila the truth of the girl's own words regarding the cruelty of siege. The troops, angered by civilian casualties they were powerless to prevent, turned out in large numbers for the funeral of the little maid who had been a popular figure at those cottage meetings. The girls from the chorus of *The Hungarian Heiress* also went to the graveside, some in tears for a comic little character so loyal to her mistress.

On the surface, Leila was calm and controlled, accepting a rôle she had never dreamed of playing. Sally had grown used to seeing her mother's mistress as a protective figure in her life, so now happily transferred her childlike dependence to "Lye-Lye", as she had often called her. One of the girls from the chorus, named Florence, gladly took on Nellie's paid duties, but the child turned to Leila for maternal attention. The years she had spent with a rector and his family in her own late childhood stood Leila in good stead as she took charge of the orphaned girl, knowing in her heart that Sally was now her adopted daughter.

The surface calmness hid a deep sense of escalating loss, however. Throughout the tumultuous stifling days and humid noisome nights, she was conscious of that element having dogged her whole life. First the mother she had never known; then her father, killed in an accident when she had been no more than a year older than Sally was now. After that, there had been a succession of Christian people who had taken her into their homes until they, too, died or moved on—always people going from her in some way. Then Frank had entered her life, taken her virtue, and sailed off leaving her bewildered, and alone once more. Rose had been the first person she had ever really loved, and the last person she had imagined losing. Yet, that lively beautiful creature had gone, like the others. Vivian had been different, because she had known all along that their love would have to end. Even so, knowing it had not eased that terrible sense of loss, the pain of separation when it had come. Now Nellie was gone. Pain had been revived to show her how dangerously foolish she had been.

307

On a night two years ago, she had vowed never again to let any man touch her emotions. That vow had remained unshaken, and her career had prospered, until she had come face to face with Vivian here. In the four months since then she had loved him again, knowing that it must end once more in loss. All might have been well, the relationship kept on a reasonably cool basis, if he had not been there when she had emerged from that lane, broken and bleeding. The clear proof that her beauty had not been at the root of his feelings had so overwhelmed her, she had forgotten all else in her response to his declaration of lasting devotion.

Since then, she had cast aside all she had worked for, had ceased to think as a leading lady who took theatre audiences by storm wherever she went, and had become simply a girl once more dazzled by a soldier. Her injuries had prevented him from seeking fulfilment of their desire for one another, and she thanked God for the fact. When they were finally freed, he would ride away to fulfil his obligations to his duty and his wife, leaving her alone and desolate. Nellie's death had reminded her of the anguish of love and loss in any form. Better, by far, to revert to what she had been before this captive world overtook her, and be in love only with the magic of theatre.

In those days following Nellie's funeral, she drew again on the inner strength she had discovered several years ago, which allowed her to direct all her emotions into the only outlet for them which had brought her joy. The change in her mental attitude appeared to prompt a minor miracle. Perseverence with her vocal exercises brought a return of her singing voice within a week. Nellie would no longer have claimed that she had allowed a group of bigoted women to silence her, and that thought spurred her to further effort. Franz was delighted, offering her every encouragement as they resumed their daily practising together. She suspected that his delight partially stemmed from her lessening dependence on Vivian, of which he had never approved.

Vivian's own attitude was difficult to analyse. Although he had supported her throughout the distress of Nellie's death and funeral with total love, understanding and authority, he accepted with surprising lack of protest her return to a routine which brought to an end their intimate interlude. Even so, when they met in company with others who had been permitted to resume their visits to the cottage, she caught him watching her speculatively. Sonic scales and duets with Franz could not immediately banish those few incredible days of pretence that the world outside Kimberley did not exist. All the while she could glance across a room and see Vivian there, all the while she could be part of a crowd yet be conscious of just one person in that crowd with her, all the while she could watch him talking to someone else then be electrified when his gaze lifted to hers and his smile caressed her, the pain must be felt. Only when he was gone could she deaden longing with concentration on her work. Meanwhile, she was grateful to him for making her gradual withdrawal easier. It was some while before she realised that he, too, was withdrawing, and the haunted look was starting to return in his eyes.

The complexities of relationships were suddenly swept aside when the big gun which George Labram had designed was completed and successfully tested. Nicknamed "Long Cecil" in honour of Rhodes, it delighted not only Labram and his colleagues, but the military gunners who operated it. By far the deadliest piece of artillery they had, the invested army bombarded the Boer positions which had been beyond their range before. Reprisal was inevitable, and Kimberley was ruthlessly attacked from every gun-emplacement circling the city. Residents grew afraid to leave their homes, yet it was little safer indoors. Deliberate shelling of the city centre, rather than the mines or military targets, was translated as a Boer attempt to force a swift surrender. It was also taken as an indication that the enemy must have sure knowledge that the relief column had abandoned any attempt to break through to them.

Day and night, the Kimberley guns thundered, and Boer shells whistled overhead in return, to explode in a successive series of roars. The air was filled with dust, smoke, and the smell of cordite. Typhoid fever ran through the starving, depressed population, filling first the hospitals, then the cemeteries. Food had become so scarce, most people were now eating horse or mule, cooked with a curious collection of edible weeds to supplement those few vegetables available. The native people, suffering more than most from hunger, were consuming cats and kittens snatched from domesticity and sold to them by enterprising coloured dealers in shanty stores.

Heliograph messages flashed back and forth between Kekewich and the relief column, but the advice was always the same. Hold on a little longer! The stationary force had apparently been given a new commander, Lord Roberts. The move was seen by British Army men in Kimberley as an encouraging sign, for "Bobs", as he was affectionately known, had a reputation for success. But even he asked the beleaguered people to be patient and resist surrender.

January passed into February hardly noticed. The days were all the same, and no one bothered to look at a calendar. Then Kimberley suffered a particularly poignant blow with the death of George Labram, when a shell entered the Grand Hotel, killing him instantly. A true hero of the siege—as Gunther Von Grossladen longed to be—the American had been a popular, much-respected resident. Ridiculous though the idea was, it was believed by many that the Boers had singled the man out as a target because he had created "Long Cecil". When his funeral, held after dark in the hope of greater safety, became the centre of furious shelling for several hours, a rumour flew around that one of the Boer residents had informed his countrymen of the time and place, so that retribution could follow Labram to the grave. Public feeling against Dutch people within the city grew worse than before, segregating them completely.

In the second week of February, another rumour hatched, then grew at amazing rate. Everyone knew for certain that a message had been flashed from Magersfontein, announcing the start of a relief operation on the very next day. Everyone knew for certain, yet no one had seen the signal. Even so, there was general quiet confidence in the veracity of the information, and faces almost brightened. Then, notices began appearing in the streets that same day, signed by Rhodes, recommending all women and children to seek shelter from attack in the bowels of the diamond mines. Advising arrival at the mine shafts that evening after dusk, the notices stated that cages would lower people all through the night to the various working levels, where guides with lanterns would be on hand to conduct them to places of complete safety.

The notices were taken to indicate that Rhodes had advance information of a concerted attempt by the enemy to storm the city, or bombard it into submission before relief could arrive. Total panic ensued. Women, convinced that Roberts would arrive to find them all massacred, having first been raped, snatched blankets and valuables before swarming to the mines to await the first sight of darkness. Those with children demanded to be the first lowered, and the organisers of the planned descents into that most obvious of shelters were hard put to prevent a female riot at the entrances to the shafts.

Leila had been alone all that afternoon. A serious headache had kept her on her bed during a particularly stifling period, made worse by the choking smell of cordite. The constant thunder of guns matched the pounding in her head. She rose as the sun sank, feeling listless and dispirited, with the headache reduced to a dull throbbing behind her eyes. Florence, who had once worked in a tea-room before becoming a chorus-girl, produced the last slices of their bread ration, toasted and smeared with the grease in which she had cooked the small portion of meat at lunchtime. The beverage accompanying it was merely boiling water poured onto old tea-leaves, but it was hot and effective in washing down the toast. Sally had her ration of milk to drink, and the remaining half of a beaten egg. They took as long as possible over the meal, because eating had become an important event in days during which there was little else to do.

They were still sitting at the table when heavy footsteps on the stoep caused Leila to glance up. Vivian, fully armed and wearing a serious expression, stood outside the fly-screen door waiting for her to unbolt it. A spurt of alarm stabbed her as she went over to let him in.

"What has happened?" she asked quietly.

He glanced over her head to the pair at the table, and drew her away to the far side of the room. "I met George Peek. He told me that you were indisposed today, so I suspected that you hadn't seen the notices. Are you all right now?" he asked urgently, in undertones.

"Yes. Which notices, Vivian?"

"Women and children are being lowered into the mines this evening. I've come to escort you all there."

"Into the mines?" Swallowing down her sudden fear, she asked, "Is Kimberley under imminent attack? Tell me the truth, please."

"I don't know the truth," he admitted. "There is definite evidence that the relief column is finally on the move, but we have no idea what to expect from the Boers. If they are confident of repelling Roberts and his men, all their attention will be turned toward the road from Magersfontein. There's just a chance, however, that they'll do *anything* to prevent the failure of their long siege. They are a foe particularly reluctant to lose men in open battle, but it's possible that their commanders will risk rushing defences held by men nearing starvation in order to capture a prize they have boasted of seizing. On the other hand, they may mount an artillery attack which they believe will force Kekewich to surrender in order to save lives and the destruction of the city. Either way, you will be safer in the mines with the other women and children." He took her arm again, adding, "Find rugs and pillows quickly. My horses are outside for you."

She resisted his attempt to lead her back to the table. "Are you saying that Kimberley may fall—even at this final hour, it may fall?"

He shook his head, his expression almost unreadable in the shadow cast by the pith helmet he had not, in his urgency, removed. "We dare not let that happen. The British Army would be disgraced. Please collect your rugs. I have to return as soon as possible."

Putting Florence, clutching the bedding, onto Tintagel, Vivian then took Leila and Sally up before him on Oscar to ride to the mines on the other side of the city. She experienced deep inner fear despite her reassurances to the child in her arms, as they embarked on a bizarre journey through fast-darkening streets where shells whistled overhead, and the ground all around them trembled. From her childhood came a sudden memory of something the rector used to recite to them all: *Yea, though I walk through the valley of the shadow of death, I shall fear no ill.* It seemed to her that the streets of Kimberley came very near to that description now. She wondered if the man holding her close against him as he rode was afraid at that moment; wondered if his mind was also full of the thought that any moment might be their last.

Then, like a beam of light through the darkness came the realisation that death now would ensure that they remained together forever. If they should be killed tonight, she would not have to face letting him go again. All reason and common sense flew at the beckoning thought. Love for him flowed through her unchecked, as she leant back against his solid strength, all fear subdued by this wilful yearning for fate, which had brought them together again here, to ensure that they never again parted.

For the length of that careful but urgent ride, she lived that yearning to the full, hardly aware of others' movement around them as the city prepared itself for the worst. Turning her face into his tunic, she felt the steady thump of his heart-beat against her cheek, which grew wet with her tears. Why had she denied them both the fulfilment of love two years ago? Why had she denied it again here? Rose had died heart-broken, yet regretting nothing she had done for love of Miles Lampton. All she, herself, had done for love of Vivian, was to hurt them both, and drive him into a marriage destined to destroy him. If she died now, she would regret so much.

Soon, they neared the mines to join the stream of people from all directions, converging on the shaft entrances which were areas of pandemonium. Women were arguing in high desperate voices with the men trying to organise them by waving their arms and shouting hoarse instructions. Children were wailing from fright, weariness or hunger; mothers abstractedly tried to quieten them while they struggled to maintain their places in the vague queues being formed by emaciated miners trying to control the operation.

"Dear God," rasped Vivian, drawing rein. "Don't they *want* to be helped?"

Glancing up by twisting her head, she replied quietly, "They're afraid, Vivian, that's all."

"So, no doubt, are you," he pointed out with rough tenderness. "If you can remain perfectly calm, why can't they?"

She had to say it. "Maybe they don't share my willingness to die at this moment."

He gazed into her face for a long time, his silence saying more to her than any words. Then he let out a long sigh. "I'll try to organise places for you all."

With that, he dismounted and lifted them down from the saddles, telling them to remain there until he returned. Then he strode off toward a surging group by the nearest shaft, the entrance of which was lit by swinging lanterns. Despite the humidity of the night, Leila shivered. Florence was still clutching the rugs as she stared wide-eyed at Vivian's tall figure, just discernible on the outskirts of the group.

"I've never been down a mine," she announced in scared tones.

"None of us has," Leila countered calmly.

"I mean under the ground—I've never been down a hole. That's what it is, isn't it? How will we breathe?"

"I don't know," she murmured, the thought never having occurred to her. "The men who work there manage it, so we shall." Sighing, she added, "I hope the other girls from the cast are here."

Florence glanced across at her in the darkness. "Someone will have fetched them, same as your friend fetched us. He's a bit . . . a bit *grand* for me, so will you tell him I'm grateful for what he's done?"

Leila managed a smile. "He'll know that without being told . . . and he's not a bit grand really." Through a thickening throat, she added, "He's very used to chorus-girls, as it happens."

He was back before them, speaking rapidly in the tones he probably used to his men—concise, authoritative, and calm. "Those with children are being given priority: there will be room for you in the next cage. You are to go over to that man wearing the white armband; he will ensure that you know the procedure when it returns to the surface. There are men on all levels ready to help you make yourselves as comfortable as possible, and to deal with any problems you may have. There are also several doctors down there, in case they are needed by anyone. Food will be provided by De Beers; there will be an adequate supply of hot drinks, day and night. You should be completely safe and secure while the emergency lasts."

Leila turned to the girl beside her; knowing that the next moment was one she desperately needed. "Take Sally over there and wait for me. I shall join you very shortly."

They went, Sally crying and holding out her arms to Leila as the distance between them widened. She turned back to Vivian, however, and looked up into his face, barely discernible in the darkness which had descended with African suddenness.

"Is your mother already here?" she asked.

"No. Von Grossladen has vast cellars beneath his mansion. He has installed her there, along with the Weldons, in great comfort. Mittelheiter is included in the party, you may care to know."

"Where will you be?"

"All military personnel will be on continuous duty."

This, now, was the parting she had dreaded. If Kimberley fell, he could fall with it. She owed him the truth.

"I married Frank Duncan because I feared that I was to have his child," she began, in confessional tones. "Thank God, I did not, but the shame of what I had done remained with me. Your attempt to buy me with Julia's earrings doubled that sense of shame. When you found Frank with me in that basement, I had just survived his attempt at rape the previous night. As you stared at me across that filthy room, I felt that you could see the same girl he saw, and the sense of degradation was complete."

At his expression of pain, she hurried to add, "That meeting made me vow to take revenge. I used men ruthlessly, forcing from them adulation which left me totally untouched. Occasionally, men like Sutton Blaise would remind me of a girl I tried to forget, but my determination was mostly successful, until you walked into the Baron's house that evening. When I began to receive a succession of vile letters, it was easy to believe that you saw me as no more than the creature they claimed I was. Shame revived. It culminated on Christmas Eve, when a band of virtuous women branded me as a whore."

Her voice began to falter as she finished what had to be said. "When I crawled from the undergrowth and made my way home that afternoon, I knew that they were right. Frank had looked at a servant-girl and seen a whore; lords and earls looked at Leila Duncan and saw the same creature beneath the fine clothes and cultivated manners. I longed for the streets to be filled with people, who would stare and point fingers openly at my naked body as I walked past. But . . . but the only person in sight was . . . was the one man I . . ." She broke off momentarily to clear the thickness in her throat. "Seeing you, at that moment, was more than I could bear."

He seemed incapable of speaking as he gazed down at her in the flashing light from gunfire, so close yet so out of reach. Knowing that final farewells should be brief if they were to remain controlled, she made a desperate effort at composure.

"When you came to my bedside that night, your vow of eternal love banished any creature but the one you see before you now. No man could speak of love for a bruised, swollen, near-bald girl unless it came from his heart, not his eyes. You gave me dignity and pride, for the first time in my life. I shall never lose sight of it, whatever may happen in the years to come."

Seizing his hands as she felt her control vanishing, she said unsteadily, "Rose gave Miles Lampton everything, and had no regrets when they parted. I have given you very little, and I do have regrets, darling. *I do have regrets.* Forgive me for hurting you. Forgive me for making you ever love me. But take mine with you now, or I shall be filled with regrets for the rest of my life."

Heedless of the danger around them, heedless of the world looking on, he took her in his arms and kissed her with the urgency of all soldiers going off to battle. Three years of a tangled passion had to be pacified by that one embrace, but they finally broke apart, each to gaze, stricken, at a beloved face for possibly the last time. Then he pulled her close again, the buttons on his tunic digging into her cheek as he murmured into her hair, "God go with you, my only love."

Turning abruptly from her, he mounted Oscar and trotted off into the night, leading Tintagel beside him. Shaken, knowing that footlights, grease paint, and wild applause were nothing compared with the love of that one man, she walked toward the head of the shaft, lifting her long skirt clear of scattered debris and fighting the yearning to run after him. When she was almost there, the babble of the waiting women increased as the cage appeared from below, and the gates were dragged open. Fighting and jostling, they rushed to enter it, forcing Leila to increase her pace for fear of losing her chance of a place in it. By the lantern-light, she saw Florence being ordered in by the man with the armband. The girl, holding Sally in her arms, tried to indicate that she was waiting for someone to join her. Impatient, irritable, the man took hold of her arm and thrust her forward to join a batch of white-faced women, some of whom had as many as four children with them.

Instinct made Leila break into a run. When she arrived, panting, beside the organiser, and made to squeeze into the huge, dirty cage, she encountered ferocious opposition from the women about to be left behind. Hands dragged at her clothes, almost pulling her off her feet. Female voices shouted at her that she had no child and must wait, as they must. Others claimed to have been there for hours, and began pushing her to the back of those clustering the shaft entrance. Next minute, the iron gates closed, and the lift dropped from sight on its descent into the earth. Leila watched helplessly as she was pushed and elbowed to the perimeter of the group left on the surface, thankful only that Sally was now safe, and had Florence to care for her.

Knowing that it would be some time before she could follow, she sank down onto a jutting piece of masonry to wait. Once there, however, she discovered that she really had no desire to leave that tumultuous night; no desire to be shut below ground with a fortune in diamonds lining the walls of her subterranean prison. Up here, in this darkness filled with the sounds, sights and smells of conflict, she felt closer to Vivian. Somewhere out there, he was preparing to lay down his life in defence of this city, if he must. Here, where they had said goodbye, was the place to pray for his safety. If there really was a person who listened to prayers, it would surely reach Him quicker from here than if she prayed several hundred feet below the ground.

A hand fell on her shoulder, a voice spoke in kindly urgent tones, but she was so much a part of that night it was a little while before she became aware of the man wearing the white armband. It did not matter that her ears were so full of the sound of thundering guns and explosions that she could not hear what he said. It was clear that he was urging her to go with him to the shaft entrance, where no more than half a dozen women now stood clutching shawls around them as relief from the chill of fear rather than that of the night. Leila walked to join them, stiff after her vigil on the masonry, and was surprised to see the large clock at the shaft-head indicating midnight. Had she been so long lost in regrets for her lack of honesty, her surfeit of pride, and for chances missed?

Moving into the cage, all she could hear was Vivian's farewell, all she could see was his silhouette as he rode away on the horse which had effected their first meeting. As the surface of the earth slid out of sight, and the war-filled night was replaced by no more than the rattle of the plunging cage in the silence of the pitch-black shaft, her spirit cried out against leaving those who remained up there. The silent women with her must be sharing that outcry, for their menfolk would also be uniting to defend the city which had resisted surrender for so long. When next they saw the sky above them, and smelt the fresh air, would it be emergence to freedom or captivity? Would the streets be filled with rejoicing defenders, or with aggressive bearded Boers? Would the men from whom they had recently parted be weary smiling victors, or weary humiliated prisoners of war? Or would they be in one of a long line of boxes beside a mass grave?

That last thought instilled swift claustrophobic fear of this incarceration deep under the ground. The sour smell of earth was strong in her nostrils; the continuing plunge accentuated their distance from the surface: panic overwhelmed her as silent destructive voices began to question her chances of ever reaching it again. Memories of enclosing undergrowth, and blows that rained on her to drive her further into it, were suddenly revived. Surrounded as she was by unknown women in a

316

confined space, her skin began to crawl with real fear. Only Vivian's description of riding onto the exposed plain, going forward just because to go back was out of the question, calmed her enough to allow her to walk with a semblance of composure from the cage when it halted.

The scene reassured her further. Far from resembling a tomb, the large vaulted chamber was electrically lit, reasonably cool, and filled with women chatting quietly together beside their sleeping children. Gone was the aggression and selfishness they had displayed on the surface. Now there was an air of sisterhood, a sharing of resources at a time of danger. A shawl loaned here, an extra cushion offered there, all marked a return to neighbourliness, which made the abnormal surroundings appear less sinister. Even so, the rocky chamber leading to the many narrow tunnels cut through the diamond-bearing soil was so full, every available space on the ground was occupied save a tiny path through the centre. Two or three of the miners walked up and down this clear area, determinedly keeping it free of overlapping rugs or mattresses as the women began to lose the battle against sleep and settle for what remained of the night.

Those who had descended with Leila searched for a spot for themselves, but she, not immediately recognising Florence, began walking through the press of women to look for her and Sally. The children were mostly curled up beneath blankets, so Leila did not attempt to identify Nellie's girl. It was little easier to recognise just one woman from those huddled into shawls or rugs as they tried to sleep on that hard stone surface, and she stepped carefully between outstretched legs, and heads cushioned on arms, whilst peering at the sleeping faces. Knowing that Florence would have identified herself straight away if she had been awake, Leila only concerned herself with the recumbent forms, hoping to spot the rugs taken from the cottage.

Frustrated, she began searching anew, apparently having missed the obvious. A second scrutiny, with particular attention paid to those with blonde hair, was also a failure. Careless placing of her foot brought a complaint, and her apologetic backward movement instigated a cry of protest from the mother of twin boys who had been disturbed by Leila's heavy skirt·dragging their faces. Next minute, one of the miners laid hold of her arm, insisting in low tones that she must cease walking around.

"I am searching for my maid and my . . . my daughter," she told him quietly. "We were separated at the top. They came down much earlier, yet I can't see them here."

Leading her along the narrow path between sleepers, the man said, "I daresay they're down below."

"Down below? I don't understand," she told him as she followed in his wake.

Back by the vertical shaft, he turned to face her, the strain of this culmination of a four-month ordeal showing on the planes of his thin face.

"The first batches went down to the fifteen-hundred-foot level. When that was full, we started up here."

"Up here?"

"We're at twelve hundred feet here—and this is now full, as you can see."

"How can I get down to the other level?" she asked, in some dismay.

"You can't—not now. You were the last to be lowered. The cage is up top now, and will stop there until they bring us breakfast."

"Can I get a message down to them. Just to reassure them that I'm safe?"

"Only if it's an emergency," he said with a shake of his head. "Look, miss, I should get some sleep. I'll see what I can do in the morning."

The clatter of the cage journeying up and down the shaft was the only indication that morning had arrived. The activity served to rouse those few who had managed to sleep on through the prolonged wailing of children, whose instincts provided an inner clock to inform them of mealtimes and other highlights of their daily routine. Leila had only dozed fitfully in a narrow cleft which had provided some support for her back. As Florence had taken the rugs and cushions with her, there had been no comforts to ease the cramped sleeping quarters, and garish dreams had flitted through her confused brain to leave her feeling leaden and depressed. Aching in every limb, she nevertheless lacked the incentive to move. There was nowhere to go, nothing to do. The chill of sleeplessness and hunger settled on her despite the fetid closeness of the atmosphere, and it was difficult to realise that hundreds of feet above her head a battle was being fought to its conclusion.

Soon, the cage stopped at their level, and the gates were swung open to reveal men of the De Beers ambulance company with huge buckets of tea and coffee for the women, and fresh milk for the children. They also had boxes filled with sandwiches. Such abundance of food had not been seen for many weeks, and it gave credence to the rumour that De Beers had held back supplies which could have been made available to the population much earlier. No one complained, however, as she accepted the very welcome sustenance with an eagerness that would have been taken as greed in other circumstances. Those with children were served first, and Leila was almost licking her lips with anticipation by the time she was handed two sandwiches and a tin cup containing hot tea.

The atmosphere instantly changed. A babble of conversation and laughter filled the lofty chamber; the children's wails were silenced. A woman beside Leila offered her a cushion to ease her discomfort, then launched into an ode of praise to her husband, who had led a daring raid on a Boer position three weeks before. Leila listened with envy. The most she could do was praise the courage of another woman's husband.

Once breakfast had been consumed and the boxes and buckets returned to the surface, Leila attempted to reach Florence and Sally. Both were probably worried and unhappy. It was some time before she gained the ear of the miner who had replaced the one on night-duty, because the women were clamouring for news of what was happening up above. It was not encouraging. The shelling was still severe; several fires had started in the city where there was a great deal of destruction. The hospital had narrowly escaped direct hits, but the theatre had been damaged by flying shrapnel. There was still no sign of a Boer attack, neither was there any sign of the relief column.

The excitement created by breakfast faded again. Children grew restless, therefore troublesome. They were all so closely confined no one could move without great care, and youngsters intent on play never exercised great care. Thus, it was against a background of noisy youthful disturbance that Leila explained her case and requested that she be allowed to go down to the other level. The request met with a negative and the advice that it was cooler where she was now. Protestations got her nowhere. The man merely repeated that there were over a thousand souls sheltering in that particular mine, and it was difficult enough trying to accommodate and feed them without shifting them up and down whenever they felt like it. Frustrated, angry, and depressed by the inability to wash and change her clothes, Leila returned to find her place in the cleft occupied by two small boys pretending to be soldiers firing at Boers.

Time passed slowly until the cage arrived with more buckets of tea to be distributed. In the cage with the helpers was a man Leila recognised, so she went to him immediately before he became occupied with other things.

'Dr Treeves, may I beg your assistance?" she asked urgently. "If you have the slightest influence over these men, would you be kind enough to use it to allow me to join my maid, who is on the lower level with little Sally?"

He looked at her closely for a moment or two, curiosity colouring his grave expression. "Miss Duncan? My dear lady, I did not expect to find you here."

"I wish to be elsewhere, as I have just explained," she told him rather sharply. "Sally has grown dependent on me since the death of her mother. I am sure you will agree the child should have me near in this situation."

"Yes . . . yes, of course. I will certainly do what I can," he promised. "If you will be patient while I check that all is well here, there is no reason why you should not accompany me down to the other level. However, I had supposed that Mr Rhodes would have arranged better facilities for a lady who has helped so tirelessly at all his concerts. There are several very strong shelters above ground, you know."

"So I understand," she replied coolly. "Perhaps I am in better company here."

The lower level was hotter, stuffier, and even more crowded than the one she had just left. Her initial recoil was forgotten when she spotted Florence to the left of the wide vaulted cavern, sitting with the full complement of chorus-girls. Greeting them gladly, she learned that they had all descended with the first groups to take charge of children of women with several. Sally was sleeping peacefully beside the others, tired from games devised by their temporary nursemaids, of which there could hardly be a more beautiful collection even if their features had grown as gaunt as any woman in Kimberley, and their shapely bodies were now board-thin.

The afternoon passed more pleasantly in company with these girls who spoke of all that was familiar, and helpers soon arrived with buckets of Siege Soup, as it was called to avoid any mention of horse which was the main ingredient. The welcome ration of hot tasty soup, augmented by more sandwiches and fresh fruit, which had been absent from their diet for some weeks, broke up the conversational groups. Along with the mothers, Leila concentrated on ensuring that the child in her charge was given all she could manage to eat before starting on her own rations.

It was whilst she was drinking her soup from the tin cup that her roaming gaze fastened in shock onto a group of faces she would remember as long as she lived. The blood seemed to drain from her veins leaving her icy cold in that unpleasantly close atmosphere, as several pairs of hostile eyes stared at her across the underground cavern. Even there, surrounded by several hundred women, she again felt a helpless prey faced by predators. For countless minutes, the sensation of paralysing fear held her immobile, the tin cup halfway to her lips. Then the suspended moment passed as her returning sense told her that both she and they presently shared just one fear—the fate of the men they had left above the ground.

The news from the surface remained unchanged: continuous shelling from static Boers, and no sign of the British supposedly advancing. A prolonged period of wailing from overtired babies and children before sleep finally overcame them wearied the women further. They settled for a further night underground with depression heavy on them. By now, the air was excessively stale, and each longed for the opportunity to wash and change into fresh clothes. The yearning to brush one's teeth became almost overwhelming and, for Leila, the discomfort of the heavy, clinging theatrical wig she still had to wear over her short hair, made her long to snatch it from her head.

The tea and coffee distributed early the following morning was declared by everyone crammed into that cavern to be the best ever tasted. They all took as long as they could over the drinking of it, because it relieved the boredom of facing another day in acute discomfort. Nerves and tempers were now being stretched unbearably, yet any woman heard complaining was immediately shouted down by a chorus reminding her of what their menfolk must be enduring as they continued to hold the city.

The news, when it came, was bad. A scout had ridden in to report that Lord Roberts' relief column, greatly swelled by fresh troops from England, was marching away from Kimberley in very determined manner. The women fell silent, their discomfort forgotten. Those with babies rocked silently back and forth, clutching them against their breasts bared to feed them. Others, with older children, drew them down to be circled protectively with a loving arm. The childless stood quietly together, their faces drawn and grey. Were they to be abandoned? Were they, after all they had endured, to be left with no alternative but surrender? Worst of all, were the soldiers overhead in that devastated city going to be foolishly heroic enough to fight to the last man?

That last consideration was one which haunted Leila during the interminable morning, which finally turned into afternoon. Dr Treeves came again, accompanied by another of his profession. They walked carefully among the mattresses and cushions, giving soothing powders to children feverish from anxiety and the lack of fresh air. The doctors' attempts to relieve the cramped conditions, by requesting permission for the women to walk along the tunnels leading from the chamber, were met with opposition. The tunnels branching off in many directions all led to working surfaces, the mining staff told them. Not only were they networked so intricately it was easy to become lost, the working area was out of bounds to anyone save De Beers staff with permits to enter. Even they were subjected to rigorous searches each time they completed their shifts, frustrating any attempts to conceal diamonds on their persons. It was out of the question to allow several hundred women, with as many children, to wander at large where a priceless rough diamond could possibly be gathered without much effort. While Mr Rhodes had most generously opened his mines to provide a haven from shelling, he had not also offered a tidy fortune for anyone lucky enough to pick up a pebble that dazzled when polished. The hopeful women all sat down again, renewed depression settling on them when the medical men explained the security restrictions.

"Damn the diamonds," muttered a disconsolate redhead beside Leila. "All I wanted was the chance to stretch my legs and practise my high kicks. Why should I want to make away with a large lump of dull stone, when I might get the final brilliant gem, nicely set in gold, from a generous admirer?"

Leila tried to smile. "I shall never again look at a diamond without recalling the sights, sounds and smells of this place and wondering if they're worth it."

"I think I'll have emeralds instead," chaffed a brunette gloomily.

"I expect they come out of the ground, too," put in another girl. "I'm telling you now, girls, that any future admirers can keep their jewels. What I want are extravagant suppers—lots and lots of them—washed down with ice-cold champers."

As she expanded her theme with descriptions of succulent chicken and wafer-thin slices of ham, the redhead picked up a cushion and put it over the speaker's face. Silence fell, the short return to the kind of dressing-room banter they all understood serving to bring thoughts of when or if they would ever resume the life they knew and enjoyed. Lost in such reminiscences herself, it was almost an extension of them which caused Leila to start singing softly to the fretful Sally when the child scrambled onto her lap for comfort. Then, as she grew aware of what she was doing, a Christmas Day from three years before returned in such clarity, it was as if Rose were there with her again.

*"It's foreign. Miles used to say it beautifully. Leeberstrowm, he used to call it."* Love's dream! Little had she guessed, that day with Rose, that she would be singing the same lilting melody to Nellie Wilkins' child fifteen hundred feet down a diamond mine in the heart of South Africa. If Rose should be watching now, her inimitable comment would surely be *"Oh Lei, what a laugh!"*

Unable to control a smile that began to curl her mouth, she caught herself singing a little louder, swaying from side to side to lull the fractious Sally as she relived the brief precious friendship with a girl who had shared such a momentous period in her life. It seemed almost part of that time when the melody was taken up by the girls around her.

The sound began to fill that chamber which had known only the rattle of the cage, the shuffle of miners' boots, rough, masculine voices, and far-off clanking machinery. The past merged into the present, as Leila looked around at the girls' faces and realised not one of them had done the Lindley Stroll with her and Rose Heywood, at that time which now seemed so long ago. Yet they had the same spirit, the same yearnings and aspirations that she and Rose had spoken of together. They, too, came truly alive when doing what they were destined to do.

The song ended; the sound of choral singing died away. It was then Leila noticed how the restive atmosphere had calmed. Children were sitting rapt, infant cries had decreased into drowsy gurgles, women were starting to relax a little. The miners on duty were smiling with pleasure: their request for more was echoed by the women sheltering there. The girls were happy to continue. There was no stage, and their weakened condition made their performance pale by past standards, but that cavern provided splendid acoustics for their voices in unison as they sang popular songs of the day, encouraging their listeners to join in with them. For maybe half an hour, the voluntary captives found a pleasure they had never thought possible in the corridors of diamonds, and the performers were able to release some of the pent-up yearning in a venue they were never likely to forget. Leila was asked to give several ballads during the general singsong, then received the inevitable request to perform the solo from *The Hungarian Heiress*, which was so popular at all the Kimberley concerts.

> "My faraway love I long just for you.
> These lips, still unkissed, whisper my sighs.
> I wait and I dream, to hope I am true
> Till you come to me here with love in your eyes."

Nothing could follow that. The words were too poignant, too heartbreakingly relevant to their present situation. Yet, the silence wrought by the song united them all as nothing else had since their virtual incarceration. Even those women whose piety had led them to attempt to destroy what they had regarded as her wantonness, were as one with every person crowded into that chamber. Each woman there had a loved one up in that city being pounded into submission. It made them all sisters.

Evening heralded the arrival of more soup, more sandwiches, more despair. The bombardment was virtually unceasing; several soldiers had been killed when an ammunition truck had blown up. Another night in the mine loomed. More babies grew feverish and sick. The atmosphere was becoming unbearably unpleasant and odorous. The doctors were worried. Before long, it could become more dangerous down the mines than up above them. An epidemic of fever racing through the crowded chambers could take more lives than the shelling.

Leila grew anxious about Sally, who was unnaturally hot and restless all that night. She slept very little herself, haunted by the past and by a future that promised emotional emptiness. The claustrophobic sensation was strongest when everyone lay silent with thoughts for company, and it was difficult to smother the longing for open darkness with the joy of stars above. Other torments beset her, like the desire to tear off her clothes and wash her whole body with cool water and sweet-smelling soap, to fling away the elaborate wig and lather her short fluffy hair until it felt and smelt as fresh as a summer day, to be in her airy bedroom at the cottage and sleep until her body was totally refreshed. Those yearnings for the world above her, and for the creature comforts, were only containable by thinking of Vivian who must be enduring far worse in company with his military comrades.

The third morning underground was distinguishable only by the distribution of breakfast by men with grey, lined faces.

"How do we know it really is morning?" asked Florence tonelessly, wiping Sally's face with the skirt of her dress. "They could be telling us a pack of lies. I swear we've been down here a week."

"They wouldn't tell lies," Leila retorted irritably. "What would they gain by it?"

The girl shrugged. "I don't know. Perhaps the city's surrendered, and they haven't told the Boers we're here."

"For heaven's sake, girl! Start that rumour and we'd have a pack of hysterical women around us. If you can't say anything sensible, stay silent," scolded Leila, half inclined to agree with her, nevertheless. There was no way of telling what time of day it was, or even *which* day it was, save believing those who came down from the surface with their meals.

Many others appeared to be feeling the same judging by their expressions as they questioned the helpers. There was a new aura of suspicion, of mistrust. If the relief column had marched off, why were the Boers not taking the city? It was of no use to them totally flattened, so why were they allegedly still bombarding it from a distance? None of it made sense. Were they being given the truth? What was really happening fifteen hundred feet above their heads? Where were their menfolk? Was anyone still alive up there?

A mild revolt caused one of the helpers to go for the doctors on duty.

They, on hearing the facts, sought out one of the military surgeons and descended in the cage to reassure the fearful women. Between them, they managed to convince everyone that it was, indeed, the morning of February 15th, and that the city was still in the hands of their own troops who had definitely not been wiped out to a man. Their quiet, confident manner, in addition to their bromides, improved the situation considerably, while the assurances of the army surgeon that he had had a quiet time for the past three days partially comforted those who feared for their husbands' safety. One of the civilian doctors, whom Leila knew only slightly, approached her to ask if she would help to ease tension.

"I heard that you staged an impromptu concert yesterday," he confessed with a smile. "Is it too much to hope you might repeat it?"

"It was not a concert," she protested wearily. "The girls were singing a lullaby, and it met with such approval, they continued with some well-known songs, that's all. It was a spontaneous affair, not a public performance to be repeated."

"I see," he commented slowly. "Miss Duncan, in this emergency we have all been driven to spontaneous action. It may last for many more days, in which we shall be driven to further spontaneous action. Most of the women here are simple ordinary souls who can do no more than herd together for comfort and safety. You have been blessed with a gift which makes you special, which sets you above the others. Use it for their salvation, I beg you."

With a bow, he rejoined his colleagues. Leila was totally disarmed. A concert—here? The idea was ludicrous! A lullaby sung to a fretful child had been taken up by some chorus-girls, who had been encouraged to sing a few popular songs everyone knew. It had been a way of passing time; an outlet for young girls who enjoyed singing and for bored worried women whose minds needed an antidote to constant fear. A concert—what nonsense! Yet, throughout the morning, Leila could not forget what the doctor had said to her. Lester Gilbert had insisted that she should "maintain the magic at all times", but would he include the fifteen-hundred-foot level of a diamond mine in that maxim? Something told her he would be appalled at what she had been asked to do, at what she had done yesterday. However, he had never been under siege, or been so hungry he had been forced to eat horses in order to stay alive.

As her thoughts continued along such lines, she realised that no words of hers would ever convey the reality of the past four months to a man safely distant, continuing the life which was actually an extension of his personal dreams. With a slight shock, it occurred to her that no one who had not been in Kimberley since October would understand circumstances which had bred fear, sacrifice, spite, greed, heroism, despair, hunger, and emotions which looked no further than the following day. How would she eventually return to the world outside this present one?

The short break from monotony created by the arrival of the men with food and hot drinks at midday did less than usual to raise spirits. A baby had died during the morning, every woman present somehow feeling its loss personally and deeply. Any manner of impromptu concert was out of the question, in such circumstances. Yet, as Leila listlessly watched the older children, who were bored and disobedient after three days of appalling restriction, she saw a way to fulfil the doctor's request. Noisy, quarrelsome boys and girls were driving the women to distraction with their restless antics which had them treading on hands, tripping over outstretched legs, and waking infants just lulled off to sleep. They were a nuisance to themselves and to everyone else. It was understandable enough, except that understanding had worn too thin for anyone to make allowances for youthful frailty.

Speaking swiftly to the girls around her, Leila told them to collect the children into a circle by herself and Sally. Glad of any action to end the aggravation, the girls soon complied, one even bringing a particularly objectionable boy by the collar and the seat of his trousers. With a grin, she explained that she had several young brothers, and force was the best persuasion she knew. Even so, it was not easy to capture their complete concentration, and several had to be coaxed back into the seated ring after attempting escape. Seeing that quick action was essential, Leila told Sally they were going to sing her favourite nursery rhyme. She began it, with the child joining in, as she always had. The result was astonishing. The chorus-girls each encouraged those nearest them to take up the beloved refrain, and they did so with an eagerness which betrayed their delight in the return of something they understood in the midst of an unnatural situation. There was no doubt of their ability to respond to authority in its gentlest form, despite the upheaval to their ordered lives. The sound of young voices echoed in that high-ceilinged chamber as they put their restless energy into the singing of rhymes, songs, and even favourite hymns.

Gradually, some of the women began to join with them, softly at first, then with the pleasure of such a natural feminine pastime. When the discordant voices first began, they were hardly heard above the melodious, echoing chorus. But the shouting grew louder, more insistent. Leila, lost in her occupation, turned her head irritably at this disturbance to harmony, but her voice tailed into silence at the sight of the miners' faces and their excited gesticulations. Other voices faded all around her, until the shouting was audible enough to make sense.

*"The relief column! It's coming. It's coming. Kimberley is saved!"*

Several hundred women rose almost as one from the stone floor. Babies and toddlers were snatched up as they began pressing forward. Mattresses, cushions, and rugs were kicked aside in the concerted rush to the shaft where the cage was the only means of returning to those left on the surface. Exhaustion and filth were forgotten; sickness, fever, and hunger were no longer causes for despair. Hastening feet trod carelessly over the trappings of survival in the subterranean cavern, in the desperate scramble to leave that site of the source of wealth which had built the city above their heads. Overemotional, the women began to fight each other, screeching hysterically as they clawed their way to the front of the surging crowd waiting for the cage which could take no more than a dozen at a time. The miners tried to organise them, in vain. Rhymes had given way to uproar.

Leila was left sitting on a cushion, with Sally in her arms, surrounded by the abandoned refuse of incarceration. The siege was over. She could not take in the fact, could not accept the enormity of its significance. There was nothing to keep her in Kimberley; in this land of beauty, heat, and diamonds. Life could now return to normal. This world within a world would be forgotten. The company of *The Hungarian Heiress* would return to London; Vivian would return to the arms of his wife.

As the women clamoured and fought, it came to her that she was one person there who could not rejoin the man she loved up in that reprieved city. Putting up a leaden arm, she pulled the wig from her head to leave exposed the dark fluff of tiny curls. No one would notice them now. No one would care if the magic were no longer maintained. Leila Duncan had served her purpose and was free to move on. It was over. Putting her cheek down against the soft hair of Nellie Wilkins' illegitimate child, she began to sob—a solitary seated figure in a jewel-lined vault.

# CHAPTER SEVENTEEN

At first, it resembled a mirage. After four months of scanning the broad empty plain for the slightest sign of movement, their bleary eyes stared, blinked, then stared again in disbelief as the mirage confirmed its reality. Riding across the sun-baked earth in splendid disciplined ranks on huge horses, the uniformed men could be none other than the flying column of the relief force. The siege was over; Kimberley had been successfully defended and military humiliation had been averted. Yet there was no rejoicing from the gaunt, exhausted, sweat-stained men in khaki who had stood on continuous guard for three days and nights, ready to repel an attempt to capture the jewel of the veld. They stood quietly behind the sandbagged outpost, their sun-darkened faces registering just one emotion. Pride. Several were blinking back tears. Most were swallowing down such unmanly weakness as they unconsciously straightened their backs, or twitched crumpled tunics into a semblance of smartness.

Vivian slowly lowered his field glasses after studying the heliograph message which had been flashing from the distance. When he spoke, it was into the incredible silence which had fallen now the guns had ceased firing.

"The Boers are on the run. They have abandoned all hope of Kimberley." Swallowing to clear his own throat of the lump which was forming, he added thickly, "I think you may safely stand the men down, Mr Crawford."

As the youthful subaltern performed the unnecessary ritual, Vivian turned back to Henry Sinclair, who was commanding the gunners manning the small outpost weapon, and shook him by the hand.

"We managed it—even without the artillery you and Blaise recommended."

The Gunner officer nodded, removing his pith helmet to wipe the grime from his brow with a weary hand. "Our communiqué will no doubt now continue on its way to Cape Town, where our recommendations will be dismissed. We managed it, as you said, and that will be their greatest argument. No matter that proper defences would have saved several thousand lives lost in the attempt to reach us, and several thousand more from shells, hunger and fever within this city. We managed it. Kimberley will return to its former state after a little rebuilding, you will rejoin your regiment in Cape Town, and I shall push on with Lord Roberts' force. I just hope to God I never experience another siege. There is the most appalling sense of impotence, of being in the hands of fate. I cannot wait to shake the dust of this place from my heels. What say you?"

Vivian made no reply as he turned back to study the plain ahead. It was impossible to comment on his feelings at that moment. For four months, the world had been no more than that city and those enclosed within it. He was not sure he was ready for these approaching horsemen, and all their arrival implied. There had been times, particularly during the past three days, when he had welcomed the notion of never leaving this place. Now, it seemed he had no other choice. It would take a while to accept that.

Although the sun beat down relentlessly, and he felt a tiredness bordering on physical collapse, he remained where he was—as did the rest of that detachment—sitting propped up against the sandbags, silently watching the distant horsemen draw nearer and nearer beneath the brilliant deep blue sky. His brain seemed incapable of thought; his limbs too leaden for movement. He had been so long in his clothes, even the yearning to strip them off for fresh ones had become deadened by lethargy. Sinclair's description of having a sense of impotence, a feeling of being in the hands of fate, had never been more strongly in him than at that moment.

They sat on, refreshing their thirsts from their water-bottles as the afternoon wore on. Weary lids dropped over eyes aching from the glare of the sun, which flashed brightly here and there as it caught the metal of horse harness or rifle. Yet, when the men of the flying column were almost upon them, Vivian and Henry Sinclair rose to their feet, assembling their respective men into regimental ranks fit to greet those who had been so long in coming to their aid.

The trotting horses were raising a great cloud of dust as they approached, but the waiting men cared nothing for that. Vivian's first impression was that of a cavalryman as he gazed in envy at the strong healthy animals, comparing them with the skinny beasts he and his men were now riding. Then he looked at the riders—big, well-fed men wearing the broad grins that befitted those bringing salvation. Yet those grins began to fade as the first ranks slowed and an officer broke from them, cantering across and leaping from his saddle to grip first Vivian's hand, then that of Henry Sinclair.

"By God, we were not a day too soon," he declared in consternation as he studied their thin frames. "You have earned our unanimous admiration, gentlemen, and may now take a well-earned rest. Our supplies are a day's march behind us, but we are here in some force and can promise you a better dinner than you have had in some weeks, I'll wager."

Neither Vivian nor his companion replied. They found it impossible to take in such geniality, such vigorous health, such self-confidence as this officer displayed. Curiously, Vivian caught himself regarding the man almost as an upstart; an intruder. An emotion strangely akin to resentment washed over him, at the calm assumption of command by someone at the head of a squadron of complete strangers. The men of Kimberley had fought for it over a period of one hundred and twenty-four days. It was *their* city, not to be instantly wrested from them by those who knew nothing of its streets, its people or its sufferings. The long siege could not be dismissed by a well-fed man with a handshake and the promise of a good dinner.

The accompanying ranks now pressed forward, dismounted, and treated the rank and file defenders with much the same kind of hearty attitude as their leader. It was met with a similar dazed inability to respond. After the initial emotion on sighting their comrades, reaction had been setting in as they had waited. The moment they had anticipated so many times had finally come, and it did not seem to be the shining victorious occasion they had envisaged. There was a strong suggestion of "Oh well, that's that!" which no man could immediately accept. They took the proffered plugs of tobacco, the apples, the other gifts of small luxuries they had not seen for many weeks, but it was done in automatic manner from men whose exhaustion would not allow them to believe what was happening.

The main part of the column had ridden in to the city, and the rearguard was just passing the outpost when the officer, who had introduced himself as Major Clunes, said to Vivian, "There is no longer any need to man this place. Ride in with me, and I'll give you an account of the trials we have had in endeavouring to reach you."

Vivian heard nothing of that last sentence as he found himself staring up at the face of a dark-moustached lieutenant, who had broken from the ranks to trot across and rein in a few yards away. The horse was from Shenstone's stables; the rider was his brother Charles. For some moments they looked at each other in shock, then Vivian pushed past those surrounding him to walk the short distance separating them. Charles climbed slowly from the saddle as he approached. Neither brother smiled or offered his hand. Nor did they speak, at first, as they subjected each other to wary scrutiny.

Vivian then voiced the only cohesive thought to come from the confusion in his brain, caused by the meeting with his estranged brother. "What madness! If you are killed, there'll be no heir."

Charles regarded him grimly. "Dear God, you stand there like a semi-skeleton with sunken eyes, the effects of your ordeal etched on your features, and still all you can think of is the damned inheritance you can never have."

As he began turning away, Vivian said to him wearily, "The damned inheritance is all *you* should think of. It's your responsibility, as the heir. War is mine, as a soldier. Don't try to shoulder both. *Charles,*" he called sharply as the other looked set to mount again. "It is good to see you again, after all this time."

Charles nodded, pulling himself up into the saddle. From there he said, "Julia told me that both you and Mama were in Kimberley. I have been in an agony of concern for her safety. Is she well?"

"She was three days ago."

After some slight hesitation, his brother asked, "Do you care to ride in with me? We have items of news to exchange."

Deeply disturbed over Oscar's poor condition, Charles was even more so when told that military chargers had, at least, been spared the fate of being served up for human consumption. That Vivian had knowingly eaten horsemeat was something Charles could not believe or understand, so he changed the subject quickly.

"Tell me of your experiences to arrive here," Vivian invited, finding it strange to ride alongside this placid gentle person now dressed in the trappings of a warrior. Whatever had driven him to take a course so at odds with his nature?

Some understanding came as Vivian heard that his country had been plunged into gloom over the three swift sieges, and the succession of heavy defeats suffered by the relieving armies. In consequence, young men had flocked to volunteer in their hundreds, and troop-ships had been bringing them out to reinforce the stationary columns as soon as their decks were filled.

"We were only in Cape Town a week," Charles said, "and even that was simply because so many were waiting for trains to take them to the front lines. Believe me, there must be enough troops in South Africa now to end this war very speedily. In his force, Roberts has New Zealanders, Indians, and local regiments in addition to the biggest British army ever known. You've no idea how violent patriotic fervour is at home. Girls are competing to offer their services as nurses; titled ladies are collecting funds and comforts for the troops, then bringing them over here personally. Julia is working ceaselessly to that end despite . . . despite her . . . uum . . . condition."

Vivian rode on slowly, swaying wearily in the saddle as he fought the effects of three days and nights with little sleep. Charles had delivered a blow by reminding him of something he had deliberately put from his mind, and which had remained from it during events which already began to seem unreal in company with this man who had arrived with the rest of the world in tow. As their horses picked a way through the devastation near the defensive perimeter, the captive freedom he had felt appeared to be falling in ruins like the buildings around him.

"The news of our breakthrough will send everyone at home wild with excitement," Charles continued, with a touch of pride in his voice. "Buller is almost on the outskirts of Ladysmith, so must relieve the garrison there in a day or so. That will remind the world of our invincibility, my word it will."

Disconcerted by his brother's military fervour, Vivian asked, "Have you seen battle yet, Charles?"

"Hardly," came the retort in injured tones. "I only met up with Roberts' force at the Modder River last week."

Vivian nodded. "Of course. We had a runner in, who reported that you were all marching away from Kimberley. For a while, we thought we had been abandoned."

His brother cast him a shocked glance. "You thought . . . ! I can't credit that statement. You must have known Roberts was moving heaven and earth to reach you."

A cynical twist of his mouth greeted that. "After four months, it did just occur to us that if an average force of Boers could not be moved, 'heaven and earth' might prove to be a little too much. Oh, don't give me that prune in the mouth look, man. Since October, we have been cut off here with no notion of what has been happening anywhere else. It's very natural to expect troops from the finest army in the world to come to one's aid with ease and alacrity. Instead, there appears to have been a David and Goliath situation—something not readily understood by a community being shelled, starved and decimated by fever. The good name of the British Army has suffered a severe reverse in this city, I must warn you, the feeling having been greatly encouraged by Rhodes himself. The man will doubtless proclaim himself the Saviour of Kimberley, giving no credit to the military defenders." He nodded toward the badly damaged Crown Hotel. "George Labram was killed there shortly after successfully testing the great gun he had designed and built. I think you have been so busy impressing upon me the patriotism and energy of the Empire, you haven't noticed the devastation around you. After several months of such things, Charles, people are inclined to believe anything."

To further impress his point, Vivian reined in, causing his brother to do the same. Charles grew quiet, his good-looking face beneath the pith helmet losing some of its indignation as he saw the slithering buildings, the great craters in the streets, the printed notices concerning Siege Soup and horsemeat, the skeletal people starting to flock into the market-place to gaze at the relieving troops for some sign of why they had taken so long. Then, apparently beginning to realise the grave implications of what he saw, he turned to Vivian in great consternation.

"Do you tell me that *Mama* has been subjected to danger from shelling; that *she* has been eating horsemeat?"

Impatient with this neatly-laundered, unblooded temporary soldier, Vivian said bitingly, "Are you totally ignorant of what siege implies? As one of our gallant, unshakeably loyal saviours, I thought your generals would have enlightened you on the reasons why your salvation was so urgently required."

Charles flushed angrily, trying to steady his horse who was taking fright at the approach of a large group of waving, cheering women. "Your ordeal has done nothing to cure you of the need to put me in my place whenever the opportunity offers," he snapped, as his dancing horse brought him round to face Vivian. "I am not here due to a desire to match your military rank, which consoles you for the loss of the civilian one I now hold, but because I saw it as my plain duty. Rest assured that I have no envy of your status in life, or any urge to strike a blow at it. You have shown that you are perfectly capable of self-destruction, which would have been successful but for the selfless efforts of a wife you do not deserve. You have not even enquired after her health and well-being, or if I have any communication for you from her." Swinging round again as the horse shifted restlessly, he went on. "It was my intention to put aside the anger between us, in view of the circumstances of our meeting, but you seem bent on maintaining it."

Realising that the large numbers of women and children flooding the streets meant they were coming up from the mines, at last, it was with only half his attention that Vivian replied, "If there was anger between us, it was all on your side. I tried to explain; you would not listen. I tried to see you; you banned me from the family home. I tried to give you back the land which was rightfully yours; you flung my offer back in my face." Urging Oscar forward for fear of encountering Leila amongst the dishevelled, haggard, but rejoicing women, he said over his shoulder,

"I am heartily sick of your martyrdom, Charles. After long confinement in this city, I can only compare your attitude to the self-indulgence of a prima donna."

After several minutes of careful riding through the debris of shell splinters, which would certainly be neatly cleared away before the bulk of the relief force came cantering bravely in, Charles came up beside him once more. His brother had no comment to offer, so it was Vivian who eventually broke the silence.

"Mama has been completely safe in the cellars beneath the home of Baron Von Grossladen during the final bombardment. I escorted her there myself," he added in brittle manner, unable to forget his mother's adamant refusal to offer Leila the comparative comfort of a private shelter, in company with Franz Mittelheiter. Her aristocratic insult at a time when life itself was endangered was something he could not forgive. Because of it, he had been driven to take the girl he would have made his wife to safety in conditions which must have grown desperately unpleasant in three days and nights. With that thought uppermost, he said, "I suppose it is my duty to tell you that the reason why we were both in Kimberley when the city was invested is that the Baron has asked our mother to become his wife."

"*What?*" breathed Charles, curiously horrified.

"I was summoned to Kimberley ostensibly to advise Mama on her decision, but Von Grossladen had already made it for her. They plan to wed the minute the siege is lifted. Your arrival could not be more fortuitous. The presence at the nuptials of Lord Brancliffe, one of the first heroes to enter the stricken city, will grace the event with the kind of distinction on which our prospective stepfather thrives," he finished sourly.

Charles was practically choking. "Dear God, she cannot marry that man!"

"He has instructed her that she will. It's all settled." Struck by his brother's expression, he asked, "Is something wrong, man?"

"*Wrong?* Do you tell me that neither of you has heeded what is in the newspapers?"

"We have seen no newspapers. We have been *totally cut off*, as I have been trying to impress upon you for the length of this ride."

Charles brought his horse to a halt and, despite the throng of people cheering the remainder of the rearguard which surged past, ignored Vivian's thrust to say, "Von Grossladen's family in Germany has not only sent rifles and ammunition to the Boers, but two of its lesser members are over here with an ambulance waggon bought and fitted out at their own expense, tending our enemy's wounded. The fact has made

334

world headlines, Viv," he said emphatically. "We cannot have our mother allying herself with such a family."

The news did not surprise or shock him too much. All he considered was the irony of that man obliging his bride-to-be to censure her son's friendship with an actress, which might touch his name with scandal, while his high-born Prussian family was the whole time destroying Gunther's yearning for siege heroism by ensuring his ignominy. The more the fact registered in his tired brain, the more amusing it seemed. Whilst the Baron had been consoling the captives of Kimberley with concerts and garden parties, his relatives had been bombarding them with shells! Gunther Von Grossladen would certainly be mentioned in history books. How would the wily Cecil Rhodes extricate himself from *that* association? How very, very funny!

"I find nothing in the situation to promote humour," grated Charles. "You have just told me Mama is engaged to marry a man, at present the subject of notoriety far exceeding any earned by our father, yet you sit there laughing. The sun has addled your wits!"

Wiping tears of mirth from his bleary, aching eyes, Vivian tried to control himself enough to say, "As the legal head of the family, yours is the duty of ensuring that our pliable parent is dissuaded from disgracing your noble name. I wish you luck, dear Charles." Pointing with his whip, he added, "There is the villain's residence. Go to it!"

"Now, wait a minute," protested his brother. "You can't ride off like that and disclaim any responsibility."

"Yes, I can," he responded, sobering fast. "Mama has shown her opinion of my filial concern. What's more, I'm tired, hungry and in a filthy state. You have my permission to take over, Lieutenant Lord Brancliffe, whilst I strip off, take a bath, and sleep for at least twenty-four hours. Our mother's future, in addition the defence of Kimberley, I willingly place in your hands. As soon as I am rested, I shall be duty-bound to return to Cape Town and my regiment," he concluded, humour swiftly being replaced by heaviness of heart.

"No, Viv, there's no need for that," came the grave comment. "The 49th form part of the relief column. They'll be here in a day or two, bringing the entire force with them."

The streets were now full of cheering emaciated people, who had emerged from shelter under ground like rabbits from a warren. Like them, Vivian felt a sense of sudden reprieve from something unacceptable. It was more than he could take, in his present state. Without a word, he turned Oscar and began walking the horse back through the streets he had ridden three nights before with Leila, heading for the tented camp—or what remained of it.

335

Life had drastically changed. Shops were filled with produce of every description, the streets were filled with troops, waggons and guns. The relief column had arrived in full force, sweeping away the remnants of despair and privation, yet leaving a curious vacuum in those who had endured the siege. Their weak constitutions rejected the glut of rich food; their months of seclusion left them bewildered by the pace of the new bustling community. The red-faced soldiers from the British Isles, the colourful Indian sepoys, the brawling extrovert Antipodeans had burst into that city and somehow taken it over. They were full of tales concerning the fearful battles undertaken *en route* when hidden Boer marksmen had mown down rank after advancing rank, to leave those still alive, and those hideously wounded, pinned down in the killing sun until darkness allowed them cover to withdraw. They spoke of kopjes, seemingly innocent, which had concealed overwhelming numbers of the enemy who had only revealed themselves when the column was caught in a narrow nek between the heights. Inconspicuous without uniforms, mounted on hardy veld animals, and completely familiar with the territory, the Boers seemed able to materialise from nowhere and vanish just as expertly after slaughtering the rigid ranks of professional troops.

The more those who had been invested heard, the more they realised how fortunate they had been to escape conquest. Those with sharper perception realised that their good fortune had probably resulted more from a tactical error on the part of the investors, than from any suggestion of invincibility that they, themselves, might have fostered. With successes against the fabled British Army to boost their morale, the Boers could surely have overrun the diamond city at any time. Single blunders had often lost wars. Would their neglect over the capture of Kimberley cost the Boers that dearly? When news of the successful relief of Ladysmith arrived several days later, that second major tactical error pointed to the probable sealing of the Boers' fate.

The danger over, the celebrating done, time then came for counting the cost and apportioning blame. Cecil Rhodes, never a modest man, laid claim to the title of saviour of his city. With ruthless determination, he extolled his own virtues to the finest degree, whilst flinging mud at Colonel Kekewich. Such was the extent of Rhodes' prestige within government and influential circles, the sacrifice of the good name and reputation of a worthy, diligent and very capable officer was made in order to appease the great man. Kekewich was relieved of his command in Kimberley, and returned to his regiment with a speed which precluded any ceremonial thanks for the difficult job he had tackled with great merit. The civilian population of Kimberley hardly cared.

The erstwhile military defenders were highly indignant. They were now in a minority, however, and their protests were but a ripple on a sea mountainous with the waves of revenge.

Leila and Franz spoke of one as they drove in a carriage from the damaged theatre, where they had been supervising the packing of their costumes and props to await the carrier from the railway station.

"I did not care for the Baron personally," Leila confessed, "but it seems most unfair to run him out of the city. He is not responsible for the actions of his family. While I concede that he almost certainly considered his own personal esteem when arranging concerts and other diversions during the siege, one cannot escape the fact that they did help morale. How can people forget so quickly and tar him with the brush of treachery?"

Franz leaned back in the seat to study her. Already, he looked amazingly robust, confirming Leila's suspicions that he had contrived to eat better fare than most during the weeks of their ordeal. Her own diet had been augmented by officers who had given her some of the edible spoils of their daring raids on enemy camps, but Franz had mixed with the Rhodes enclave known to have stores accumulated before hostilities actually commenced. He was a tenor, first and foremost. There had never been any secret about that.

"*Leibchen*, you are in a profession which is one of the most precarious in the world. One day you are the darling of the West End, the next day there is a new face, a new voice singing a song which catches at the hearts of theatre-goers. Fame is so fragile. Gunther courted it too openly. His fall was correspondingly dramatic." Doffing his hat to several ladies who were waving handkerchiefs in his direction, he treated them to his flashing smile before turning back to Leila. "Those same creatures most probably listened to rumours that my own interest in De Beers workshops was potentially treacherous, and nodded their agreement. Now they have a better traitor, I am once more the dashing stage hero."

"But the Baron wasn't . . . isn't a traitor," she protested.

"He will never disprove it. Who can ever say whether or not he had contact with the enemy?"

Staring in astonishment, she said, "You can, Franz, surely. You were his friend."

"*He* was *my* friend," he contradicted calmly. "There is much difference. I always denied his claim of compatriotism, as you well know. In any case, it was impossible for me to continue any contact with the man after his treatment of you. This I can never forgive. When I learned that you had been overlooked, that you had not been asked to share that shelter with him and his associates, I was distraught."

"Yet you made no effort to come to the cottage," she reminded him quietly.

Unshaken, he continued expansively, "We were assured that all ladies and children were in the mines—a far, far safer place than the Baron's cellars, you know. It would have been senseless for me to leave what little shelter I had in order to confirm something I knew to be true." Bowing toward a group standing on a street corner, he straightened up to add, "It was the insult to you which I could not accept, and it is my pleasure that his windows have been smashed with stones, his garden trampled, and threats painted on his walls to frighten him into leaving Kimberley to join his treacherous family in Germany. I think he will not be allowed to return here for many, many years. It is of great amazement to me that he escaped personal attack by those intent on vengeance."

Leila turned her head to gaze from her side of the carriage as she recalled the vengeance practised on her. The memory of it had been partially exorcised down the mine with those responsible, but it remained to haunt her on silent, humid afternoons.

Franz broke into her thoughts as he continued his theme. "The Honourable Margaret will not, of course, now become the Baroness. I hear it is of much satisfaction to her sons. The lordly brother is unlike your major in appearance, but it is said that he is in greater favour with their parent."

"He's not 'my major', Franz," she said quietly.

His lazy attitude changed. "Then why did you suggest that he was? You disregarded my advice and warnings; he treated me to insults. With such result that you were spoken of everywhere, and removed from the privilege of Mr Rhodes' circle. It is clear you have no care for your own career by allowing scandal to surround you, so it also means you have no care for his. That last is not for me to worry," he continued, growing heated. "I have tell him he is a fool, and he chooses to remain so. I have tell you of the dangers, and you have called *me* a fool. So now, Miss Duncan, you will discover the rights of it all. The Major has the wife, who will hear of it now we have link with the outside world. He also has the colonel, who has just arrive in Kimberley. There will be much explanation demand from him. For this I do not care," he declared sharply. "For you, I do care. Yes, even when you ignore me. For a leading lady it is necessary to have many gentlemen admirers. She must be always surround by the wealthy and famous. What have you do here? Stay alone after curfew with just one man—many times, not just once. He is not wealthy; he is not famous. *He is not a bachelor!"*

Carried away emotionally, his command of English suffered badly. "What will you do when we reach Cape Town? Will you be surround by admirers? No, you will be at the end of pointed fingers: this is the creature who stole Veasey-Hunter from his wife! Huh!" he exploded, shifting angrily in his seat. "I think you may soon find fame is so fragile."

As he fell silent, Leila caught herself recognising in him the embodiment of his own strictures. Whatever the situation, whatever the conditions of it, passion would always be removed with the grease paint where Franz Mittelheiter was concerned. He had no understanding of any love other than that of his art.

"All you have just said is probably true," she told him. "But after witnessing the death of a girl who was very dear to me, after watching people wait for hours under the blazing sun for a small ration of some poor beast slaughtered by men who revered it, after seeing daily funerals for fever and shell victims, and after knowing that Vivian could be out there dying in a sun-baked wilderness while I was singing songs, fame does not seem fragile to me, it seems totally unimportant."

He sighed heavily, wagging his head in complete lack of understanding. Yet he said no further word as the carriage bowled along toward her cottage. Leila smiled automatically in response to salutes, or doffed hats and nodding heads as they passed old acquaintances, or newly-arrived eager military men. She longed to be gone from this city, yet knew a part of her would remain. Freedom had brought its penalties; everything had changed, and she saw her own life and that of those around her with clearer vision than before.

They were nearing the cottage when impulse led her to tap the driver on the shoulder with her rolled sunshade, and instruct him to pull up. Franz asked sharply what was amiss, but she merely opened the little carriage door and stepped down determindly just a few yards from the entrance to that lane leading to the road where she lived.

"There is something I must do before leaving here on Friday," She explained to her disconcerted companion. "Please drive on."

"Do?" he queried. "Here . . . and now? I do not understand."

Her smile was touched with sadness. "You wouldn't, Franz. Unless it concerns the theatres or vocal entertainment, you don't understand anything."

Telling the man to drive on, she opened her sunshade and held its lacy protection over her head as she stood watching until the carriage and its disgruntled passenger had turned the corner. The street was by no means deserted, but she felt alarmingly alone as she turned to face the lane, knowing that she could only banish the lingering fear of it by walking through once more. Defiance could not have been more evident in her appearance, for she was wearing an elaborate gown in deep apricot, with a layered collar which hid her diminished bosom and accentuated the siege narrowness of her waist. Cream gloves matched a toque of alternate cream and coffee-coloured stiff ribbons, finished off with two tassels in deep apricot at the left side. Seductive it might be, but surely far too elegant for a whore, she decided in a cynical attempt to bolster her confidence.

The lane was empty. On the point of turning back, Leila told herself she would be gone on Friday and would forever regret her lack of courage if she did not now go on. Stationary, she fought irresolution until a thought she had had on many such occasions returned once more. *Rose would do it.* Tightening her grip on the handle of the sunshade, she acknowledged that Rose would walk through this place, regretting nothing that she had done, and proving the fact with her defiance. Taking a deep breath, she set off at a slow pace, and had covered some yards before realising that she had subconsciously adopted the Lindley Stroll. It somehow strengthened her resolution, so that it was then also easy to adopot the haughty look which had accompanied that mesmeric walk across the stage, reducing an entire audience to breathless silence.

Some women entered the lane at the far end, and momentary terror rushed through her. They were chatting together, however, and carried nothing more sinister than shopping baskets. She strolled on toward the place where a small clearing gave the deceptive impression of a path through the undergrowth. The two women passed her, smiling shyly. A military officer, with a laughing girl hanging on his arm, then turned into the lane, so she kept her concentration on them as she neared the dread place, knowing she must stop there and confront her fears.

There was nothing there to suggest pain, terror and humiliation. Shrubs were producing early autumn flowers; birds flitting about them suggested the usual moving rainbow. Sun filtered through branches onto a normal dappled glade filled with peacefulness. Enormous relief washed over her. Aggression had left no mark there; hatred had vanished on the breeze. Turning away, she continued on her way, filled with a strange sense of triumph comparable to that of the inhabitants of Kimberley on hearing that the Boers had vanished into the distant hills.

Sally toddled to greet her when she opened the gate, but Florence was so full of excitement she made no attempt to bring water for Leila to wash, or to make tea.

"Look at this," she cried, waving a newspaper. "They came up from Cape Town this morning on the train bringing more troops. Dr Treeves dropped it in on his way to the hospital. Do you think they'll hear about it at home, Miss Duncan?"

Slightly abstracted, Leila took the newspaper, still holding Sally by the hand. With her mind full of what Franz had warned about scandal, with Julia hearing the distorted truth and fingers pointing at the "creature who stole Veasey-Hunter from his wife", she could not take in what she saw written in headlines on the front page.

## HEROINE OF KIMBERLEY SIEGE
## FAMOUS ACTRESS SINGS TO WOMEN IN DIAMOND MINE WHILE CITY IS SHELLED

Incredulous, Leila read the remainder of the highly exaggerated piece of patriotic journalism to discover, to her own great surprise, that she had defied starvation, fever and severe mental stress to entertain the women and children of the diamond city during their ordeal underground. She had, apparently, put aside her own sufferings for the sake of those sheltering with her, and had organised the girls from the chorus of the musical show in which she had found fame to provide musical relief during three days and nights of non-stop terror from Boer shelling, which had nevertheless failed to defeat the gallant defenders of Kimberley. It surprised Leila even more to read of the gratitude expressed, on behalf of his city, by Mr Cecil Rhodes when she emerged from the mine, weary but smiling bravely.

Lifting her gaze from the newsprint to Florence's flushed face, she said, "This is absurd. It's totally untrue. How could anyone write such nonsense, much less publish it? Who, in Cape Town, knows anything of what happened here in the mines? Oh, Florence, what am I to do about it?"

The girl laughed gaily. "Make the most of the unexpected publicity. Ooh, I do hope they read about it in England."

"But it's . . . oh, it's the most outrageously sentimental piece of fabrication," she cried in protest. "Whoever can have done it?"

"Almost any man who works for the *Diamond Fields Advertiser*, I should imagine. A piece like that would earn a fortune right now," Florence said, still full of excitement. "You'll have to stick to the story."

"I certainly shall not," she declared. "If anyone mentions it when we arrive in Cape Town, I shall deny it."

"We're not going to Cape Town," Florence informed her, as she turned away toward the kitchen to make tea. "The railway is now open right down to Durban, and troop-ships are coming in there. I don't mind. I liked it there, and we'll have a few extra days at sea to rest on the voyage home."

Leila sank slowly into a chair, still holding the newspaper in her gloved hands. There was another item of news connected with the siege and, as she read it, it seemed that her life was always being unfolded in the columns of newspapers. Beneath the picture of a striking woman in a low-cut ball-gown partnered by a man in uniform, who was half turning from the photographer, was the story of Mrs Veasey-Hunter, wife of the gallant Lancer officer who had been visiting his mother when Kimberley was invested. Whilst Major Vivian Veasey-Hunter had been engaged in dashing sorties against the enemy, his wife, a popular and celebrated equestrienne, had worked untiringly with other society ladies to provide medical equipment and comforts for the troops, in far-off Cape Town, where the fate of those under siege was unknown. Three days before the relief of the city her husband helped to defend, Mrs Veasey-Hunter had given birth to a premature child. Close friends of the convalescing mother had hinted to newsmen that the lusty boy was to be christened Kimberley. Major Veasey-Hunter was reported to have stated that he was thrilled and delighted by the news, when it was relayed to him on the reopening of communications between the two cities.

"I have tolerated your claims to greater affiliation with Mama as her doomed first-born," Charles declared hotly, as he faced Vivian in the sitting-room of the Weldons' home. "I have, for years, deliberately stood aside to allow you the compensation of being the favoured one with the right to give our mother any support and protection she might need. Whilst you have been flamboyant in verbal and active defence of her reputation, suggesting the most ardent filial devotion, I have merely maintained a regular correspondence informing her of all I felt she would wish to know." Taking a deep breath, he snapped, "So much for your professions of everlasting regard! Wasn't it enough for Mama to suffer the privations of siege, that you must also hurt and humiliate her in this manner?"

"You said no word of it! For four whole months, you made no mention of Julia's condition," cried his mother in distress, from the *chaise-longue*, where she was supported by a pile of cushions. "The

342

affair was reprehensible enough before. Now it is plain your wife was enceinte when you arrived here, your behaviour must be seen as that of a complete blackguard. Your career will be in ruins; your wife will suffer the very greatest humiliation."

"I could not believe what I heard from those who had been here during the ordeal," Charles declared, taking up the attack again. "It was appallingly clear to me why you had really made the journey to Kimberley, at a time when war was certain to overtake the city. Thank God others are not aware, as I am, of your earlier liaison with that woman."

"Had I known of it, I would never have given you the perfect excuse to come to her here," Margaret vowed in despair.

Charles moved about the room, working himself up to say more on the subject. Vivian waited silently for him to do so.

"We both spared Mama the sordid facts surrounding your marriage," his brother said eventually. "You through feelings of guilt, no doubt, and I from consideration of her blind love for you. I felt it my duty to acquaint her with the truth, this morning, before you arrived here. The distress it caused her was, unfortunately, necessary in order to alleviate her feelings of responsibility for what went on here. She now sees that your ungovernable passion for that woman takes no account of the feelings or reputations of others. You have used Julia in the cruellest manner; you have rewarded Mama's devotion with treachery. Toward me, you have consistently practised the most refined form of punishment for inheriting what should have been yours. I have borne it out of sympathy for your position.

"I frequently asked your advice and help, so that you would feel some sense of sharing the family responsibilities. You took advantage of my generosity to treat it all as your own, even bringing your mistress to Shenstone when I summoned you to Brancliffe's sick-bed. You further obliged Julia and me to entertain her. I confided to you my earnest desire to marry Julia, and Brancliffe's determination on the match. You responded by deliberately compromising her in the most cold-blooded fashion, blighting my expectations, and killing our grandfather with the subsequent unavoidable marriage.

"You then attempted to mollify me by offering a piece of land intended to be restored to the estate when Julia became my wife. When I, with every justification, declined your offer, you promptly locked your gates and deprived me of access from the west. The name of Veasey-Hunter was further besmirched by the scandal surrounding your murder of two Englishmen, one of whom was an officer with whom you had quarrelled publicly over a woman. I, to say nothing of poor Mama, suffered the backlash from that affair until the wife you have treated so inexcusably won society's forgiveness with her loyal support of you."

Flushed with rage, Charles could no longer control himself. "By God, Vivian, you did not deserve it! You do not deserve Julia for your wife. You do not deserve Mama as a parent." Breathing heavily, his immaculate khaki patched with the dampness of his raised temperature, he finished what he had begun. "By God, nor do you deserve me as your brother!"

As the prolonged silence suggested that the outburst had ended, Vivian said calmly, "Bravo, Charles."

His brother goggled at him, as he dabbed his wet brow with his handkerchief. "Is that all you have to say? Is that really all you have to say?"

"No," he admitted, "but I was not certain you would wish to hear it."

"We are entitled to some answer to your brother's charges," pleaded his mother. "You owe us that."

Charles glared at him. "Yes, you owe us that, at least."

"Very well." Folding his arms in relaxed manner over his well-worn starched tunic, he said, "If Miss Duncan were here now, I believe she would agree with me that you had both missed your vocation. I have witnessed few better played dramas than the one you have both just enacted. It can only be the greatest histrionic talent which allows you to brush aside four months of death and destruction as if they had been nothing, to concentrate on the wounding to your delicate constitutions caused by my attentions to someone who has never been my mistress."

Smiling at their expressions, he continued in the same calm manner. "The so-called scandal linking Leila's name with mine was perpetrated by Von Grossladen in order to take attention from the one concerning his loyalties. It circulated only amongst his friends—or should I say, *former* friends? Ask any military man, or any civilian resident not included in such exclusive circles, and you will be told that Miss Duncan entertained, in gracious and dignified manner, most lonely gentlemen in Kimberley at some time during the four-month siege."

Turning to address his mother, he said accusingly, "You, Mama, are wallowing in a delicious mire of long suffering martyrdom, unforgivably embellishing this contrived 'scandal' in order to cover another. Von Grossladen has been unfairly pilloried and forced to flee to his homeland, leaving you deserted in his reflected disgrace. You suddenly find yourself with no one to make your decisions or arrange your movements. Your ordered future has fallen around your ears, so you have retreated into feminine frailty in the hope of attracting a fresh broad shoulder to cry on, and a strong will to guide your movements." Unfolding his arms to support himself as he leaned across a chair to emphasise his point, he went on. "They will no longer be mine. You have here with your your legal son, who has just very pompously championed you and confessed that he has always stood aside in my favour where you are concerned. I give him my blessing to come forward now and take over the task of getting you out of your present predicament." Straightening up, he added, "Leila once told me that she thought very little of any mother who would stand aside and let her sons be bullied by a vindictive old man. I see now that Brancliffe shared that opinion."

Into the deathly silence that had fallen in the room, Vivian crossed the few feet to confront his brother. "You asked my help and advice only because you could not cope with your responsibilities alone. Your 'earnest desire to marry Julia' was no more than spineless acquiescence to Brancliffe's attempt to put some character into the line of inheritance. It was a sense of guilt, for ever allowing it to be detached from Shenstone, which prompted your insufferable refusal of my gift of Maxted's Farm and the surrounding acres. Blighted expectations, be damned! If you had had an ounce of red blood in you instead of pure blue, you would have told Brancliffe to go to the devil, chosen a bride with high spirits and a fortune, then produced an heir as swiftly as possible. The old man would have been reassured and handed over the reins, without reservations. He had no faith in you, Charles. You are weak, and I hope to God you overcome it in battle or the name will suffer a scandal far worse than it has ever known."

Allowing a short while for the inference of that remark to sink in, Vivian continued. "When you have experienced a situation in which men are falling around you, bloody and screaming; when bullets whistle past your ears, enemies rush at you with murder in their eyes and cold steel in their hands; when your ears are deafened by the thunder of cannon, the shrieks of agonised horses, and the repeated sound of the 'Charge!' in the face of almost certain death or mutilation, you will understand the meaning of being a soldier. Only then will I consider you just the very slightest part entitled to express an opinion on the actions of another soldier, especially in circumstances of which you know absolutely nothing."

Walking past his brother, then thinking better of immediate departure, he turned back to say, "In Brancliffe's day, you would have been called out for expressing such an opinion of the Ashanti affair as you have just done. I shall make allowances for the fact that you have inherited Mama's propensity for feminine frailty, which forces you to counter those things of which you have little understanding with bursts of immature outrage. You are right, Charles. I do not deserve the brother and parent I have. Neither do I deserve Julia for a wife."

Walking back to his stunned brother, who had swung round to face him, Vivian finished, still with calm control of himself, "To correct that situation, I intend to dispense with both you and Mama. I wish you well of each other. Julia, unfortunately, I am saddled with 'until death us do part'. The only factor which will prevent my courting that blissful state in forthcoming battle, is that I do not intend to abandon my son to her sadistic domination. I will come through this war for his sake alone."

Walking swiftly over to the door, he again hesitated on the threshold, driven to say one last thing. "It may interest you both to know that my 'ungovernable passion' for Leila Duncan led me to beg her to become my wife three years ago. I would give half my life, if my new-born son could be hers and mine. He would have been assured of the unselfish love of both parents . . . and blessed with a total lack of relatives."

Nodding to the manservant waiting outside to open the door for him, he took up the pith helmet and whip before running down the stairs to where Oscar was being held ready, that last thought so strong in him it was a source of true pain.

# CHAPTER EIGHTEEN

Vivian did not take advantage of Colonel Messenger's offer of leave in order to visit his wife and new-born son. The officers of his own regiment, when they rode into Kimberley with the main section of the relief force, were so full of elation and fervour none appeared surprised at his decision to push on to Bloemfontein with them. Although born prematurely Vivian's son was apparently a strong, lusty child enjoying the same degree of fitness as the mother who had produced him. This obviated any need for Vivian to rush to Cape Town on compassionate grounds, for which he was heartily thankful and, since Julia could do little to influence their son's character at such an early stage, he was happy to remain away from her for as long as possible.

Knowing as little as most men of pregnancy and birth, he was nevertheless astute enough to guess at the cause of the early arrival of the child when fellow officers told him that his wife had continued to ride Mountfoot St George over difficult country, against doctor's orders. They gave verbal admiration of her spirit and pluck, but Vivian saw her behaviour as defiance of what she would regard as feminine weakness. There was no doubt in his mind that, if Julia could have copied Ashanti women by retiring into seclusion a short time before producing her offspring, then walking back with the infant in her arms to continue as before, she would have done so. For once, nature had shown her that she was not entirely mistress of her own body. What if the child had been lost through her heedlessness? Would he have been glad? Would he have felt freer? The existence of his son, the child of loveless passion, tied him as never before. After the clarity of vision the siege had brought him, he might well have walked away from Julia at the end of the war. He would not walk away from his son.

Reunited with his own regiment, Vivian found it curiously difficult to recapture the old camaraderie with those from whom he had parted only four months before. A lifetime seemed to have passed in that span of weeks. Relationships formed under dramatic and stressful circumstances were hard to sever, and he found himself missing those men of the Kimberley Regiment and the Diamond Fields Horse with whom he had trotted beside the armoured train, or ventured so often across that

347

deceptively empty plain. Additionally, he felt excluded from the reminiscences of skirmishes experienced by the 49th *en route* from Cape Town. During the march on Bloemfontein, those men who had mounted the defence of the diamond city tended to seek each other out. Vivian was more often in company with Henry Sinclair, Sutton Blaise, and those officers who had been with the four companies of the Loyal North Lancashires in Kimberley. One man he meticulously avoided was Lieutenant Lord Brancliffe.

On reaching Bloemfontein they were ordered to rest, rearm and wait for reinforcements coming up by train. New shiploads of troops were arriving to swell the ranks of the existing columns. Volunteers all, these men were untrained, untested and more enthusiastic than efficient. Some regular soldiers despaired. Half their new comrades rode like farm yokels, or were unable to ride at all. In a country such as they were in, even the infantry had to be mounted in order to move around it. The horses sent with the volunteers were destined to suffer like those already there. Unable to withstand the heat, and the prolonged marches across dust-dry terrain, the poor beasts had grown thin, sick and broken.

Even so, Lord Roberts' army in Bloemfontein could have been ready to push on within two weeks. Instead, it remained there for two months. The Boers rejoiced. Eight wonderful weeks in which to reorganise, re-equip, and take up strategic positions all along the route to Pretoria. The failure of the sieges no longer appeared to have sealed their fate. In open veld, all advantage would be theirs against great cumbersome columns which could be seen from miles ahead by a few mobile men with field glasses. The longer the rooineks, as the British were called by them, remained stationary, the greater the disaster they courted for themselves.

The delay irked Vivian unbearably, haunted as he was by memories only action could dispel. Leila had returned to England with the cast of *The Hungarian Heiress* two weeks after the siege had been lifted. Although he realised he had lived a fool's dream there, it had shown him once more that any place or circumstances could be lit with hope when she was beside him. He had seen her just twice after relief had arrived. They had passed in the street, and he had known by the way she had looked at him that the news of the birth of his son had erected barriers between them again.

On the night before her departure, he had been present at the company's farewell concert. Gazing at the makeshift open-air stage, with the stars like scattered sky-diamonds above them, he had watched her prove that his rival for her love was more worthy of it than he. She had never looked more out of reach; her voice had never contained such

348

melodic sadness. The entire audience had seemed mesmerised by what was happening in the city so lately a scene of fear and misery. A virile, handsome man in a chocolate-box uniform, and a willowy girl who sang from the heart, had held a mass of people from diamond lords, to yeomen soldiers, to shopkeepers in thrall under that African sky. When Leila had yielded to roared demands for "My Faraway Love" and had stepped forward to sing it, the hush that had fallen across the veld must have enabled even their hidden enemies to hear and thrill to it. So Leila had gone, but the vision of a blue-eyed girl in a yellow gown, which had reminded him so strongly of their first supper together, remained with him.

His mother had left Kimberley before the concert, Charles having arranged passage for her on a ship from Durban on the first leg of her journey back to Rhodesia. Lady Weldon had accompanied her, only too willing to leave Kimberley until the war ended. Vivian had not said goodbye. She no longer needed her illegitimate first-born, and he vowed he would no longer accept the allowance she had always made him from his father's share of the estate, even if she were prepared to continue it. The umbilical cord was totally severed.

Not so the marital one. A letter had finally arrived from Julia. Reading the several pages of vigorous sentences describing their son, their horses and their future, in that order, Vivian could visualise that strong face with its huge assessing eyes, and he could hear that confident challenging voice. With his decision not to visit Cape Town already proving to be the wisest, his mouth twisted on reading her last sentence: "All I hear suggests that you have been terribly brave, darling, never more so, I suspect, than down the diamond mines during the last three days of your ordeal."

It was Julia's way of telling him that she had read about Leila's presence in Kimberley, and would wage subtle reprisals for any hint of gossip linking him with the girl she had never succeeded in exorcising. That letter increased his longing for action.

Finally, at the beginning of May, with winter advancing swiftly, orders were received. The march to Pretoria was on. The troops cheered and set out in high spirits across land burned brown by the heat of summer, little realising what lay ahead. In contrast to the terrain around Kimberley, the great snake-like columns had to cross vast areas of grassland which rose in ridges and hills. These had to be scaled by means of rough tortuous tracks or skirted through narrow neks between heights. In the magnificent clarity of a veld winter, it was possible to see for an astonishing number of miles around. Distances, therefore, became deceptive. The absence of maps of the area caused many

349

problems for military commanders of marching columns stretching for up to seven miles in length.

A relentless summer sun had parched grass and dried up the rivers, presenting a dire shortage of water and fodder for the beasts on the move. Large numbers of fine horses, which were nevertheless unsuited to the job they were forced to do in this alien country, fell ill and died all along the route. Many more grew so weak and broken, it was clear they would be of no use in actual battle. Alarm increased when soldiers also began falling victim to the hazards of this land no one knew. Fever raced through the ranks, felling men with appalling swiftness. Particularly vulnerable were those who had been debilitated in Kimberley through privation and exhaustion. Those men who welcomed the magnificent crisp blue days with temperatures comparable to those of England's gentle summer, found themselves huddled into greatcoats around camp-fires at night. Darkness came early, and with it came a drastic drop in temperature. Tents gave little protection in huge exposed areas: all too often there was not even tented protection, when encounters with the enemy concealed in the hills meant an open bivouac at the end of a day's fighting.

The force which had set out enthusiastically for Pretoria then began to realise that the war was nowhere near over. The troops began to dread nearing every kopje or ridge. There were Boers in every one of them, hiding behind the giant aloes, or in shallow depressions—anything providing cover while they picked off, with skill and ease, the khaki-clad men toiling across the vast distances. Those ordered to climb the slopes and flush out the enemy did so with apprehension. Mown down relentlessly as they moved up the exposed hillsides, those few who finally won through to the top found no one there. The Boers came and went as if by magic.

It was just as bad when passing between the hills. In higher positions, with perfect command of a narrow nek cutting through the great ridges, a mere handful of men could pour a hail of bullets down to hold at bay several thousand. The confusion amongst the British and Common-wealth ranks in such situations was increased by the order which had demanded that officers must remove their badges of rank, due to the Boer habit of picking off all officers first. The order ensured that the attacking troops were not immediately deprived of leaders but, in the heat of battle when so many commands were shouted, the bewildered men were unsure who to obey first. Every one of them looked the same in universal khaki, stripped of insignia.

The exhausted, dispirited, fever-stricken column slowly advanced until it came upon an even worse enemy. The rain began. The vast

South African skies flung it down relentlessly, in thundering downpours that turned tracks into mud, and filled dry watercourses with rushing torrents which could rise as much as six feet in an alarmingly short time. In accumulating misery, the long khaki snake slithered, slipped and struggled as waggons sank deeper and deeper into mire churned up by thousands of hooves and wheels and trudging boots. More beasts died from the effort of trying to pull laden waggons and heavy gun-carriages from submergence in sucking pools of liquid mud. More men succumbed to fever and pneumonia and sheer exhaustion. They came upon rivers, now swollen by the rains, and sought for drifts where the shallow stretches would enable them to cross. During the time it took for an entire column to splash laboriously to the far bank, the water level often rose so fast men and animals were swept away and drowned before the eyes of those waiting their turn. During the long winter nights, their bivouacs or tented camps merely extended their misery as frost hardened the ridges and penetrated to their bones. Those who had been captives in Kimberley began to feel that freedom was little better.

Although Vivian suffered as much as any man during the advance to Pretoria, he felt a new inward sense of peace which counterbalanced the hours of riding against blinding rain, the struggle to advance over miles and miles of mud, the frequent dousing in icy rushing rivers, and the danger in every encounter with the unseen enemy. It did not take long for him to realise that the peace came from acceptance of a man called Vivian Veasey-Hunter. Gone was the ever-present drive to banish the social stigma of his birth; gone were the erroneous impressions of a vindictive unloving grandfather, a sweetly devoted mother who had been cruelly persecuted, and a brother who would remain staunchly loyal. No longer did he feel the compulsion to prove that he was better, stronger or more courageous than any other man in order to be accepted on equal terms with him. Best of all, he knew the truth about Leila, which gave him the sensation of standing alone as a man and as a soldier.

Feeling free to order his own actions, choose his own life, he bore the long hours in the saddle, he dismounted to heave and push alongside his men each time their waggons stuck fast, he fought his way through swiftly-flowing rivers encouraging those with him by words or a helping hand, and he charged the enemy at the head of his lancers with no thought of standing with a board strapped to his back while he recited his shortcomings. Every man with him in that column had human failings. At last, "Veasey-Hunter's by-blow" could accept his own.

Those who had fought their way to Kimberley had discovered that the Boers hated open hand-to-hand battle, and particularly dreaded a charge of Lancers. Knowing this, the British commanders sent their cavalry regiments into action whenever possible, although the enemy seldom gathered on flat areas where they could be routed in such manner. The 49th were more often employed in searching dongas, ravines and gullies in order to flush the hidden marksmen out. So many of such places were death-traps, the regiment lost a number of men including several valuable officers. John Kinson, Vivian's most staunch supporter in the past, was killed by a bullet in the head. The youthful Piers Jeffries, who had never wanted a war in South Africa, had his sword-hand shot off before dying of multiple wounds several hours later. Theo Fennimoore, blue-blood and friend of the prince of Wales, who had betrayed details of the Ashanti affair, met the hero's death his ancestry demanded of him, when he executed a solo charge at a shallow pan giving cover to several vicious marksmen keeping his troopers pinned down in a cleft between rocks.

So many killed or wounded, so many victims of the terrain and climate, yet the snake slithered steadily onward toward Pretoria and ultimate victory. At the end of each day, Vivian enquired by all manner of means about his brother's safety. Lord Brancliffe remained healthy and unharmed, apparently acquitting himself well enough in brushes with the enemy. Vivian still believed Charles should have stayed in England, leaving the fighting of wars to the warrior of the family. If he should fall, the title, the estate, and all other properties would pass to their cousin Gerard, who had a title and lands of his own. The line would be broken; the family continued only through what was legally considered bad blood. He prayed Charles would survive the war.

The rain stopped. Once more the undulating land stood out in clear relief, making distances look shorter, and giving riflemen perfect vision of a target. Vivian again experienced that sensation of loneliness he had felt on that plain outside Kimberley, on a day when his company was acting escort to an artillery battery as they crossed a particularly exposed approach to a ridge of hills they must cross. Riding alongside Henry Sinclair and Sutton Blaise, he voiced his thoughts.

"They are in those hills, for certain, but where and in what strength?"

"Watch for the dazzle of sun on metal," advised the serious Sinclair.

"To hell with that," swore the younger more bellingerent Blaise, who approached the enemy with the same arrogant assurance he displayed toward women. "The minute our guns are within range, we should bombard those slopes and make them run for it. You could then go pig-sticking with your lancers, V.V.H."

"Waste of ammunition," Sinclair murmured. "They'd run, but it would be down the far side of that ridge to lie in wait for us as we trundle down. All we would achieve would be the destruction of a very nice hill."

Vivian grinned. "It is rather nice, isn't it? Pity we can't hack over it and enjoy the view."

"Pah!" cried Blaise in disgust. "Give me the thrill of the chase. You may hack like two maiden aunts, if you choose, but I ache to pursue our quarry."

"Really?" queried Vivian deliberately. "I heard a rumour in Kimberley that the quarry once refused to be pursued, and sent you away with your tail between your legs—or was it with your diamonds in your pocket?"

Totally disconcerted, for once, the younger man stared at Vivian while his colour slowly darkened. "How the deuce did you . . . ?"

"Watch for the dazzle of sun on metal," Vivian reminded him, amused by the success of his taunt. The man was likeable enough and a splendid soldier, but the temptation to slip in a thrust on behalf of Leila had been irresistible.

They fell silent, watching the looming slopes for any sign of the enemy they sensed were hidden there. The track had been baked hard again by the winter sunshine, and their progress was not only perfectly visible, it was also considerably noisy. The guns and their limbers rattled loudly as the six-strong teams of horses dragged them, bumping and shaking, over the stony surface. The long line of waggons carrying supplies of ammunition creaked and groaned beneath the heavy loads, the plodding oxen somnolent with warmth after so much rain. The curious continuous rumble of a million hooves hitting the ground was augmented by the thundering tattoo as officers cantered back and forth along the column, checking, taking messages, changing duties. Added to that medley of sounds were the whinnies of horses and mules, the cries of native waggon-drivers, the voices and laughter of men on the march, the squeak of leather, and the metallic clanking of a thousand cooking-pots.

Thus the British announced their coming to men in hiding— men who wore their ammunition in bandoliers and carried their rations as dried strips of meat in saddle-bags slung across beasts bred for the rigours of the country.

It was well into the day before they reached the ridge and began their ascent. Advance cavalry scouts flashed the comforting message that it was safe to proceed, so the snake slowly undulated up the winding rocky path providing the only means of crossing to the next open plain. They had been on the move since first light, and backs were now aching from hours in the saddle, eyes were aching from the glare of the lowering sun in a vivid sky, and throats were aching for a mug of refreshing tea. The hillside, thickly dotted with the universal spiky aloes, was tinged with the pinkish-gold of mid-afternoon. The plain below and behind them was the same shade, vast, empty, and curiously humbling in its immense deceptive isolation. Yet, once the clamorous human column had gone from sight, the creatures of Africa would return to graze, leap and prey upon each other, their common predator forgotten.

"God, but it's beautiful!" breathed Vivian, as they crested the hill and saw the flushed continent stretching away, ridge upon ridge, ahead and behind them. "I'll come back here when the war is over . . . and I'll bring my son," he added before he knew it.

"Beautiful, wild and slightly cruel," mused Blaise. "I've known women like that."

"You've known women to suit every description," his colleague Sinclair commented dryly. "You two may keep your females and your paternal vows. At this moment I am more interested in the demands of my stomach, and the thought of a good hot dinner washed down with a decent wine. I've a few bottles left in my waggon. I'll split several with you when we set camp."

"Generosity?" teased Vivian. "There must be a snag somewhere, wouldn't you agree, Blaise?"

"Not at all," Sinclair assured him with a shake of his head. "This is the first day in a long while on which we have had neither rain, nor a brush with the Boers. That deserves some little celebration, surely?"

They began the descent in the wake of advance waggons, going on confidently because the scouts had not returned with warnings. The far side of the ridge was steeper than the one they had just climbed, so the gunners were obliged to walk beside their teams, holding the harness and reassuring the animals struggling against the pressing weight behind them as they trod the uneven track. Progress consequently slowed. Vivian dismounted to lead Oscar beside the lumbering gun, resting the horse he knew like a friend, and easing his own stiff limbs by walking. The track zigzagged so that for stretches at a time the sinking sun blinded them, then it was on their backs to give a last touch of warmth before the chill of night. Men said little to each other now, all thoughts on the meal they would have when they reached the plain below. The only sounds were the snorting of agitated horses, the rumble of wheels, the frequent rustle and bump as stones were dislodged to career downhill, and the nervous cries of native drivers as their spans of oxen rebelled against the steepness of the track.

The chill increased as the way cut through the hill on the lower section of the descent, and the steep sides of these cuttings hid the sun completely. Vivian shivered involuntarily, but the relentless downward stream of men, horses, waggons and guns prevented any opportunity to stop and don his warm cloak. Now the track was winding more tortuously. Progress slowed even further until, near the base of the ridge, a long easy stretch led to what appeared to be the final sharp bend into a gully that spilled onto the plain. With the end in sight, some of the men spoke of a game of cards after their dinner, or a singsong if someone would play the concertina. Vivian thought only of a meal, some of Sinclair's wine, and time on his camp-bed to think of Leila before sleep overcame him. It was a pleasant preoccupation as he led Oscar around that final bend between high rocky walls, beside the team of six valiant horses braking the gun and limber to which they were harnessed.

The sense of shock dawned slowly; his wandering thoughts prevented recognition of what his eyes registered in the ruddy glare of setting sun. It must have been the same for every man, for progress had continued to where the track widened out onto the plain before reaction touched them. Lining the track on both sides were men in rough clothes, slouch hats, and well-worn boots, with bandoliers around them and with rifles in their hands. Those in the advance section of the column had been detached from their waggons and guns, and were standing captive while their vehicles were being moved away by enemy drivers before their stunned eyes. The cavalry scouts, now minus their horses, were herded miserably together to watch those they had been unable to warn flood into the trap. There was no sound, no shot as the mesmerised troops obeyed the commands of several thousand rifle barrels pointing downward into the pass.

It might have gone on forever, except that one man just ahead of Vivian was either a fool or a heedless hero. A shot rang out; a Boer fell from his place on the rise beside the cutting. Then all hell broke loose. Those lines of silent rifles rent the air with a thunderous fusillade. Those on the track became a clawing, screaming mass as men and horses fell beneath the ongoing press of hooves and vehicles which were unable to stop their downward way. Another fusillade, and the track became blocked by overturned waggons, horses entangled in the traces of their dead partners, and guns which had jack-knifed with their limbers. Confusion and noise reigned as those in the rear half of the column ran on into those ahead of them, the panic-stricken animals beyond restraint.

All around Vivian was pandemonium as the gunners fought to turn the long weapon in the narrow spot. It was well-nigh impossible, for the horses were so terrified they had grown dangerous. Knowing there was nothing he could do to help them, he mounted Oscar and pushed his way through the tangle of oxen, mules and laden vehicles until he had turned that final corner once more. The scene there was even worse. Ignorant of the facts, yet warned of danger by the shots, desperate men had succeeded in turning a gun further up the slope. The weakened, exhausted horses had been unable to hold the weight on an upward gradient, and had lost their footing. The gun had careered down, dragging the poor beasts with it, and crashed into another, setting that one off down the hill into yet another.

Seeing an infantry officer nearby, Vivian went to him. Shouting to be heard above the tumult, he explained the situation as concisely as possible, declaring that he could not send his lancers against the enemy without infantry to support them and drive the Boers into the open. He returned past the groups of men heaving and swearing as they tried to right the upturned waggons, guiding Oscar through spilt supplies, and thanking God for a horse that remained calm in battle. Rallying his own scattered men, he told them they would ride as soon as enough infantrymen could be gathered to flush out the marksmen on the slopes. His men looked sceptical. How would several thousand troops struggle clear of that tangle to their rear?

They could not, of course, so they went another way. Having scrambled up the steep sides of the pass, they crept down the hillside, pushing painfully through the aloes, to come up behind those Boers concentrating on the mêlée below them. Their fellows on the opposite side of the pass were blinded by the angle of the sun, so did not see what was happening until volleys of fire came from fresh guns.

The battle entered a new phase. Fighting was hand to hand and particularly merciless. Slowly, the Boers were forced to retreat, leaving the mouth of the pass free and abandoning their positions of advantage. Only then did Vivian see the moment he had been awaiting, and led his men out onto level open ground in hot pursuit of the veld horsemen. Once more, fear of the lance demoralised them. Some of the enemy at the rear slowed, and offered surrender before they could be pierced through, but Vivian could do little with just half a squadron, and was forced to call a hasty retreat when those of the enemy who had got away with the captured guns turned them and began firing with disturbing accuracy at their erstwhile owners.

Reaching his own lines again, he was relieved to find that Sinclair and Blaise had extricated their weapons from the tangle and were preparing to fire from the left flank, while several from another battery had been dragged to the right and were already operating. The thunder of the guns grew deafening as the engagement turned into a battle between

356

opposing cannon, with additional rifle fire from Boers who had somehow managed to move back to their cover on the heights and were firing from the late-afternoon shadows. As Vivian watched, small groups of kilted infantrymen tried to approach the area from where the accurate fire was coming, but they fell to a man each time until their commander realised that it was a useless waste of lives. Freed from attack, the hidden Boers then concentrated on the guns on the right flank. These were bombarding the distant enemies making a stand with the captured weapons, and with several hundred captured British troops beside them in danger of being hit by their own shells.

The sun sank lower, and the battle raged on. Slowly, those manning the guns on the right flank were being accurately picked off by the enemy marksmen dodging from cover to cover above them. Soon, the weapons were being operated by wounded, bleeding men who heroically continued to fire until a final bullet killed them. Fresh gunners galloped out, but they, too, fell beneath the hail of bullets and shells. One by one, the teams of horses also became victims of Boer accuracy, until it grew obvious that the guns would have to be withdrawn before they were destroyed. Having already lost half their artillery, it was imperative to save what they could. Yet to go out there was to invite death or mutilation.

As Vivian and those on the left flank watched, repeated attempts to bring in the guns were made by men whose vain courage was cheered by their comrades. The number of lifeless and bleeding bodies surrounding the weapons increased, yet still there were those who were willing to risk adding their own to the carnage. At last, two supremely courageous men succeeded in harnessing a depleted team of horses to one of the cannon and began bringing it in. Encouraged by their achievement, a clutch of men led by a boy subaltern raced out for another, finally running it in by hand when their horses had been shot under them and two of their number killed in the effort.

Before they were safely back, a fresh sortie was mounted by two officers who galloped out, each leading a spare horse, to attempt a rescue of a third weapon. Under a veritable hail of fire they harnessed the team to the gun, despite the nervousness of the animals. Then, one of the officers staggered and fell lifeless, leaving the remaining man to scramble into the saddle on the leader of the front pair. On the point of wheeling them round, a shell exploded a few feet away, throwing up clods of earth to fly through the air with large splinters from the shell casing. It proved too much for the horses. The officer, hanging lifeless from the saddle, was eventually thrown as the maddened beasts bolted, gun and limber leaping wildly behind them. So much had been done in

357

an effort to save it; two lives would have been lost in vain if the heedless dash took the team toward the Boer lines. They raced on unimpeded straight for the distant enemy, however. Watching them in the fading light of day, Vivian heard an urgent inner voice that had spoken to many that day. He turned to Henry Sinclair, saying, "Do you care for that race we one day promised ourselves?"

The man was so lost in speculation of all that was unfolding before them, it was a moment before he acknowledged that challenging invitation. Then he nodded. "No better time for it."

They spurred their mounts and were off, galloping side by side onto the open stretches of the plain toward the runaway gun. Oscar covered the ground like a giant, racing unhesitatingly over ground potted with shell craters which jumped with bullets. Vivian's heart was pounding with excitement and fear as he bent low over the charger, his gaze on the careering horses they chased. His hammering heart-beat merged with the heavy thud of shells, the spattering tattoo of bullets, and the thunder of flying hooves to produce a deafening orchestra of sound in his ears. Still they raced on unharmed: miraculous survival amidst raining death.

Instinctively, he and his companion swerved in a united movement designed to turn the direction of the terrified gun-horses from their present course to the safety of their own lines. They closed in fast then, and Vivian could see the wild eyes and foam-flecked mouths of the runaways clearly, even in that half-light. The greatest danger was the gun itself as it bounced and swung from left to right. If he attempted to draw alongside from the rear, the team's slightest swerve could send the gun arching outward into Oscar with a force that could kill them both. Yet, to approach at right angles meant taking a wide curve on nearing them. Time and ground would be lost; Oscar's stamina diminished. The risk would have to be taken.

The gun horses sensed the two coming up on their outside flank, and veered from possible impediment just as they were meant to do. Pressing in closer and closer, Vivian and Sinclair forced the runaway animals into a wide turn which would eventually put them on a direct line to the mouth of the nek and their own defences.

All went well until Henry Sinclair, neck and neck with Vivian, appeared to fold up slowly, then just as slowly slip from the saddle as his horse faltered and fell back, leaving Vivian to continue alone no more than yards from the dangerously jumping cannon. All thought and emotion appeared to have deserted him at that stage. He drew inexorably nearer danger as if motivated by an urge that took no account of reason. Now he was racing hard beside the long sinister muzzle, the spinning wheels, the thick metal shaft—a compound of dangerous, uncontrolled weight—yet he neither slowed nor veered. With his gaze on every lurch and leap of the weapon, with its limber, he continued so long beside it, it seemed that Oscar had no power to outpace it and draw up with the team.

Gradually, however, Vivian realised that the gun was falling behind in that desperate dash, then the limber. Oscar's great head was now alongside the haunches of the rear pair of the team—a long brown nose, gentle loyal eyes, and tall ears flattened for speed, as he nobly responded to the effort demanded of him. Vivian was spattered with the foam of hysteria from the gun team as he inched ahead to the leading pair. Something thudded against his shoulder to produce the burning sensation of a bullet entering his flesh, but the agony of such supreme effort absorbed the separate pain of the wound so that he galloped on with that sense of purpose still uppermost. There was another thud. The bullet had entered his neck with no immediate sensation of anguish, yet his throat began to fill with the hot thickness of blood which set him coughing and retching. His face was running with the sweat of exertion; his entire body was wet with it. His head, from which the pith helmet had fallen some minutes before, was full of thunder. It might have been guns or drumming hooves. He was up with the leaders now, however, and must keep going.

Closing as much as he dared toward the charging, foam-flecked offside leader, Vivian bent in his saddle to reach out his left arm, now in a blood-soaked sleeve, in an attempt to grasp the traces linking the team together. In that precarious position, endless moments passed while his groping fingers sought for a hold on the chain attached to the horse-collar. Touching it, losing contact, touching it again, Vivian established contact with the big black stallion, continuing alongside the beast while he gathered all his strength for the attempt to slow the runaways. Just as he felt ready to do so, Oscar gave a shriek, faltered, ran on, then pitched forward helplessly, leaving Vivian clutching the traces of the gun team as he automatically freed his feet from the stirrups.

The ground slid past at a furious speed as he clung on with a strength born of the drive to survive, his legs twisting and bouncing agonisingly whenever they hit the surface of the plain. He was choking on his own blood, and there was no longer any feeling in the upper part of his body, when his dazed senses realised that the four black legs beside him were slowing, slowing, slowing. The pounding of hooves diminished; the horses snorted their dying fear as they subsided into first a trot, then a walk.

Still clinging to the chains, Vivian was dragged slowly across the barren ground until progress stopped completely. Then he grew aware of two very strange things. There was a sound remarkably like cheering from somewhere near by, and his legs were both bending at impossible angles. Next minute, men were surrounding him. They were smiling, mouthing words he could not hear for the thunder still in his ears, and prising his fingers from their hold on the chains. The blood filling his throat prevented his telling them not to help him to his feet. When they did, the world quickly grew dark and faded into total blackness.

Time passed in strange alternate periods of awareness and bizarre dreams. Often, it was difficult to distinguish between them. He only knew wakefulness in the night by the bright springing lights of camp-fires; he only recognised consciousness in the day by the relief from pain as the hospital-waggon jolted and lurched over the interminable distances of wild country. The old fever seized him once more, blotting out several days completely. Loss of blood weakened him further when torrential rain again brought mud, and the efforts to free the waggon tossed him from the stretcher to reopen his wounds. A doctor regularly dripped liquid into his mouth. Most of it ran out again. There was a burning fire in his throat, and the craving for water constantly tormented him. Friends, even complete strangers, came to him speaking of courage and impossible deeds. He could not answer. The power of speech had deserted him.

One evening—it could have been a year later for all he knew —Charles appeared from the fire-dotted darkness to stand beside him. His brother looked neat and handsome in a clean uniform, seeming tired, perhaps, but mercifully whole. Vivian tried to express his gladness at his survival, but the other's expression showed that even if words had come they would have been useless to a relationship broken beyond repair.

"We'll be in Pretoria tomorrow," Charles informed him briefly. "When you reach hospital, you'll doubtless be told that you are to be decorated for bringing in that gun." His mouth twisted. "You have always felt the need to prove that you are the better man of us. Your point has been publicly made, never fear. Even Brancliffe might have been impressed. I trust you will find yourself able to live with the knowledge that you sacrificed Henry Sinclair's life to satisfy your drive for social acceptance. I could not, and therein lies the difference between us. I became a soldier from a sense of duty, not a desire for self-glorification. My greatest comfort is that, should I be killed, it will be Cousin Gerard who will fill my shoes, not you." On the point of turning away he added, "You are out of the war now, and will return to

Julia the wounded hero. Nothing will ever change the fact that you are a bastard, however, and you know it."

The hospital was spacious, comfortable and blissfully stationary. Doctors told him the multiple breaks in both legs would keep him bedridden for some months, and that he would then have to learn to walk again. They added that the fever, and his inability to eat solid food, had reduced his physique to such a dangerous degree it was out of the question to transfer him to a hospital-ship for England. He lost all count of time in that white room striped with bars of sunlight through the slatted blinds. He lay a helpless prey to his thoughts, fighting to swallow the nourishing liquid that would keep him alive. Even in his desperately weak state, he somehow knew the truth before they told him his vocal chords had been irreparably damaged; that he would never manage more than a whisper, if any sound came at all. His critical condition mercifully deadened the blow of facing an end to his military career, which had been so controversial, yet so prized by him. With survival his main concern, there seemed little point in fretting over a future he might never have.

Day after day he held his own, defying the fears of the doctors. Almost imperceptibly he began to improve, to grow a little stronger. One evening, the doctor came to his bedside with two items of news, and Vivian could not decide which depressed him the most. His visitor first relayed what he considered the bad news: that Charles had been taken prisoner by the Boers whilst investigating a farm suspected of hiding rebels. The supposed good news was that Julia was so determined to come to Pretoria, she was all set to win a fight with the military authorities controlling movement in an area still used as a battleground.

"A lady of great strength of character, I understand," Dr MacVay concluded with a smile, as he left the room. "I have no doubt Mrs Veasey-Hunter will be with you in a wee while."

Despite MacVay's confidence, Julia did not appear that week or the next, and Vivian began to hope that she had met her match, for once. However, a regimental colleague came to see him with the assurance that Charles had been captured unharmed, and was being treated reasonably well in a prison-camp regularly visited by neutral doctors and churchmen. Other military news was that Sutton Blaise had been recommended for a Victoria Cross. Wounded, yet the only man left alive, he had defended a gun for four hours and saved it from falling into enemy hands. A supremely brave and dedicated soldier, yet Vivian could still see the man's expression as Leila had dropped his diamond carelessly back into his pocket. A smile touched his mouth at the memory, but it was a bitter one.

The young officer's visit brought home to Vivian the full import of his own forced severance from such men and their very individual way of life. What lay ahead for him? Without the funds previously diverted from the estate to him by his mother, there was a pressing obligation to earn enough to keep a wife and son in comfort, if not in luxury. He was no budding politician or businessman. If he could not be a soldier, he would have to engage in some work connected with horses. An hour of deep thought brought him no solution and exhausted him to the point of bringing tears to drench his lashes, as he stared at the enclosing walls growing so claustrophobic after countless weeks scanning vast sobering distances. Soldiering had been his life for ten years. It was not easy to surrender a career which had given him friends, status, equality and an awareness of his own mortality that had put his past into perspective. Without those things, without the woman he truly loved, was there any point in this long drawn-out struggle to emerge as a crippled survivor?

When he opened his eyes, he found Dr MacVay beside the bed, studying him gravely. Afraid the man could see the moistness on his lashes, Vivian put up a hand to draw across them, saying, "That damned sun reflects on the walls in dazzling fashion."

Moving to close the blinds against the spring brightness, the medical man then sat beside the bed, frowning.

"All my years in this profession have taught me that there is only one way to say what I must say to you now, Major," he began. "Your wife will not be visiting you here—at any time. Three days ago, she met with an accident. Although everything possible was done to save her, I regret to tell you that she died shortly before noon today."

Vivian could not take it in. *He* was the one fighting death. "She died? Julia? There must be some mistake."

Shaking his head, Dr MacVay said, "No mistake, my dear fellow. I wish to God there was. I am hardened to telling ladies that their men are gone, but I'd make no mistake over telling a man in your present condition that he has just lost his wife, believe me."

Numbed of any identifiable emotion, Vivian lay staring at the Scottish army surgeon for so long the man decided to continue.

"Mrs Veasey-Hunter was a dedicated horsewoman, apparently, and inclined to believe that her constitution was stronger than that of the average female. That might well have been the case, but childbirth produces certain frailties which are unavoidable, Major. Regrettably, your wife ignored the advice of her doctor and resumed her practice of taking an energetic ride each morning, far too soon after the birth of your son." He sighed heavily. "Such needless tragedy!"

"Mountfoot St George," Vivian murmured, recalling the huge beast Julia had revelled in controlling. "Have you the details?"

MacVay nodded. "Enough to be certain that everything possible was done by her companions to try to save her. You must lay no blame. Your wife was thrown by a temperamental grey startled by a sudden storm in the hills around Cape Town. The fall was not fatal, in itself, but it induced an internal haemorrhage. The unavoidable delay in transferring Mrs Veasey-Hunter to a hospital gave her no hope of recovery. She held on bravely but, in the end, her weakened constitution could not equal her determination. I am deeply sorry," he concluded, getting to his feet. "You will wish to be alone for a while, naturally. I'll return in a wee while. Perhaps you will then be able to give me your instructions for your wife's interment, and nominate someone—presumably a fellow officer—to officiate on your behalf."

With his mind in chaos, one item emerged strongly enough to make him ask, "What of my son? Who is caring for him?"

At the door, the doctor gave a faint reassuring smile. "The child and his nursemaid have been installed with one of your wife's numerous friends in Cape Town, until passage to England can be arranged. Sir Kinsley Marchbanks has declared his intention of rearing his grandchild in Cornwall. You may rest content on that score, Major."

As the man went out, Vivian thought of his son being claimed by that family, and vowed that Kimberley Veasey-Hunter would be given the love and freedom a long-ago small boy at Shenstone had been denied. That vow was the incentive to recovery Vivian had been seeking.

*Epilogue*

For the British, the war in South Africa was finally over; for the Boers, it would never be over. The cost in British and Commonwealth lives was more than twenty thousand, with an even greater number wounded or maimed. The cost to British pride and world prestige was as severe. Even with the fall of Johannesburg and Pretoria, the Boers had not considered peace. For two years more, the "farmer army" had roamed the veld in small groups, harrying the virtual victors with their ability to appear and vanish without warning. They killed the khaki-clad troops in ambushes, silently stole their arms and cattle, forced them to cross the many rivers over drifts notorious for their tendency to flood, and broke their spirits by leading them a grim dance back and forth across a land baked by the sun and demoralising in its vastness.

With no hope of ever winning the war, the Boers had simply continued it with the aim of humiliating their massive enemy in the eyes of the world. In an attempt to shorten the humiliation, the British had started to burn those farms providing food and shelter to the roaming Boer marksmen. The homeless women and children had then been taken into camps until their menfolk decided to surrender, causing an outcry from those nations supporting the Dutch settlers. Finally, realising that the extended hostilities were resulting in too many losses and the destruction of those very acres they were fighting to preserve, the near-starving Boers had begun to split into factions. Many had surrendered individually to the nearest British camp or outpost, taking an oath not to fight on. Known as "hands-uppers", their countrymen who refused to give up the battle became their worst enemies, and many were murdered by their erstwhile comrades.

That last drawn-out stage of the war had seen the end of the element of fair play, which had typified the early days. The spirit between opposing sides that had led the Boers to fire plum puddings into the beleaguered garrison of Ladysmith on Christmas Eve, and had allowed the British to unhesitatingly meet a request for medicaments for Boer wounded, had been dispelled by a further two years of needless bloodshed. Bitterness had replaced chivalry; hatred had evolved from aggression. The peace terms gave control of the two former Boer states to the Empire, as Rhodes had wanted, but huge sums paid to the conquered race in order to restore their farms and communities suggested that acquisition of the Transvaal and the Orange Free State might have commanded too high a price.

In England, the end of the war in May 1902 aroused less jubilation than had the lifting of the three sieges two years earlier. Aside from those who still had loved ones on active service in South Africa, the conflict had grown stale for most of the island race. The patriotic fervour which had sent young men off to fight by the thousand, and had driven women to volunteer as nurses or helpers in fund-raising projects, had long since dwindled. Three years in which to bring a race of farmers to their knees seemed excessive to those who had remained at home. It was less embarrassing to play the whole thing down, and concentrate instead on the new era of gaiety promised by King Edward VII, who had finally mounted the throne on the death of the redoubtable Victoria. The repressive years were over; *naughtiness* was thriving.

The new king's fondness for theatrical extravaganza had brought a boom in musical comedies and operettas. Speculation grew when he especially requested the inclusion of Leila Duncan and Franz Mittelheiter in the cast of a charity concert to raise funds for the wounded of the Boer War. His partiality for the leading lady who had suffered siege in the war was no secret. He had been spotted at Lindley's Theatre for the fourth time at a performance of *The Princess of Budapest*.

The lovely dark-haired actress had returned from South Africa to mass adulation from a public in the grips of patriotic fever over the final relief of Mafeking, the tiny garrison north of Kimberley which had held out even longer before being rescued. The immediate revival of *The Hungarian Heiress* by Lester Gilbert, who had encouraged exaggerations of the story concerning Leila's three days and nights down a diamond mine, had brought his leading lady a following never before experienced by an actress at Lindley's. Her song "My Faraway Love", which had become a sentimental favourite of troops and those they were leaving behind on the dockside, had been greeted with cheers and tears on the first night of the revival. The show had been halted for a full fifteen minutes, until Lester Gilbert had broken his own rule and signalled an encore. No one that night, save perhaps Franz, had known what it had cost Leila to sing that song once, much less twice.

*The Princess of Budapest* was the finest show Lindley's had produced, filling the theatre with patrons each night, and filling the impressario's pockets with revenue each week. The lilting, teasing waltz sung by Leila to Franz, her errant fiancé who mends his ways only just in time, suited the new mood of frivolity so well, it superceded the wistful "My

Faraway Love" in popularity, becoming a firm favourite at court balls, and prompting more and more gentlemen to imagine themselves in love with the girl who sang it so provocatively. Lester Gilbert could not have been more pleased. The war was over, the troops would be returning, and he had the girl they would all rush to see. *The Princess of Budapest* was set for a long run.

Vivian saw the title of the show, and the names of the most scintillating vocal partners in London, as he passed Lindley's on his way to his meeting with the family solicitors. He had not seen the capital for over three years. Although spring sunshine brightened the streets, and the parks were filled with flowers, the city in which he had once roistered seemed shabby and claustrophobic after the vastness of the veld. Only now, when returning to the scene of those heedless youthful years, did he realise how much he had changed. Many months of painful struggle to recover had taught him different values. At a time when the taking of several laborious steps without the aid of sticks had been a major triumph, the frivolous things in life had been subconsciously discarded.

He had remained in that Pretoria hospital for almost a year, waiting for the multiple breaks in his legs to mend, and learning to walk on them when they did. During that period, he had installed his son Kim, along with the nursemaid caring for him, in a set of rooms not far from the hospital. She had brought the boy each day to see him, providing the greatest spur to recovery. On difficult, depressed days, it had been the thought of the Marchbanks family claiming control of the child which had kept Vivian fighting.

The boy had been taking his own first faltering steps by the time doctors gave their reluctant permission for their patient to leave the hospital, but it had been given on the proviso that he attend twice weekly for checks on his still-vulnerable legs. Willing to promise anything in return for freedom from the long medical captivity, Vivian had then fully realised his status as a father. Watching the blond youngster day after day, he had vowed to give his son an inheritance fit for a legitimate Veasey-Hunter. With the income from that area of the Shenstone estate including Maxted's Farm, Vivian had purchased some land north of Cape Town, with the intention of establishing a stud-farm. Before he could move on to it, however, Boer rebels had occupied the simple homestead, and the buildings had been destroyed during a battle to drive them out. Without the allowance previously diverted to his account by his mother, he had been unable to rebuild at once. He had also been reluctant to do so in case the same thing happened.

Repeated requests from the family solicitors to return to London had gone unanswered, initially because he had been too ill, then because he had been so involved with plans for an estate to rival Shenstone. However, financial matters had to be discussed now the war was over, and his affairs transferred to a firm in South Africa, so he had sailed for England with Kim and the nurse, taking rooms in a private hotel not far from the Veasey-Hunter home in which he had taken Julia into his bed. It seemed particularly poignant that the route from there to the firm of Rundle and Hawthorne should lead past Lindley's Theatre.

He knew of Leila's total success and was glad for her. The theatre was in her blood: Franz Mittelheiter had emphasised the fact. That was only one reason which had governed his decision not to approach her after Julia's death, however. He was a man whose life was now restricted by stiff, weakened legs, and the inability to speak in more than a laboured hoarse whisper. He was a man of limited means, all of which he intended to use for the establishment of a stud-farm miles from any civilised city. He still loved Leila, he knew he always would, but love was not enough to offer a woman in place of what she had now. Then there was Kim: Julia's child, who would surely always stand between them. Even so, he was filled with yearning to see her again, as the carriage passed Lindley's that morning. He could book a seat in the stalls for the evening before his return to Cape Town, and she would never know that he had been so near for a few short hours. The negative came almost immediately. He would prefer to remember her as he had last seen her, on an open-air stage beneath the veld sky, in a city filled with weary but jubilant people.

Horace Rundle was a small self-effacing man of seventy-six. Three generations of Rundles had handled the Veasey-Hunter affairs, the account proving to be demanding and complicated on many occasions —none more so than the scandal surrounding Vivian's illegitimacy. The partners in the firm had always been most sympathetic to the ousted heir, even when his wild youth had constituted further complications for them to unravel. In consequence, the junior partner greeted his client with warmth as he was ushered in.

"Major Veasey-Hunter, how truly pleasant it is to see you after so long. We, of course, read of your gallant action for which you were decorated, and we have been exceedingly anxious for your recovery over this incredibly long period. Mr Hawthorne has been reprimanding me on the subject of your continuing absence, but I trust that you will confirm my diligent flow of correspondence asking you to arrange a meeting with me."

Vivian smiled back. "Yes, the fault is entirely mine, Rundle," he confirmed in the slow rasping tone that served as a voice.

Visibly shocked at the sound, but too professional to comment, the solicitor saw his client comfortably settled and provided with a glass of Madeira before taking his seat behind an ancient desk.

"I imagine the formalities are straightforward," Vivian began. "As I wrote to inform you, it is my intention to make my home in South Africa, with my son."

Rundle replied with a nod, before saying, "Yes, sir, but I venture to opine that your plans might be revised when you have heard what Mr Hawthorne and I have been anxious to disclose to you. Will you give me permission to proceed, before we discuss the transfer of your capital to South Africa?"

Vivian studied the round face now embellished with rimless spectacles, and grew curious at the hint of furtive excitement in the other man's expression.

"Certainly, if what you have to say is relevant."

"Indeed, Major, it is. *It is*," he repeated emphatically, tapping the outspread fingers of both hands together as if playing a pair of silent cymbals. "Your grandfather, sir, added a codicil to his will shortly before he died. You and your late wife were not present at the reading of the document, as I recall, and I confess that neither myself nor Mr Hawthorne realised the full significance of the content of that codicil, at the time. We have since debated at great length—even consulted distinguished colleagues on the subject—and are certain our interpretation is correct."

"Go on," invited Vivian, growing even more curious.

"While the Brancliffe title *must* pass to the legitimate heir, the properties can, in fact, be willed away at the deceased owner's directions. It has never occurred before in the Veasey-Hunter family —possibly because the line of descent has been straightforward— but your grandfather was deeply affected by the unfortunate circumstances surrounding your father's marriages, and by his early death. It appears that he wished to compensate, in some direction, after his own."

Alarm replaced curiosity as Vivian asked, "Are you about to disclose that the old man has given away the Veasey-Hunter land?"

"Not all of it, Major," Rundle assured him, almost smugly. "The present Lord Brancliffe still owns the London house, the shooting-lodge in Scotland, and the surrounding forests."

"And Shenstone?"

"Ah, that is the subject on which we have been debating for so long. Our conclusions are the reason why we have been so anxious for you to return to England."

371

"Shenstone is no concern of mine," he said slowly, yet with a stirring of excitement at impossible thoughts.

Rising to his feet at that point, Rundle said, "It is of the utmost concern to you, Major. Your grandfather's will ruled that the legal heir should continue to manage the estate, until the birth of the first Veasey-Hunter great-grandchild of male sex. The estate would then pass to the ownership of this boy on his twenty-first birthday. Until that time, it should be administered on his behalf by his father." Walking round the desk to stand by Vivian, he went on, "Sir, it is our confident opinion that your son Kimberley Meredith Veasey-Hunter has inherited Shenstone Hall and its surrounding acres, and you are the appointed administrator until he comes of age in 1921." A broad smile covered features unused to such extremes of emotion. "As you were already married when the old gentleman added the codicil, and your brother was not, the chances of the first male child being *your* son were very high. It was, perhaps, a slight gamble, a challenge to fate to right a wrong, but Mr Hawthorne and I believe it was your grandfather's gesture of reconciliation, sir."

Vivian sat in the familiar office, near to tears. To the end, the old man's pride would not accept a bastard as master of Shenstone, so he had gambled on there being a son from the union of two strong personalities, who would take over that great house on the moor in place of the heir he did not trust. Small wonder Charles had been so vindictive after the old man's death; how understandable, in the light of this news, his brother's venom after learning that Julia had given birth to a boy child.

"Mr Hawthorne and I would like to express our gratification at the turn of events, Major," said Rundle, drawing Vivian's attention back to that room. "Lord Brancliffe will be returning to London now that the Boers have released all their prisoners, of course. We shall inform your brother of the new situation as soon as we have contact with him." Vivian remained gazing as if in a trance, and the little man ventured to ask, "May Mr Hawthorne and myself rest assured that you will be taking up residence at Shenstone Hall instead of the farm in South Africa?"

Already seeing that old house on an evening when a chorus-girl in a pale-lilac dress had shown him it could be beautiful, he murmured, "Yes, Rundle, you may rest assured that I shall go home as soon as possible. I want my son to enjoy the freedom of running through those gardens, and riding across that wild, spectacular moorland. I can't wait to hear his laughter echo through that house. The sound of it should drive away any ghosts lingering there."

Leila left the theatre quickly, and returned to her luxurious apartment alone. These days, she often shunned the post-performance gaiety. Flowers galore had been delivered to her dressing-room; they had been thrown at her feet during the numerous curtain calls. Boxes of fine chocolates, and *glacé* fruits, had been piled on the table by Mrs Marks, her dresser. Leila had given instructions for them all to be delivered, as usual, to a home for fallen women near Mirtle Street, where she had once taken such pride in a dingy basement. It was her tribute to the ghosts of Lily Lowe and Nellie Wilkins.

On entering her apartment, Leila found more flowers, in baskets and bouquets. Running her glance over hothouse roses, orchids and camellias, she thought suddenly of orange and lemon blossoms, jacarandas, flame-of-the-forest, and other huge rioting blooms lining Kimberley's wide streets. Several baskets of fruit stood in a corner of the room. She paused to gaze at them, thinking of the time when a single orange had been a priceless gift. Passing through the sitting-room into her boudoir, Leila flung off the lamé cloak, sat at the dressing-table in her shimmering pink gown, and began to unfasten the diamond collarette and bracelets. They dropped onto the polished wood in a glittering, winking heap. The City of Diamonds! How did it look now?

Since their return to England, Franz had used his experience in Kimberley to the same end as Lester Gilbert used it. He seemed supremely untouched by it now. Leila could not forget any aspect of those four months, and "maintaining the magic" had grown more and more difficult. After all she had seen, and heard, and done in Kimberley, the life she led seemed increasingly false. Franz lived only for his art; she found it impossible now. Their relationship had changed. The natural rapport of the past was slowly vanishing beneath the weight of their differing outlooks. In the middle of singing the teasing waltz song to Franz, she would remember the morning that a baby had died down the mine from fever and malnutrition. Halfway through Act Two, she would suddenly think of the queues for horsemeat. On some evenings, every girl in the chorus seemed to have the face of Nellie Wilkins.

Those two years since Kimberley had taken Leila to the top of her profession. She was now wealthy, accepted by everyone save a few die-hards of the aristocracy. The epithet "whore" was never, ever used in connection with the fabulous Leila Duncan. Pictures of her were in newspapers and periodicals; her life was an open book to anyone who cared to read of it. She broke hearts, and set fashions. Hardly a month passed without a proposal of marriage, and occasionally one of the other kind. Some men attracted her, some made her laugh. Others put her up on a pedestal and became her virtual slaves. Nothing they said or did touched her as much as the memory of Vivian gazing at her battered, bleeding face, with the hair shorn from her head, and saying, "*I loved you then, I love you now, I shall always love you.*"

Julia had been dead for more than eighteen months, yet he remained absent. One evening some months ago, a convalescent officer from Pretoria had said, at a party, that V.V.H. had finally recovered from serious wounds received in an action which had earned him a DSO. Rumour suggested that he had elected to remain in South Africa, and had bought a veld farm where he lived with his son. But the officer had been unsure of the truth of that information.

What was certain, because it had been headlined in the daily press, was that Lieutenant Lord Brancliffe had become a prisoner of the Boers soon after the fall of Pretoria. Leila could imagine such a fate demoralising the mild-mannered, unworldly man she remembered. Shenstone still had its heir, however, and Vivian would be glad of that. She often wondered about Margaret Veasey-Hunter, who had produced two such contrasting sons, and who had been deprived of the chance to become a German baroness. Gentle, lovely, indecisive, how different that woman's life might have been had she married for love. That thought always brought reflection on her own future. Nellie had often repeated the advice that necklaces and bracelets would not keep her company when she was lonely, or look after her when she was old and sick. Yet Leila persisted in the belief that one day, somewhere in the world, she would look up again and Vivian would be there. When that happened, she wanted nothing to stand between them at last.

Lester Gilbert was planning to send *The Princess of Budapest* on a tour of America next spring. No risk of war in that very stable country. Her career would reach its very peak, if she and Franz captured the hearts of American audiences, as they had done everywhere else they had appeared. After America, what? A new show; another tour. More fame, more riches, more proposals of one kind or another. At what point would a new face appear, a new talent capture attention, a new vogue sweep the West End? Most of her contemporaries were marrying into the aristocracy or the professions, ready for that day. Leila clung to the hope that her fateful meeting with Vivian would come before the magic began to fade altogether.

Putting aside the supper tray brought by her maid, Leila sat while the girl took the pins from her hair, then brushed it so that it hung long and shining. Had it ever been cut from her head to lie scattered in a clearing by those who saw only evil in its beauty? Millicent was efficient; calm, and well used to waiting on celebrated ladies. She addressed Leila as "madam" or "Miss Duncan", and knew her place. Millicent anticipated her mistress's wishes, knew when to admit or discourage gentlemen visitors, spoke in genteel manner, looked attractive without appearing provocative, and was utterly trustworthy—Leila had no idea whether or not the girl liked her. It hardly seemed to matter, so long as she did what she was paid to do. There were many times, however, when Leila longed for Nellie, with her pinched face, deplorable accent and comical ways. Or even Florence, who had shared those days in Kimberley. They constantly haunted her.

Dismissing Millicent, Leila donned a satin wrapper and went to Sally's room, as she did every night before retiring. The child was plump and rosy now, still a merry little soul, and still very plain. Leila loved her deeply. First Rose, then Nellie, then Nellie's child had given her what she had never found in her own childhood. As she looked down at the sleeping girl, she prayed that Sally would not also be lost one day, snatching away the only probable hope for happiness in old age.

It was while she was bending over the white counterpane to kiss the child's warm brow, that Millicent entered the room quietly. The silver tray in her hand held a piece of folded notepaper.

"Could it not wait until the morning?" asked Leila irritably.

"The gentleman refuses to leave until you have read it, madam," the maid announced in a tone of disapproval.

Knowing Millicent would never refer to a footman or valet as a gentleman, she grew curious. "He brought the note himself?"

"He asked if you were at home—I think he had a sore throat—then wrote the note and insisted that I give it to you now." Her mouth tightened. "I closed the door, but I know he's still there, madam. He's the sort who won't leave until he gets a reply . . . or until I send for a constable."

Leila sighed, unwilling for company that evening. "I've no wish for a scene with the police. The foolish man is probably slightly inebriated, that's all. I had better scribble a few words of discouragement."

Taking up the note, she opened it and read the single line in handwriting she knew so well: "I have no large horse with me this time, I swear."

The paper fluttered to the ground as she went from Sally's room to the door of her apartment, and flung it open. Pain had etched itself on his features, and there was a puckered scar on his neck that the silk scarf did not completely hide. Yet, despite that legacy of battle, his eyes were again alive with confidence, having lost the haunted look put there by Julia, and he seemed even taller and stronger than before.

"I knew this meeting would come," she confessed breathlessly, "but I am still taken unawares. I think it will always be that way when we come face to face." Putting out her hands to take his, she drew him inside, saying, "I'm glad Oscar is not with you."

"The poor beast was killed outside Pretoria."

A sense of shock filled her at the sound of the wheezing whisper which came from that scarred throat. *The kind of voice to get a girl into bed quicker than anything.* Growing cold, she said, "It could have been you who was killed. I think I would have died, also. Died inside." As he stood regarding her with the look she recalled so well, that moment became vitally important. "Vivian . . . nothing has changed."

"No, nothing has changed," he agreed, gazing at her with all the hunger of a two-year absence. Then he put up a hand to touch her cheek with great gentleness. "So much time has been wasted, I vow I'll waste no more. This morning, I learned that my grandfather had willed Shenstone to my son, nominating me as custodian of his estate until he comes of age. I intend to take up residence in Cornwall immediately, then travel twice a year to South Africa to establish a stud-farm. That farm will be my legacy to future children—*our* children." He put up his other hand so that he was cradling her face between them. "Leila, our marriage need not interfere with your career, I swear, but for God's sake, let us find that elusive happiness at last."

As she gazed up at him she saw the wide veld sky full of stars, and smelt the mesmeric scents of rioting blossoms filled with a rainbow of birds. She also saw a primrose-dotted Cornish moor, where she had been handed one black sheep by another, and her spirits sang sweeter songs than her voice ever could.

"There's just one thing," he whispered huskily. "Kim is my son, but he is also Julia's. Can you accept him?"

"He is a child," she said simply. "I have Sally Wilkins. She is not my daughter, but I think of her as such. Can you accept her?"

He smiled, and it was the familiar light-hearted one she had known so long ago. "Of course. I have a particular fondness for bastards."